For Jim and Nick

# CROSS OF FIRE
## A Pirate Devlin Novel

# CROSS OF FIRE

## A Pirate Devlin Novel

## Mark Keating

HODDER &
STOUGHTON

First published in Great Britain in 2013 by Hodder & Stoughton
An Hachette UK company

1

Copyright © Mark Keating 2013

The right of Mark Keating to be identified as the Author of the Work has been
asserted by him in accordance with the Copyright, Designs and Patents Act 1988.

A CIP catalogue record for this title is available from the British Library.

ISBN 978 1 444 72788 3

Typeset in Simoncini Garamond by Hewer Text UK Ltd, Edinburgh

Printed and bound by Clays Ltd, St Ives plc

Hodder & Stoughton policy is to use papers that are natural, renewable
and recyclable products and made from wood grown in sustainable
forests. The logging and manufacturing processes are expected to
conform to the environmental regulations of the country of origin.

Hodder & Stoughton Ltd
338 Euston Road
London NW1 3BH

www.hodder.co.uk

*—little Villains must submit to Fate*
*That great Ones may enjoy the World in State.*

Samuel Garth
*The Dispensary.* 1699.

# Prologue

## *London. February 1721*

*H*e had been called back. Not to Walsingham House as he expected or even to Whitehall. The victualler's house at Tower Hill was where the coach from Portsmouth had carried John Coxon.

The first frozen grey days of February and the former post-captain was coming home, or at least to London. Home was a parsonage in Norfolk, a dead father and mother, a brother perhaps still preaching from a stone pulpit somewhere.

He had never known London as now, in the midst of winter, and he wrapped his boat-cloak about his face and snapped the ice from the window frame of his carriage. It was as cold as the Massachusetts Boston colony he had left just weeks ago. He had thought of the Caribbean then, when the two men in black cloth had come to him to request he return, and he thought of its warmth again now, a memory hard to recall when the frost numbed him so.

He could not remember being cold in the wars, or in thirty years at sea. His duty had kept him in warm climes all the year and all the world round and he imagined he might die if he stayed here much longer.

His skin was dry. He could feel his joints move. His hands were chapped; he owned no gloves. He had never needed them, and he was not gentleman enough to wear deerskin just for colour.

*I am no longer English*, he thought. *I have come to a foreign land.*

He had retired to Boston after it all. Retired and withdrew to open a store as he had always thought to when the sea finally let him go. At first it was just a chandlery and then, over the months, he had come to sell all manner of general goods as the homes around him matured and one by one brickwork replaced wood.

Last, before, he had been with Woodes Rogers as part of his colonisation of the Bahamas, of New Providence, where colonisation had truthfully meant the eradication of the pirate crows nested there. Coxon had gone with Woodes Rogers because it was the challenge of the Caribbean, as ever. Because he saw a white star-shaped scar on his right forearm every morning when he woke. Because Devlin might be there. Because Coxon could have his revenge.

And then Devlin beat them again.

But he had been promised that was all at an end now.

For years the name Patrick Devlin had pursued John Coxon with ridicule and rumour. He was Post-Captain Coxon now, his rank granted following actions he had taken when an Irishman in the Marine Royale stepped forward to save the lives of his French officers by translating for them. That was Devlin. Coxon had been fascinated to discover what adventure could possibly have brought an Irishman into the service of the French fleet.

It was a tale beginning with injustice, as in all good stories. But a father's injustice: the little boy sold to a butcher and working at eight years old for a burlap bed beneath a counter and beer for breakfast. Bloodied hands all his life. Butcher-boy grown up to poacher until a hypocrite magistrate's judgement had forced Devlin to flee to London. Then the murder of a fellow countryman who had taken him in set him running again, as only the poor are able, now to St-Malo for dread of accusation and the rope. A few years of fishing along the Breton coast and then war had saved him from starvation until the day Coxon captured his sloop.

Devlin became his steward. For years the younger man stood at his shoulder and, charitably, when he found that his ward could read and write, Coxon gifted knowledge and books to him. The Irishman absorbed the intricacies of navigation and became a valued acquaintance if not quite friend. Yet Coxon had much in common with the ex butcher-boy despite his officer's strut. For Coxon, son of a clergyman, had succeeded through sheer hard work and grasping opportunities. The servant, with the same application, might one day make a fine bosun's mate – and more than that, Coxon was sure, had it not been the fellow's misfortune to have been cursed with Irish birth.

But no matter now. Instead, the loss of his ship, the loss of Patrick Devlin to the pirates, to the Devil. And now Coxon's promise to give the Devil his due.

The unevenly worn heels of his shoes added to his poor gait and marked him as a man before the mast as he clacked his way along the black-and-white corridor. But he walked towards the closed double-doors confidently, assured they would open by the breeze of his approach.

And they did.

He entered the dark room, naked candles at the four tall, shuttered windows on the right, a blank wall on the left, and enough light from the open door and the flames to discern the smoky outlines of picture frames recently removed. There would have been portraits hung up, portraits that he supposed he might have recognised.

The glare from the corridor threw his shadow to the back of the room, and then the unseen hands closed the doors and only the narrow candlelight remained.

Coxon was not a man for ghosts and melodrama. He had lived too long.

He turned and faced the men by the door, their lower faces hidden by cloth. He nodded at them to no response. He removed his hat.

'Post-Captain John Coxon,' he announced to his echo. 'I have returned under orders of the king. From the colony of Boston. I came with Messrs Duke and King, summoned here before I am to Walsingham House. Whom do I address?' He let his words hang.

'Walsingham.' A covered voice rose slowly from the darkness. 'How apt. The spymaster of Elizabeth. Our gratitude to you for attending, Post-Captain.'

He saw them now. Two figures that had seeped from the far corners, their cloaks and blank Bauta masks shimmering in the candlelight.

Coxon sneered at the foolishness of the secrecy.

*Masks was it? Is that what it had come to?*

'I asked whom I address. Mark that I will take orders from the Board only.'

'Not from your country? Is that what you say?' They drifted towards him, their luminous faces floating in the gloom.

'Aye,' Coxon said. 'From the Board. From my king.'

'You judge that the same as your country?'

4

Coxon said nothing. His weariness with the scene was visible in his shifting stance. He turned his hat in his hands.

'What have you been told, Post-Captain?' One of the masks leaned into a cocked pose, neck bent to a shoulder.

Coxon's instinct was to turn from the room or pull open the doors and throw light on these badgers and watch them scamper away. Or better still pull their masks and have them face him like men. If they could.

This was not Coxon's world, or anything that rang of the sea. This was old courts and secret signs. He had heard of such things but did not know them; but he understood how the world turned and why his kind would never make admiralty or high office. It did not hinder his bread so let the world to it. He did not fear them.

'I am told that I have been recalled to capture the pirate Devlin. That he has embarrassed you all long enough. That I am the man to bring him.'

'Just so,' one said, but Coxon could not tell which of the blank masks had spoken and on they came, drawing closer all the while.

'There is the rumour, Post-Captain, that you may have . . . *acquired* some of the pirate's gold. To furnish yourself in the colonies. Something of a French island? Gold to fund Louis' colonies. They do love to build on swamps do they not?'

Coxon rested on his sword hilt. His old sword, older than their voices.

'I resigned my commission. I earned all that I had.' He offered nothing more and there was no apology in his voice.

'Devlin was your man. Your steward. He has caused you much dishonour. It is attested. Twice he has bested you. And his king. You would like to end this pirate's . . . *ways* – would you not?' They stood together in front of him. 'Would that not be beneficial to you? To your king?'

'Would it be more beneficial to the companies he has hurt?'

The masks stood back. Their heads angled unnaturally, pivoted as if they had no necks, as if their marionette strings had been cut. Coxon stood fast. His words had struck a chord. He knew nothing of Devlin's adventure of the diamond. That history was as secret as the conclave of hand-shakes and the symbols that scored the walls of gentlemen's clubs which ran off of London's alleyways and met above her coffee-shops and taverns. But Coxon was aware of the South Sea Company that had collapsed like a house of cards, and with his ear to the sea had noted Devlin's absence from the pirate round.

Even from his hideaway in Boston the pirate atrocities ran and rang along the post roads like the horrors of an Indian massacre – except accompanied by grins and whispers, not howls and the wringing of petticoats. Coxon had noted the colonists' curious admiration for pirates; he marked it as nothing more than a new country devoid of heroes but with infinite space in which to celebrate any deviation from the order forced upon them. But Devlin had vanished from the Americas and during his absence a financial cataclysm had shaken every coffee and chocolate pot from London to Amsterdam.

And soon after it all two men had come for John Coxon to demand he eradicate a pirate, with no questions asked. Coxon did not need a map to spy the lie of the land.

'You are a shrewd man, Captain,' the masks agreed between them. 'We have chosen well.'

'Your games do not impress me, gentlemen. I will do my duty as ordered and if that is of benefit to you, I have no mind in that regard. If my king wants the pirate . . . that will suit.'

A white packet appeared in a gloved hand and floated in the air in front of him.

Papers to his hand. Good. Real weight at last.

'Whatever you hear from Walsingham House, whatever happens at sea, this is your only order. It will be seen by no-one, not even yourself. It is to be opened should you fail, for then you will have need of its power. It is to release you from blame should you have to deviate from orders to make an end the pirate. Anything you do will be warranted and conceded. And concealed . . . if necessary. From the highest. From the *very* highest. You have only one order. Whatever the cost. You understand this?'

Coxon put the packet in his coat.

'And I have my store in Boston? To keep without question?'

They retreated.

'We will forget you.'

'Am I to be certain?'

'Nothing,' they repeated the word between them. 'Nothing shall remain.'

'It has been nigh three years since I have known him.' Coxon put back his hat. 'I will need to peruse the Board's papers.'

'Full warrant, Post-Captain,' they assured him. 'All doors will be open to you, though you will not know who has opened them, nor question how or why. For . . . security. For protection. For you and your country.'

Coxon sighed then tapped his forehead, and the doors opened behind him. The masks backed into the shadows. He spoke to an empty room.

'Full warrant? Are you sure on that? You may regret such. And I hope you gentlemen have studied him also.' He smirked at the silence. 'You may have found that he has left less of you every year. He has probably saved the country a fortune.'

He turned on his heel. Gave them no further thought.

# Chapter One

*May 1721.*

Three months later.

*I*t was the Principal himself who hauled Walter Kennedy along the corridor to the Master's side of the Marshalsea. The gaol was not only a debtor's last card but also the biding place for those to be tried for crimes at sea; Southwark its home, south of the river, the wrong side of the Thames.

Once a butcher, the Principal was as beefy as his past and scrags like Kennedy, no matter how much they struggled, were blown before him. Still adorned in his leather apron of old, large enough to serve as a blanket to most, as good for wiping off blood as it had ever been, he now coupled his breadth with a capstan bar for a bludgeon and a rusty ring of ward keys that may well have been the originals for the medieval doors within.

Kennedy stumbled with each shove from the man of meat, his bare feet stubbing on the rough limestone, his cursing and whines lost on folded cauliflower ears. At least he was out of the Hole. His words had gained him that much; they had bought him an audience in some better air for a while.

The Hole in Marshalsea was a fabled early grave. Below ground, scarcely more than a stone alcove next to the sewer of the gaol, it was not uncommon for a man, woman or child to lose an eye or a cheek to rats while they tried to sleep there; more common for the miasmas and the damp to produce men rotting from the outside when they finally emerged with swollen flesh, white, carrying the miasma back up to the other unfortunates.

Three hundred men and families slept in the common debtor's side in rooms made for thirty, an hour's light in the yard every day their only respite, charity and church plates paying for their keep. But now Kennedy was seeing the other side, the side for those who had means and family enough to eventually pay off their debts, but not too soon that the director's profits should suffer.

White-washed walls, doors without keys, wax candles in the lanterns along the walls – not stinking whale-blubber stumps as in the wards. The inmates here could be released to work outside for their debts and garnish, pay for women to attend them. They had their own taproom and chandler for extra food. This was a gentleman's gaol, a place where Kennedy could reside if he played his hour well enough.

The Pound now, quarters where prisoners were first brought until an inmate 'vacated' his room. The butcher pushed Kennedy through the door before him, slamming it hard and fast so that its planks caught the spit Kennedy had intended for his gaoler.

The room was dark, windowless, but Kennedy could make out a hat and figure sat at a table. A strike of flint and steel, a candle lighted. A crock bottle and two clay cups. Enough invite for Kennedy to sit. He thought on the figure sitting in the dark awaiting him. Be a cold man to sit and wait in the dark so, but a friendly enough hand waved to the bottle for Kennedy to help himself.

The flame grew and spat. A leather folder, red-ribbon tied, was the only other object the rising light revealed. Kennedy poured and drank before the liquid even lapped the brim, and the watery red wine washed away his swollen tongue and rinsed his teeth of the scum furring them.

Now men could talk, the civility of wine waving away the differences between them. Only food could do better at clearing the air.

A hand to an outer pocket and Kennedy flinched. A lump of charred brisket fell from the hand to the table and again the hand waved Kennedy to partake.

Kennedy snatched at the meat, as gaols teach. His teeth wobbled as he chewed, but no mind. His mouth ran wet as the beef sucked at his gums and his belly tried to pull it down even before he could taste the savour, and he had to fight his own throat against the swallow.

To the man opposite, the beef was part of his old habit. He had a compass in his other pocket and even without introduction young Walter Kennedy could smell a man of the sea, albeit one from the other side of the waves.

'Thanking you there, Captain,' Kennedy beamed, his Irish voice not lost even after years of other realms, of a thousand shores and colours of the world that other men did not have the imaginations to dream of. The saddest prisoner was the seaman. His whole world may only be contained in a small brown box, his shoulders touching another as he slept and ate, but his sky and garden were infinite. Take that away and you would have no need to kill him. He'd gladly make his own rope to be free again. John Coxon understood this, the answer to why so many of them went so well to the gallows, made merry speeches to the crowd and thanked their hangman for the show.

He let Kennedy enjoy his bovine chewing of his meat and opened the folder.

'You are Walter Kennedy, are you not?'

Kennedy nodded, his eyes stuck to the meat.

'Late of the pirate Bartholomew Roberts?'

'Well late, Captain. And Bart's his pirate name to protect his priest brother. John Roberts he be. See, Captain, I know all to validate my claims!'

'And you wish to turn evidence against those who once served alongside you? To buy yourself from the noose?'

'I can name at least ten I know to be in England now as freemen. But I can't write them down, Captain. Head's no good for schooling.' A small choke on his meat as he grinned and drooled.

'And you sailed with Woodes Rogers for New Providence three years gone?' Another affirmation. 'And when Howell Davis turned pirate on the *Buck* out of those islands you were of his crew?'

'Aye,' Kennedy chewed slower. 'But do you not want to know the names of the men I have to give you, Captain?'

Coxon reared up, the candle lighting up the plate buttons of his white waistcoat and his face blazed under his tricorne.

'You sailed with Howell Davis did you *not*?'

Kennedy swallowed the chum in his throat.

'Aye, Captain. Forgiveness, Captain. That I did.'

Coxon settled.

'Very well. And when Davis met his end and Roberts elected captain how did you end up in Bridewell gaol?'

Kennedy sat back and appeared to find a window in his eye to sigh out of.

'Sounds mighty simple when you says it like that, Captain.'

In one sense Walter Kennedy's past did not befit his end. Generals and admirals had seen less. It had glory and violence richer than the most vulgar Spanish novels. Defoe himself would have struggled to pen a more fitting tale of folly and just desserts. Drama and dudgeon sat together like cheese and bread to pirates and were marked on Kennedy's face with lines and wistful eye as tamer men carry lost loves.

Coxon had been on New Providence, although Walter Kennedy's existence was unknown to him then, for the young man was still of the ordinary world. Coxon arrived with Rogers's fleet in July 1718 when the king resolved to end the pirates' reign over the Bahamas. He had been privy to the order that sent out Howell Davis to trade with the Spanish. And Davis had turned pirate, as all Welshmen seemed willing to do, and his death had spawned the greatest pirate flotilla ever to threaten trade from the Indian and African seas. It was the 'Great Pirate Roberts', as Governor Hamilton of the Leeward Islands had christened him, that now drew costly blanks in the ledgers of Leadenhall street and Whitehall.

Walter Kennedy, still in his twenties, had pirated with Davis and Roberts. He had helped avenge Davis's death at the hands of the Portos and sailed with Roberts as one of his captains for over a year before slipping his cable from Roberts's fleet and roving alone with a crew of other traitors. Trying to shape home to Ireland, navigation not his best dancing, he fell into Scotland instead where, even among a drinking people, this special band of men startled the countryside with their rumbustion.

His men caught and hanged, Kennedy took to his heels to London, where he had been raised, and used the coin he had left to open a brothel in Deptford, close enough to the water and wharves to still have the spirit of the oak near him. Using his book of clients to work out the best-heeled he returned to the occupation of his formative years and housebreaking became his new piracy.

Some bad dealing with the ladies of his house had his name squawked to a beak and Walter Kennedy found himself dragged to Bridewell, the house of correction near the Fleet gaol, a fairly comfortable prison, until one of the other inmates recognised him as the pirate who had taken a ship from under him – and then the Hole in Marshalsea became Walter Kennedy's new home.

Now it was a silver oar, the pirate's last memory of the sea, that would ride with him to Execution dock, being the judge's mark of a pirate for the crowd to torment. But Kennedy knew names, and those names had bought him this beef, this weak wine – had brought him a gentleman captain to talk with young Captain Walter Kennedy, just twenty-five. And not dead yet.

This man of the sea had time for Walter Kennedy.

'Would you submit that your pirate days are over, Walter? That by giving up these names you wish to return to the proper world?'

Kennedy rapped the table. 'That I do, Captain. I owes none of them anything except for the fate that awaits me due to them.'

'I am glad to hear it. It is a small world for evil men. Their end ever the same.' Coxon watched Kennedy savour his final swallow.

'However, the names of these men will not save you.' He calmly observed the drop of the young man's greasy chin.

'You will hang. These names you hold in regard are worthless to me.' The candle flame rose as Coxon let his words test Kennedy's nerves. 'But your past interests me. It is your younger days that may save you yet.'

The brisket stuck in Kennedy's chest.

'How is that, Captain?'

Coxon looked down to the sheaf of papers and pulled from the others the one in his own hand. The one with the name.

'What can you recall about Patrick Devlin? Your time with him?'

Coxon already knew the most of it. Devlin had related it himself.

For five years the man who would become the pirate Devlin had been his valet, his steward, his servant. Coxon had liberated him from the Marine Royale where Devlin had found himself during the war. Before that a Breton fisherman, before that, in London, apprenticed to a Wapping anchorsmith.

The anchorsmith had been murdered – the reason Devlin had run to France. Coxon had always believed the boy's innocence but then Devlin had become a pirate and left dead men behind him wherever he went.

The vellum in Coxon's hand said all of this and one thing more that he had pulled from memory. The anchorsmith's name had been Kennedy. He had had a son named Walter, a housebreaker who shared the home with his father and Devlin. The paleness of the face in the candle-light, the hesitancy to answer as wheels turned in the pirate's head, seeking the safest reply, revealed to Coxon that he had found the right Walter Kennedy.

Post-Captain John Coxon had been removed from his retirement in the Massachusetts Bay Colony and summoned hence by royal decree, which did not impress him more than the subject of his orders.

Get Devlin.

Four pages of the summons but the gist of it simple: the pirate had embarrassed the kingdom once too often, hurt the right people this time, hurt their pockets. Devlin had twisted away from them and sunk their schemes along with the first great diamond of the world, the Pitt Diamond as was, the Regent Diamond as is. Only now the world would look unknowingly upon its replica in the boy king's crown when he finally ascended, Devlin having 'lifted' the original. Coxon had arrived in London to hear that surreptitious gangs under government sanction still dragged the Thames daily in the hope of finding it. Mudlarkers' dreams.

With his final defiance against the good, the pirate Devlin had caused the devastating crash of the South Sea Company to become inevitable. The greatest diamond in the world, that might have saved the fortunes of the many – the righteous were merely seeking to protect the interests of those they had encouraged to invest in the great companies, after all – had vanished along with the pirate they had sent to fetch it. This pirate who had spurned them, had cast away what the diamond might have achieved. It could have saved the Company, saved the whole country. The pirate was too ignorant to understand. What had it cost him? Some men, some flesh? What concern was that to governments and fortunes?

In January, just as Coxon was receiving the Navy Board fellows 'Duke' and 'King' in Boston, the Committee of Inquiry in London published its findings into the deceit and chicanery woven by the Company's directors. The loss to the general public and even those of greater means was catastrophic to the world. Devlin's part in it was only one of the torn seams but at least it was one could be repaired, could be restitched, and Coxon would be its tailor.

He repeated: 'What can you recall about Devlin, Walter?'

Kennedy trod carefully for a hundred nooses hung in the room to catch a wrong word.

'I never have come across Devlin as a pirate. Had none of his doing, Captain.'

'What about in London? What about Wapping? The Pelican stairs. What about your murdered father, Walter?'

Kennedy coughed the tough brisket down. This man he had never met had the knowledge of a judge, and all of it about young Walter Kennedy.

'I never did for my father, Captain, I swear. I gave up all he had to my mother and sisters and went to sea.'

'So you think Devlin may have done for him? Could that be the case? As you might remember it?'

At Coxon's words the nooses snapped back into the ceiling; Walter Kennedy was free to run again.

'Aye. Aye, Captain, that it could. Devlin lived with me and me old man. Me father found with a knife in him and Devlin gone.'

'And you distressed so that you fled to sea yourself?'

'Aye,' he poured more of the warm wine. 'Distraught I was. The sea my saviour. I am only sorry that I was led astray.'

'Of course. And what if you had the chance to redeem your life of wickedness, Walter? What if I could take your repentant soul from this place?'

Kennedy wiped his chin. 'You want me to find Devlin, Captain? I told the truth, as always I ever have, I never sailed with the man.'

'You sailed with Howell Davis. You sailed as captain with Roberts and I need a man who knows the pirate islands of the East Indies. The Americas are not the place for pirates now.'

'That's not easy, Captain. Hundreds of islands for a man to hide on.'

'You're a pirate, Walter. One of the worst. A pirate to catch a pirate.' He supped his own wine for the first time, his chest rising.

'A chance for you to have revenge on the man who killed your kin ... or silence those who may know otherwise – depending on your own objective of course.'

'He to be dead then, Captain?'

Coxon became a portrait. 'Do we have an accord, Walter?'

Kennedy could discern the first wails of the morning seeping through the damp ancient stone as those in the sick ward came to life and were dragged to their labour.

'I'd be a poor son, Captain, if I didn't seek justice wouldn't I?' He thought on the man who had become the pirate, the pirate Devlin, the cemetery in his wake. 'Mind, it might be too painful in my sorrow to actually meet him again. Perhaps leave that part for better men. Such as yourself, Captain.'

Coxon squared back his papers, bid Kennedy finish the wine, stood to leave, even nodded a sententious smile before rapping on the door.

'I would have it no other way.'

# Chapter Two

*1*721. A good year to be a pirate. The purge of the pirates from the Bahamas in 1718 under Woodes Rogers' cutlass and the pardon bestowed upon the rovers by King George had broken the spell for most.

Some returned to the life, to be sure, finding the hoe and the taxes lesser reasons to own a putrid shirt than times under the black flag. But the amnesty proved what amnesties only ever prove:

> *The ones that don't take it, the ones that defy,*
> *you can accord that thems will be the worst, Your Honour.*

The Americas were now unfriendly shores. With the gruesome end of Blackbeard in 1718 the bell had begun to toll the end of the Caribbean's 'Golden Age' of piracy. Hundreds had been hanged, notorious names swinging or staked out for the tide. For those bold and lucky enough to still sail, new climes were needed. The 'pirate round' was growing ever smaller.

Africa proved the course to shape, the Indian Ocean, Madagascar and her islands still a free world, a mysterious world of old gods and untold wealth. What was once the edge of the pirate round was soon to become its prime corner.

The Lion Mountains. *Serra de Leão*, West Africa. The Rice Coast. Some twenty miles upriver lay the Royal African

Company's fort, a slave fort, on Bense Island. And like Cape Castle further up the Guinea coast her twenty-two guns faced the sea rather than inland. Any attack on her would come as a European assault not an African one.

In front of Bense's cannon, Tasso Island. Larger, harder to defend, her Dutch fort abandoned for more than a hundred years. It had been foolish for the Dutch to desert such a fertile area, for now Governor Robert Plunkett and his forty-strong garrison processed the most valuable slaves for the New World. By all means let Cape Coast Castle and General Phipps send hands and backs to the Caribbean – any fool can cut cane. Bense fort was built for a superior breed of slave. Bense fort was built for rice: slaves to grow rice for slaves.

The natives had grown the precious crop for thousands of years and now it was the Carolina colonies' largest export. But whereas white hands had yet to learn to cultivate it well, the slaves from Bense had rice in their blood. Plunkett's slaves were farmers, a machine for the plantation owners of His Majesty. Chosen men. Valuable men. Their final journey to the Americas would be more survivable than most.

The slaves ate well aboard – better than the crews, whose worth was less, the slave ship being the last rung for a sailor before disease or old age ended him. There was even malt liquor for the males whilst the 'blackbirders'' officers drank palm wine. In fine weather the prisoners were taken on deck in the morning where they could remain until sunset separated from the crew by a wooden wall athwart. Pipes of tobacco were allotted on Mondays and, most distinctive of all, no chains once at sea.

Aye, Robert Plunkett of Bense island kept his stock well. In 1719 he had defended his small world against Howell Davis, Thomas Cocklyn and Olivier Levasseur – *La Buse* or 'The

Buzzard' as he had become, one of those rare men to gain a pirate name in his own lifetime.

Against this pirate triumvirate, formidable for even a nation to hold against, Plunkett only surrendered when he ran out of shot and then impressed the pirates so much with the Irishman's fearless temper and swearing while tied and kidnapped that they let him live.

A year later and even the 'Great Pirate Roberts' decided to career further downstream rather than go against the furious governor. But upstream, in Whiteman's Bay, the mouth of the river, pirates of a darker breed found a home and the farmers of the tribes found a harsher side to the white man.

Here a former Royal African Company man had himself turned pirate. John Leadstone saw no profit in waiting for the tribes to pawn their unwanted criminals, captured enemies or their own indentured as the companies dictated. An armed gang 'panyarring' – kidnapping – from the farms, proved quicker for Leadstone's turn of coin.

Leadstone found willing trade in the visiting Bristol and Liverpool 'interlopers', those ships that had also decided the Crown's slavers had too much of the business than was good for them.

With smaller sloops and pinks these low men, sunk below the level of honest merchants in a poor world since the South Sea Company's collapse, needed harsher controls for their violently procured cargoes to prevent mutiny on their short-crewed ships.

First they would identify and dismember the strongest in front of the others. Without them knowing your tongue the captives would understand what would be their punishment should they resist. Any assault against the crew and the assailant's heart and liver were to be fed to the others; or if a woman was found disrespectful she would be hoisted by her thumbs from a yardarm to be whipped with knives attached to ropes in front of the rest.

'That's the way you do it, Cap'n.' Leadstone, 'Old Cracker' his pirate name, pointed his thumbs at the ceiling of his shack, demonstrating to the young captain with the black hair, dressed for cooler climes in his Damask waistcoat and dark twill coat and tricorne, the close heat invisible upon him.

'They'll do what you says then, so they will!' Cracker twirled gleefully, his arms close to his head as he mockingly sobbed and mimicked the screams of the women until he could take it no more and doubled over laughing and drooling. He looked up at the captain who was coolly unimpressed with the pantomime, or indeed the heat. Leadstone sweated like a whore in comparison, a shine of grease matting his clothes to his arms and back. The man had introduced himself as Captain Devlin, and he was in a buying mood.

Leadstone wiped his face, the sweat on his linen just shifting the dirt around. A good Bristol man at one time and somewhere under the grime a friendly face, but drink and easy living had turned it wasted and sallow, and evil never seeks mirrors.

'Rogues of dignity be the black, Cap'n. Treat 'em as any mutineer, they understand little else. Mind I don't deal with Kormantine blacks. Those fellows will kill you or themselves once your back's turned. Be assured, Cap'n, my chattel be willing and true.'

He came from around his counter, nailed crudely from barrels and decking; Devlin noticed the short legs under the normal length body. He had watched a gypsy baiting dogs in St-Malo with the same disproportion, an ugly waddle like an old circus ape.

22

'I'm sure you'll do me well, Cracker.' Devlin took off his hat, looking for somewhere to place it that wasn't too filthy. Leadstone's stone-built quarters and store were scarcely less than a stable. Barrels for tables, milking stools for seats, straw-and-mud floor. Devlin kept hold of his hat.

'Drink, Cap'n?' Old Cracker uncorked a green bottle from the sill beside the door. Two windows had been chiselled out from the stone either side of the plank door with just a sack-cloth curtain for slowing the biting insects and a lump of tallow to distract them. Cracker slugged a draught; held out the bottle.

Devlin waved away the rum. 'Let's to business, Cracker. Ten good rice men I'll take if you haves them.'

Cracker swigged again, taking Devlin's round for himself. 'Ten? Take twenty, Cap'n. Get yourself some Gromettes. Why wipe your own arse with rope? Look at this.' He weaved back to his counter and grunting as he bent below pulled up a young girl with roughly chopped hair, her eyes wide and white, a calico dress half off her scrawny body.

Gromettas and Gromettes. Male and female servants, paid at least. The females had the worst of it.

'Not bad once you get past the stench.' Cracker licked the girl's neck, she stared straight ahead, not a glance at Devlin. 'And it likes it well enough once it gets going, Cap'n.' He slapped the girl's rump and shoved her back to her straw below.

'Business is good, Cracker?'

'Aye, Cap'n. I can sells me fifty a day if I wanted to keep hours. Old Cracker will retire a rich man. Get me an inn in Jamaica I wills, and sell you a drink so I wills.' He raised his bottle again to his lips.

'So how much?'

Cracker gave a deep breath, thought long to the ceiling, calculating a special price for the man he had only just met.

'I say fifty pounds each, Cap'n. Get you a hundred and twenty in Charles Town, that will. Leave you a mark for if some of thems dies.'

Devlin put back on his hat, walked to the window. The *Shadow* sat out in the bay anchored fore and aft. The only ship save for several dories on the shore for victualling the ships that visited. No visible company. Old Cracker's shack stood the closest to the cliff, three 'thundermugs' outside his door for greeting his pirate traders. The thundermugs were miniature cannon, shaped like pewter mugs and pointing skywards, used for testing the quality of powder or as small signal guns. No threat there. Behind the shack stood the barracoon, large enough for a hundred slaves. Scattered around the trees lay some other cattle sheds, now brothels and taverns, good pirate trade but Devlin had seen no other travellers. He turned back.

'I'll see them. See what you have. Quality 'fore I pay, Cracker.'

The shack had been cooler. Outside, once the sight of the sea and its breeze had gone and Devlin walked behind to the barracoon, late May hung heavily. The torrential rains would arrive in July but even now the ground was sodden, the air was like walking through a hot cloud, the sky an iron weight about to fall, pushing down on a man's shoulders. The *Shadow*'s deck needed swabbing twice a day to keep her wood from warping.

Devlin baulked audibly as the barracoon met his senses and his hand involuntarily flew to his nose. Cracker snorted his amusement.

'Tells you about the smell didn't I?' He pulled Devlin along. 'You gets used to it, Cap'n.' From about his waist, doubling as a belt, he pulled off his *manatee* strap, a strip of sea-cow hide fashioned into a whip. 'They needs this,' he winked at Devlin. 'You have to get 'em to expect it, see?'

More than ten years ago Devlin had seen such a strap in Don Saltero's 'Coffee house of Curiosities' in Chelsea. He had gone there to see a stuffed crocodile, an Irishman disbelieving that such a creature existed, but the strap had been there as well. He had run his fingers down it. Rough as a bastard file. He had rubbed his scraped fingertips and wondered about the flesh on his back, then moved on to the crocodile with the rest of the crowd and never saw such a thing again until this morning. Like a scent from childhood long forgotten that returns from nowhere making the years and miles fall away, Devlin rubbed his fingertips together and felt the rasp.

The barracoon had no roof save for a shroud of flies. Around it a moat of mud and effluence bubbled, something honey-sweet beneath the stench that made Devlin back away as instinct draws one back from banded spiders and snakes. Cracker snorted again and Devlin was bitter that the man was not carrying a pistol. But at least he could tell everyone afterwards that the beast had been armed.

For five days the *Shadow* had sat west of the bay, had watched ships go in high of the water and come out low. If Black Bill had still been with them, had not died last year in the adventure of the diamond, his head for numbers would have calculated the wealth that Old Cracker had accumulated in just that week. *Think about the coin*, Devlin thought. *I will not look into that tomb.*

Old Cracker heard the click of the gun-lock behind him. He would swear that there was silence from the cicadas and the fire-finches as in the first moments of an eclipse; but he swivelled round, braved the pistol's stare with a grin.

'Now, now, Cap'n. That's hardly friendly, like.'

'Needed to concern myself that you were alone out here, Cracker.'

'A snatch is it? Do pirates lift their brothers now, is it? Is that what counts for a surprisal for you, Cap'n.' He weighed his strap.

'I'll measure against any. Any on the sea. I don't know what *you* are. I'm for your tin, Cracker.' His pistol pointed like a line straight to Cracker's head.

He could justify that something as evil as John Leadstone deserved to be robbed but still it was not a tale that Devlin would wish transformed into ballad. This was low work even for a pirate and especially for one who had known princes to whisper at his collar and won at cards against nations. But times were hard even for the wicked and robbing this shite of its flies gave him no pride.

Cracker opened his arms, his whip loose. 'You can't kill Old Cracker, Cap'n. He got friends all along the coast.'

'I don't have to kill you.'

Devlin's gunshot sent a hundred birds screaming to the sky as the Diana monkeys crashed away and howled to everyone of what they had seen. Old Cracker fell with a squeal, slapping his hands to his shattered shin where the blood soaked and smoked.

Devlin pulled his second pistol.

'I just have to slow you down so you don't bother me none.'

As much as two thousand pounds, judging by the sacks hefted by Hugh Harris and John Lawson making their way back to the longboat. Devlin shouldered his own bag. The young negress was emptying John Leadstone's green bottle down her throat at the counter. Devlin paused, shared one look with the girl, had nothing to say that she would understand, saw nothing in her eyes that he knew. The best he could do was leave the door open behind him.

John Leadstone, 'Jolly Old Cracker', was on his knees. His sweat could have been tears now. He rocked, cursed and spat when the black coat came back to meet him.

'No hard feelings to my coat, Cracker,' Devlin dropped the sack. 'I ain't got time or men for dealing with slaves and I aims to stay around these climes for a while. You should be careful how you make your money when you meet the genuine.'

Cracker heard the sway of leaf behind him, the boots of large men creeping through the grass. The pirate had not heard. Cracker shouted to cover the approach.

'I been here years, *pup*! I'll tell every brother about you! And not for the good!' He spat on Devlin's boots. 'The Pirate Devlin! Big in England is it? Big in America? Hah! I got Roberts and Davis as friends!'

'Davis is dead.' Devlin checked his favoured pistol's fresh load and snap, the pyrite flint good for ten first shots so keep an eye on its edge. No-one would give you the time to cock again.

'They're all dying,' he said. 'We're all dead men.'

Cracker turned his head to the big leather-clad man with the Sibley blunderbuss emerging from the greensward at his side. A brother. A big, bald brother with red beard and steam rising off his shoulders. A straggler from the taverns who had heard the shot. God bless those who missed their ships for drink.

'Friend! Ho!' he yelled. 'This man be robbing Old Cracker! Shoot him down for gold!'

Peter Sam, Devlin's quartermaster, thumbed back the dog-head on the maple and brass gun.

'This hogshit be dead, Cap'n?'

Cracker felt the cold lip of the gun's barrel at his cheek. The chill of it was oddly pleasant.

Devlin had not looked up from checking his pistol.

'Just slowing him down, Peter. Free those inside that hole. That'll keep him busy.'

Old Cracker found a protest. 'Ah, come now, Cap'n. That's a months *work*! Leave a man a something!'

Devlin aimed back to Cracker's face.

'I'm leaving you work ain't I?'

Peter Sam tried not to tread through the moat but his massive frame was not one for moving so delicately. Three paces in and the stench had him decided that the Sibley hand-cannon was the way to go. He pushed it into his shoulder and blasted the door's lock, and Devlin ground his teeth at the gunshot that trembled the trees.

If there were still slumbering heads about in the taverns and brothels *that* would bring them. He thought once about closing down his trigger into John Leadstone's face, but other long-dead faces filled his eye. More every year. Every pull of his pistol they came back, but only until the shot blew them away again. He lowered the pistol.

Peter Sam looked into the black hole as the door swung free then stepped back, pulling a fresh apostle from his bandoleer as *things* began to move forward from the dark within.

'*Devlin?*' He threw his voice behind, waiting for the word, right or wrong.

Cracker shifted on his knees, his eyes turning to the mumblings behind him.

'Ah, now . . . ah, now, Cap'n . . .' Cracker found himself caught between judge and jury. He let his strap fall.

The green almost disappeared as dozens of shining black men filled the close garden. Peter Sam stood next to Devlin, both loaded, weapons downward to appease. A swift black muscular arm picked up the sea-cow strap and Cracker tried to wriggle closer to the pirates, leaving his blood like a slug's trail.

A scuffle broke out between the black men over the strap, their excited voices arguing in their rapid tongue, a firing of vowels, unintelligible surely even to them. Hands pointed to Devlin while others shook their heads and slapped their arms at Cracker, even their feet stamping out their passions, their chains rattling the while.

'*Devlin?*' Peter Sam said again. Never any fear in Peter Sam, his dog-head tight until his captain gave word. Devlin said nothing, hoped that what he saw, what he read of it was just a to and fro of blame and vengeance.

They would have seen Cracker on his knees, seen his blood, have heard Devlin shoot him, known that it was the big man that had broken their gaol. But when these people painted the Devil they painted him white. Best not think about that. But Cracker did, could see the argument not falling in his favour as a circle began to form around him and backs began to turn toward Devlin and Peter Sam.

Cracker's last chance, his only chance: the man who had shot his feet from under him.

'*Cap'n!*' he called between the bodies surrounding him. '*Cap'n! I has something for you! Something to tell! Listen to me!*'

Devlin did not move but watched Cracker's face creep and plead.

'*Please*, Cap'n! I can makes you *rich*! Rich I says!'

The African voices had ceased their gibbering. Cracker watched the strap pulled tight in the arms of the largest of them, the face vacant.

A shot over their heads and the crowd jumped back. More nervous chatter, all eyes to Devlin as through the smoke he pulled his second pistol and Peter Sam's cannon marked them all.

'How rich?' Devlin kept his pistol on Cracker's face.

# Chapter Three

## *Walsingham House, London*

**W**alter Kennedy sat nervously. The oak bench ran almost the length of the wall but he squeezed next to Coxon like a boy to his mother in the hours before she sold him to the sea. Coxon had been here many times, here and Whitehall. In 1717 with the Earl of Berkeley – the First Lord of the Admiralty, as he was still, Coxon had taken orders at sea signed by these men. That was when Captain William Guinneys' orders had differed from Coxon's in the taking of the gold from The Island – when he and Devlin had first crossed as enemies instead of master and servant. Coxon was not destined to return according to Guinneys' papers. He had faced the oak table and wigs with his account of the tale; denied any knowledge of Guinneys' orders. Now he was meeting the same signatories of new orders.

He had once sworn to be loyal to these men all his life, but then he had even trusted an Irishman once.

The doors opposite opened and a scarlet-clad steward beckoned them up. Coxon dragged Kennedy to his feet.

They had summoned Coxon this time, so different from the years after the war when young captains hovered around Walsingham House like hopeful bridesmaids. Masters and commanders had sought patronage, pleaded for prize money long unpaid or begged for a ship to keep ahead of their creditors on land. Still, those had been the best years. Not this mirror of life, this uncertainty. No war. No need for warriors.

He unclasped his sword from his belt, took off his hat and laid both in the valet's waiting arms, then took his hat back as he was sure he should and the valet did not correct. He signalled to Kennedy to follow, habitually smoothed forward his rabbit-grey cropped hair and walked into the room. His own anxiety was perhaps not too many degrees below the pirate's.

The steward dipped his head to the table.

'Post-Captain John Coxon, My Lords.'

A cursory glance up from the ink wells and ledgers from two of the three wigs. Five red leather-backed seats stood available, two empty. Coxon bowed and clicked his heels together; Walter Kennedy hovered at his shoulder and swivelled his eyes about cautiously. The oil paintings hung all around the room looked down at him disapprovingly and the white wigs in front of him scraped the hour with swan's quills. Rarely did such occasions go well for one of his birth. He kept his eyes down and his mouth shut.

One of them put out a friendly hand.

'Come forward, John. Sit down.'

Viscount Chetwynd. Not a man with fighting history Coxon recalled, a junior of the office, younger than him at least. A landsman. Coxon looked at them all as he sat.

Sir Charles Wager and Sir John Jennings, the older hands at the table. Both in their late-fifties, they had oak in their bones and the red, dry faces of seamen. They would not drag this out. Good. Get along with it.

'Who is this you have with you, Captain?' Chetwynd asked.

Coxon looked at Kennedy behind his shoulder as if he had forgotten he was there.

'Ah. Sirs, this young man is Walter Kennedy. I intend to take him with me. A special envoy of mine.' He looked along the three faces. 'That is if I am still here for the purpose of why I was recalled from my retirement? That is to say . . . to make an end? Make an end to the pirate Devlin?'

Sir John Jennings leaned into the others. 'What did he say? *Who* is it now?' Sir John had been part deaf since the Spanish guns.

'Never mind,' Sir Charles patted Jennings's hand. Coxon noted the two golden-liveried scriveners, one to his left at a desk against the wall, another behind the lords. It was only when they picked up their pens as Sir Charles first spoke that their movement made them apparent to him. His words were now marked by their audible scratching.

'Captain. You resigned your commission in the Bahamas three years since. You should consider that if the Board has requested you in particular that it would be for no small matter.'

'No, My Lord,' Coxon blushed. 'I meant no disrespect. But I am aware how circumstances can change. I have been on a packet three weeks since from the Americas. Then been in London months more before being called here. As I said, I know how things can change.'

The deaf Sir John leaned in again. 'Change what now?' He cupped a hand to his ear as if his ailment needed emphasis.

Sir Charles carried on, thumbing through the pages of vellum.

'Aspects have indeed changed somewhat. No doubt your assumptions are part of the instincts that have kept you alive for so long, Captain.' Coxon nodded his thanks to the compliment.

'And we are all well aware that your recommission will be a short-lived affair – if you will pardon the expression, sir – and you can return to your ambitions in His Majesty's colonies with no mark against you.'

*Mark?* Coxon's mind leapt on that one word. *What mark?* He brushed his hair forward again, flattening it down like a man trying to hide thinning hair. He had no marks against him unless there was still the embarrassment of his servant turning pirate, his failure to stop him the first time, his bowing to let him go the second, although that decision had brought the secret of porcelain to the king.

*It is the gold they refer to, John. The gold you buried on Providence, remember? Devlin's gold from The Island. The gold that you took up to start your new life. That is the mark they have against you.*

His feet had risen up on his toes as he tensed. Chetwynd looked down at the sound of the shoe leather creaking and Coxon put his heels back to the floor.

'Yes, My Lord,' he said. 'Aspects have changed, you say? In what way?'

Sir Charles shifted, ruefully shook his head, some of the words to come distasteful judging by his sour expression.

'You may be unaware that the pirate nuisance has become exasperating in the African and Indian waters. These fiends have become overtly wealthy, ever more resourceful. They hamper everything. From resupply to the trade of the African companies and harassing His Majesty's forts to Mogul treasure fleets. And there is one, above them all, who has become almost ridiculous in his disregard.'

Coxon did not get the name he was expecting.

'The Pirate Roberts! The "Great" Pirate Roberts as he would have it no less, would you believe! *The Admiral of the Leeward Islands,* he has penned himself to our governors! You know of him?'

Coxon had obviously become the font of all knowledge where pirates were concerned and some of that had to be conceded. He had found Walter Kennedy, after all.

'Something, My Lord. My first inclination when I returned was to try and gain some leverage over the pirate Devlin – other than using myself – to which end I withdrew from my memory some members of his past from our time spent together.' He put his hand back to bring Kennedy to their attention.

'May I present Walter again? This time as one of Roberts's former captains. Former acquaintance of the pirate Devlin. A young man who left Providence under the wing of the late pirate Howell Davis who, after his death, was supplanted in power by Roberts.'

The men in the white wigs exchanged looks, studied the young man. Chetwynd put down his pen.

'He is known to Devlin *and* Roberts?'

'That he is, sir. He has been gaoled. I have had him removed under my property. In exchange for a sentence other than the noose he is willing to aid me in the capture of Devlin. We will draw him out, sir. We may draw out Roberts as well.'

Kennedy knew nothing else to do except tug his hair down in salute to the table.

Chetwynd leaned back.

'How "draw" him out? What does that mean?'

Coxon thought carefully. So much of this was private to him. So much of this could be perceived as madness and that would be the end of it. Softly now. He had the papers previously conferred on him to back him up. One of the masks he had met probably sat before him now. Testing him.

'Walter, and myself – now that we have discussed it – believe that it was Patrick Devlin that murdered Walter's father. Before he was the pirate. Before he was with me. When he ran from his criminal life in Ireland. They all lived together here in London. The father was killed one night and Devlin ran. Devlin told me this story also – naturally not implicating himself – which is how I knew of Walter. Before I came here to attend Your Lordships I reviewed some recent records to see if I could discover any member of Devlin's crew who may have been facing trial or death. A piece to play that I could use against him like a lodestone. Draw him out, as I say. Fortunately I came across the name Walter Kennedy . . . and here we are.'

Sir Charles raised himself in his chair.

'And where are we?'

The air in the room almost crackled as Walter Kennedy found some nerve that came from his old life. A low growl.

'He killed my father. I know pirates. He'd have to face me to settle that. If his crew know their captain wants for a backbone he won't be a captain no more. Mark me on that, Your Honours. And if it's Roberts you wants then I'm your man. I betrayed him and he'd swim to find me. I reckon some of that might be worth more than just a rope about me neck, sirs.' He tapped his forehead again and took a step back. The faces on the paintings seemed to look down on him with more disdain now the names of pirates soiled their brush-strokes.

Coxon could have done no better. He brushed his hat as he waited for the table to speak.

Sir Charles looked to his colleagues. 'Well . . . I suppose that shapes as a plan of sorts, gentlemen.' He scratched at the paper with his quill before continuing.

'Captain Coxon, our information is that since the pirates are no longer welcome in the Caribbean they seem intent on turning Madagascar and her islands into a new Bahamas. Do you concur?'

'It would be my first drag, My Lord.'

'*Drag*? Is that what we are calling such actions now?'

'No, My Lord. I mean that the best place to find sea-scum is in the netting when you fish. I intend to fish for pirates. My bait will be myself. And Kennedy here.'

Sir Charles sniffed deeply.

'As you may, Captain. Viscount Chetwynd? Orders if you please for our . . . "fisherman".'

Chetwynd opened a folded sail-cloth packet, pulled his head back to read the blurry script and summarised as best he could.

The pirate Roberts had become England's new priority. Along with the other pirates who had found the Caribbean too warm for them he had made for Africa, his black flag first being seen off Senegal according to French reports. Now he targeted Royal African ships and was costing tens of thousands in trade. Two warships had been sent to intercept him, were out there now, sweeping the Bight of Biafra. If they should have no luck in his capture then at least Roberts would know that the navy was more intent on protecting the African trade than in its lacklustre performance around the Caribbean, where the pirates had almost ruled.

Coxon's orders were to sail to the Cape Coast Castle, the Royal African Company's slave fort on the Guinea coast. Both warships, the *Swallow* and the *Weymouth*, had ported there. Any word the ships had of Roberts would now be with General Phipps, the castle's governor. Coxon was to take any information and act accordingly then meet up with the

*Swallow* and *Weymouth*, join forces with captains Ogle and Herdman. Full warrant.

On the arm of his chair, as Chetwynd went on, Coxon had found his thumbnail irresistibly drawn to an imperfection in the wood. He raked at the splinter trying to smooth it back down. Perhaps a decade of this filing would solve the problem. The act served no further purpose, as did Chetwynd's wind, and he looked up.

'Pardon me, My Lords,' he twisted his hat on his lap, fingered the trim to distract him from the irresistible chasm in the arm of the chair. Chetwynd paused.

'Yes, John?'

'Well, I am confused, My Lords; yes, that I am.'

Chetwynd smiled. The first smile of the room.

'How so, John?'

'Well, I have traversed thousands of miles, requested in particular so I was to believe, to hunt down the man who has caused grave embarrassment to His Majesty's ministers and that of our allies. Yet – sitting here – I am chasing the wake of other men after this . . . this *Roberts* that you all hold in such high regard.' He stopped, took in their unmoved expressions.

'Devlin is who I am here for, am I not?'

Sir Charles folded back his ledger, the scriveners' pens hovered in the air above their pages.

'If you would be patient, Captain, you would understand more.'

Coxon scratched his hair again, combed and spliced his fringe with his thumbnail. Chetwynd put down the orders and went for a more personal approach.

'The secondary part of your orders, John, is that after you establish from General Phipps the current circumstances of the *Swallow* and the *Weymouth* you are to proceed down the coast. If Roberts is aware that there are three men-of-war on his tail he may run for Madagascar and the Amirantes. We shall corner him there, and if not him then we will certainly bag some game.'

'And what of Devlin, sir? What about the notion that it was him to be most removed?'

Sir Charles tapped the table to draw Coxon's eye.

'That has not changed, Captain. You will hunt for him as much as you will join the hunt for Roberts. I'm sure you will invest as much time in engaging for news at our forts and from passing ships as you will spend drilling your men. You should also think on the opportunity that you have of ingratiating yourself back among the African Company's good books.'

A small dig at Coxon's ribs from the Sea Lord. Four years ago Coxon was to escort a blackbirder of the Royal African Company to America from Cape Castle. While victualling he had become ill, indisposed with dysentery, the 'vacuums' as the sailors put it, the curse of the white man in Africa. He had sent his ship home rather than sail to the Americas without him. His ship. His ship that in peacetime might as well have been the property of the companies that profited from the peace that men like Coxon had given them.

Without a war the Navy kept afloat by loaning out their men and their ships to the royal-warranted companies. Coxon's blackbirder waited expensive weeks for a new escort. His own ship was taken and burnt by pirates. His own man, Devlin, now one of them. That was how it began. Coxon's first taste of shame.

'Very well,' he said. 'A hunt it is. From where do I sail? What ship have you for me?'

Chetwynd picked up the packet and held out the orders for Coxon to stand and take. The appointment was settled. All the detail therein for an evening's study. Coxon obliged swiftly, remembering to click his heels as he tucked the packet under his arm and placed his hat back on his grey hair.

'My Lords,' he bowed and turned, Kennedy ducking out before him.

Sir Charles's voice lilted from behind.

'And John?'

Coxon paused. 'Yes, My Lord?'

'Welcome back, John.' His tone carried the inflection of a man meeting a trouserless friend in the street and enquiring if he is well. 'Good luck.'

Coxon dipped his brow. 'Yes, My Lord.'

He took back his old sword, carried it rather than try to attach it back to its frog, his hands trembling too violently to attempt it.

The first step had been taken on a journey that would end in blood.

Blood at last.

# Chapter Four

*O*ld Cracker was calmer now, seated in his shack with Devlin and Peter Sam. His girl gone, he poured his own rum into his blackjack leather mug. His stock had run off and the night would be a sleepless one with pistols primed to prop up eyelids lest revenge be in the minds of the negroes.

However, for now, his company as dark in humour if not in skin, Cracker would have to come up with a fair old tale to live even to see the night. Peter Sam was especially distrustful of every word that any man said.

Peter Sam, a terror in brown goat-leather jerkin and breeches, a scowl for even when his captain spoke to him. Six foot and more and broad as a door, his grizzled red beard hid both snarl and smirk. Old Cracker felt easier looking away and to the calmer aspect of the man who had broken his shin with lead. Cracker searched for charity in that face.

Ten years Devlin had been at sea. If he stood still the whole world continued to move. His shoulder-length black hair tied in a bow showed some sun bleaching at the sides. Cracker put him at no more than thirty-five, his face still ready to slope into an Irish grin at any time but his eyes slipping from confidence to guilt almost each time he spoke, and every breath of wind and creak of wood in the shack made the eyes snap hard as flint, every inch of him constantly ready. Cracker saw he didn't have the drunken sheen of a pirate but instead, with his voice and clean-shaven manners, something of the naval officer about him.

'You said rich, Cracker,' Devlin said. 'Mind that you and I may have different measures of that.'

'Aye, Cap'n. Reckon so. I knows all about you and your gold. Four years now ain't it? The French island and the gold. Four years and I suppose that's all gone and dust now ain't it, Cap'n?'

'I do just fine, Cracker. Now tell me why I saved your hide.'

Cracker watched the flint eyes fall, then they were gone, back to intelligent and warm. The desire to keep that look on the pirate's face was deeply encouraging.

'Well, Cap'n, what I say will make that island look like beggar's pockets, so it will. If you've come this far, I'd dare say you heard of Captain Roberts?'

No need for Devlin to answer. Bartholomew Roberts had become a pirate of infinite success. He had taken over Howell Davis's crew almost two years since and, after exacting bloody revenge on the Portos that had killed him, he had treated the Caribbean and the Spanish Main like his own garden. It was rumoured he had taken four hundred vessels in those two years. He had now come to Africa, like the rest of them, except for Roberts it was more home than climate of death and disease. He had been on a slaver before being pressed into piracy, knew the coast well, and his constitution matched the baneful tropic.

'What of Roberts?' Devlin put his pistol down heavily on the table. The rum and mugs jumped, as did Cracker at the closeness of it. A Bohemian pistol with a left-sided lock and octagonal barrel, at least a half-inch bore. Its shot had almost split Cracker's shin and the pain of it came back upon him like sympathetic magic of a voodoo poppet at the sight of the gun.

'Nice pistol, Cap'n.'

Devlin placed his hand over the stock, his finger tapped the guard. 'No it isn't. Talk.'

Cracker looked between the two, sure that what he had was worth his life, not so sure that he would be allowed to keep it after he had spilled his guts – and hoping that the phrase was just a metaphor.

'Well, I sees Roberts only last week, Cap'n. And he's in a fury. He's on his own, see? Just the one ship. His mate, Anstis, makes off with his consort in the night on his own account, and this after last year and his other captain, Walter Kennedy, doing just the same.' A flash on Devlin's face at the name Kennedy but Cracker was animated now, his forehead glowing, paying no mind to the flies dancing on him.

'Now, turns out Roberts needed Anstis because old Bart Roberts has never dropped anchor in the East Indies and Anstis was an old hand and—'

His voice was cut by the flying away of Peter Sam's stool and the click of the Sibley's lock as the giant towered over him, the blunderbuss filling his vision.

Cracker could see the paper wad down the gaping barrel, holding back the shot.

'*Enough*! You're wasting! Tell, you bastard!' Peter's arms shook.

Devlin saw that Cracker's life would end and he had been foolish to forget why the big man had become so.

Three years ago Peter Sam had been held by chain, his freedom taken, his great body thinned and broken, a world of darkness and beatings until he felt that he deserved them and even liked the man that hurt him when he did not punish him.

All was reconciled now, but Devlin had not realised the power of the sound of chains.

43

Devlin rose, used the voice he had found in the garden in Charles Town that had brought Peter back from his abyss.

'Easy there, Peter. I need this man for a while, mate. Easy, brother.'

Peter Sam's fist tensed on the gun. Cracker closed his eyes, couldn't remember a single word of prayer. He blathered out some plea, Peter Sam was clearly a softer man than he looked when it came to the slave.

'They be pawned by their own kind some of 'em! They're proud to wear the chains for their family's debts, I swear!'

The shot blew the stale air from the room like a bellows.

Part of Cracker's wooden wall behind his head vanished in splinters and the green shone in through the gap as a new window lit them all.

'A *million*!' Cracker screamed. 'A million! At least! Roberts is going after The Buzzard!'

Devlin gripped Peter Sam's arm, pulling him back from the cringing Cracker.

'Levasseur? Olivier Levasseur? Roberts knows where La Buse is?'

'Aye,' Cracker shivered. 'The Buzzard. The treasure of the *Virgin*. A million and more!'

The *Virgem do Gabo*. In almost two months the haul had already become legend. The largest prize ever taken on any sea.

*Ever taken.*

Large words for a pirate, and all without a single shot. And all of it gone silent. No trace of it in the whispers around the taverns. Levasseur and Taylor the pirates who had done it, and them gone too.

'Tell. Make sure I believe.' Devlin let go of Peter Sam and sat back down. Cracker watched Peter Sam slowly reload, and desperately gave all that he had.

Olivier Levasseur, one of the pirates at Providence when Woodes Rogers arrived with the king's proclamation of amnesty. Dyed to be a pirate, not one who saw its drunkenness and easy living as the reason for the life. He was just a captain without a war, too frayed a coat for the Marine Royale. A Calais privateer in the wars, on the right side of the world as long as the cannon was hot and the English and Spanish needed cold steel to cool their blood.

His father had been an administrator in the court of Louis XIV and had garnered for his son a privateer's commission so that he might make the family rich from the wealth flowing through the Mediterranean. He had been a learned young man of formidable strength and without fear; one of his more rugged interests as a youth was to descend rockfaces into valleys and climb back up again. Alone. A climbing accident had damaged his right eye but not his lust for pitting himself against mountains.

But like the hundreds of captains who found not even the shake of a hand in gratitude after the peace of Utrecht and only unemployment their future, Levasseur saw some sense in the Devil's lot.

Levasseur. La Bouche, La Buse, la Buze. The Mouth, The Buzzard, The Nozzle. Whatever the name, he had been a pirate of moderate success under the flag with Ben Hornigold's rogues until the new ownership of Providence sent him to Africa and the Indian Ocean with the rest. By then the injury to his eye had festered and forced its removal. An eye-patch did not harm his standing amongst his brothers even though the manner of its gaining would have impressed them less.

For a time he joined up with Howell Davis and Thomas Cocklyn and that could have been the end of the world with the terror that three pirate crews, a force of over six hundred men, could have blasted upon the bastions. But, as ever when pirates combine, the enterprise went the way of argument and braggadocio.

Levasseur coursed to try his luck in the East Indies with Edward England and John Taylor and that may have been history's last call for Levasseur, if not for one Portuguese carrack anchored off of Bourbon after becoming holed east of Madagascar.

Levasseur was now single partner with Taylor after marooning Captain England on Île de France, the former Dutch colony of Maurice where two failed attempts of patronage had only resulted in the extinction of an indigenous flightless large bird and gave the world a phrase that would come to exemplify anything dead and gone. The pirates were now almost living up to the legend themselves as the world grew smaller around them.

The stranded ship that Levasseur and Taylor happened across, the *Virgem Do Cabo*, carried two imperious men: the archbishop of Goa and the departing viceroy of Portugal; and like the Moguls they were also escorted by their wealth.

The arrogance of the appointed was always that the lowly should know their place. Even pirates would understand the sanctity of the noble. They had even waved the two black ships in to assist them.

'More than a million, Captain,' Cracker swore again. 'Levasseur and Taylor went their ways. Parted for retirement and cream and wine, all their crew rich as lords. Three times

46

what Avery caught from the *Gunsway* thirty years gone, and Avery almost a *king*!'

Cracker lowered his voice, slowly dragged his words as if telling a fairytale to children.

'Taylor to Panama and vanished. The Buzzard gone from the earth! Spirited himself away to the east they says. On his own island they says.'

Devlin grew less impressed. To say that Levasseur had hidden himself in the Indian Ocean would hold no bones. Its islands were as numerous as the stars that shone down upon them, set in fifty million square miles of ocean.

'What of Roberts? What is he in this?'

'I had Roberts here ain't I? He himself tells me about his mate slipping cable. Him all alone and asking Old Cracker if I knew any that could make the islands. So Old Cracker says Levasseur be the man for that and Roberts gives me a laugh, says it is him he's after! Says he knows where he be but not the shaping of it nor the men to do it, down to one ship and all!'

'How would Roberts know?'

Cracker laughed, Peter Sam raised his gun at the sound but Cracker did not drop his merriment.

'He sailed with Davis didn't he? When Levasseur was his partner. Long nights on a ship, Cap'n. Long time to tell of where you've been and what you've seen!'

True enough but Devlin had heard the end of it. Time to leave. Too long would bring some ship into the bay and company to Cracker, the *Shadow* seen. Cracker could tell all when they had gone.

Or not.

Devlin looked at Peter Sam then to Cracker's nerves. His cold expression was like a door slowly closing in Cracker's face.

'Ain't that all to the good, Cap'n?' he pleaded through wide rotten teeth. 'You kept Old Cracker from those blacks. He tells you what he knows.'

Nothing from Devlin. Peter Sam's impatient breathing was the only draught in the baked, quiet room. Cracker's hand went carefully to his rum, trembling as he raised it, and Devlin tapped again at his pistol. If Cracker had known him better he would have known the thinking stillness of the pirate as the sign of promise more than threat.

When he moved was the time to worry.

Roberts alone, Devlin thought. Him of no mind to shape the islands. Looking for a partner to go against The Buzzard and relieve him of the largest fortune ever to cross a pirate's palms. A good year to be a pirate.

'The ships' names?'

Cracker did not need to think. 'The *Victory* for La Buse. The *Royal Fortune* for Roberts. He left a week yesterday, Cap'n. Third of his crew be black now Anstis be gone. He needs white sailors and company.'

Devlin watched Peter Sam's cooling. The big man at the door, looking down at the *Shadow*, and keeping a watch for any bodies on the grassy paths. He turned as Devlin's stool scraped.

'We'll be off, Peter Sam. Old Cracker has given us something that might be of use. We're back to the boat.'

Hugh Harris and John Lawson were at the beach with the longboat and the rest of Cracker's coin, their triggers itching with waiting for Peter Sam and Devlin to return. Each delayed minute could bring a sail. Any and all company was the wrong company for pirates.

Peter Sam looked down at Cracker then back to his captain picking up his sack of coin.

'You believe that shite?'

Devlin reflected on Peter's doubt as he shouldered his bag.

'I'm inclined to it, Peter. Who's to say that Levasseur isn't burdened with all that gold? He may need some friends to help him spend it or protect himself. Protect himself from his sin.'

Peter Sam's beard rose. 'You sound like Dandon,' he said. 'And what about *him*?' The grin gone.

Cracker gulped his rum.

'Now now, Cap'n!' His voice grabbed the back of Devlin's coat. 'I told you all I know. Catch up with Roberts and all. Find The Buzzard. And his treasure.'

Devlin tugged gently at Peter Sam's leather.

'Come Peter. We're away.'

Peter's gun sank despondently.

Cracker went to stand, then his shin reminded and he winced back down again.

'Wait! Cap'n! Don't be leaving Old Cracker without any penny surely? Leave a man a something!'

Devlin turned his head from the door.

'The gall of it! Here's me leaving the man his life's work and a tale! Come now, Cracker. Don't be greedy there.' He dipped his eye to the bloody stocking. 'It don't suit your shoes. I'll let you tell anyone what we've relieved you of, and how. But not where we be going. If I finds a ship to my quarter I'll know who sent them.'

Peter Sam went ahead, to guard the path. Peter Sam behind when needed, in front when danger neared. Peter Sam and his captain. A little man who needed him. A thing to be protected.

Devlin tipped his hat as he left. Repeated for the stage. 'I'll be back, if I has to. And you know what they say about dead men, Cracker.'

Alone, Cracker limped up and to his counter; a pistol beneath the bar top of decking, unloaded should his concubine ever have found her nerve, but that would take seconds to correct. He picked it up as a voice yelled out from the path.

'And I can *hear* lead, Cracker!'

Cracker slung down the pistol to the bar and hoped Devlin could hear his curse.

# Chapter Five

'It is done, then?' A gold mask muffled the voice at the round ebony table, round so no man could sit at its head. Yet surely some superiority was implied over the others who sat in the corners of the room above the Greyhound tavern, suitably situated in St James's, close enough for any gentleman to travel thence discreetly from Westminster or Cornhill.

'It is done,' the white mask replied with a bow and sweep of black velvet cloak. 'Coxon is on his way. All is set.'

The gold mask nodded, sipped his black port. There was some shifting from the other figures in the room, similarly masked. Red and black, white and blue. One of an Apollo aspect with curled fringes of plaster hair, others distinctively feminine or bestial: almond eyes, red lips or whiskers and pointed noses.

A figure rose to his feet, white gloves pushing back his cloak to reveal a gold and sapphire hilt. His was the Apollo mask, also of gold.

'And our revenge? Is that promised?'

The seated mask raised his hand dismissively. 'All in good time, sir.'

'My satisfaction is paramount. That must be stressed, sir. The pirate has hurt me more than just in estate and purse! I seek blood!'

A hand went to the back of the neck of the seated mask to rub away some tension, his blond wig shifting. His other hand reached into his pocket. A brass token was tossed across the table to the white mask, bearer of news. A slow obeisance was displayed and then a gloved hand dragged the coin to the edge of the table, unable to pick it up with beaver-lap gloves. An intaglio of a bull's head with a serpent's body was on the coin's face, and a papal cross on its reverse. White mask scraped it into his hand and then his waistcoat.

'Privacy, gentlemen,' the seat ordered. 'I must discourse alone with our wounded fellow.'

The room emptied so that only the two gold masks remained, a glass of port for each. Both stood now, removed and put their disguises to the table.

'That is better,' the one who had been seated perched on the table's edge. 'Can't see the rim of yer damn glass with those things on! Now, George, explain your outburst. What riles?'

Sir George Lee, Earl of Lichfield, also took a perch at the table.

'Philip, you aspire to be a poet. I find it demoralising that you purport to not understand.'

'I do understand, dear friend. Albany Holmes was close to us all. But such scenes do not favour our sentiments. The Hellfire club aspires—' he lifted his hand above their heads and George's eyes followed '—to debase such,' the hand dropped to below the table. 'Are we not beneath all men who think otherwise?'

George conceded, drank his port and filled his goblet again. 'That is the pretence, Philip. Walpole gives us no mind whilst he thinks us a rakes' club for fools and scoundrels.'

Philip, Duke of Wharton, opened his palms, declaring modesty and innocence. 'Precisely, George. The Hellfire club is a child's folly. Walpole knows me for a Jacobite but knows me more as feckless and libertine. What possible harm could we inflict?'

'Your political notorieties matter less today, Philip. I need only your promise that my investment will ensure Devlin's death.' George drained his second glass. 'You have lost only money.'

George Lee and Albany Holmes had been young gentlemen on a grand tour, taking a repose on Madagascar when the pirate Devlin had need of a ship. Their ship. He had robbed and abandoned them on Ascension island, sure that a passing party would acquire their unfortunate company. Eventually. That had been three years ago.

Returning to England, George resumed his education at Oxford while Albany rejoined a lascivious life in the court-yards and passageways of London. Inevitably Albany had shared shoulder and tankard with Wharton, Duke of Wharton, Irish peer and Duke of Northumberland, that title bestowed upon him by the exiled James Stuart, to be taken up on his return to the throne. And with Albany's companion-ship so followed a friendship with the new Earl of Lichfield, George Lee.

Somewhere, over beef and burgundy, under tobacco and turbans, Albany, George and Wharton had envisioned a club to annoy Walpole's government, ridicule the masonic doctrine and to mock the House of Hanover and indeed the very hand that fed them.

With the South Sea Company's collapse and the financial travails of all Europe that followed, even peers of the realm found their carriages and tailors actually needed paying and

Wharton discovered that he had something more than just an exemplary eye for horseflesh in common with his young friends.

The pirate Devlin, with his failure to assist the bearing up of the South Sea enterprise, had cost Wharton his fortune. Wharton had even held a funeral parade for the company and for England, to further humiliate Walpole's Westminster, when it transpired that the government and Bank of England had backed a consortium of thieves.

The arrogance of the worm of a pirate in casting the diamond into the Thames! His dilettante's whimsy with other people's fortune. The idiotic gall of him.

Wharton may have been a wastrel and profligate but he knew the purpose and value of money. Pleasure until death. The only purpose in life. Peasants knew nothing of entitlement. The pirate had most probably laughed at the sound of banks falling.

But it was more than that. Along with the loss of the diamond Devlin had mercilessly, cowardly, taken the life of Albany Holmes when he came to the diamond's defence. There had been a wherry boat on the Thames, under the fog, that two-of-the-morning fog that clings to your coat and lungs. A blade had ground into a liver, a body was dumped on the water, even more casually than the diamond.

The Hellfire peers would have their revenge, for they were Hellfire in more than just name.

'George,' Wharton drew his friend's shoulder close. 'Our friends have secured the only man who surely could find the dog. He has his orders from Whitehall for the same.' He tapped the masks in turn. 'Ridiculous, ain't it so? Masks. Cloaks. But they insist. And they have considerably deepened our purse.' He lifted his goblet. 'And mine host's cellar.'

54

George sniffed. 'They could be anyone in our group. I think the anonymity gives them pleasure. The little shits.'

'But they wish to return the true king.' Wharton pulled another one of the tokens from a pocket, twisted it in his fingers. The bull with the serpent's body. The papal cross. 'They fear the Hanoverian will ruin the colonies. The Stuart has promised independence. The Americas allied with Spain.' He put back the coin. 'The pirate has had dealings with them before. There was the porcelain.'

'Aye,' George said. 'Myself and Albany were in the opening act.'

'Exactly.' Wharton stretched and yawned. 'A dream that the "white gold" might provide them with their own industry. Fools. They are merely England's lumber yard. Slave paragons. They should be grateful for that.'

'As we should be grateful. For the pirate denying.' More port, a chime of glass this time.

'Just so,' Wharton said. 'But we share a common purpose.'

'The extinction of the dog.' George drank.

'Ah, ah,' Wharton lifted a hand in objection. 'The return of the king.'

George corrected himself with a salute of his glass.

'And the man Coxon?' he said. 'He can be trusted?'

Wharton's thin lips twisted. No sneer; just disinterest.

'I think it of no matter. His hate will see him through. To the end.'

'But orders from his king? From Whitehall? And from masks? Is that not too much?'

Wharton lifted his rear from the table with a snort.

'He is farmer stock. Impressed that one seal is as valid as another.' He crossed the room to the shuttered windows and opened them out onto the night of St James's, the jovial sounds of the inn travelling up from beneath his feet. 'He sees them all the same.' He turned back.

'He probably adores the feel of paper at his breast. Needs it like wine.'

George stepped across the floor.

'But if he fails ... paper will hang someone for sure ... when it is discovered.'

'Oh, George!' Wharton shook his head. 'Do you take these masks for imbeciles? Even I, with brandy for breakfast, understood how that poor little play closes!'

'And how is that?'

Wharton ignored the question. 'What matters, George, is that Walpole has demonstrated the idiocy of the Hanoverian. How his government does not work. Our friends have ministers, lords in every quarter, who are willing to turn to be in credit again. Walpole failed with the pirate. He sends Coxon to correct that error. Our friends and their lords intercede and send Coxon also. If he succeeds our friends will claim satisfaction for those who have lost their fortunes, and turn *more* coats.'

'And again. What if he fails? If Coxon does not bring the pirate?'

'Then that will be the false king's failure yet again. And *more* will turn. And we will promise to send out another to correct.'

'But our incrimination? I mean our "friends'" incrimination. His orders?'

Wharton sighed. 'Trust me, George. I have confidences that I cannot share even with you.' He looked back out onto St James's awakening from its long luncheon, choosing its evening coats and hose.

'Have no concern. I'm sure the failure will not stain.'

# Chapter Six

*Portsmouth. Monday 2 June, 1721*

John Coxon had spent a woeful Sunday night at the Ship Inn on Portsmouth Point. He took a meal of broiled beef, beans and one green potato in the wet, plaster-smelling room. The buttered beer, however, was good as would befit an inn in Portsmouth if it was to make any trade.

Below his floor several crèpe-makers had found brothers-in-ale in a group of young shipwrights and he had watched from his window as some formerly respectable ladies, judging by their dress, were carried from the tavern shortly after six to their carriages.

The rowdiness continued past two of the morning, after which Coxon drifted in and out of sleep, his brain too fervent to rest, his anticipation too keen for the dawn. Thoughts of the weeks ahead fell before his eyes as if already past and mingled with the true – impossible echoes but plausible in the deep of the night. Memories yet to come.

Dreams. First there was Coxon, watching himself, a Norfolk parson's son, sent to sea at twelve with an apple, a Bible, and a wet-cheeked kiss from his mother who ran inside with a howl he never forgot when the coach came for him.

A veteran of two wars; real wars when the sea turned red and the skies blackened and doomsayers bewailed the end of the world. Then there was the pirate. A man Coxon had taken an interest in, had shown patronage to when he took him from a French sloop-of-war almost a decade ago. For half that time the young man had been his steward and willing pupil. In his frowning dream that had all been part of the pirate's plan. Devlin had accepted Coxon's tutelage, taken what he could like the pearl from an oyster and now laughed at him from across stormy waves tinged with gold.

And then the laughter grew.

The gruesome faces of his peers laughed in the dark as papers fell and blew over the sea with his name, and the pirate's, joined together.

Coxon's dream body, a younger, slimmer body, went for his sword, to cut away the paper, to wade through the sea to the laughing pirate sitting far away on an island of gold. But the sword had rusted in its scabbard, his body naked, and the sand sucked him down.

He struggled to lift his legs free from the silt but only sank deeper. He tried to pull up with his arms against waves thick as mud.

The tide at his chest now, salt water splashing in his mouth and gold dust dribbling out as he tried to yell the name. The sinking sand around his thighs and then the water over his head in one huge wave, the laughter deafening and then Coxon rolled up awake, sweating and blinking at the cobalt blue of the coming dawn and the unfamiliar shapes of the room shifting back to lucid, friendly forms and hearing the last laughs of the patrons of the inn finally bidding a raucous good-night.

He wiped a hand down his cold face and took in the room, his chest heaving. He saw the room was empty, the key in the lock, the bed away from the window and clear from clawing hands coming through the glass, he drew back down into the warm blankets, assured that doubt was his only fear. The night, it was only the night after all. Only children fear it.

Confidence comes with daylight, bright June daylight, like the first Day, and suddenly Englishmen forget that they ever had a winter and months of damp clothes and cloying sea-coal fires.

Joy and a conquering spirit comes with bacon, poached eggs and a mug of hot brandy and milk hippocras, the Ship Inn's kitchen not stretching to tea or coffee.

He made his way to Portsmouth harbour, a fair stroll from the Point but a soul-enriching walk for a seaman, poet, or painter as dozens of ships stretched along the walls and even more sat out in the harbour mouth. The giants lay there, the ninety-fours sitting and waiting. Waiting to lumber out again when the Spanish or perennial French thought their cards stacked well enough and Englishmen would yawn and roll up their sleeves and get on with it as always.

But along the harbour jostled the smaller ships, latent promise in their furled sails, the oak straining at the bit as men tended to the seams and yards with mallet and caulk, slapping tar like whitewash, and over it all a cacophony of whistles and curses in equal measure oft from the same mouth in a single breath.

Blocks squealed like piglets from the derricks and shrouds and the smaller dories and barges milled around the mother ships like ducklings as goods passed from shoulder to rope, to ship's hold or deck. Curses and thanks.

This the best part of the venture, always. The shine of it. The coming home and the pulling out. The happy blushing wives and the shy children of men they had not seen for a year. Some toy made of wood or painted shell pushed into their chubby fingers. The weary returner looking for a still bed, and the laughing voyager about to leave, one month from knowing and wishing better.

Coxon inhaled it all, the colour of the goods, the noise and the endless tramp of backs and urgent feet. This he had missed. If he could draw it he would, if he could write it down that would be better. But to live it was the keepsake of envy.

He touched his cockade in reply to a couple of boat-cloaks saluting him. No uniform to ascertain the navy man but he had wet and brushed the dust off his old silk cockade and attached it to his hat with a pin asked from the buxom land-lady of the Ship Inn.

The cockade was more green than black, aged, but perhaps that was to the good. It had aged with him, along with the pitted sword, its gold wire beginning to fray. He should have made to get it repaired. Never mind. A man on board surely had some skill that did not belong at sea. Over the years he had seen men with tremendous gentleness at quite the most delicate arts. They carved monkeys and seal pups, cut silhou-ettes, collected images of birds and treasured them like chil-dren and pontificated about beaks and wing-tips to anyone who would listen and Coxon had listened to them all, could remember their faces and names. Distant or dead sons now.

'Captain Coxon? Will you give me the honour of carrying your bag for you, Captain?'

The voice startled him out of his musings. He braced at the pale face of a striking youth – no – a *man*, but the boyish face topped with coppery hair now revealed as he whisked off his modest hat.

His dress was wonderfully new but not extravagant, perfectly perfunctory for the work ahead, less to polish, to be brushed rather than cleaned. Coxon had yet to locate his ship. The familiarity required to be recognised had thrown him.

'Do you know me, sir?'

The man grinned. 'It is I, Captain. You may yet recall.' He stepped back, as if the act would move him back in time and stature to be remembered like an etching in a book.

His voice chimed like a bell. 'Thomas Howard, sir. Lieutenant Thomas Howard I should say. At your service and proud to serve.' His grin faded but the eyes carried it still. 'I was on the *Starling*, Captain. Midshipman. I acted Lieutenant . . . for the day.' The eyes dropped. 'On The Island, Captain.'

Coxon had grey hair now amid the black but it darkened as he brushed memories away from his eyes like dust from a painting's glass and he saw again the mottled, nervous-brave face of Midshipman Howard, sixteen once again and handing him his quarter-bill for the hour against the pirate. A tearful child recounting how he had found the murdered body of Edward Talton. The first act of betrayal from Lt Guinneys, who did not live to see the end of the day. But Howard had survived. One of the pirates had protected him when the demons had boarded and killed. The yellow-coated barber-surgeon had shown some compassion – to Coxon's mind just to save his own hide if all went wrong. The pirate doctor had hugged Howard close to his chest, surely to protect himself, and had stared down the axes and cutlasses that swung across the faces of Coxon's crew. Perhaps some sodomite plan for the boy that was never realised.

So Thomas Howard had sailed back to England with the crippled *Starling* and Coxon. Howard had been there, fought there, and the officer's reticence left Coxon as he dropped his sack and clasped the man's shoulders and laughed at the new height and breadth of him.

'Bless my soul! It is Thomas Howard so it is! Lieutenant Howard now, is it?'

'It is, Captain,' Howard glowed and picked up the hemp sack without demur. 'When I heard of your return I begged myself from my Bristol packet to see you proper. Especially when I heard of your purpose.'

He put out a hand for them to continue and they walked abreast; the carriages and their passing click-clack over cobbles and the discord of the dock were unable to drown their words, not when seaman can throw their voices like ropes when they wish.

'So it is the pirate then? That is true?' Howard asked.

'Aye,' Coxon tugged at his nose. 'But chasing after the *Swallow* and the *Weymouth* first. There is a man, a Roberts, who is more vital since I was called.'

'Ah,' Howard sighed. 'The pirate Roberts is doing terrible harm to the right people. Thank the Lord that the Royal African Company keeps us all in her debt so we may keep busy.' Howard stopped, pointed out into the bay.

'*There* she is!'

Coxon followed the arm as Howard drew his head in close to his captain's.

'The *Standard*,' Howard declared and Coxon walked to the edge of the seawall so his toes peered over; nothing but a straight line of sea between the tips of his shoes and the black freeboard.

'Mister Howard,' he called behind, 'what of her? She is a two-decker?'

The *Standard*. Of the 1706 Establishment, Howard informed. That would make her the youngest ship Coxon had ever sailed. A fifth-rate frigate. She would have had some use in the Mediterranean during the Spanish war, a victualler or guardship perhaps. Forty guns, almost twice as many as the pirate, if Devlin had kept to the same ship.

Twenty twelve-pounders on the lower and twenty six-pounders on the upper, according to Howard, but none on the fo'c'sle or quarterdeck.

Coxon had never commanded a separate gundeck and they were heading to Africa in June, in the rains. He had heard many bemoan that rough water kept the lower deck ports closed, a whole battery ineffective. It depended on the wind and the rain; more often a heavy downpour could be gracious, and smooth the water like glass; then the gundeck's portholes could be used for sweeps, long-oars, to speed her along. He asked Howard if she carried a complement of such. Howard confirmed.

They continued to the gig awaiting them. 'And oil, Thomas? Does she have plenty hogs of whale oil also?'

Howard was surprised at the seriousness of Coxon's face at what seemed like the dullest factors of a supercargo's mind.

'Some, sir. For lamps, grease and such. We should carry more?'

Coxon spied their man with his red oars and slops, surely theirs, the only gig not loaded and a man not impatient to be so.

'Oh, no concern. We will meet many tides. We are entering the coasts during the wrong season, that is all.' His words were too cryptic for Howard to follow and you only questioned your captain once.

'But I should like to know how much oil she carries by and by, Thomas. And what you have been up to these past years. You will dine with me tonight?'

'Of course, sir. Thank you, sir.'

They found steps and clambered into the gig, with the tightest-lipped greeting from Coxon to the man of whiskers and Monmouth cap who rowed them off.

'Did my man find his way aboard, Thomas?' Twenty more minutes and the familiarity would drop. It would be Mister Howard again until supper.

'Your man, sir?'

This had been the first test for Walter Kennedy. He had coached down to Portsmouth with Coxon but had been sent to find the ship and go aboard alone. It raised a level of trust that Coxon would need if the mission were to go well; but after seeing the Marshalsea he had confidence that Kennedy stroked his neck carefully at every deliberation.

Howard settled Coxon's doubts just so.

'Oh, yes! Scruffy fellow with darting eyes, kept his head low. Used to a ship. Good man, Captain?'

'I'm very much afraid not, Thomas,' and he leaned back to relish the bright morning, the sounds of life drifting off behind, the lap of waves at the gunwale and the mesmerising stroke of the oars drawing the frigate closer. Thomas Howard felt sure that his captain's utterances were hieroglyphics that only needed experience to decipher and a nod of the head to at least acknowledge that one had heard.

One turn of the glass later, the final grains tapped loose by a black fingernail, and the *tang-tang* of the bell coincidently marked Coxon pulling himself through the entry port. He forsook any introductions or piping; the ship was busy, and noon, for their departure, only two hours off. Taking his bag he gave Howard his muster instruction that he would address the ship ten minutes before the noon bell but that he would like to see his First Lieutenant, Christopher Manvell, in his cabin as soon as he was free from his duty. Coxon ducked beneath the quarterdeck and went to his coach, to his new command. His first for very near three years.

He gave a brief study of the wine cradled in the rope beckets just inside the door and a twelve-pounder at his left knee and another just past his cot. A breath of his cot: clean, no trace of powder, an emery starchiness to the sheets, a compass set into the wood above for him to read on his back. He slung his sack and entered the cabin. Dry, beeswax-scented air was just overpowered by the coffee pot sitting in its gimbal on the table and squeaking to and fro with the tide.

He tossed his hat beside it and stared out the slanted windows to the grey horizon and a picture of the crosstrees and furled sails of a dozen ships in the pool as if painted on the walls of a child's bedroom.

He was home.

Even the sound of feet overhead and the hammering from the fore was comforting. The crash of the man stumbling through the coach shattered Coxon's reverie, the reparation coming before Coxon could scowl.

'My apologies, Captain,' the young man made to salute, instinct over sense, forgetting that his hands were full.

His hat was under his arm amongst a large parallel rule and rolled-up charts sticking out from every angle like spines on a porcupine. The salute precipitated the clanging fall of brass instruments and notebooks and another profuse apology as the man bent to gather his detritus.

'Most sorry, sir!' More metallic pieces of him seemed to fall off like a clock flying open as it tumbled down a staircase.

'I am most dreadfully sorry, sir.'

He bundled some of the tools and charts to the table with his hat which collided with Coxon's and the coffee pot, agitating it across the table. He slapped his hand on it just in time for the save and just in time to scald his palm, which he now blew on and shook before handing it out to his captain.

'Lieutenant Christopher Manvell, Captain! At your service, sir!'

Coxon looked down at the hand and watched it slowly withdraw as he left it hanging.

'*You* are my appointed First?' Coxon's eyes dragged up the slender body of the man. A handsome if somewhat chalky face under queued auburn hair the shine and thinness of which gave the man a feminine appearance to Coxon's mind, although it probably merely contrasted with his own coarse grey. The thick long eyebrows were dark and raised giving a permanently astonished look to the man's face.

'I am,' Manvell said seriously. 'Please forgive my brusque entrance, Captain.'

'You did not knock, Lieutenant.'

'No. Unquestionably I did not. For my innocence I did not expect you to be here, Captain, so soon. I had hoped to set up my charts in anticipation of your arrival.'

'You are clumsy, sir!'

'Indeed. But I am blessedly thin which has limited my propensity to disturb I find.' He smiled and then pulled it back behind his lips as Coxon glared.

Coxon moved away to the window lockers, turned his back. 'Take up your hat, Mister Manvell. Leave and enter again. Correctly if you please.'

Manvell backed from the room, sliding his hat from the table along with a divider which clanged like a dropped anvil behind Coxon's back.

Moments later Coxon heard the faint rap and bid enter. Manvell slunk into the room; Coxon watched his first lieutenant's dejected reflection in the diamond shaped panes.

'Come in, man.'

Manvell stepped forward. 'Lieutenant Christopher Manvell, Captain. Reporting for duty.'

Another rap from the other outer coach door, the official entrance for visitors where a cot lay for gentlemen not of the crew, botanists or political advisers and such, and where a stool and marine and a hanging lighted lantern indicated that the captain was within.

Coxon held up a hand for Manvell to be silent and called the party in. Thomas Howard swept through the door, his hat already neatly under his arm. His voice stalled as he saw Manvell.

'What is it, Mister Howard?' Coxon asked.

Howard looked between them both.

'I . . . I merely wished to inform the *Standard* that I could not find Lieutenant Manvell, sir.'

Coxon introduced the lieutenant with an open palm.

'It seems I have found him myself, Mister Howard. That will be all.'

'Very good, sir.' Howard clicked his heels and spun around out of the room, glad at that moment that he was not the First after the sight of Manvell's flushed face and the mess of instruments and papers on the floor.

Coxon scratched his hair, smoothing it forward as he spoke, his concentration on the polish of his floor.

'Now, Mister Manvell,' his eyes flashed upwards again and Manvell jerked as if shot. 'You wished to set up your charts for some account? Explain, if you please.'

Manvell gingerly bent to the remainder of the papers and brass and began to gather them up.

'Yes, sir. I had hoped—' he stopped as Coxon came down to help. 'I had hoped that I might demonstrate my diligence to my duties to the *Standard* by comparison of notes of her previous endeavours and—' He rose with Coxon, who passed back pencils, rules and an ivory compass card with a kindly look as if handing a dropped handkerchief to a blushing housemaid in the street.

'You know, you may find that if you took the purchase of a barber-surgeon's etui, such for the storing of probes, you might find your tools less liable to jump from your arms, Mister Manvell.'

'Of course, sir. Very good, sir.' Manvell carefully set the instruments down. 'I believe I did have such an item but . . . made loss of it and since—'

'Made a good splash did it?'

'Quite, sir . . . and since such event I have found it gener-ously sensible to lose only one card at a time rather than the whole suit, as it were.'

Coxon went for the coffee.

'Sound reasoning. But perhaps you can explain to me why you need such a compendium?'

Coxon poured then held out the pot for Manvell, waiting for him to notice that there was only the captain's cup at the captain's table.

'Well, man? Do you expect me to pour it over your hands! Fetch a *cup*!'

'Of course, sir. Very good, sir.'

Manvell found a decanter and glasses behind a brass guard above the writing desk. Coxon grimaced as he measured a small shot of coffee into a port glass.

'So what is all this?' He waved over the sprawl of tools. 'You are more mathematician than seaman, is that it?'

'Oh no, sir, but accuracy in all things is the measure of how men's lives are saved.'

Coxon bowed to that with his cup as it went to his lips.

'But we are on an easy run to Cape Coast Castle, land in sight all the way. Are we not?'

The old instinct in Coxon scratched at his collar as he studied Manvell over the cup. It should be only Coxon's knowledge of the pirate hunt; beyond the traversing to Cape Castle to resupply General Phipps with victuals and deliver post, all the crew should be ignorant. He trusted Howard; the boy had bled with him and that counted enough, but after feeling William Guinneys coil like a snake around him on The Island those years ago when Guinneys' orders had differed, Coxon now preferred to sniff his food well before he ate. He had more officers to meet. He would test them one by one.

Manvell bowed. 'Of course, sir. Perhaps I just wished to show off apace. I am aware that I appear unimpressive at first sight, Captain.' Manvell gingerly passed the scalding glass of coffee from hand to hand and finally placed it down to cool.

'Modesty and duty impresses me more, Mister Manvell. I am more taken by a horse of the field than one of the course.' He passed his cup arm over the table. 'You have two compasses here. Why?' Coxon could indulge the young man a little.

Manvell picked up one wooden and brass box.

'For variation of the compass, Captain. I mark one compass "A" the other "B".' He picked up the other compass and demonstrated the etched 'B' on its base to his captain, who had been at sea for over thirty years.

'At the binnacle I compare the readings for all three and allow for the true north. I then take my reading of the vane outside on the chains – to allow for minimal disturbance from the movement of the ship and to be as low to the earth as possible – and take a reading for both sides of the vane so that there will be two observations for both compasses. After which I am able to ascertain that any fault that may be in the construction of the compasses can be eliminated and a true bearing calculated.' He paused for some compliment from Coxon but he only refilled his cup with eyes more firmly on the pot than the instruction.

'Very well,' Coxon said. 'But for Cape Castle we will use the rhumb lines of a Mercator projection. I have all the readings I need for such a course. Do you have Moll's map of Africa?'

Herman Moll's 1720 map was as yet the most detailed description of the continent. Gibraltar at its tip, part of Brazil at its left side and Madagascar and the Amirantes to its right. But it had no rhumb lines. The rhumb lines, the loxodrome spider-web patterns that criss-crossed mariners' Mercator charts were paths for ships to tread. But the Moll map served more as a land map than nautical chart, its detail for the coast exceptional to this end. Manvell rustled through his papers until he found it.

'Good,' Coxon said. He put down his coffee and picked out of Manvell's collection a parallel rule, the compass card, divider and pencil, then with a sweep of his sleeve like a broom sent the rest to the floor. Manvell jumped at the sudden crash.

'Does that offend, Lieutenant? I was beginning to accept that such disturbance was common in my cabin.'

Manvell watched his compasses dance on the floor like dreidels. A thousand images of their new imperfections spinning through his brain. Earnestly his voice was shamed.

'My apologies, sir.'

'The map to the table.' Coxon cleared his coffee to a safer surface as Manvell set the paper.

'Now, with no rhumb lines, and just Moll's single compass rose, I want you to chart me a course from Cape Vert point – an easy start for it sits on the fifteenth parallel, is easy to sight and with the Verdes to our starboard you'd be a fool to not know where you are in the world – all the way to Cape Coast Castle. If you please, Mister Manvell.'

Manvell began to sit.

'How long do I have, if I may request, sir, to measure my aptitude?'

Coxon took up his coffee.

'Until I finish *this*, Lieutenant.' He took his first sip.

Manvell did not take a seat.

The dividers first. He took the nautical mile reading from the latitude scale down the side of the map and set the legs; three attempts, his fingers unable to steady and Coxon on his second taste.

Manvell marked Cape Vert, a nice neat hook like a parson's nose hanging off the coast as if God had created it just so for mariners to mark.

Taking up the rule and pencil he drew, assured and swift, a line through the archipelagos and past the Grain Coast, his second mark. Next he walked the rule to the rose near the edge then replaced the rule with his compass card and penned the bearing in the map's margin. Next, he swiftly brought back the rule and drew again, traversing into the Gold Coast and Cape Castle clearly marked amongst the other factories. His third mark.

He walked the rule back to the rose, its hinge treading the way like pigeon steps and again with the compass card took and wrote his second bearing as Coxon's cup lifted higher.

Provident that he had set the divider first. He danced it along the lines with one hand and pencilled his calculations with the other, dropping the brass instrument the moment Coxon placed back his cup.

'Well?' Coxon wiped his top lip. Manvell resisted wiping the shine from his forehead.

'I believe, Captain, that from Cape Vert, south-east by south at thirty-five degrees for ninety miles. Then east by north for seventy miles, eighty-one degrees into Cape Castle.'

'And if we maintain four knots from Cape Vert? You have us at how many hours?'

'Forty-eight hours at twenty-four hour sail . . . if we are in need of urgency with our post, that is.'

Coxon looked down at the pencil marks and scribble that scrawled in their anxiety to finish; the numbers and letters falling over each other.

'Good. Good. Although I prefer Waghenaer's projection.'

Lucas Waghenaer, the Dutch cartographer who gave the seaman the term, 'Waggoner' for his collection of charts.

'Far before your time but good sense to rely on the work of a Dutchman when this was all their land before us and who most surely copied his works from the Portos'. Their very language infects the negro's tongue.' He finished his coffee. 'I think by the Waggoner you be twenty miles out. Your correction should be to compare both before making your decision, as you compare your compasses. What one man can do wrong another man can do wrong also. Where the lines meet is your cocked hat to throw your ship into.'

'Indeed, sir. That would be my course also but the cup was not so deep for me to divine any further.'

Coxon was satisfied. This man would do. His reach extended his grasp.

'And suppose I had used your Port glass to time, we would be still at Cape Vert no doubt?'

Manvell raised his glass. 'Mine has become colder, Captain. You would have drained it in one.'

Coxon slapped the man's shoulder, spilling Manvell's coffee on the map, and he laughed and surprised himself at the noise that he had not indulged in for years as if it had come from some other corner of the room.

Manvell would do. Find out more about him at supper. But the man could course on the fly; Coxon's coffee and eye upon him was as noisome a distraction as cannon and storm. He *would* do, and Coxon went grim as he remembered the last time he had taken to a young man so. He clasped one hand into the other behind his back.

'Away with your Bibles and Testaments, Mister Manvell. Ten minutes to noon beside me on the quarterdeck.'

Manvell took up his hat, gathered his instruments crudely like scrumped apples in his arms.

'Very good, sir.' He left by the correct door, unsure of the laugh, even more unsure of the dour look of unpleasant recollection on Coxon's face.

Ten minutes before noon and the ship's company assembled. Tarpaulins secured over the hatches gave comfortable seating for some but they stood with the rest when the bosun piped Coxon from his coach to the quarterdeck rail, his five footsteps up the stair echoing all over the ship as eighty-five men waited on his first words.

He looked over them squinting at him with the sun at his shoulder. Young men for the most with shorn hair to stop the spread of lice. Three or four with their badge of service in their long hair or pigtails. Eighty-five men and officers. The pirates the same if not more as was their way. And what of the ship?

The *Standard* had been under Royal African Company service for over a year. The men had probably had a fortnight's leave and cashed their pay ticket in Portsmouth at a money lender; the Admiralty in London too far and costly for their full payoff.

They would have lost forty-percent on the deal but as long as there were no wives waiting that was sweet enough. But this would not be a Royal African commission to come. This was navy work, and the embitterment of being paid a quarter of what the Company had waged them looked back at Coxon.

'Gentlemen!' he began stiffly. 'My name, if you did not hear of it, is Post-Captain John Coxon.'

He tried to show an attitude of war in his assured eyes and lined face; he hoped it carried across the deck.

'You are all now king's men again. The *Standard* is no longer a ship buoyant by the grace of the Royal African Company. She floats alone – proudly – and by your arms and by your loyalty.' He paused, looked to the fo'c'sle over their heads as if for inspiration, then down at them again like Mark Antony upon the crowd.

'You may all have heard that we are to sail to Cape Coast Castle. Heard that Africa at this time of year is a disease for Englishmen. And you may all have concerned yourselves that you are being paid too little to risk the bite of a fly or a drop of water that may bring you to a stitch through your nose and a coffin in a sail that you made.'

A rumble arose now and he freed himself from the lectern of the rail and the company of his officers to address the deck from the stair. He hoped they noticed the poor cut of his breeches and the dull pinchbeck buckles on his shoes that they shared.

'But I will give you more than just a post-run and the opportunity to fill fat General Phipps's plates and keep merry his sots of clerks and lobsters.'

Manvell leaned into Thomas Howard's ear from behind Coxon's back. '*Friends, Romans, countrymen* . . . Lobsters. Sots. Very good.'

Thomas hid his smirk with his hand.

Coxon picked out the largest men, held their eyes one by one.

'I am a fighting man. I have been summoned from honest retirement for a single purpose. Chosen by "Turnip" himself for sword and cannon.'

He could almost feel the blinks of eyes fanning him at the use of the national insult for the monarch that paid their wages and his.

'We are to Cape Castle to be sure. That is but a fortnight of your hard work. From there we are a-hunting. Hunting for bounty. Bounty and prizes. Easier than when you were at war and waiting months for your share. This will come to your pockets as soon as we empty theirs. Legal as a judge!' He slapped the rail.

'We are after *pirates*, my boys! Their holds will be your holds. Their riches your riches. That I swear!'

A circle of looks from the officers around the quarter-deck, only Thomas Howard straight-backed and confident; privileged before them in the knowledge of his captain's words.

Coxon came down two steps, the men at the fo'c'sle gaining higher ground to see him, those closest to him beaming now as their captain came into handshake's reach.

'Weeks I spent from America to England. Weeks, and more weeks, choosing my ship as to the king's instruction. Pick wisely, John, he told me. Pick well the ship and crew you will take. Which of the ninety-fours will you choose?' He pointed aft to the first-rates bobbing in the offing.

'No, says I. No, Your Majesty. I want speed and experienced men. I want men who warrant reward! I hear good things about the *Standard* do I not? She is young. Her crew is able. I have been through all the rates and I choose her!'

A roar from the deck. A nod and a wink from those with pigtails who now definitely recalled to their fellows they had heard the name Coxon before, had served with him in the Spanish war – and who would doubt them?

The first of the guns from Portsmouth harbour signalled noon; instinctively the officers went to their pocket watches.

Coxon went back to the rail, the rail above the belfry and the hour glass, the rail of *him*.

'The pirate Devlin, lads! *Him* we are after! A belly-full of gold for all!'

Across the harbour every ship sent a waft of cannon marking noon, marking Coxon's words, even the ninety-fours respectfully punctuating his speech as if ordered like fireworks, as if planned, their resonance more empowering than cloak and ermine cape.

'Pirate hunting! And that's the best trade for honest men! I came back to be rich!'

He did not say the name Roberts. He glanced back to his officers. No eye showed they knew different. Perhaps they held steady afore their men. Query them all at dinner. Wine better than a Bible for swearing allegiance.

The *Standard* fired its own signal, the glass turned with the ringing of the bell and the bosun yelled for the sail. Noon. The powder salute for those about to sail. Their day beginning, the capstan drawing up the anchor like the ticking of a giant watch and before the fluke met the cathead the *Standard* began to drift impatiently.

Those of the ninety-fours raised their spyglasses to the little fifth-rate dropping her sails like the white faces of a winning hand of cards.

She began to move, a child's paper boat on a stream under a wind that barely lifted their hair from their collars. To their five hundred tons Portsmouth's shallow draft would need escort and towing, for giants lumbering to war.

Let the little pup go to her adventures, escort her slavers, carry her shaky clerks who had drunk the last of their employer's gin at their final post. When war burned, as it should, as it will, they would saunter out. When Admirals wrote the word they would come.

Do not begrudge the fifth-rate her duty to service the factories and forts of the slaver. Even the greatest houses need cleaners and servants.

Yet still, they watched her enviously.

She was going somewhere.

She had orders beyond holy-stoning the deck and drilling marines to stop men deserting.

A fifth-rate two-decker heading out of the mouth and catching the wind like a fisherman's yacht.

The captains studied her like the boys they once were when they first made the promise to themselves, once they realised they were born on an island and had stared out to the horizon at the ships rolling by.

*Where is she going? What shall she do? With what shall she return?*

'To Cape Castle!' Coxon's voice boomed. 'Then to the pirate! George has requested you to empty pirates' pockets! I have known him, this pirate Devlin. He knows and fears me, my boys! He cleaned the blood of Spaniards from my coat and shined my brass. He fears me and he shall fear you!'

A huzzah. Coxon had not expected one. His head dipped to hide the blush at his collar. 'I am to make my plan!'

He came down his triumphant steps once more; happily shook some of the hands that were offered to him, admiring the gall of the men to do so, and disappeared back to his cabin leaving the quarterdeck to Manvell and the others.

Manvell checked his compass, could see the Verdes on its face, the bearing burned into him, then passed it to the sailing master, Richard Jenkins, with the order to set them out of Portsmouth. He gave the deck to Thomas Howard, his last words as he stepped down the stair for every officer and gentleman on the deck.

'Supper will be interesting, gentlemen. Pirates indeed. *What dreams may come.*'

# Chapter Seven

*A* world away, more than a thousand miles and two weeks' sail from Coxon's speech, Patrick Devlin faced his own men from his own quarterdeck. And, just as far, a different breed looked up to their captain before the same noon sun that blinded Coxon's earnest men – men only a bad spin from being on Devlin's side of the line.

The pirate's, the rover's life, was a coin to be tossed for most common seamen. Most, at their trials, would plead they had been forced into it. They had been plied with heady drink and cajoled into the black flag's service and bided their time until a good ship freed them again. They swore on the Bible and priests' robes that the Good Lord had finally saved them from the wicked and – may the saints preserve them – they were now back within the realm of the righteous.

But, like the judges that hanged them, the pirates knew these men well. Fish in a barrel.

The sailor was the most-needed man on the earth. Without him the world failed to turn but to pay him his worth would cripple the enterprises that relied on his back. It is always labour that suffers and the sailor accepted his lot for the promise of steady work.

But then a pirate comes along.

Despite the best efforts of the Just, the stories swab below deck. Common men had become rich as sultans overnight with the flash of a pistol's frizzen.

Why work for bread when meat is a mere blow of a fist away? Honesty was a rich man's sentiment. True honesty is knowing what your arms are for, why God gave you strength and will.

And then a pirate comes along. To it all he says 'No'. The smallest word. The most powerful word, the word of the Lord himself at the temple when he throws the merchants aside.

'Gentlemen!' Devlin's arms spread wide. These were different men to Coxon's band of sailors marked by their petticoat slops.

Long hair throughout, worn so because to cut it meant the first mark of the slave. Gentlemen had long hair but lice favoured them the same.

*They cut mine to cut my place. Pride has long hair. I am filth and they love to cut it from me.*

No uniform clothes.

*I wear the waistcoat and shirt of a gentleman. I took them from him when he shat himself in front of me.*

*My trouser is silk and washed in Chamberlye. An Italian duke bequeathed them me when I didn't cut his throat.*

Pistols about their waists.

*I hang them from silk took from a Maccaroni epicene ponce. I earned them when I swung across to his merchant or spied the ship first from the tops.*

Pistols not bought.

*I own them because I took them. And despite his blood and right he could not keep me off. I earned them. He only bought them from a man who simpered and bowed at his purse.*

Pirates did not take from the poor, for what would be the point of risk for nothing. And their mark was their ports, the places that they took for their own where good ships learnt to shy from. The islands where their names are written forever

were the lands of the dispossessed and the slave; their ceme-
teries, in corners barely trod, told a measure of success.

*You did not catch me. I did not bow my head once nor choke
for your pleasure and indenture.*

The shame of nations was piracy. England was hated
throughout the world, for wherever she spread her coats the
pirate was the flea riding on her back.

They had almost lost the Caribbean and now the East
Indies lay under the same threat from the same men who had
nearly buried America – Devlin one of them. Aware that his
captaincy, elected as it was – a mad democracy that further
showed the pirate's deviance – hung on the morrow more
than his past.

*Where do we sail? What prize can you bring me before I am
cut down, still in my youth?* Enough pirate captains had been
marooned for lack of heart, or compassion on the wrong side.

He had opened his mouth on that June midday wide-armed
with the word 'Gentlemen'.

That would be his last use of the word.

Beforehand he had taken a drink, and that had not been
unusual for he was addressing a hundred killers that followed
him. The unusual was after the rum and lime. He had craved
tea, of all things. A porcelain cup of black tea that you could
stand in. And there was a man with one hand who brought
these things to him, a remnant of a man who never fought in
their boardings but received the same share as all. He was
probably richer than all of them together but he never asked
to be put ashore. On land he would be a crippled sailor wanting even for a cup to beg with. Here he had a worthy place.

Devlin had stood in front of his stern windows and sipped.
He opened a pane, breathed in the blue sky, listened to the
tide pushing against the anchored ship, watched the insects

dive and hum about the stern, the gig below chinking against her chains as the water ebbed.

The unusual came then.

Something content settled over him. Not happiness, that was wrong, but something. He closed the window to stop the moment forming in his memory as he did when he unloaded his pistol into a man's face and concentrated on the reload and moved past the body. Bite, pour, click, snap, click, pour, ram. Gone.

Now he would tell the hundred what they were about to risk all for. *Again.* Again and again. Four years now. Too long to chance your arm. He winced as his right leg reminded him of the bullet and the sword from last year, the most recent chancing of his luck. Too long to chance. Always strange that he had been shot on the left of his back yet the right leg had the memory, and always in the damn morning, nagging like a whore outstaying her coin. A small limp now, but he would rather be a dead man than allow it to be seen.

'We're to the Indies, lads.' He spoke as if standing among them all, no need to shout or bully his words.

'Back to Madagascar and then some. We made out poor last year and lost good men. But that was then.' He moved along the rail, scanning for resentment, finding none.

1720 had been a bad year for all and not just those with their breeches stocked into the South Sea failure. Devlin had come away from the year with nothing but lead in his back.

He had risked his ship, and his crew, for the promise of amnesty from the Crown, and the Crown and black-clothed ministers had wanted a king's diamond that could save the world. But Devlin had lost men in its getting.

Black Bill Vernon, one of the old-standers, one of a handful of the originals, him missed most of all. Devlin and Dandon bloodied and scarred, limping still and stretching their white scars awake every morning. Devlin had sent the greatest diamond of the age back to the earth. Lost as they had lost. He had been called to London and Paris, blackmailed, threatened – as ever the recourse of the appointed over the oppressed. And the pirate had proved too depraved to be swayed by notions of honour or duty. Some coin, the promise of pardon, that would be the limit of his understanding. But that was then, as he had said; last year. Now it was June on the African side of the Atlantic, the season of typhoons and monsoons; but there was work to be done if a quiet winter in the Spanish Main was a prospect or, as Old Cracker had sworn, to become rich again.

That part was important. The crash of the South Sea Company had been a glorious revenge for his men that had died, but now the seeds that he sowed were not even worth reaping. Ships rotted in harbours, companies were unable to trade, goods were not sailing. Bad news for a pirate. The *Shadow*'s coffers were almost spent and not for want of trying – simply for want of lading. Almost any man is one or two bad months from the compter. The threat of bad debt was a strong motivator in the normal world, and how the mighty conspire to keep the lowly in their power. And when all pockets are empty charity dwindles and crime increases. Crime becomes work and those who lived by it before must work harder for their piece.

Aye, work to be done, and murderers and thieves the tools of Patrick Devlin's trade.

'We're after La Buse – "The Buzzard", as he has it. Though I'm minding that's for the mark of the beak on his face than for a talent for prey!' A welcome laugh. The opening of the pocket. Pick them up and place them in – but careful now.

The purpose of the narrator on the stage is to pull the audience into trust, assure them that the play about to start is the best entertainment to be had for their penny.

'The Buzzard took the *Virgin of the Cape* in April. We've all heard it. The inns are full of little else. A gold bounty that no man can measure.' He watched the crowd anticipate his next words. 'But we can measure a lot. Don't we always?'

Whispers now from the deck, a scowl from Peter Sam not enough to quiet them, but Devlin knew what word went round.

La Buse had vanished. He could be anywhere.

'I have good word he has taken his spoils to the Amirantes. And there is the pirate Roberts after a partner to relieve La Buse of his wealth.'

A doubtful voice hidden by the wall of men chirped up.

'How did this "good word" come to thee, Cap'n?'

Peter Sam broke from his lounging against the gunwale to seek the head that spoke, a path opening up before him, but no need: Devlin had been a poacher since childhood and more than once something of those days had saved him and others.

The shot thudded between the man's bare feet into the deck, now split apart. The sailor jumped away from the splintered hole as if the spent ball might still leap up and bite him.

'That's how I got it, George Leary!' Devlin shoved the smoking pistol back to his belt. In his mind's eye a fat fox with Devlin's rabbit in its jaws winked at the fourteen-year-old butcher's boy. '*You'd best get better at this, fool,*' its tail flapped at him before loping away into the dawn. Hunger and beatings had trained his ears as much as his eyes.

The ship cheered at George Leary's impudence but questioning the captain was a pirate's right. It might mean death for the common sailor on merchant or king's ship but Leary had his entitled answer. Devlin's speech carried on as if he had only pointed out Leary from the crowd.

'What's to happen? An easy cruise. Until the end of it. But an eternity of wealth waiting. Roberts knows where La Buse might be but he don't know the Amirantes.'

Another voice, and why not now after Leary had his heard? A shot between Leary's feet made him special. Questioning was now a badge of honour.

'*Might* be? Where Buse *might* be? And how do we know the Amirantes, Cap'n?

Devlin arrowed a finger at the accusing head, which ducked as if the pirate could smash it with a lightning bolt.

'Sam Morwell! You *know* I could find you in hell and steer you to the saints. Ain't I kept your raggedy hide alive all these years?'

More laughter. Rum and laughter as good as the wind to a pirate ship's sails. Keep them hot. Damn hot.

'The Buzzard won't give it up easy, mind. 'Course, we could head back to the Carolinas then up to Trepassey for the summer. Then winter in the Caribbee or Maracaibo. Back here in the spring. The same pirate round as ever. Or would you like one last hunt? And when we're dull and fat, with grease on our chins and virgins at our feet shall we pity what other men do with their lives? Or shall we go? Summer in Newfoundland? What say you?'

This was the hardest part, the thinnest thread. The pirate captain might have the plan but it was the ship that decided.

There were fishermen near the shore, their rafts bound with strips of bark, no hemp or tar to hold the loose wood together, just trust in the father who had taught them. Their teeth were sharpened and their faces painted red and the most golden-bowed missionary riding his chariot of fire would have found it hard not to sweat and shirk in their presence.

They ducked at the joyous roar and the pistol-fire from the black and red ship in the offing and chattered and panicked like birds; they pushed their poles to the coral and away from the ship that was about to rise up and swallow them whole with the great mouth that had made such a fury.

Aye, thought Devlin, that'll do.

Away we go.

# Chapter Eight

*S*upper on the *Standard*. Eight bells. Early, but Coxon retired at ten and he would need the hours to prise from his officers their pasts and any futures that differed from his own. He started lightly, over tongue and potatoes greased with a salty gravy the consistency of pitch, making comment on how he wasn't sure whether to eat it or brush it on the shrouds. Monday a banyan day for the men, no meat; not so for the captain's table. His company chortled through the gravy. Pease, potatoes and bread for those below. He lulled the table more, caused snorts into their wine, as he described his last steward, Oscar Hodge.

Hodge, pitifully amusing in that he had a disorder of the nerves which caused one or the other of his eyes to be half-closed and always made him appear deep in thought. Coxon never sure, he told them, when Hodge was silent, whether the man was having some grand epiphany or passing wind.

He studied them over his glass as they roared. He had them now.

'Drink up, gentlemen,' he said, 'for I will hold to the rule that officers shall only drink in company. And I will hold you to the tradition that you will be expected to bring your own wine tomorrow.'

'No strap in our beds, sir?' This from Doctor James Howe, corpulent and scarlet. Coxon had already surmised that he was not long for the world. Every breath was nearly a gulp, every bite of food scooped and swallowed was barely chewed. The man obviously accepted that indigestion was now the natural state.

'As I say, Doctor Howe, no drink without company.' He watched the man drain his glass and reach for the carafe, a belch held back through puffed out cheeks.

'But no less for that I assure you, Doctor.' Coxon smiled.

Each man stifled his amusement with napkin or glass, with the doctor the last to laugh and just polite enough not to query what the joke was, and still managing to pass the port to Coxon on his left after pouring for young Thomas Howard at his right.

Coxon's glass was as full as he intended and he sailed the carafe on to Lieutenant Manvell, who topped up and offered the toast: Monday, so the glasses raised to their ships at sea. The table repeated with a rap to the wood, no glasses clinked for that would cause the death of a sailor, and no standing – for the beams overhead and several dead soldiers of wine might cause unfortunate injuries. Even the sovereign had to deign to permit his captains to sit when saluting his health as per the tradition. Coxon, not privileged to ever have been in a king's presence, wondered if such a right was ever asserted and voiced this to test what company his table had kept before he came. But this sitting was not wide enough. There was Howe, a sot of a doctor, no doubt only aware of the blue and the black draught that settled most problems or at least stopped men coming back for seconds. Thomas Howard, no dissatisfaction there, but Coxon knew his own weakness for sentiment. Judge him by his actions. He had thought Devlin as loyal as a dog once but carried a star-shaped scar on his forearm from when the pup had bit the hand that fed him.

Sailing-Master Richard Jenkins. Quiet, another one in his fifties creaking towards pension like Howe. God, how will I fight with these men? He looks like his hair is that of a horse stuck on with glue of the same. No captain for the dozen marines, only a sergeant, so no seat for him here.

Manvell then. Feign a giddy openness due to the Oporto you have only sipped. Coxon put down his glass.

'I should like to know how you entered the service, Mister Manvell.'

Manvell cleared his throat as he dabbed at the corners of his mouth. 'Well, sir, I must admit it is not the most honourable of appointments.'

'Explain.' The humour fallen from Coxon. He sat back with his hands entwined across his waistcoat and stretched his feet beneath the table until they touched Manvell's. He felt Manvell's pull away as he hemmed again.

'My stock is not the greatest, Captain. My father is a Deal publican, but a tremendous man with a sword. I have fenced by his instruction since I was seven. I know not where or why he acquired such a habit and I thought it ordinary for all boys. Fortunately, due to my father's humble nature, I have not boasted of this aptitude, which I'm sure has led me to be a modest and healthy sort.'

'No shame in being an honest publican's son, Mister Manvell. I myself am a parson's second. Had one pair of trousers until I was twelve and the queen gave me another. Go on. When did your service begin?'

'I am afraid I am a bit of a late bloomer, sir. Not that I should wish for the *Standard* to consider me less for it.'

Coxon shook his head and Manvell gave up his journey like a confession.

At eighteen he had fallen into a romance with the Duke of Beaufort's daughter. This was not to the duke's pleasure and the prospect of his dearest and his lineage living with a tavern-keeper's son was beyond the pale.

Coxon winked to all the table: '*Both, Dove-like, roved forth beyond the pale to planted Myrtle-walk.*'

Manvell saluted with his glass and carried on.

He had fortunately relieved the duke of this embarrassment by providing him with another scandal to remove it completely. Foot followed foot and Alice, seventeen, tripped and fell pregnant, which surprised everyone except the birds on the bough who witnessed the act beneath their tree.

At first the duke considered a duel until he considered better the advice given that young Manvell could peel the skin off an apple while it was still in your pocket with any strip of steel you gave him.

So marriage then, and a commission for Manvell so that he might at least have some future.

'Unfortunately our daughter was not born, sir, but, as is the way, the Lord is apt to plan these things to bring love closer. I am in two families now. The duke has mellowed to me, and I am blessed to say that Alice is expecting again. Although I am considerably nervous on my part as twins do fairly run in the duke's family. I'm sure I believe we will be successful this time.'

The table was quiet, forks were laid down.

It is difficult to commiserate and congratulate in the same voice even though all men share at least some of the same paths. The only relief is the hope that the path when you meet it will be just that. A path. A short tread through the dark, and not a road.

Coxon kenned Manvell shy of what he had said: the man had come to terms with his loss and now did not want to embarrass others. Coxon locked only two words away for when the time came to measure him.

Manvell had said 'daughter' not 'child'. There was a terrible shared day there. And he had said the name 'Alice' to strangers as if they all recalled her. As if anyone could not know her. Coxon had only ever spoken of his first ship in the same voice. He almost felt envy at the tone of it.

'Then we will make the duke proud of his son-in-law,' he said. 'And your father will have your portrait above the hearth of his tavern.'

The bell outside rang once and Coxon glanced at the clock. Eight-and-a-half hours since they had set sail. The Lizard and even Brest at their stern. Lonely water now to the Verdes. Eleven days he planned to Cape Coast Castle, the trade winds at their back. Worthless to consider the pirate before then. But Manvell had not forgotten the noon address.

'Captain?'

Coxon sniffed himself out of his thoughts. 'Yes, Mister Manvell?'

'This pirate, this . . . Devlin, you mentioned, whom we are to chastise. You indicated that you knew him.'

Coxon played his fingers on his full belly. 'Has Mister Howard not told you of our experiences together?'

Manvell explained that Howard had only come into company the day before and that he was confident that neither of them trucked in gossip.

'Very well,' Coxon said. 'For some years this man was my steward.' Elaboration on those years was not tasteful to Coxon and his embarrassment well known. But they needed to know about the pirate.

'I would like to say that he is a drunken, misanthrope idiot. But that would give you the impression that all you will have

91

to do is walk into a tavern and lift his head up from a table.'
He watched them all shift in their seats, study him judiciously.
The tradition of Aesop was his duty.

'What I can tell you will be meaningless against what he
*may* show you. And if you give him the opportunity to "show"
you . . . it will be too late.'

Howe scoffed into his glass. 'You make him terrible,
Captain! I'll wager he doesn't even wear shoes!'

'He will be wearing *your* shoes if you continue to
appraise him so, Doctor. Make no mistake, Devlin is intelligent and bold. He has not survived so long by mere luck
and nor is he a great warrior. If he were in this room now
you would not see a remarkable man,' he pointed to the
door, to the deck. 'You would see one of *them*. The men
we trust to follow us, who rely on our instruction to bring
them home. And I guarantee that a similar discourse is
flowing below. Only *they* will show a little more respect,
some of them even awe. And you may live longer if you
gain the same.'

Manvell was intrigued.

'You sound as if you admire him, sir.'

Coxon leant on the arm of his chair, pitched forward so
that Manvell could see nothing else but his face and taste the
meal on his breath.

'And so I should. If I did not admire a man who has bested
me twice, that would make me a fool who any boot-wipe can
lick. And I take pride in the knowledge, gentlemen, that the
one time I was not there to break him he triumphed over the
royal houses and governments of *two* countries, sirs!' Coxon
fell back. He had said too much. He looked at his glass. Wine
proved always the culprit. Devlin's grin piercing him was
always the spur. He blurted an apology.

'But I can say no more on that, gentlemen. Forgive me. But, yes, the part of me that knew him would be foolish to not admire.'

Thomas Howard had been conspicuously quiet. He cut his meat silently and sipped his wine as Coxon had spoken. He had seen pirates fight. Seen the boarding axes fly with blood, seen the cannon fire two to their one, and the green veil of smoke that heralded their coming from their cauldrons on deck. He shared a glance with Coxon who now sank in his seat.

Doctor Howe smirked.

'*Admire,* sir? You sound positively proud!'

Coxon tapped his glass on the table.

'And should I not? I taught him everything he knows. Shame and praise me.'

Silence around the table and the sound of music, an agreeable Cheshire voice and a fiddle, from far below, gentle as whale song. Something about lasses and fairs as always. Coxon picked up the decanter with a chime, poured for Howe and himself then passed it on.

'Shame and praise me. I am the fox and he is the crow.' He raised his glass to the table. 'And we are both equally hated.'


Devlin entered the cabin and threw his coat onto a chair; the relief of his men's acceptance was as heavy as the twill. Dandon watched him from the locker seat, an amber bottle between his legs. He watched him limp to the rope beckets that held back the wine from falling when the deck pitched. Neither of them had sought a light first. Just the liquid. Drinking in the dark and alone was what counted for privacy on a pirate.

Dandon watched him pour a fist's worth of wine. He knew Devlin had seen him. He would wait to be acknowledged and listened to the wine rush and bubble into the mug.

For four years now Dandon had known Patrick Devlin. They had both been near thirty then – old for pirates at even that age. Devlin had once saved Dandon from a drunken Blackbeard's rage on Providence island, where Dandon had fancied himself a barber-surgeon. In truth he had joined Devlin's rag-tag crew for the drink and the joy of it and, besides, he had nothing better to do.

It took little more than that to become an enemy of mankind.

But Dandon, in yellow wide-brimmed hat and justacorps, asides from the scraping off of arms and thighs what did not belong and cauterising that which he could and offering laudanum when he could not, was not fully of the crew.

He took no part in boardings and no share and only asked that someone bring him back any powders, draughts or chest of medicines that might aid them. He was Patrick Devlin's friend, and counted himself rare to be it. Rare to be anything alive around Devlin for long.

Devlin did not even know Dandon's real name – one of the ways of the pirate. Sign the articles and be baptised anew. Your name belonged to the old. You were on the account now and born again. The purpose was two-fold: Protect your family and your old crimes, or the past that tied you to a king's ship and the regular.

Dandon's name came from 'Dandelion', a mockery of his bright yellow coat and hat worn when he had first arrived on Providence and dreamt of operating a saltern and selling gout pills to fat rich men and romancing their soon-to-be widows. He had ended up a pox-doctor in Mrs Haggins's brothel, and then Devlin had entered his world.

He lived amongst murderers and thieves but being secure in himself he never carried pistol or sword. He had no need.

The pirate Devlin was his friend. No-one could keep count how many times one had saved the other.

'Are we well, Patrick?' he enquired when the first sup had been sighed away.

'Aye,' Devlin said. 'Well enough. We have a new game.'

Dandon had not seen him since the hours when he had given the men their needed speech. That time was for the planning of a course, the listing of sailcloth and cordage, the counting of hogsheads and sacks and as ever the bottles of brandy, rum and wine to keep the men hot, fit for the Devil. Dandon did not belong when those plans and lists were made; that was for Peter Sam, the quartermaster, and for John Lawson, once the bosun and now sailing master since the death of Bill Vernon. That death had come when the ship had been taken by the great René Duguay Trouin.

But Devlin had taken it back.

All for the taking of a diamond.

They had stolen the first magnificent diamond of the world, the great Pitt diamond, originally stolen from the Regent of France himself, to save a kingdom from the collapse of a company that had valued itself more than all the coin in Europe. There was nothing small in Devlin's world any more. Once his horizon had been brushing shoes and cleaning plates, steward to John Coxon for four years after Coxon had taken him prisoner from a French ship. He had run to France when the murder of old man Kennedy had made London no place for an Irishman to be found near a corpse. He ran for the second time, as first he had run from Kilkenny to London when his poacher's shot cracked the wrong tooth and a magistrate swore against him.

But running was not in Devlin's nature now. That image was all done.

Dandon saw the drain of enough wine for him to question further.

'What "game" is it now, Patrick?'

'The old one. All the gold in the world.'

'How is that now?'

Devlin moved to look out of the small window closest to him. Dusk now, the best time to be on the sea. Anchors soon, the smell of hot stew, the last cries of the petrels and then the stars softening the whole world as if nothing evil ever happened or would again. Until the dawn.

'I'm going after Levasseur. He took a Porto carrack in April. Loaded to the gunwales with gold from Goa. The pirate Roberts is also after. He knows the island where he may be but not how to get there. He's been abandoned by his captains. I reckon he needs a friend.'

'And you feel you can find that which Roberts cannot?'

'Give me a map, a star and a rule and I'll show you your mother's belly.'

Dandon saluted with his bottle.

Before becoming the pirate, Devlin's master, Captain John Coxon, had taught him the art and intricacies of navigation. Coxon had hoped to help the young man. After all, he had stepped forward from his captured ship of the Marine Royale to speak for his officers in strange Irish vowels under his French tongue. Saved their lives. Gave information that had made Coxon a post-captain.

On finding he could read and write Coxon had given the Irishman study and measure. Perhaps an instructor he could be? Or an hydrographer's assistant? There would be no officer for the Irishman despite his brains. Coxon and the world were both now paying the price for his teaching of the Irish upstart.

Most of the pirate's contemporaries were now dead. The Lords of Providence, the Kings of the Caribbean and the Pirate Republic that they dreamt of had been wiped from the earth under King George's proclamation of *Hostis Humani Generis.* Enemy of Mankind. Pirates were placed beyond the law as far as fair trial and punishment were concerned. Kill on sight. Devlin was no longer an antagonist.

He was a survivor.

Only Roberts seemed able to douse the fuse lit against them. As underestimated as Devlin, a seaman from a slaver, almost forty, a forgotten man until Howell Davis found him and Roberts turned pirate.

In two years he had taken nigh on four hundred ships. That did not make him a pirate, that did not make him an admiral – that made him Poseidon himself, and the most wanted man on the sea.

'Though every soul will be looking for the treasure. And for Roberts too,' Devlin said, to the window more than to Dandon.

'And us to swim into the middle of it all. As always.'

Devlin cocked his head.

'I swear Dandon, sometimes I thinks you want to live forever.'

A cry from outside snapped them upright like gunfire.

*'Sail! Deck there!'*

They both sped outside and straight into the backs of dozens all straining for a glance. Peter Sam stood to Devlin's side.

'There,' he pointed off the starboard quarter, and Devlin called for a spyglass.

He saw a snow through the glass. The smoky blue lens was dark in the falling light as if it too, and not just Devlin's eye, were squinting . There, under his gaze, two masts and the jibs. Low in the water.

'She be fast,' Devlin said. 'And three miles from us.'

He passed back the scope to the hand that gave it. 'Lawson!' he called for the bosun. 'Close up on that ship before dark. An hour now, John.' He climbed the five steps to the quarter-deck, Peter following, Dandon gone back to his bottle. No worth for him outside.

Here be pirates.

Devlin looked to the coast. They were three miles from land, the snow a further three miles away. If you attacked a vessel within five miles of land it was an act of war not piracy and that would not do. He had enemies enough already.

'She's ours,' Devlin said. 'Stores are low even after taking Cracker's lot.' He had a lectern by the helm with a map always out and marked their place now and where an hour would put them at five knots.

'No more than five, John!' he called to Lawson. 'She's making three. But she'll raise when she sees us coming.'

'Aye, Cap'n!' and Lawson yelled at his mates to move like apes into the rigging. One more square of sail.

'What you reckon on her?' Peter Sam asked. No flag, but then ships rarely sailed with colours until they closed for news.

'A snow. Out here. Too small for Spain. Porto, maybe.'

Devlin pushed Peter Sam to his work.

'We'll ask them when we catch them.'

# Chapter Nine

*T*he triangles of white had still not changed. Devlin, no need for a scope, could see few men upon her, but small traders often sailed light.

'More than an hour. She still runs under staysails and jibs. She's not fleeing. No mainsails.'

Peter Sam held his hand over his brow as the setting sun lit up the little ship. 'So she's a merchant letting us close for words.'

'Then she'll have it. We'll ride into her lee. Raise a Porto flag. I'll gamble that's what she is. I see no guns other than swivels. Tell the men it's a surprisal.'

Peter Sam left the helm, left just Devlin and the timoneer on the higher ground of the quarterdeck.

This would be the old game. A pirate's methods of taking a ship varied as much as the ships themselves or as much as that of the pickpocket and highwayman.

The drunk who bumps into you on the street, apologises and wheels away with your watch and purse. The crippled old man who begs for alms and then pushes a pistol into your belly, or the sweet girl who asks for aid and her lover stoves your head in from behind with a chair leg.

Disguise and deception were more powerful than arms – until the last minute and the great reveal, the magician's 'praestigium' and the cannons that rip into your world.

Another ship springing up from the sea like the dove from the hat.

For larger ships, for the *Shadow*, for those rovers who sailed the square-riggers, the tactic was to appear fully laden and slow.

The chase, the prey, would be ahead, would see you at their stern under full canvas, your courses stretched fat and tight but barely crawling.

No need for them to make any more sail. Just a fat merchant lolling in their wake.

What they did not see was the log over your stern trailing a grinding-stone or 'stop-waters', a sea-anchor pulling you to a slow crawl.

When the time was best judged, up would come the stop-waters and your fat merchant would charge under full sail, run over them like a rogue wave as they fumbled to raise even a half sail under the onslaught.

That would not work today. The ships were on a parallel and the snow was more than capable of running like a deer from the bullish frigate.

The smaller ship was the more weatherly. Devlin's angle of sail could only make twelve of the compass's thirty main points to the wind. The snow with her staysails and flying jibs and narrow beam could almost double them. She could turn and run at forty-five degrees before the *Shadow* turned a point.

So the *Shadow* had to run ahead, the parallel closing. Run a friendly flag and then time the angle to cut off the ship.

'Stand to her forefoot!' the cry.

Cut her bows, and as the daylight vanishes that will be your time, for whereas pirates relish the dark to cover their work, were trained to it, the common sailor fears it.

They will panic, become clumsy, may lay on too much sail, worse as too little for losing a mast.

If the other captain kept his head, fought against his instincts and, instead of running, slowed, heaved-to and aimed for the pirate's wake the pirate would overrun and he would wave them away with a sweep of his hat and could drink to his smarts for the rest of his days.

That too would not work today.

The snow had taken the bait of the flag and within minutes the square white and red of the Porto came up from the ensign at the snow's stern. Both ships heaved-to and the earth stopped turning, and they bobbed together like gulls riding the waves.

'We have her,' Devlin announced to the timoneer. 'Peter Sam! Men below! Weapons loose!'

The sun had flattened her edge along the horizon, the men now merely etched out across the deck, barely there.

Dozens of them crouched below the hammock nettings with pistols slung by lanyard or silken ribbon around their necks. A coil of rope nearby with grenadoes and stinkpots lay ready to throw to the prey's deck. Each man held a smouldering match fuse safe in a tin in his waistcoat or wrapped around his wrist. They giggled to each other like children.

The final subterfuge.

One of the finest weapons of the pirate was the international nature of his crew. Regardless of the captain's original caste he could within a year have Dutch and Spanish, African and Indian, French or Portuguese on his quarter-bill. The lines of war did not matter. This was a democracy for all.

'Mateo!' Devlin called, and a shirtless brown youth bounded to the quarterdeck where Devlin passed him the speaking trumpet.

Devlin's chest beat hard, his eyes staring wide and not because of the fading light.

It would be a cutlass to break a bottle-neck by evening's end instead of just pulling a cork.

The thrill of trawling your hands through other men's gold, pulling their rings from their fingers, taking the pistols that they never used, and the pistols grateful for it. The laughter and the dining on fear. New maps to add, log books to check for your name or news of riches yet to be taken in new ports. Hogsheads of meat, ankers of wine. How do you measure your world?

'*Hoy, lá. Quais são as notícias do dia, Capitão? De onde você é?*' Mateo called over, and waited with Devlin crouched beside him.

'From the Holy,' the call came back in English and Mateo did not understand but no matter, the ships were close enough. Devlin stood to the falconet at his rail and Peter Sam stood with him and gave his order to the men low on the deck.

'Sling your hooks!'

Grappling irons were hurled at the prey's gunwale and into the rigging, should someone have the mind to wield an axe to cut them.

The hooks bit, more men ran to the ropes to haul as the snow groaned and Devlin fired the flintlock on his falconet.

It was only filled with powder, just a startling warning like the stinkpots that flew over now before the ship could react.

The clay-pots smashed and the fuse crawled over the brimstone, char-cloth and tar inside and a cloud of foulness spread around the deck.

These were the harmless weapons, less than the 'fireworks' to follow with the grenadoes of glass and nails and musket balls. Give them first a chance to surrender. Let them mark the next part.

Nothing. No boarding pikes or muskets, no shouts or screams. Devlin's smoke cleared and he looked down onto the deck below.

Half a dozen men in black robes wiping their streaming eyes, pouring water from the gourds around the mainmast on the ticklish fires from the pots or stamping them out with sandalled feet.

No weapons met them and Devlin's men stood up from the nettings and pointed their pistols and musketoons at a deck ignoring their presence.

They looked back to Peter Sam to direct them. He held his Sibley gun against his hip and watched the robed men mill about as if the fires were grapes to be picked and the pirate ship just a light disagreeable rain. He turned to Devlin, who had pulled his pistol and looked back just as baffled.

'Priests?' Devlin said. 'It's a ship of priests?'

A bearded tall man span against the rail and shouted up in a scornful Irish voice which instantly took Devlin back to his boyhood.

'Of course we're bloody priests, you shite! Now come and put out these bloody fires, damn you! Do you not hear a Father when he calls you!'

# Chapter Ten

Another hour and into darkness. The snow, the *Santa Rosa* it transpired, now ran consort to the *Shadow*, a pirate crew upon her.

The priests walked to the *Shadow* over boarding planks under pistol and lantern. The pirates were pleased, for although Whitehall would have laughed at the thought, pirates held priests and tracts in high regard. The pirate Roberts even kept the sabbath and others had begged clergymen to join them as they burnt their ship around their feet.

Perhaps it was still due to the ingrained Bible of their youth and service and the sailor's wont to respect anything supernatural, knowing how thin the border lay between life and death.

They swore on the Bible as much as pistols.

Seeing his men's joy at them Devlin gave the priests freedom upon the ship. He ordered them to be fed, to have a table made up for them below; but the pirate ship was sparse of furniture. Their attitude was more to remove wood and bulkheads. Remove to clear more space for more men, for lading, for fighting. But the men adapted well for their guests. A couple of hogsheads and boarding planks for a table, some carpenter's half-barrels for seats.

Devlin at least had real chairs and a table in his cabin and he invited the Irish priest to join him and Dandon once the heat of the evening had died down.

The priest carried aboard with him a sailcloth packet and Devlin recognised the shape and the fondness for books and so let them be.

They would raid the ship in the dawn.

They broke a bottle together, beginning as all introductions should begin. The priest, to Devlin's mind, acted uncomfortably too genial for a man who had just lost his ship.

'Hugh O'Neill, Captain,' he sent out his hand and Devlin took it.

'Ah, I discern that there is still enough of your home in you to recognise that name.' He swept his hand on to Dandon who reached over and took it warmly; for so long had such a conviviality been absent from his day.

Devlin let the priest sit and wanted more on the name.

'You take your name from Irish kings, Father?'

'And why not that for a Donegal man, Captain? And where are you back home?'

The question was the same from all Irishmen who meet for the first time no matter where they have ended up or how dubious their social standing. For Devlin however this was the time for interrogation not banter, Irish or not. He had played the same scene with dozens of captains before this one.

The pirate would want to know where the ship was coursing for and from and the nature of her passengers.

Was she expecting to meet anybody? Was she already a part of a convoy that might lead to more riches? And what was the news of the world as the captain knew it?

News was paramount. The pirate spent most of his life at sea. He could often be the last to know of a new war. It could be fortuitous to know which kings and queens were at each other's throats if only to draw new lines of where the best-laden would be sailing.

'I'm a Kilkenny man, Father. But that was too long ago. What's a Donegal priest doing out here? A snow with six priests coursing against Africa. What's the game of it?'

'So it's definitely the pirate I am meeting? Not a chance to let us on our way?'

Devlin noticed he had cruel black eyes to match his thinning hair and close-cut beard greying on the jowls. A thin face and frame but his gown was tight and showed muscle more than bone.

An Irish priest shaping a course on the Atlantic showing no fear of the pirate in front of him. Devlin could change that. The look of confidence never lasted long.

Dandon spotted the next thoughts and interceded as he often did when he could feel the air warming.

'Father,' he said. 'It would only be considered as prudent that you avail us of any information. In the first instance – over drink and pleasant company – it would be considered polite. In the second instance it would be simply . . . *unwise* to not do so.'

Dandon anticipated the open mouth about to object and raised his hand.

'It has nothing to do with fear. I'm sure your faith in Your Lord is ample enough that you're little afraid of any villainy. But perhaps consider that it will be better for other souls. That is to say should we come across other ships who might be attached to yourself.'

O'Neill cocked his chin to Devlin.

'He goes on a bit, this one.'

'I don't,' Devlin said coldly. 'He means that you can't be out here by yourself. By dawn the others will show themselves. That might go hard for them. Hard for you. If you don't tell what I want to know.'

'And who says I won't tell? I've been hoping for the opportunity. Waiting for it. You're just what I was looking for, so you are!'

'And how is that now?' Devlin watched him stand and pour them all more wine.

'Captain,' he watched his pour and spoke slowly. 'I've not been back home for a long time. Maybe as long as you, my son. I come from Lisboa with my brothers. Before that, I served in Goa and left that place with my archbishop and the viceroy in January.'

He sat and looked mournfully into his mug.

'You may have heard something of that, being pirate yourself? A viceroy's ship taken, that is.'

Dandon saw Devlin glow and hold his breath, and O'Neill had seen it also.

'Ah, now, so that would be of interest to you?' He drank long, savouring his power over the cabin.

'Aye. I was on the *Virgin of the Cape* when the pirates took her. A carrack of gold with the departing viceroy.' He drank and gasped at the fullness of the wine.

'Would some of that story be the kind of thing you were after?'

Dom Luiz de Menezes was the departing viceroy, he explained, and it would take almost five months to return to Lisboa from Goa.

Accompanying him aboard the *Nossa Senhora do Cabo* was Sebastiao de Pessanha, the archbishop, and several millions in gold, rubies, diamonds and emeralds for their king, for India was the birthplace of gems. But the most precious tribute, the greatest symbol of the Christian over the Hindu, was the solid gold Flaming Cross.

Crosses of fire represent the Son and the Father. God the Word revealed himself to Moses through a burning bush foretelling his coming incarnation. But the bush was not consumed by the fire. This God, over the old, had no desire to punish man. His power would be to save.

The bush is not consumed.

When the Messiah is consumed by the cross the unification of the Father and the Son becomes complete. That was the prophecy of the burning bush.

See the Son in the cross, in the flames, and see the Father.

The Flaming Cross of Goa held this tradition. It was from the Se Cathedral of Santa Catarina and destined for the cathedral of the same name in Lisboa.

Gold mined by slaves and moulded by priests into a seven-foot cross adorned with rubies and mounted on diamonds and emeralds, the rubies emulating the fire of the burning bush, the incorruptible fire. The Cross of Fire.

Recently removed from the heart of a smaller cross, and placed within its heart as it cooled was a small gold box no larger than a forefinger. It had been brought from Lisboa by a group of priests to be conjoined with the new cross under the blessing of King João of Portugal. Its destiny was to return home to the king, to show the world Portugal's wealth in India and to demonstrate the conquest of Christian over Hindu.

It was the incarnation of the Word and the Son, and that part O'Neill hoped Devlin still had soul for.

'You see, Captain, my name is no coincidence. I am descended from *the* Hugh O'Neill. I am an heir of Tyrone, if you would believe it.'

Dandon looked to his captain. He knew nothing of the relevance of O'Neill's words but Devlin was listening and so

Dandon would also, but not dry. He reached for the bottle but kept quiet, even polite enough to draw directly from the bottle lest his pouring disturbed the story.

O'Neill accepted that the bottle would not be returning to him.

'I, in my journey, at least made it to Spain, Captain. I had more luck than Earl O'Neill. And on to Portugal and so to India. A pilgrimage.'

'For what?' Devlin asked.

O'Neill took a breath and sent the pirate a look of pity.

'Do you remember your Sunday education, Captain? The Irish kings leaving us to the English. Leaving to raise a Spanish army in 1607, a Catholic army that never arrived. The end of our country?'

Devlin did not share that his school had been books that servants had stolen from their masters to pay for meat.

His father had sold him to be a butcher's boy far from home. His mother had left, for whatever reason. That was done. Him his father's only child. Guineas for a boy. That all done now. He had shot enough pistols to make peace with it.

'I read something about it, Father.'

'Ah, then you know of the cross. The *true* cross.' O'Neill gave the *signum crucis* in the air before him and glared at the pirate when he did nothing but stare right back.

'The earl, my ancestor, had a gold crucifix about his neck. Inside, protected by the gold, the cross held a piece of Our Lord's *own* cross.'

Devlin gave the rest.

'And a storm came up. And O'Neill took the cross and had it dragged behind the ship and the waters calmed.'

O'Neill nodded proudly. 'Aye. And the waters calmed.'

'Do you believe all fairy stories, Father?'

O'Neill took his seat.

'So you wouldn't believe me if I told you it was the cross that pulled me to Lisboa? That I took it with me to Goa with Our Lord's cross within on Holy order?' That I travelled on the king's command?

Dandon's eye caught the glitter and silent fall of a star from the window. He had wandered from the conversation and into his bottle, but the star had brought him back.

'How does a piece of wood get inside a gold cross?'

Devlin snatched the bottle.

'It doesn't. It's a story. Irishmen are raised on songs and stories. That's why they're all hungry.'

O'Neill's voice lowered. 'You should hear the rest of it, my son.'

'I'm not your son.' Devlin sank a drink.

The priest had made him think of home, of being young, of being quiet, of being left. Of watching his father's back go out a door with coin for his son in his pocket and the boy carrying the memory like a boulder from then on.

The priest saw the pirate's mind wander. 'But it is a good story. And you a part of it. That I know.'

Devlin stiffened.

'How am I a part of it?'

'The cross went with me to Goa so O'Neill's cross could be joined with the Flaming Cross. So to preserve the Holy Cross, the True Cross, the relic of Our Lord, forever. And return with it to Lisboa.' He crossed himself.

'The True Cross within the gold. The divinity of it, Captain! And you to play a part! A pirate with the Lord's cross. Your poor life elevated to glory! This is why you have had your tribulations and troubles. The Lord has shaped you to his purpose!'

110

'And the pirates took it,' Devlin said. 'And you in mourning.'

'The True Cross is within that cross. It must be returned to the world. If this pirate melts the gold, the True Cross of Our Lord will be lost.'

Devlin had heard enough. He stood and took up his glass. His back to the table, his front to the black outside the stern windows. He spoke to the sea.

'I come across you who carried this cross from India and had it taken by Levasseur. That is too short. Too thin, Father.'

'How so, Captain?'

Devlin did not turn. 'I am after that treasure. How is it I come across you?'

O'Neill stood. In the mirror of the window Devlin saw the strength of him. Formidable for his kind.

'I am a simple priest. I left a king – though I am sure that means nothing to you – and I told him that I would return with the cross. I told him the Lord would provide.' He looked down at Dandon.

'I have faith.'

Devlin came back and held out his hand for Dandon's bottle. He sank it long and gasped his words.

'Levasseur took the *Virgin of the Cape*. Left it as a wreck. How did you make it back?'

'Oh, it was quite a month, Captain, to be sure. But it was on the snow you have now. A friendly ship come for us. Her captain handsomely paid back in Lisboa.'

'I have sworn to get back the cross. The only truth I knew was that I would find men to help me take it back. What else would I hope for with but six priests? I care not for the treasure, for the rest of it, just the return of the cross.'

Devlin turned.

'You think I'll help you? I've pirated your ship. I want to empty you, not fill you up.'

'I can pay, Captain. If that is your only wish.'

'With what?'

O'Neill rose and went to his sail-cloth packet.

'When I meditated on my mission, and the king granted me anything to take with me to aid my journey, I asked only for entry to his library.' He brought three books to the table. One an enormous tome and two smaller. Dandon pushed aside the obvious Bible and picked up the pale hardback of a new copy of Woodall's *Military and Domestic Surgery*. He leafed through it with a gleaming eye.

'My word!' he laughed. 'I have never seen it complete!'

Devlin was drawn by the large, square, blue book. He lifted the cover.

'The *Neptune Français*.' He repeated the title as his hand stroked the colourful plate inside. 'In English. A Mortier translation.'

Most complete mariners' charts were French; France, just last year, had been the first country to dedicate an entire government department to hydrography. A seaman would know the French name for an island before he knew his native one.

Dandon peered over from his own study. 'An atlas?'

Devlin folded out one of the charts as gently as if it was made of gold leaf.

'It is *the* atlas.' He thought on his waggoner of charts from different nations, in different scales and varying meridians.

O'Neill took up his Bible.

'It is yours. These were the books my prayers told me to find. I was to seek a surgeon and a seaman and gift them to aid my mission.'

Devlin closed back the atlas with a slap.

'It is mine anyways. Along with anything else you have.'

'But do you not see, Captain?' He came close to the table and pulled all three books together.

'The trinity of it. A Holy Trinity! The Bible, the maps, the surgeon's treatise! All we will need to bring back the cross! It is your destiny! The spirit of St Brendan inside you!'

'You set out on the sea and guessed you might meet a sailor and a surgeon. Well done. None of this gets you your cross. I do not know where it is.'

'But *I* do.'

O'Neill let his statement sink deep into both men's lusts, smiled at the pirate captain's hunger.

'Say that again?'

Devlin dropped his hand to his sword hilt as his back bit with its old wound.

'You know where it is? With the rest . . . the rest of . . .?'

He could not say it.

Treasure is a fragile word. It travels out of open windows and is blown away like smoke. A word to be whispered over candlelight and small round tables in private corners.

The mouthing of it was sacred, for it longed to speed to the ears of others.

'How know you this, priest?'

# Chapter Eleven

*O*livier Levasseur had captured the *Virgin of the Cape*, a Portuguese ship full of nobles and priests.

He burned the ship.

She was holed and grounded and he sailed in his caravel, *Victory,* taken with Taylor months before. He left the ship. He had the *Virgin*'s treasure. That would do.

The pirate and his crew delighted in using the priests' backs to shift his new wealth. Porto Catholics fresh from their inquisitions in India. Let the bastards sweat. With Taylor he discussed the dividing of their haul.

John Taylor, English; Levasseur, French. The Portos would understand French and Spanish so they spoke in English as the captives ferried past with their goods.

'That is how I know, Captain,' O'Neill declared. 'The wretch did not suspect that there was an Irishman within his earshot. I know where he is going.'

'But not how to find it,' Devlin said.

O'Neill waved his arms over the books.

'The trinity. Together we will find it. You your treasure, and I my cross.'

'And why would I do that?'

'But why would you not?' O'Neill displayed himself the priest amongst the rogues, gave the glare that shamed.

'Would you not see some worth for yourself in being an

114

instrument of the Lord? Is your soul so wretched, my son?'

Devlin said nothing. He took up the bottle and moved around the priest out onto the deck and slammed the door behind him.

O'Neill looked at Dandon who did not appear puzzled at all.

Dandon sighed.

'He will need to contemplate,' he offered. His words did not remove the confusion from the priest's face.

'There are the men to consider. Patrick is not the master of their fates. Every decision must be agreed. He has lost many good men on the whims and motives of others.'

'So more the need to gain some redemption.'

Dandon closed his eyes and shook his head.

'You do not understand. His contemplation is not on whether to help you or not. It is on whether to *cut* from you what you know. Or – and this the more probable – how to convince the crew to not do so.'

O'Neill paled for the first time since he had come into the company of pirates.

Devlin took himself to the gunwale, his bottle hanging over the sea as he leant over to study the black water below. A few men were smoking above, lost in their own memories, and the ship was slumbering at anchor for the night.

A song arose from under his feet but not a great chorus, just one or two with a fiddle and a shared voice, a spoon rapping against a stool; 'Jack Hall' the song, a variation of the Kidd ballad that the pirates often sang.

'*And my neck will pay for all,*' they sang, and Devlin spat to the sea.

'*When I die, when I die.*'

'When I die!' Devlin drank and laughed into the bottle.

But he pondered as he played the bottle against the wood in time to the song.

If the priest knew the name of the island they could forego having to find Roberts. Go straight for the gold and the ridiculous cross. That would save time. And time was of the moment; the money all of the moment, for the world was poor.

The South Sea collapse had been bad for all. Devlin recalled himself throwing the diamond up and over the heads of Walpole and the Prince of Wales, no less.

It had felt good then but now the trade on the waters had slowed, the ship's holds were thin, and him with a hundred men to feed, the purse lower every month and a pirate captain's tenure only as happy as the bellies he filled.

Their gold was low, their silver already broken into pieces of eight. The years of fat were dwindling down to a scraggy stew.

He had thought the coin would last but avarice surprises even the richest of men, but the thief and the viscount were both only a bad month or two away from the compter.

He had met dozens of vagrant pirate captains who had once been gods. He had never seen himself as toothless and tobacco-stained like them, begging rum for their tales of past glories.

He weighed one hand with the other, not seeing it as palms closing for prayer, and he did not hear Peter Sam come to his side.

'What ails, Captain?' The rough quartermaster stood with his hands tucked into his broad belt, a pipe drooping from his mouth.

'Nothing,' Devlin said. 'The priest has surprised that's all. How go the rest of them?'

Peter Sam breathed in the night air.

'They ate. They don't speak English but it'll be good to have some holy luck on the ship for a while. The men are pleased about it anyways. The parsons seem mighty calm for captured men.'

Devlin offered his bottle without a word and Peter Sam swigged short for its liquid was in the last quarter. You can't drain a man's last.

'We're almost broke, Peter,' Devlin said, taking back the wine. 'Every ship we come across is thinner than water.'

'But we're after The Buzzard's gold. That'll do. The ship talks of nothing else.'

'Aye. But I feel like a gambler on his last coin. Going broke for the toss.' He drank until he choked and went on.

'It's desperate. A myth. Chasing a fortune. We could be starving by the end of it. Never find a thing.'

Peter Sam had never heard his captain talk so. He was older than Devlin but they had both seen the end of the Spanish war. The boy was no pup.

Peter Sam had killed more, had seen more, and learnt to judge his day by what he had drunk and ate, by full belly and bleary eye. Morning was another country.

He knew his captain to be a quiet one. A man who read, who killed easy and well but slept badly for it and drank fast to drown his humour. And Devlin did not sing. And he would dance awkwardly, and then pretend to be breathless and leave the others to the jig. His was not an easy take to the life, so Peter Sam, the true, the actual, had to show him the way.

If Peter Sam was not this, not the brigand in goat leather with apostles of powder about his chest, not the giant of the deck, he would still be the cod fisherman in Newfoundland earning less than he owed his masters for their black bread and cod-bone mash. Those men who had set themselves above him would fear him now if they ever saw him again. He had often thought that he would return to greet them, one moonless night.

He knew that Devlin needed his word. His word as pirate. He needed to be reminded. Reminded that *they* would enslave him for a coin and hang him for a stolen spoon if he let them forget the fear. 'You have your pistol about?' Peter Sam held out his hand.

Devlin lifted from his belt his favoured left-lock Bohemian pistol. It had taken the life of more than a dozen men and grew heavier for it as all arms do when you weigh them. New, they are like babes. As they wear, as the lock and breech show each firing, they tell more about their owner than his eyes. They show the terror of every man that stared into the muzzle. Sweat from the hand turns the wood to an amber shine on the wrists of a well-used pistol. There is aught so melancholy as an old gun.

Devlin passed it over and Peter Sam twisted it and showed Devlin its wood and the deep cut.

'This is where I hacked at you, Patrick Devlin. Tried to kill you. I thought you'd done for Seth that night. For my Thomas Deakins. You remember we fought?'

'Aye, Peter.' Devlin could see the storm again. The lightning flashes and the cutlasses running wet with the rain as he beat back the big man but saw his death. That had been on the island of the Verdes. St Nicolau. Four years gone. Still almost yesterday. Where he had become the pirate and been born again.

'You had me then, Peter Sam.'

Peter gave back the gun.

'Aye. Had it not been for the gold that you screamed in my ear.' He patted his captain's shoulder.

'You don't have to yell no more, Captain. If you say there is gold we will come.'

Peter Sam wanted one more thing. He wanted to pull the younger man towards him but that would not do. A squeeze of his shoulder was as much as he would bestow.

Once, the pirate Devlin had traversed the oceans to rescue another Peter Sam, a broken Peter Sam, a dead Peter Sam. That had been in Charles Town. That Peter Sam was now long put aside but still not forgotten. They never spoke of it but it roped them together. He pushed his captain away like a boy to be bullied and Devlin rolled against the gunwale.

'Fuck it, Patrick,' he snapped. 'Let us to the gold. Shoot 'em all. What else are we here for?'

Devlin tucked back his pistol.

'This priest. He says he knows the island where Levasseur is. He was on the ship. He wants me to believe that there's a gold cross. That's all he wants. We can take the rest of it.'

Peter Sam puffed on his pipe. 'Sure. And why not?'

'That's mighty thin, Peter.'

'Were you not in chains in Newgate? And chained in Providence before that? Ain't it always thin? You could do with chancing it a bit more, you fat fuckster!'

He wheeled away to go below and close down the lamps and punch any drunk smoking near the wet baize curtain of the magazine.

Devlin fumbled for his own pipe.

One smoke before he returned to the cabin.

'Aye,' he announced to the sea. 'Why not? Who's to stop me?'

He scraped his striker, sucked his Meerschaum pipe, the wine and tobacco soothing his head.

'Ain't they all dead?'

O'Neill was pouring, measuring not the wine but more the greasy yellow-coated fellow left in his company.

'And you, sir? How are you come here?' He passed a glass that was not his, from a bottle that was not his. 'You are a surgeon?'

'Not at all,' Dandon chimed his glass against the priest's exactly as seamen are not meant to do.

'I was an apothecary's man. First in Louis' American lands and then in Bath. My master was French and I learnt his tongue and I tore through his books better than he. I can make a fine draught and powders to keep you in or out of bed. Whichever is best required.'

'But how with the pirate, my son?' O'Neill's face grew warm and welcoming. Extracting confessions was his métier.

Dandon recounted. The tale almost a myth to him now so long had he been on the sea.

It was as if he were his own father, and the son still back there somewhere dreaming of owning a saltern on New Providence and selling salt pills to gout-ridden gentlemen in the Carolinas.

The priest shook his head and apologised on his God's behalf as Dandon explained how the rum had claimed him and he made his living in a brothel for a pile of straw on a floor and popped, pierced and scraped what was beyond poultice.

'The pirate – as you call him – saved my life. I imagine that even in your world the name of Blackbeard filtered through. My tongue had slipped badly again and the rogue Blackbeard was about to vent my spleen. It was Patrick who took him

120

down, and with an empty gun at that.' Dandon held a finger at the priest.

'Mark that, Father. An empty gun against Blackbeard. And he has pulled down loaded on the Prince of Wales and the first minister of England. Killed king's agents and Porto governors.'

He drank to his captain.

'If you want your cross you have found the right man.'

O'Neill saluted his glass.

'The Lord has found me the right man, my son. And it is the Lord's humour and his love for the Irish that he brings me a fellow countryman.'

Dandon scratched his eyebrow with closed eyes and sniffed away a laugh.

'Don't play the countryman with Devlin, Father. I suspect there is no love in him for his home.'

O'Neill poured again, the bottle in a losing wager against his mood.

'Nonsense! I have been across the world and still measure every blade of grass against that on my mother's own porch.'

He was cut by Devlin crashing back into the room. Pipe in one hand, bottle in the other, a boot kicking the door closed. He strode forward and bit on his words as they came through narrow lips.

'My mother left me before I knew her face. My father drank. Left me that as a trait. Sold me to a butcher before I was nine.' He handed Dandon the dregs of his bottle and Dandon tipped it to O'Neill.

Devlin still came on and O'Neill backed up.

'An English magistrate bid me hang for poaching fowl that he ate. All I know about being Irish is that we're the last to eat and the first to hang.' He pushed the priest's chest.

'I don't know about a "flight of earls" and their sons and any Irish kingdom and your God gave me nothing.' He turned his back and went for the ropes that held the bottles.

O'Neill watched him select a wine and pitied the boy inside the man.

'My son,' he spoke as in his pulpit. 'Can you not see that it is the Lord who has given you this path for this very purpose? He has given you your strength and your fortitude and your nature so to be his sword. This is His work for you. To bring back the True Cross for the worship of the world!'

Devlin pulled the wax and the cork with his teeth and spat it to the priest.

'I'll let you live. Give me the name of the island. If your cross still exists I'll bring it to you and take as much treasure as my men can carry.' He drank with the bottle high and gasped it from his mouth and wiped his chin.

'And that's all I'll give your God.'

O'Neill bowed his head, a balding pate revealed to Devlin, the first weakness. He went to the table and the *Neptune Français*.

'I will need you to read it, Captain.'

Dandon coughed as Devlin crossed the cabin.

'Is there no ill, Patrick, in going after the wealth of another pirate?'

Devlin glared but Dandon knew how far he could go against his friend.

'I only ask because I was believing that our ilk are dwindling in number without our assistance. Is there no loyalty other than to the ecstasy of gold?'

O'Neill's shoulder stood at Devlin's, both looked down at Dandon.

'How can you be so?' O'Neill's tone completely assured. 'This is about the cross of your saviour!'

Devlin pushed him aside, away from the table and the charts.

'No it isn't. He's right. You look on us all the same. One set of evil men after another. Always useful ain't it, father? When the Church needs something done.'

O'Neill's sanctimony came back, something about righteous men and forgiveness, but Devlin put his hand up. Dandon was his only interest.

'And you,' he pointed down to Dandon. 'You should know better,' he held up the wine. 'These bottles represent the last for your thirst unless you want to start making your own. The ships are drying up if you hadn't noticed. Honest merchants lie rotting in the harbours. Just a small bite of kings and moguls with any tin to sell. And did they work for it?' He gave Dandon the bottle.

'The world's burst its purse. Tew became rich. Avery and Captain England like kings. They did it by Indian waters and princes' ships. Why not me? If The Buzzard has it and I'm starving and can work at finding him who's to say I don't deserve it?'

Dandon drank and wiped his lip.

'*He* may have argument against your deservedness. I would think that pirate against pirate would not be a bloodless encounter.'

Devlin snatched back the bottle.

'You!' he pointed O'Neill back to the atlas. 'Tell me this island. Make sure I believe.'

'*Believe*?' O'Neill smiled warmly. 'Faith, Captain, so it is. Faith is all we need.'

# Chapter Twelve

*Cape Coast Castle, West Africa.*

Three days later.

John Coxon had been here before. On the *Noble*, the ship he had commanded through the Spanish war, he had watched the bleached white walls and embrasures of Cape Coast Castle roll before his bow. All the castle's guns faced the sea, from where the only threat would come. Africa would not attack the companies that took their unwanted criminals and prisoners of tribal war for iron and cloth.

He had watched from the castle's cloistered rooms the escutcheon of his ship sail away. It was the only time he had watched a stern he commanded leave him behind. He had been sick, possibly dying, snared by one of the tropical diseases that befell the foreigner, and as armies had discovered often killed more men than warfare.

Once revived he had left the coast of Africa on the *Starling* and embarked on his first adventure against the pirate Devlin, the steward who had become his enemy. That ship had limped back to England months later showing what a boot-wipe could do. Now it was the *Standard* rising and falling towards the slave factory.

Castle was a strong word for the peeling building. It had been built as a garrison and prison decades before, then the slave fortunes had turned it into England's workhorse of flesh. Its master for almost the same number of decades had been Governor General James Phipps, and Coxon divulged into Thomas Howard's ear two mysteries.

One was that the title 'Governor General' should no more be respected than that of Wagon-Master General in the land army. There was no grand deed in Phipps's past, just high friends and money. Second, that he was most surprised that the thirty-stone man was even still alive. His renown should be his constitution that kept him fat when others had become ghosts along the coast that whittled down white men into toothpicks.

'You will see a feast such as you have never known, Thomas,' and Thomas beamed at his captain's familiarity. 'But you'll have to move fast. Phipps will suck in plates like a hog. It is a marvel to behold.'

Howard looked over the bow at the coast painted brown with the effluence of a hundred thousand ships.

'You have been here before, Captain?'

Coxon grabbed a man-rope as the ship started its backing of the sails a mile offshore; they would take the longboat in.

'Aye. Almost died here. Mind, you may see me take a formal tone to this dog. Pay no attention. Company men expect it.'

General Phipps was in charge of the castle, acting on behalf of Whitehall and the Royal African company. He knew that the navy kept afloat only due to the company's magnanimity. The only defence of a naval captain would be to treat Phipps's office as if he were in front of the lords themselves. You did not have to like him.

'Be official,' Coxon gave his word to Howard. 'And we'll be on our way soon enough.'

Thomas Howard would carry only one thing from his visit to Cape Coast Castle. Coxon informed him with an outstretched arm that just a few miles south down the coast the Dutch at Elmina Castle ferried the blacks to South America also. This was the joint reward prised from the Spanish at the end of the war. The Dutch and English had insisted on the transport of slaves most of all.

'See that door, Thomas?' he yelled from the bow of the longboat, and Thomas looked on the double-door and shingle path and steps from the castle's bowels down to the beach. 'That is where they take them to the ships. Many hundreds of them in a space for one-hundred fifty. You can smell it from here. The floor is raised almost a foot with their excrement. They stand for weeks waiting for their ships. And see here now,' Coxon pointed to the black shapes spinning beneath the water and Howard drew himself in as men do when they first see something the length of a man cutting through the water and the black dorsal fin more fluid than the wave that breaks over the shark's back shining in the sun. A devil waiting.

'They follow the boats taking the slaves,' Coxon yelled back almost gleefully. 'They are expectant that some of them will roll themselves over into the sea before they meet the ships. They only chain them together once on the ships do you see? Else they will pull the others and the boat over with them.' Coxon looked side to side at the fat black shapes. 'They follow the ships for miles afterwards before returning here. They are quite smart.'

Howard watched the sleek dark fish buck at the splash of the oars, their anticipation tangible, excited by the presence of men, the potential in their roll that revealed their white bellies like a puppy and the soulless black of their eyes as they weighed him.

'Quite smart,' Coxon said again and pushed one away from the bow like a cow. 'Quite smart.'

Coxon had left Manvell as his First in command; he considered that the officer might have attitudes that could sway in front of General Phipps, for the general would remember that he had dealt with Coxon before and had found him wanting of respect. Manvell was a gentleman by proxy and Coxon, although sure of his loyalty thus far, did not know how deep he had fallen under the spell of men like Phipps.

Howard however had bled with Coxon, and with the aged captain that counted more. He turned back with a reproachful glare at the giggle of Walter Kennedy as an oar slapped against one of the sharks. But he forced himself to smile at the lad and looked back to the shore ahead. He had brought him for other reasons.

You had to carry some shit in on your shoes.

'General Phipps!' Coxon said it as if greeting an old friend. He pulled off his hat and dipped his head. That was enough pleasantry. He squared his hat back just as swiftly and Howard mirrored him. Walter Kennedy had no hat but tapped his forehead; that would always do. He had done it all his naval life, not sure what it meant, only that it was required when men wore wigs.

This was the dining room of the house, where Phipps met all his dignitaries, and where a meal seemed always present. Its entrance was through the chapel and this had been designed just so, for if there was ever to be a slave rising or native attack they would not come through the church. The respect for the gods, even a white one, was too powerful to challenge.

General Phipps did not stand. He lounged in his chair at the long table and waved a napkin in response. It had been four years since Coxon had left the man and from this same room. Perhaps he had never moved.

Thomas Howard's eyes widened at the sight of General Phipps. When they had walked from the longboat – and he had noted that Coxon had splashed into the surf rather than be carried on the seat by the oarsmen – the humidity had hit him like a hot cloud. Ten paces and he was wet. By the time he entered the dining hall his shirt was plastered to him and his wool coat felt heavy as lead. This explained the fat man in shirt open to the chest and silk pantaloons more fitting for some Parisian whore, and that expanded over his gut to his guinea-sized belly button.

'Post-Captain Coxon,' Phipps nodded. 'A pleasure to see you again, sir. Glad to see you are still alive in the world.' He waved loosely to the other side of the table. 'Take a seat do, take a seat, gentlemen. Please help yourself to some bread.'

There were chargers of boar and beef sitting in gravy and potatoes, as well as pineapple and paw-paws and other fruits that even the sailors did not recognise. Black and white grapes were afforded their own bowls and in them were piled high. And there was a fresh loaf and butter for the seamen.

'My gratitude, General,' Coxon praised, and led the others to their chairs. Howard heard his name in the introductions as he sat and closer now he could see the bracelets of shells and charms about Phipps's wrists and neck as the fat man nodded his greetings. Phipps had long embraced some of the cultures and traditions passed onto him by his native concubine. Coxon had seen her, and Phipps's brood of mulatto children on his last visit. In fact she had cared for Coxon in his illness. He had never even learnt her name.

'And who is this fellow?' Phipps grimaced at the dishev-elled scrawn of Walter Kennedy. 'Not an officer I hope? I should have to write back to Whitehall if he is so.'

'No, General,' Coxon said. 'May I introduce Walter Kennedy. A captain late of the pirate Roberts now attached to our mission.'

'A *pirate*!' Phipps went scarlet and rolled himself against his chair; almost managing to stand. 'A damned pirate! Are you mad, sir? You bring a sea-dog to my castle!'

Phipps had suffered badly over the last two years by those pirates who had left the Americas. Davis, Cocklyn, La Buse and now Roberts had ridden the coast and harangued and raided the forts and ships with impunity. Coxon reminded him why they were there.

'General, we are set to capture pirates. Your troubles are what brings us, as requested by yourself – as ordered.' He removed his hat to the table; the humidity was simply too great. 'I designed to bring a sailor with me who has knowledge of both the pirates and the Indian sea. Kennedy is my choice.'

Phipps scoffed. 'Bah! *Knowledge*! What knowledge can scrap provide? Nonsense, sir!'

Coxon stroked his lip to hide his thin smile. He stood and crossed the room, his attention drawn deliberately to a curi-ous wooden box standing on one of the commodes beneath the windows. Phipps's neck craned to spy the object of Coxon's interest.

'Ah, my Fruit of the Sea! A gift from the ambassador of Maputo.'

Coxon had recognised the cabinet's origins; he would make a criterion of it for Phipps, in Kennedy's cause.

The box was made from a Coco de Mer, the rare seed of a fabled tree. It sat on silver lion's paws, and in its erect position could cause embarrassment to even the bawdiest of men for its shape resembled the shape and size of an ample woman's lower half, front and back. This one had silver repoussé mountings framing the doors which opened out of the buttocks. Princes loved them.

'What do you know of this, General?' Coxon asked.

'Ah, it is a mystery of the East,' he sang. 'Some espouse that its tree grows beneath the sea for the seed is oft seen rising from beneath,' he leant forward and winked at young Howard. 'And has risen many a sailor's ardour at the sight of it, lighting up dreams of mermaids.'

He turned back to Coxon. 'It has many legends. Of Eden, of the Roc bird. No-one knows the truth of it or where it comes from.' He widened his eyes to all of them. 'I can tell you it is worth a tidy sum.'

Coxon opened one of the blue velvet-lined doors and shut it as loud as he could to raise his voice to Kennedy. 'And you, Walter?' he called. 'What do you know of this thing?'

Kennedy dragged himself to his feet and loped to the object. He stroked it almost tenderly and certainly inappropriately to the witnesses' eyes.

'To be sure, gentlemen, it comes from only two islands. The tree that is. The seeds sink when the tide drags them and don't make for good eating 'cept for years later. Tide and time takes them out to sea. When the husk rots she comes to the surface. That's why the sailors think the tree lives under the waves.'

Coxon looked at Phipps, who was fuming. 'And where does it come from? In your "knowledge"?'

'Those islands have no name. We careen and take land turtles. You keep in the fours,' he dipped his head respectfully to Phipps. 'That's the latitude, Your Majesty. East-nor'east from the Comoros, that's the perfume islands off Africa. The air smells of vanilla and Creole whores. The sands are the colour of pearls. I don't know the degrees without tools.'

Coxon softly pushed him away.

'Thank you, Walter. Take some bread.'

Kennedy went the long way back to the table, avoiding Phipps's glare.

'I think I have my man, General, for a good run to the Amirantes. Unless you can suggest better.' He came back. 'Now, what do you have to tell me about the *Swallow* and the *Weymouth*. That's what I'm here for. I'll forego my bread. I am not a bird to eat crumbs.'

Howard put his face down to hide his smirk. General Phipps appeared relieved that the time to be polite had passed.

'Very well, Captain.'

'Post-Captain, General Governor. If you please.' Coxon took his seat.

Phipps winced. 'My apologies ... *Post-Captain*. Captain Chaloner Ogle and Captain Mungo Herdman are more than a month gone. I have copies of their logs for you as per my instruction. It is believed that the pirate Roberts will make for Madagascar. He is down to just the one ship.'

Kennedy pricked his ears and Coxon snapped to the sight.

'What is it, Walter?'

Kennedy took a knife and produced first a flinch and then relief from Phipps as he sawed at the bread.

'Not much, Captain. But I would be thinking that would be Thomas Anstis has left Roberts now. As I did. He was always threatening.' He went at the butter.

'Why are men leaving him, Walter?'

Kennedy shrugged and stuffed the bread into his mouth and sputtered through it.

'Roberts gives you a ship. Your own men. We were immortal under him. Took dozens of ships just with drums.' He swallowed and something of the pirate's pride came back to him as he remembered and as the cold stone of the Marshalsea faded far away.

'Your kind never reached us. Gave us wide passage, Captain. I never saw an English flag for two years.'

Coxon looked away. '*I* was in the Americas, Walter. Why would you leave him?'

'He wouldn't go for British. Just the old. The French and Spanish and the fat boys. Just the merchants and the slavers.' He looked across the table to Phipps. 'You might have given him a medal in years gone.' He slouched in his seat until Coxon pulled him up with his frown.

'Anyways, me and Anstis wanted more. I ran in the night. Reckon he's done the same.'

A door creaked. A stumbling scrivener, dragging his left foot, approached from behind Phipps. He asked no entrance or exit as he dumped some ribboned paper at Coxon and pulled himself away.

Phipps plucked his long fingernails through a tender hide of boar and pulled and sucked on it as he spoke.

'Your further orders, Post-Captain. You are to meet at the *Îles de Comorre*,' he delighted in his French accent over Kennedy's Irish vowels. 'All is within the papers. The captains will wait until the eighth of August. Then they will hunt for Roberts without you.'

Coxon slipped off the ribbon and ran his thumb through the papers as he kept questioning. 'Did the captains not mention Devlin?'

Phipps licked his thumb then further drew it in and sucked on it, the image of a blushing cherub with his plump cheeks and curled wig.

'Hmm? Who now?'

'The pirate Devlin. I've been recalled to hunt him. He is in these waters, it is believed.' He corrected himself. 'May be here.'

Phipps rolled his head.

'I heard no mention of him,' then he clicked his fingers and gulped some air which made Thomas Howard think of a whale he had seen do the same.

'Wait now. I think we did have some discussion of him. The name is sound.'

Coxon sat up and Phipps leaned back and picked his teeth with his littlest fingernail like a hook. 'He is the one, is he not, that was your man? Is that the length of it? "Post-Captain"? The servant who licked you? I recall myself and Captain Ogle had some amusing discourse about it over supper now that you say it.'

Walter Kennedy covered his mouth and his leg shook against the table. A choking from his throat on the bread sticking. Thomas Howard looked over to Coxon concentrating on the paper in his lap. Coxon put the ribbon clumsily back around his papers.

Phipps leant forward with a grunt.

'Am I not right informed that you lost your ship to pirates, "Post-Captain"? Does your Lieutenant not know this? I hope I have not overstepped my mark as "Governor General" with my voice. He does know that your man joined them and is now their captain?'

Coxon squared his papers and his hat and finally lifted his head. Thomas Howard spoke quicker.

'General Phipps. I fought with Post-Captain Coxon against this man Devlin. I am here because of it. I volunteered to join him. I would expect nothing less than your full devotion as befits your station to respect the trust that your king and first minister has put in his ability. And *their* faith that His Majesty's Governor General will respond accordingly to our mission.'

Thomas Howard's jaw trembled as Phipps glowered at him. He wanted to exhale but kept his head stiff as if a leather stock were around his neck.

Coxon breathed out for him. 'Thank you for the logs, General. If your information is lacking I will follow my orders to meet with Captain Ogle and Captain Herdman.'

He scraped back his chair and the others followed without order.

'Wait, wait, Post-Captain,' Phipps raised a finger. 'I neglected to tell you of the most interesting fact.'

Coxon raised his chin and Phipps's lips slid into a sneer.

'You know of the English novels of Defoe? I credit he is up to at least the third or fourth about his Robinson Crusoe chap.'

'What of it?'

'It transpires that the man who was the inspiration for those stories travels with Captain Herdman. You know the name?'

'I do,' Coxon said. 'Selkirk. A Scotsman.'

'Aye, that be it,' Phipps wagged his finger. 'That be him.'

'What interest?' Coxon's face went rigid.

'You may have much to talk about when you meet.' Phipps sat back in his seat.

'As one failure to another.'

Coxon afforded a smile beneath his hat.

'You are aware, General, that I am set to hunt pirates that have hounded your shores and your Royal African ships? That such is my purpose?'

'It is your duty, sir,' Phipps warbled, pleased with his words that he was sure had stung.

Mark Keating

Coxon dipped his hat and backed to the chapel.

'Have you not given any thought as to what might happen to your good self should we fail? If only one of us cared not enough to douse you as you burned?'

He span on his heel and pushed his men into the chapel, even winking at Walter Kennedy. Damn him for a pirate but he had played his part when a wig had mocked him. What to make of Ogle and Herdman when he met them? Were they of the same cloth as Phipps? Had they laughed over his past? He pulled Kennedy's shoulder as they walked up the centre of the church, the cross staring down at them as on a bride and groom, Howard afore them as if their priest.

'Tell me, Walter. Where would you go as pirates to find out the word?'

'I don't get your meaning, Captain?'

'Yes you do. Where are the hidden forts? Where do you speak to each other?'

Kennedy rubbed his chin. 'Madagascar to be sure. Anywhere on Madagascar.'

'But they'll shut up at a naval ship. The *Swallow* would already try there. Where else?'

Kennedy stroked his sweating neck next; felt the rope already rasping. This was why he was here, yet if he could delay the end, belay the meeting of Roberts or Devlin until he had made his escape, that would do.

'That would be Old Cracker's place. Back up the coast. Back up to Sierra Leone, Captain. If any on the account comes to Africa they stops there.'

Howard stepped between them.

'Returning up the coast, Captain, would add another week. Our orders are to meet up with the *Swallow* and *Weymouth*. We have only until August eighth.'

135

'And it is still June, Thomas,' Coxon said. 'Even with the trade winds against it will only take a week from us.'

'And a week to get back here again and three weeks to reach Ogle. That is fine shaving, sir. With respect, you speak of the coast as if it is a walk to market.'

Coxon slapped Howard's shoulder.

'That's the mark of it, lad!' Then his jocose manner dropped as suddenly as it had appeared.

'We know Roberts is around since Biafra but what of Devlin? If a pirate wants to survive he needs to know what is afore his bows and reaching for his stern. Devlin would do that.' He tapped Kennedy again. 'This "Old Cracker"? It is the first pirate place you would come to?'

'The most English one, Captain.'

'Then we will go.' He already began to leave.

Howard protested. 'But we will lose weeks, sir!'

Coxon stopped. 'I can *feel* him, Mister Howard. I know the signs. We must walk in his shoes. Devlin has kept alive for so long because he questions everything. He would not sail without having some idea where Roberts is if he wishes to join up. And if he doesn't . . . well, he would still get as much information as he could. He would question everything.' He walked on, up the church, his heels near sparking the black stone floor in haste. Howard and Kennedy trotted behind.

'How would you know that, sir?' Howard asked to his back.

'Because I told him to. When all of this was younger.'

They squinted at the bleaching sunlight as they left the chapel and said no more until their return to the boat. Thomas Howard kept his eyes to his shoes during the trawl back. He would obey his captain always but the tenacity of Coxon to want to chase Devlin, and Devlin only, itched uncomfortably.

The greater order was to meet with the *Swallow* and *Weymouth*, now confirmed waiting for them in the Comoros, east of Africa.

His education of the Cape was limited to his trade jaunts with the late Captain William Guinneys. It took only one bad day to set you back a week or more. All the seas seemed to meet at its point and now they were to head back along the compass they had already sailed chasing whispers and ghosts. Further delay. Devlin was not here at all and they had real orders to follow. He would wait until the word was given to Manvell back aboard. Give his voice if Manvell objected. He watched Coxon tut and twist his head back and forth between the castle and the ship as they were rowed away. Captains should not be anxious or tut at waves.

Faith, Thomas, he thought. In twenty years you may gain such instinct. Or else it is only madness and you are already lost.

The bell of the castle tolled noon. Coxon pulled out his watch and called for Howard to do the same.

'Set for noon, Thomas. The castle is as close to Greenwich as we will get; that is why it is here. Set the clock on the ship as soon as. We may have good longitude for a day or so.'

Howard turned the crown of his watch. Was it really noon in London as well as in this tropical hell? They seemed in another world. The earth could not be so big and yet so small that two clocks told the same time in such differing climates.

Perhaps this was how Coxon was so confident that the pirate could be found. In the vastness it was the detail that mattered. Set your watch so, your rule and compass to match, the stars against the astrolabe and there Devlin will be, hiding behind a barrel somewhere as sure as the Pole Star.

He closed the case, replaced it in his pocket and looked up at Coxon's pleased face upon him.

Faith, Thomas, he repeated to himself. Or else it is only madness and you are already lost.

# Chapter Thirteen

*T*homas Howard had not had the dream for many a year but he accepted that it was no coincidence. He was a boy again, a young man, aboard the frigate *Starling* and surrounded by smoke and hot gore. He could see the pistol in his fist, shaking at the sight of a hundred pirates with mouths as big as their heads, their yellow jaws down to their chests and howling like demons as they burst from the cabin. They tore through the paper sailors until they came just for him, towered over the boy that he was.

The boy grew smaller under their foetid breath and they blotted out the blue sky above where the mainmast had been. They raised their axes with a roar that went on and on like wind through a cave. His plea for mercy came out as a mew from a neck-slit calf. He had words but they were just sounds as if his jaw were broken and his mouth were filled with blood.

He knew he was asleep and this was but his treacherous sleeping mouth trying to speak and only mocking him in doing so. It was the sound of torment. He waited for the axes to fall.

If he awoke before this point, as he had done many times, he was convinced that he had died, and it would take moments of patting down his body and gasping like a banked fish before relief would come and he looked about at the dark comfort of his screened world behind a simple door on the lower deck aft. The snores of a whole ship and her protests against the sea echoing all around and lullabying him back to sleep.

But sometimes in the dream, as now, a yellow sleeve came out of the beasts and pulled him close. Arms enfolded him and brought his face to a damp and smoke-reeking waistcoat of yellow damask. A scent never forgotten.

He could hear music far away and knew it was from the pirate ship across that had broken them but it was soothing, as was the voice and gold-toothed smile that looked down at him and brushed his hair from his eyes and spoke to him with a voice tinged with gold.

'*Good boy*,' the smile said. '*Brave boy*.' And the axes did not fall.

Howard sprang awake to a hand on his chest and a lantern before his face. It took a moment for his shaken brain to jigsaw the features, half-lit in the amber light, back to the real world and not the other.

Lieutenant Manvell knelt beside his cot and was rousing him awake. He was in his nightshirt and his hair fell long about his shoulders.

'Quiet now, Mister Howard,' hushed Manvell, his teeth glinting in the light like those in the dream. 'You'll wake the mess to breakfast.'

'I am sorry, sir,' Howard wiped his sweating chest. 'I was dreaming.'

'A nightmare more like, lad. I thought you dying!' Manvell's cot was just across the common corridor of canvas walls, their quarters below Coxon's cabin. It was hot always, any sleep light, but they were far away from the seats of ease and the manger. A scant privilege. But Manvell was aware of men swaying and snoring in hammocks just feet from them. If an officer had nightmares, and they heard, he would be their sport tomorrow and forever. He would have a nickname by four bells. Their other companions in their domain were old men who took port to bed. They would not hear.

'I'm sorry, sir. It was an old dream.' Howard brushed down his tussled sheet.

'Of what?'

Howard slumped back. He knew Manvell little but the concern was genuine. Manvell was older but they were both men still young enough to remember the promise of summers, the sea still a means to romance and adventure and not a prelude to war. Boyhood seemed still within reach.

'It was the pirate attack. When I was with the captain before. Devlin's ship destroyed us.'

He sat up. 'Not him, you understand. Nor the captain. They were on the island. I was a midshipman, acting-lieutenant for the day. I was sixteen.'

'And what happened?' Manvell's voice hushed.

'The pirates boarded us.' He offered no more than that. Manvell would understand what those words meant. 'I was by the guns. They came out of the cabin. I was to die. They were coming to me.'

Manvell put his lamp to the floor. 'Is this your dream?'

'No. This is true, sir. But the next is most important.'

'What is that?'

'One of the pirates, sir, had coerced his way aboard.'

'Coerced?'

Howard yawned, he could not help it but would rather that it had not happened; it lessened his dream.

'That is not important. The nature of what happened has bothered me ever since.'

Manvell shuffled along the cot, his bones waking. 'This is intriguing, Mister Howard. What occurred?'

'He was a man in a yellow coat. We believed him a doctor attached to the island; he spoke French well enough and he had the accent. We thought him a fool. But he was one of them.'

'And he harmed you?'

Howard had cooled; the dream fled as it always did. These were just words now.

'No,' he made the word absolute so Manvell would not mistake. 'No. He saved me.'

'I don't understand?'

Howard wanted sleep now. This story had been part of his life, part of his dreams for too long to be of much interest, and other people's dreams were always a bore.

'He covered me, protected me, and stopped them. Nothing more. I lived. Please excuse me, sir, I am on duty soon.'

Manvell felt knees push him off.

'Of course. Sleep what you can.' He stood. 'But mind those dreams, Mister Howard.'

'I will, sir. It is only the talk of Devlin I am sure. Going back up the coast and all.'

'Aye,' Manvell took his lamp past the screen door. 'But an interesting story, lad. Just be careful that the men don't hear of it.'

He slipped the door and its tiny catch to, and turned with a start to the captain hanging off the companion stair with his own lamp lighting his face.

'What goes on, Manvell?'

'Sir?' Manvell closed the door and walked closer. Coxon was half-dressed in breeches and shirt. His rabbit-grey hair sweated forward, the chains of the deck chiming behind him in the dark.

'I was woken by distress. Is Mister Howard fine?'

Manvell imagined the wood above their heads and Coxon's cot. He would not have awoken to Howard's howls.

'A nightmare, nothing more, Captain,' Manvell's voice a smiling whisper.

'Not about our days ahead I hope. We will be on the coast at dawn.'

Manvell had not objected to course back up the coast. Intelligence would be a fine thing to court. His only note for the log was for the black clouds meeting the horizon aft: the monsoon season threatening their passage back.

'No, sir. It was about your pirate.' Manvell wished to grab the words back into his mouth but blushed and cleared his throat. Coxon showed no flinch or emotion. 'I mean he recalled something about your time together.'

'The one with the yellow coat?' Coxon nodded through thinned lips.

'Yes, sir.' Manvell was intrigued. 'He was real?'

'He was a cryptic one. Insidious. If he is still alive I suggest you look out for him. He fooled us all.'

'It seems he saved young Mister Howard's life.'

Coxon went for the step, his conversation done.

'Probably just to bugger him for himself. Pay it no mind.'

Manvell watched the bare feet climb the stair then returned to his cot. He settled and wafted into his own dreams, always aware of the bell to come so only tentatively asleep. Still, there were pirates there. In lucid dreams.

They had grown in number every night.

# Chapter Fourteen

*O*ld Cracker, John Leadstone, was beginning to consider himself unfortunate. Devlin had left him almost a fortnight before with the sweaty task of rounding up the stock he had lost. He had a couple of blacks which he kept drunk enough to be tied to him and just enough standing with the tribes to sell him their prisoners of war but he did not expect a British ship to pay him any mind. Plunkett's stock on Bense island was the limit of their interest. What harm could Old Cracker do to their trade? He did not take rice farmers, just backs and arms – and wasn't there plenty of those? So why were British muskets tramping up his path and a captain with hands clasped behind judging his dwelling?

Old Cracker wiped his hands on his breeches after laying two pistols below his counter and greeted the man in the three-cornered hat.

The sailor measured the room and drew his nose up accordingly. 'John Leadstone I am informed? Royal African man were you not?'

Cracker bowed and wiped his nose and shuffled around his counter. 'That I was, sir. That I was. Long time, long summer. Just working my way through the world, so I am now, Cap'n. Not wishing any harm to nobody, Cap'n.' He wiped a stool with his sleeve and bid the officer to sit.

John Coxon ignored the offer. 'I have left my guard

outside, John Leadstone. And I take my hat off to you.' He did so and brushed its trim. 'Do you know what that might mean?'

Cracker wiped his face of flies. 'No, Cap'n. Just hope I can be of service.'

Coxon laid his hat to the table cut rough from a tun. 'Let us say that removing my hat removes the man-of-war from your bay. Removes the king from your trade. Just two men talking. How would that sound to your ears?'

Cracker allowed himself a seat. 'That would be admirable, Cap'n. But if that be the case – nothing official, like – I should be entitled to a shilling or two if it's Cracker's brains you want.'

'Ah,' Coxon sighed. 'You may have misunderstood my implication. The removal of my hat removes myself of any responsibility of what is to follow.' He went to the door and dragged it open. 'A captain's innings, if you would indulge me.'

Walter Kennedy took his cue and steamed into the room, straight for the stocky Cracker, heaved him off his feet and slammed him to the wall where Peter Sam had made a hole weeks before.

'Ho, Cracker! Remember Kennedy? Davis's Kennedy? Roberts's Kennedy? How you been, old son?' He jabbed a fist to the soft belly and Cracker fell against the arm at his throat, hung off it like a hook. 'Ain't you pleased to see me, Cracker?'

'W . . . Walter . . .' Cracker choked but that was all he could do as Kennedy pressed harder against his throat.

Kennedy finished his thoughts for him. 'Oh, I'm alive, Cracker. Walter's back from the dead! And he's on the king's side now, Cracker! What do you think I can do with that!' He stabbed his fist again, dropping Cracker coughing to his knees.

Coxon called Kennedy back like a dog, and Kennedy wiped his mouth of the spittle that had frothed and licked it back, his eyes white on the gasping Cracker.

Coxon came forward and helped him up and to a seat. 'Don't fret, John.' He joined him on a stool and pushed Cracker's own rum towards him. 'Walter is excited to be back on the sea. I won't let him step out of line again.' He moved his hat further away and dismissed Kennedy to the door. 'But he has a point.'

Deliberately, Coxon had brought only Kennedy to Cracker's shack. When his telescope surveyed the cliff as the *Standard* sought her sounding he had seen the shack and the ragged landscape, the few outbuildings like the last tombstones at the end of a cemetery.

He had judged at that time the type of man who had abandoned Company order for such degradation. A man who traded with interlopers and pirates. He had looked down his ship at young Manvell with the astonished eyebrows and Howard who was the stalwart picture of fresh heroism. He would spare them this. Just he and Walter Kennedy. They both knew what was needed to gain respect and intelligence. And he did not want his officers to measure him so soon if the meeting went badly.

Cracker took just a rinsing of rum. 'What point does he have, Cap'n?' he asked, carefully he hoped.

'He does have the king behind him now, in a sense – a strict sense – but further than that it is the Davis and Roberts aspect that is most relevant.'

'Cap'n?' Cracker's face twisted in pain, convinced something had burst inside him. He kept an open eye on Walter Kennedy by the door.

'I want to know about Devlin, Cracker.'

'What about him, Cap'n?'

Coxon had thought this would be harder. 'So you know him?'

Cracker scratched his whiskered cheek. 'Well . . . know of him, know of him. Can't be sure beyond that. Exactly who I sees and who I remembers are different pages, Cap'n.'

Coxon flicked a mosquito from his leg and watched it settle on Cracker's face, where the man ignored it.

'Walter came here with Davis and Roberts. He tells that all the pirates come here. Roberts has certainly been seen and we are hunting him. I would like to know if Devlin is here also.' He gave Cracker a charitable look as one might bestow to a simpleton at Christmas. 'Is that too much to ask?'

Cracker sweated. His eyes shifting from Coxon to Kennedy lounging at the door. 'No, Cap'n. Not much at all.'

'If it is for fear of betraying those that you consider brethren do not concern yourself. We would have nothing to gain by mentioning it. And besides this is nothing to do with pirates.'

'It's not?'

'No, Leadstone. We require your assistance in a murder investigation on His Majesty's request. With due respect to you being a former Royal African Company man.'

'Whose murder?'

'A poor man in London. Killed in his prime and leaving his young son to fend for himself. And the murderer fled. Would you begrudge us to seek such a villain?'

'No, Cap'n. I would not. I have a son myself somewhere.'

'And would you give your pity to that boy if you could meet him now, John Leadstone?'

'I would. As a Christian man.'

Coxon watched the mosquito sucking on Cracker's face and then his eye dropped to the buzzing of other wings at Cracker's shin and a grey bandage wrapped and seeping.

'Walter?' Coxon called. 'Introduce yourself to John Leadstone.'

Kennedy sprang from the door before Cracker could move and slapped Cracker's slack face.

'That was my father that bastard killed!' He saw the smudge of blood along Cracker's cheek and looked at the crushed insect in his palm and wiped it off on Cracker's hair. 'Talk, worm!' He yanked him to his feet. 'Where be Devlin?'

'More instructively,' Coxon suggested. 'When did you see him last and what did you hear?'

He drew his hat across the table. 'Your only consideration, Leadstone, is that if I put my hat on I become His Majesty's Captain again. It would be my duty to take my licence as a protector of the royal companies and push your little enterprise here into the sea.'

Kennedy, his eyes bulbous, his teeth drawn, pulled the terrified Cracker closer, as Coxon went on.

'Or you take the lesser of that evil and tell the vexed young Kennedy where the man who killed his father might be heading.'

Kennedy shook Cracker like a doll until Coxon raised his hand.

'And you can start by telling me what happened to your leg.'

# Chapter Fifteen

*T*hey had passed in the night. Coxon and Devlin; Coxon asleep on the *Standard*, Devlin drinking long into the early hours aboard the *Shadow*. Behind Devlin sailed the *Santa Rosa*, the priest's ship now consort. Sixty-odd nautical miles lay between the freeboards of the pirate and the returned captain. Two of sand on a beach in the sea's measure, city to city for the two captains. Their only connection had been that their respective ships' watches had witnessed the passing of the same school of Southern-Right whales making their way to the cape for calving. On each ship one man had been moved enough to try and capture how the moon had shone on their barnacled hides and reflected the solemn eyes of the great creatures who were studying the humans passively. Charcoal and book in calloused hands. The same date scribbled, the same emotion scratched on the page. But if they met on a deck, each man would carve different, violent emotions and never know the majesty they had shared.

Coxon and the *Standard* were making for Sierra Leone and Old Cracker's illegal slave-hole. Devlin and his ships were sailing south to Ascension, to keep from the coast and to careen and gather food and water.

Ascension island was God's gift to the mariner south of the equator just as the Verdes was north. From the Verdes you sail west and you will meet the Caribbean; from

Ascension sail west and meet Brasil, and sail up the coast for your trade.

Run east from Ascension for the meat of Africa; or, as Devlin would, like tens of thousands before, set for one hundred and thirty-four degrees and seven hundred miles to Saint Helena and thank the Portuguese and their carracks that had discovered the islands and laid goats, pigs and trees there. Gather more water and fresh meat and set to cleaning.

Careening and caulking, 'brooming and breaming', to take a day. This was the pirate's advantage over their naval hunters. The warships would careen in port, the pirates on the fly.

Wood and water. The worms and barnacles were sworn enemies of oak, and the pirates needed to show a pair of clean heels more than most. It would be a generation before copper-bottomed boats cut through the water. Burning and brushing remained the only way to clean. If a safe island were found – and if the ship were small enough – then beach her and fire and scrape away the sluggishness. For larger ships like the *Shadow,* anchor and weigh all her guns and lading to one side. Her crew put ashore to feast and drink while the gangs allotted to the task keep to the boats, some on one side pulling her gunwales down while the others cleaned what strakes they could as the ship leant clear of the waterline. A clean keel was as fine a weapon as any cannon to a pirate.

The task done, the final scuttlebutt of water filled at Saint Helena, and one more ink line was turned dramatically up to sixty degrees for the almost fifteen hundred miles to reach the Comoros islands. Thirty-five days for Devlin with his swift girl; just over five thousand miles. Africa to be kept just off the edge of the page to be safe from the coast where the hunters lurked.

But it had been a hard month. Devlin had awoken on the first Sunday to an Angelus bell and prayer under the sanguineous dawn of an African sun. He slammed out of his cabin, fit to wound those who had woken him, pulling on his shirt only to stall with one arm still naked at the sight of more than half his crew on their knees.

Their heads looked up to him and he spat as if that had been his only intention and returned to his cabin. O'Neill went back to his incantations as his Porto brethren passed out hard-tack as jury-rigged communion wafers. At least there was plenty of wine and the pirates willing to accept its holy transformation.

Devlin closed his door, dressed with coarse mutterings and looked out at the endless horizon from his slanted windows. And the month went so.

They had used the weeks to refit the *Santa Rosa* more to their purpose. Gunports cut away, six-pounders added fore and aft, stanchions for swivel-guns mounted on every rail. She had entered the world with six four-pounders and two half-pound falconets; she would dare you to make her leave it after trebling her armament and taking cut-throats for her crew.

The *Shadow* too had dressed herself for a bride. Devlin had taken a leaf from Roberts's book and mounted guns to the fighting-tops. Half-pounders, but from the tops and firing down onto a deck it would be like hot hail to the unfortunates opposing. A rain of lead, cruel even for pirates whose rule book began with all the ways to whittle down a crew before the freeboards scraped.

And two pirate ships crossed the cape of Africa and entered the Indian Ocean and even the priests had seen it before and kept to their sewing palms and mending of sail and swabbing of wood that never ended.

So it came to Lieutenant Manvell on the *Standard* with John Coxon, seven days behind Devlin, to marvel at the new earth.

Coxon could keep to the coast, no need to shy from fort guns or passing ships. Just over three-thousand miles against Devlin's five. Three thousand miles. Down to green water and beer and all the fresh meat gone. But now, heading for the Comoros, there was the promise of water, turtles, goats, fish, birds. A garden of Eden. After two days of rain around the Cape, an early July dawn opened for Lieutenant Manvell.

He climbed to the weather-deck and became blinded by the searing white light. He reached for some wood to steady himself and with his hand over his brow looked about the deck.

The ship shone, her wood freshly swabbed and holy-stoned, the brightness off her chains and oak dazzling. Before him the men had adapted to the light and heat like moulting a winter coat. White loose shirts, rolled sleeves and pale calico slops. To Manvell they were as angels beneath the greater whiteness of their cloud-like sails. Those who had some position wore straw hats, the common sailor a headscarf if he had it. They looked over to him as they worked and tapped their foreheads to him. Some had daubed black ash under their eyes.

With Manvell acknowledged they went back to their sewing, cleaning and painting. His eyes at last adjusted, Manvell took off his hat and then the blue of the sky hit him. He took a breath and even that was sweet. The sky was a colour he had never seen. The barest blue, going on forever, irenic and dissolving into nothingness. He leant over the gunwale off a rope and looked fore, his eye falling to the water as the ship rolled.

The sea did not boil and cream as they ploughed her, the wash parted like fresh snow and the waters shone as clear as looking up a street, only it was shoals of fish hurrying along and not passers-by. He settled down and whispered to his pregnant wife thousands of miles away.

'Oh, Alice! To *see* it!'

'It is hard to believe it is of the same earth.'

Thomas Howard had joined him silently and had ignored the jump of his senior officer at his voice.

'You were asleep when we entered the Agulhas current. That is where one leaves the Atlantic. One can see the hemispheres meet as the water becomes . . . *this.*'

He enjoyed the sight with Manvell, envious that this was not his first time but warmed to share another's.

'The hue of it!' Manvell gasped. 'How so, such a sea?'

Howard looked out over the miles. Here and there a large shape on the water like black oil. Reefs and shoals seeking keels.

'I am told it is a higher salinity and an abundance of smaller life such as the whales consume. It is a warm current coming towards us. It will be slow here . . . but to look at it shouldn't that be the way? Our *Standard* with her dirty legs sullies it, do you not think? A brown scar across it.'

'Men being here sullies it.'

'Aye,' Howard agreed. 'That too. The pirates worst of all.'

Manvell moved away from the blinding panorama over the sea and studied Howard. Had he brought up the pirates for further discussion?

It had been weeks since their captain had taken them back up the coast instead of on to the Comoros and their official path. Back to Leone to chase phantoms of his past. Coxon and the pirate, Kennedy, had gone ashore alone and Kennedy had come back with bloodied hands. At dinner that evening Coxon had eaten heartily while Manvell could only see his meat swimming in the blood from Kennedy's fists as Coxon updated their orders, not requiring consent. The sail back and into the Indian had been long and even with Manvell and Howard sleeping just feet apart they had discussed nothing outside the workings of their watches and designations of their quarter-bills. Howard's nightmares grew more frequent and Manvell found them almost necessary for himself to fall asleep to, so used to them he had become.

Manvell shook the thought of pirates away and pointed to one of the men with the black eyes. 'Why do they wear those?'

Howard followed his hand. 'Ah. Yes. You may have noticed, sir, that the water and the deck is very much like staring at the sun. Ashes and grease. Keeps the glare down and prevents burning. I wish I could do it.'

'They look mean to be sure.'

'They look like pirates.'

The word again. Manvell took a breath.

'What say you on this Devlin business, Mister Howard? You are close to the captain.'

Howard looked straight ahead. 'Is that a question from the *Standard*, sir?'

'No, Thomas. Just from me.'

'In that case, sir, I see no diversion or concern. We are on course to meet with captains Ogle and Herdman as per orders. The pirate Devlin is part of the order to go after Roberts. The captain has gained intelligence on Devlin. Once we meet with Ogle and Herdman I'm sure we will compare and adjust.'

'To go after Roberts? That is the greater order is it not? Would you not agree?'

Howard stopped looking forward.

'The captain will do what is best, sir. I know that because I am alive to say it.' He tapped his hat and Manvell saw the hot flush on his face. 'Will you excuse me, sir?'

'I meant no offence, Thomas. The captain has not told me what occurred at Leone. I only saw that man, that pirate Kennedy stained with blood.'

'Will you excuse me, sir?' Howard repeated, his youth suddenly gone.

'You may go, Mister Howard. I am to the quarterdeck to await the *Standard*,' Manvell used the regulation term for the captain, as Howard had done to him. 'But I hope you will assist me at dinner when I ask the *Standard* directly what happened and what he intends.'

Howard dipped his chin.

'I will follow my orders and adhere to my duty, sir.'

'I expect no less, Lieutenant. I just want to know if the next time the *Standard* goes ashore will he bring one of us . . . or the pirate again? Do you not think it strange that the man has no duties, eats with the cook, is separate from all of us except the captain?'

Howard spoke low for prying ears. 'Pirates have a way of wooing men's ears. It is best to keep him away.'

'Even from us? Can we be wooed?'

Howard touched his hat again and backed away.

'I think something is wooing you even now, sir.' Howard span away, fore to the fo'c'sle.

Manvell watched him leave then walked along the skid beams to the quarterdeck. Two of his next four hours would be spent with the captain. Then later, at dinner, or supper as his inn-keeper father preferred it, ask Coxon what he had learnt at Leone. Howard had been primed a little to expect a difficult conversation. Perhaps a word to the doctor or the master. If the table all had an interest Coxon could not refuse without discord.

He looked at the intensity of the colourful new world that he had awoken into. It seemed impossible that night could ever come to extinguish such light and his impatience to be at dinner would not help its snuffing.

From the quarterdeck companion-way he paused and looked back over the deck at the black eyes. Maybe it was easy to woo these men who already resembled pirates. If the captain could raise huzzahs out of them with talk of treasure and prizes why not one of their own?

He stepped up and greeted Master Jenkins and the timoneer. Below them at the belfry the cord was pulled and the bell rang eight times, the glass turned on the final tang and a hand held the bell to cut the peal dead. The day begun. Manvell took out his log and called for the backstaff. He would forget about dinner for now. His concentration went to the small inked numbers and the lines of the earth. No room in his equations for the mundane.

He saw the top of Coxon's hat come from beneath the quarterdeck and bark to some slackens and his heart raced.

He fixed to his charts, his head down to yesterday's position. He would wait until dinner, when he had the company of others. Keep his conversation ordered, aware as any that a captain's instincts and consciousness of his ship were mystical powers.

He prepared the backstaff, the Davis quadrant, held it in front of his face looking for faults, and used its frame to hide the body coming up the stair. He convinced himself that it was nothing to do with doubt and all to do with that own instinct nurturing inside of him for the future, for the time when he commanded his own ship.

He felt the body and the shadow fall over his chart.

'Mister Manvell?' Coxon beamed with the day.

'Yes, Captain?' Manvell showed too many teeth.

'We are entering into pirate waters. The clouds on our star-board horizon are Madagascar.'

'And we have the Comoros a day afore our bows. Although the four islands—' the backstaff almost slipped from his sweaty hands and he danced with it '—will be new to me.'

Coxon patted his back. 'To your readings Manvell. Between thirty-six and thirty-eight degrees will gain us the highest westerly.' He turned and walked to the taffrail. 'And Manvell?'

'Yes, Captain?'

'There is something I need to talk to you about over dinner, or supper as your father and mine would prefer. Make sure no officer is absent.'

Manvell dropped the backstaff with a clang impossible for an instrument of wood. He had thought of his father, the word "supper", and Coxon had heard his thoughts. He momentarily dreaded that Coxon might also have kenned his other notions and was slyly letting him know. For the powers of captains were ever mysterious.

'Of course, Captain.' He scrambled the wood up into his arms and made his way to the chains for his reading.

# Chapter Sixteen

*A*thin supper on the *Standard*. Suffolk cheese and
biscuit for the crew – the cheese harder than the
biscuit – and a pease and rice stew. Victualling would be done
at Anjouan where the *Swallow* and *Weymouth* waited. The
stores were not low, the victualling was just a precaution
against the unknown should Anjouan prove troublesome and
they had to head west to Mozambique's forts. Three hours
were allotted to feed the messes of the *Standard*, four men to
each mess, the officers not dining until done.

It was seven o'clock before Coxon's table was prepared.
The Suffolk cheese could keep for months, skimmed of all
its cream, and the officers shaved it rather than sliced it
onto their tack. They had meat at least, braised in gravy,
and suet pudding and actually the leftovers from the crew's
lunch. Tomorrow's salt beef was already steeping to make it
edible.

The same hands at table as every night, like the hand-clap-
ping chorus of a nursery rhyme.

*The doctor, the master, the captain and his boys,*
*Sitting all together like Christmas toys.*

Except that Manvell and Howard were hardly boys.
Howard, at twenty-one, was in his seventh year, Manvell the

same length of service but older. If he did not make captain or master and commander in four years his commission would be languishing, a warrant officer to a ship yet to be built, or the merchant service for him if it went for the worst, and that might all depend if his wife Alice had a successful birth.

It was impossible for him to tell how he would accept another still-birth. Sure in his love for Alice, unsure of his faith in himself and God, and what lesson he was to take from His plan for him. And there was Alice's father, the duke.

With Manvell at sea for months on end, his letters were only written on the wind. Polite questions of health, affirmations of constancy, no reply expected for months. What words were spoken in his absence, what sighs about the man who could only father loose children that fell from perfect aristocratic wombs?

'Your thoughts are not with us, Mister Manvell?' Coxon angled his voice from the side of his mouth that was not masticating on hide.

Manvell put down his cutlery.

'No, Captain. My apologies, sir. However,' he caught Howard's glare from across the table and turned away from it like a blinkered horse.

'I am, I assure the *Standard*, concentrating on our mission at hand and considering your word this afternoon to address us, Captain.'

Coxon succeeded in swallowing the wood in his mouth. 'Quite so, Lieutenant. I'm well aware that there may be some concern about our task. Particularly in light of Kennedy's involvement.'

'Not at all, Captain,' Manvell said. 'We are behind the *Standard*, one and all.'

'I am glad to hear it. Especially as events now lead me to adapt our orders.'

The table stopped eating. Master Jenkins leant an ear forward; he was the furthest from Coxon and may have misheard, he hoped.

'Change our orders, Captain?'

'*Adapt*, Mister Jenkins. I thought it prudent to wait until we were at least in the right sea to announce.'

Howard trapped Manvell's eye this time. Manvell was unable to read the young man's face but sure that the next question should be his.

'Adapt in what way, Captain?'

Coxon carried on eating and waved his fork for the rest to follow.

'A minor addendum that is all. My intelligence serves for us not to attend to captains Ogle and Herdman.'

'*Not* to attend? On what intelligence, Captain?' Manvell asked.

Coxon chewed, brushed his hair forward, separating the strands with a thumbnail. Habit now.

'I know it has been difficult for you to approve, Mister Manvell, but Walter Kennedy has shown himself invaluable. I think the difference between our success and the *Swallow*'s and *Weymouth*'s failure will be their arrogance to not consider the value of base men.'

'So what has your "pirate" told, Captain?'

Manvell felt Howard's glare. Doctor Howe's red face almost burst.

'*Manvell*!' The doctor poured himself some port to mellow his shock; neglecting in his horror to first fill Howard's glass to his left. '*Respect, sir*!'

Coxon raised his arm across Howe.

'No, no, Doctor. My First is correct. His concern is for the *Standard*. I would expect no less.' He leant to Manvell's side of the table.

'My intelligence, Mister Manvell, is gained from my interrogation of the slave trader, Leadstone, at Leone. Thanks to the man's trust of his old pirate bonds in Walter Kennedy he has informed us that the pirate Devlin is after the treasure taken in April from the Portuguese viceroy.'

Howard spoke for the first time. 'The *Virgin of the Cape*? She was taken by pirates in April.' He looked around the table to the blank faces. 'The treasure on her was in *millions*.'

'The very same,' Coxon rapped the table. 'Which is why I have delayed so long in telling. It would fly around the ship in moments. I want the men to be inspired but not before the chase is within reach.'

'Within reach?' Manvell asked.

'Devlin and Roberts are coursing after the treasure. Possibly together. Which is why we shall adjust our orders as given, as is our duty when intelligence demands. Leadstone tells that one of the pirates that captured the bounty has run into the Amirantes with his lot. Over a million, as mister Howard states learnedly. What say you to that, Mister Manvell?'

Manvell took a slow drink of port.

'My instinct would be to question intelligence gathered from sources distrustful by their criminal natures, Captain. I also do not see how this changes our alliance with the *Swallow* and the *Weymouth*. From your declaration I have gathered that we are going after *two* pirate vessels. Roberts and Devlin. Would not the extra ships be of use?'

Coxon took the port from Howe's place and passed it left to Manvell.

'It is time that unbalances us on that level, Mister Manvell. Kennedy says that the pirate Levasseur – along with dozens of others – operates out of Bourbon island, off Madagascar's east coast. Part of the Mascarenes.'

Doctor Howe belched through the French pirate name.

'*Leva*-what now?'

Coxon ignored the interruption. 'That is where we're heading. To Bourbon. To fish for where Devlin may have gone. Time taken to meet with the *Swallow* will be wasteful. I'm more conscious of our orders to apprehend, and with a treasure to boot I would not like to consider the talk of us in England if we let such opportunity pass. Would you not agree, Mister Howard?'

Coxon attempted to nail the young man to his flag, Howard his oldest ally. Howard's face had still not revealed anything to Manvell except a disagreement with the suet.

'I understand our orders are to hunt pirates. I don't see how that's changed, sir.'

Manvell remained calm. 'But to hunt them with the assistance of *two* other men-of-war and report to Captain Ogle. Has that not changed?'

'Manvell,' Coxon shook his head. 'The *Standard* is acting on information unknown to anyone else. Know you that every packet contains the scripture, "as the captain does see fit". We are heading sooner to conflict. I should hope that it is not the prospect of assault that concerns you?'

Manvell felt the eyes of the table upon him, the eyes of the duke staring across the waves from his drawing room and judging his daughter's choice of husband.

'No, sir. And I'm sure the men will be uplifted by the word of true treasure as their goal. But this morning you bade me course for the Comoros and—'

'And tomorrow we will shape for Bourbon using Cape Sebastian.' Coxon raised his glass. 'I can do it myself if you wish?'

Manvell removed his hands to below the table to hide their trembling. 'I only voice concern, Captain, that as your First I should like to be better informed of my task and duty if I am to perform ably.' This posturing was hard for Manvell. He had served three captains, most of whom had been happy with his manner and impressed with his ability despite his stock. He hoped that his unease was only born from his lack of experience of the boldness of men like Coxon and not of a want of clashing with pirates. 'And I have never been in service when orders were changed.'

'In war it is commonplace,' Coxon said.

'But we are not in war.' Manvell regretted the words as they came, wished to pull them back in as they fell upon the table. It seemed almost his habit now.

Coxon eyed him over his glass as he drank and placed it back to the table slowly. 'What would you call it, Lieutenant, if not war? What you must remember is that I have seen pirates up close. I have seen *his* ship. No match for the *Standard* and her guns. And when I announce to the men that there is treasure to be had they will grow wings to push us on. I am sorry to hear that your service has only been dull up to now, Mister Manvell. But you claim that your father taught you how to use a sword so I doubt that is your issue.'

'I have no issue, sir,' and he meant it. 'But I would like to hear it confirmed that it is Devlin that is our target now. That Roberts is not of your concern – my apologies – of the *Standard*'s concern.'

The bowls cooled and good humour vanished. Coxon seemed to puff at a pipe that was not there and scratched his hair forward again.

'Yes,' he said at last. 'If that is how we shall have it. We are after Devlin and a million pounds of prize. I see no harm in admitting it. Why not? We have good men, a fine ship and, once at Bourbon, I'm sure we will have the key. Together – a crew such as this – we could pickpocket our hangman.'

Manvell saluted his glass. 'So be it,' he said. 'I am convinced. Then tomorrow at *him*.' And again he failed to read anything from Howard's stoic face. 'But we will need to supply.'

Howard spoke finally.

'Bourbon is a trading island, Mister Manvell. No purser's credits but we could give sailcloth and cordage for what we need.' He smiled at Coxon, the first time Manvell had seen his face shift.

Coxon returned the smile briefly then ruminated on his glass tilting with the sea.

He had not told any of them of his meeting in the Boston colony in January. A square of paper sitting in his coat, burning into him. Hidden even from the Board that gave him his orders. Manvell was a good man but Coxon could see his faith wilting. Even Howard only indulged him. How far could he push before he would have to reveal his only true order? Two black-coated men had come to him in January to call him back. Paper kept in the safety of his command. Paper even he had been forbidden to read. The seal to be broken by those who would judge his success or failure.

Devlin their only order. For their shame and their folly in having trusted a pirate. No plays or ballads for Devlin. Not even a noose.

End him. Once and for all. Ignore all else.

Doctor Howe broke his sombre mood. 'Forgive me, gentle-men. I heard something about "hangmen"? What are we about now?'

# Chapter Seventeen

*T*here exist islands that have no names, or at least no official names. That comes when a country decrees to colonise and lands a flagged possession stone, builds a fort, establishes a trade route, and claims it as their own. Until such time the island might have many titles, depending on the map the mariner uses.

Devlin used a new Mortier which gave no such names for the tiny outlines the priest had pointed to with his fingernail. But O'Neill repeated the titles for the cluster of islands that he had overheard The Buzzard use.

'The last island of the Amirantes,' O'Neill said proudly. 'The largest one. Fifty to sixty miles all round.'

Devlin bent to the map. 'It has no name?'

'Does it matter? Levasseur scoffed at Taylor for going to Panama. His, he said, was devoid of man but as fruitful as Eden. That is the island where The Buzzard has gone. That is where he has taken the cross.'

'The *treasure*,' Devlin corrected.

Dandon joined them and looked down at the island.

'Do you know this place, Patrick?'

Devlin dragged his fingernail over the string of islands.

'These are the islands that the Portos called "The Three Brothers and The Seven Sisters". Wild places. No-one wants them.'

166

'A good place to hide,' Dandon said.

Devlin concentrated on the chart. 'From Cape St Sebastien,' he covered the tip of Madagascar with the first fingers of his left hand where the rhumb-lines passed and twisted his wrist to match the line that stretched away and ended at *de Roque Pires*.

'Sixty-five degrees north north-east.' He walked the rhumb line with his first knuckle as a gauge. 'Seven hundred miles. Six days if we're lucky and sail all night.'

'And no sign of Roberts,' Dandon reminded. 'He may have already found a guide and beaten us to it.'

Devlin slammed the book closed.

'That's the craic of it! The Buzzard took the ship at Bourbon. He's taken his *Victory* and run five degrees south of the equator. West he hits Zanzibar, east, Sumatra. He could trade between them for a thousand years and Europe would never know.'

Dandon watched Devlin's confidence shine yet could not help but break it.

'It has been three months since Levasseur took the treasure. Would he not have perhaps melted this cross? Parted this island by now?'

Devlin's manner darkened.

'Do you not remember a chest that we could not move for its weight in gold? Sometimes a feast is a curse. How would you melt a seven-foot cross of gold?'

Dandon looked out a window to the night.

'I would – I suppose – need some lead cast to melt it. Tools to pour it into more manageable moulds . . .' He faltered. 'I do not know.'

'Exactly,' Devlin said and O'Neill seemed pleased beside him as Devlin went on.

'He's the richest man under heaven. And he'll need help to rid himself of it.'

'Our help,' Dandon suggested.

'But not yours, my friend.'

Dandon straightened from his usual slouch.

'Not mine? And what am I to do?'

Devlin patted his shoulder.

'This road may be bloody. I need Peter Sam and Hugh. I need the true beside me.'

He read Dandon's sallow eyes and hoped in return Dandon could see his reasoning. Devlin had lost Bill Vernon last year, and others before whom he had known since his first days as pirate. Peter Sam indestructible, Hugh Harris as novel as rat and cockroach at survival, but Devlin had learnt how death discriminated. He had stood in the guts of Sam Fletcher, who had shot men in their faces and only asked that Devlin did not tell his mother about him, as he tried to push back his insides. Others had been just as bloody and broken, their lives snuffed by powder, tipped to the sea or left on beaches where they deserved to be, to be sure. But Dandon did not carry a weapon, and they were going against pirates.

'We'll drop you with the priests and the *Santa Rosa* at Bourbon.'

Bourbon was east of Madagascar. The Buzzard, Taylor and England had made it one of their pirate bases as had hundreds of others over the decades. Dandon would be safe there, the priests would be safe there, all safe for Devlin's return with a hold full of gold. None dead. Dandon saw no argument in Devlin's eyes.

'But *I* will come with you, Captain,' O'Neill insisted.

Devlin looked the priest up and down.

'You'd better. You carried that cross once. I'm not hauling it for you. Can you fight, priest?'

'Am I priest first or Irish?'

Devlin grinned and elbowed him aside.

'That'll do, Father.'

# Chapter Eighteen

*E*xtract from the journal of Renaud Rennefort, first governor of Bourbon, 1665.

*The Isle is situated between twenty-one and twenty-two degrees of south latitude; is of a round figure and sixty leagues in circumference. The sick who were landed there recovered in a very short time from the purity of the air and the excellence of its refreshments.*

*The turtle doves, the wood pigeons and parroquets, were so far from being alarmed at the sight of man that they flew about him as to suffer to be taken without any exertion. Cattle and goats were seen in great numbers. Hogs also were in great plenty, and fed on the land turtles, which were seen crawling about in every quarter. The sea turtles visited the shore during the evening and were easily taken.*

*The land animals were inexhaustible, as well as the fish which were found in pools or inhabited the beautiful rivers that flowed through the island. Almost all the trees wept benzoin and other precious gums. The soil is so rich as to be made capable of producing two harvests in the year, and the water, which is excellent, does not nourish any venomous and mischievous animal. Ambergris, coral and the most beautiful shells in the world are found upon the coast.*

*One half of this island was formerly consumed by fire which has left very dreadful proofs of its violence. The anchorage is not good off any part of the island, nor are hurricanes infrequent. When they arise, trees are torn up by their roots, houses are blown away, and, if the ships are not driven on shore, they are sunk by its fury.*

It cannot be seen from Madagascar and in truth it was part of the Mascarenhas Archipelago, as, of course, discovered by the Portuguese and a sister to the Île de France; but to Christopher Manvell it seemed conceivable that the island's peaks could be seen from India.

Bourbon. Named after the royal house. For one year it had not held a French governor and although the pirates had enjoyed a peaceful relationship with the old one the absence of any law suited better.

Manvell stood at the fo'c'sle as the bowsprit bobbed up and down over the green mountains that stretched out of the sea. Cloud shrouded the whole of the island, the wet heat already in the air over the ship and the rise of smoke from her volcanoes created an emblem of places imagined only by sailors – a remnant of the earth before time. A place to be avoided. All the promise of new worlds, all the dangers of the savage tropics. Every sight reminded them how far they had come, how foreign they were. Even the sea was different. Yet the sound of the ship ploughing through it remained reassuringly the same, and the sight of the brigs and sloops curving around the coast was the same, if less reassuring.

The pirates, Manvell thought. Wherever God has thought an island in this ocean there be pirates and crows.

They advanced on St Denis, the main town, from the north, the wind to larboard. There was no port, nor any port on the island. The other three French settlements, St Paul, St Mary and St Susanna lay also in the island's north. The mountains and volcanoes kept the south secret. If there were towns there the French were not interested. If the French were to make the island a success it would be the north shores that the ships would divert to.

No port, just beach and shore, so the *Standard* anchored near a league distant amongst the dozens of others whose crews rubbed their chins and counted the bodies in the rigging and measured the worth of the twin gundecks. A naval ship, a bold captain flying his Union Jack from the ensign and mainmast. A visitor only.

He had better be.

Coxon, Manvell, Kennedy and two marines were quickly to the shore, Kennedy blabbing all the way. The names that he knew. The faces best not met.

'Captain England, naturally. He always favoured these waters. Sorely miss Captain England, I do. Davis and I never agreed on him, and Roberts never agreed on anybody!' He laughed, alone, then sheepishly turned his face to the beach.

Coxon called from his seat afore the coxswain.

'What is the best place to pay a visit, Walter?'

Manvell cut across the pirate's answer.

'Would we not introduce ourselves to the governor first, Captain?'

'There is no governor at present,' Coxon said. 'We're on our own, Manvell. No office to protect us.'

Another chip at Manvell's valour. His concern for propriety had come across as hiding behind duty or perhaps Coxon pricked at him for other purpose. The captain did not strike Manvell as the bullish or petty type. Another purpose then; just not perceptible. Manvell thought of questioning direct, imagined it in his head. Demanding. Accusing.

He looked at Coxon's old silk coat; green across the shoulders and in the creases where the black had faded. Cuffs, wax-stained and balding. The thick black belt cracked and limp. The aged grey shirt and steinkerk, the hat bleached with salt.

He passed down at his own suit, a suit befitting the son-in-law of the Duke of Beaufort. Aye, Coxon had another purpose. He did not see the Kent publican's son. He saw the clothes and manners and privilege of marriage and commission. The burden to prove worthy to stand on Coxon's quarterdeck was not weighed in ink or patronage. Manvell settled to watching them break to the shore, the oars brought up, Kennedy giggling again as he leapt from the boat to heave her in with the marines.

Manvell stood with the spume bubbling over his shoe buckles. Dark volcanic sand, the beach surrounded by vibrant cliffs, their majesty hundreds of feet straight up in the air and so resplendent they might have risen only yesterday. Palm trees seemed to shoo them back with their fronds, and in the distance, wild mountains pierced the clouds. Just green. Just never-ending green rolling on and on. Except at the ground. Except at head height. Black rocks, ash, the gritty sand underfoot; a paradise not quite finished.

'The town is up aways,' Kennedy waved them to him as merry as if he were at a horsefair. The sailors dragged themselves out of the sea.

'Manvell,' Coxon said. 'This could get lively.' He looked down at the sword on Manvell's hip.

'Can you use that against anyone other than your father, or did he teach you with a wooden one?' He did not wait for a reply and sharpened his pace away from Manvell and the

marines who had heard their captain's disdain for his
lieutenant.

A winding jungle path, a dust track and the squawks and whistles of the birds colourfully stark against the green like shards
of stained glass. Kennedy was the only one suitably attired,
shoeless and coat free. The others drowned in sweat but it was
necessary to show superiority. No uniform for the officers, but
the cloth of a gentleman and the chink of weapons and coin
might be worth more than a scarfed head and slops.

'It is like Providence again,' Coxon said to Manvell as they
came onto the edge of town. 'For all their talk of freedom
pirates always strive for the same wherever they go. Not one
has tried to improve the world.'

They strolled through the dirt and grass that made up the
thoroughfare. Stucco buildings, some three stories high, built
purposely as if to create and let fester dark alleyways. Blanket
awnings at every wall covered baskets of fish and fruit where
homes had become stores.

A rush of people, no-one paying them any mind, a sadness
on the faces Manvell thought, the women especially. Naked
children in doorways stared at their passing, their eyes questioning and their smutty chins wet with juice.

The pace went slower as the road climbed, always the way
in any Catholic place. All roads led up towards the church,
and dutifully Kennedy beckoned them away to a slope
between two plastered walls that came out on a canal path.
Manvell saw a watermill on the side of a house, a wooden
bridge. The French were trying to work here. But above them
the mountains. You can't break mountains. Their smallest
chagrin will crush your civilisation. A shrug and your mills
and workshops are gone, washed away like an ant's nest.

Another quarter, more timber and plaster dwellings, almost to scale like an artist's maquette of a town, a village for dwarves. Manvell sure now that he could never make it back to the shore alone, lost as he was.

A square of buildings appeared, a small stream running through it, red and muddy. Kennedy pointed to a two-level building, the largest they had seen.

Coxon approved.

'Such grandeur would be the tavern,' he said. He posted the marines where they stood and he and Manvell walked on.

Manvell could hear music now and women's drunken screeching.

'What is our course here, Captain?'

Coxon did not hesitate.

'Kennedy will see if there is anyone worth speaking to. We'll throw some coin about. An anker of brandy for information on Devlin's whereabouts.'

'Or Roberts?'

'Either will suffice.'

'What if Devlin is in there?'

'He's not,' he said, and nothing more.

The door was flimsy and crashed open but the room was used to it and few heads turned. Manvell had not spent much time in taverns. His father's inn was a country coach house. Food, beds, travellers. Coxon's confidence in striding amongst the tables and benches hinted that he had seen such debauchery before.

The stench of roasting fat, the boucan kitchen, tobacco and stale beer mixed the colour and taste of the hanging air and Manvell coughed, put back the door and put out the day. The shutters were closed, the room vague by lamplight and candles. Coxon and Kennedy already stood at a crowded table. Manvell weaved through the raucousness and kept to Coxon's back.

Kennedy whispered into ears, slapped backs and cocked his thumb to Coxon who stared down all the eyes studying him without a word.

Kennedy had deftly become separate from them. In seconds he was no longer Coxon's prisoner. Manvell was unsure exactly what he was, but sure that word of the naval men was spreading around the room and surer that Coxon would have to do something to stop their mission ending here and now.

Coxon had read his mind.

'Two jugs here!' he grabbed the arm of a Creole girl with a jug on her hip. 'The best you have. And a hen and wine as soon as you can for this table.' He put a guinea in her palm, making sure that the table saw the gold.

He pulled a stool, flapped aside his coat to sit, revealed his sword and pistol.

'Is there not a local drink of some sort of mead? Would you fellows prefer?' There was no preference given, a couple of salutes was all, and Coxon shuffled his stool closer to the table and did not waste time.

'I'm looking for word on the pirate Devlin. Any word.' The table shared lowered looks.

'I don't expect it without cost. I reward information. With brandy and gold. And I'm not saying that any of you gentlemen know anything. Just pass the word that I'm paying for any word on Devlin. Any word that I don't already know.'

'And what do you know?' A young face, too young to be halfway across the world.

The rum came – came with a lascivious look and one mug for Coxon. The others filled their blackjacks and listened hard over the row all around them.

'I know that Taylor and Levasseur took the *Virgin of the Cape* in April off these shores. Taylor has gone to Panama, Levasseur is in these waters. Roberts and Devlin are seeking Levasseur, hunting his treasure. I'm after Devlin.' He took a drink. 'For nothing more than that we have scores to settle. I hold no interest in any other man of fortune.'

The oldest of them, the blackest of them, with hands and face as gnarled as bark sucked at his rum through a bamboo straw.

'And what does Cap'n Kennedy have to say of this? Him of Cap'n Roberts's lot. Helping the king?'

Kennedy put his hand on Coxon's shoulder.

'The good Captain Coxon here comes and gets me out of a hanging to have my revenge.'

'What revenge?' Another voice.

'Against Devlin,' he borrowed Coxon's mug for a drag as Coxon shifted from under Kennedy's hand.

'That dog killed my old man back in London. Lived together so we did. Like brothers we were. My father his father. And kill him so he did, in his gratitude. That's revenge to me.'

Coxon's lips thinned at the exaggeration and doubted the table took in any of it. It was possible that Devlin could have done the deed. Kennedy and he had lived together. Every dog is capable of biting. But a man knows his own dog.

'I freed Walter from the noose,' he said. 'I have that power. I'm after a murderer not a pirate.'

The older one sat back.

'Ain't no pirates here anyways that I know of, Cap'n.'

'Nor I,' said another.

A finger pointed out from the edge of their conclave to the tailored Manvell.

177

'And who's this ponce keeping an eye?'

The finger belonged to a fellow in waistcoat over bare flesh, a skeleton of a man, impossible to judge the age of him but not his humour.

It was a long pause before Manvell noticed he had been brought into play. Coxon raised his hand.

'He's with me,' he said. 'My man.'

'He has a disapproving stance about.' The pirate whistled at Manvell. 'Too good to sit with us, lad?'

'Me, sir?' Manvell squeaked. 'Not at all. No, sir. There is no room to take a seat. That's the only ounce of it.'

The young one threw his bait.

'He looks like he'd enjoy sitting on your lap, Samuel!'

Samuel's teeth showed.

'Would that be right, lad? Would you be wanting to take a rest on my lap, is it?'

Coxon rapped the table.

'My business, gentlemen?' The hen and wine slapped down in front of him. 'Eat. And see if you can remember something I can use.'

'Your business can wait, Cap'n,' the pirate winked and began to rise.

Coxon watched the amusement grow around his company. This was tavern sport. It went ever only two ways. It would be up to Manvell to decide which and then it would be Coxon's turn to be tested. He expected something like this. He moved his wrist to rest on the pistol in his belt, assured that the rest of them saw.

Manvell stepped back as the pirate drew a dagger slow, and a cutlass slower.

'You think my arse for quim, lad? Sodomy your curse?'

None of what he heard made sense to Manvell – he was

178

unsure even if he was hearing English – but there was steel. That he understood, and his captain still sitting.

'I beg your pardon?' he said, convinced that the music of lute and fife had addled his senses.

The pirate came on.

'You having any of it?'

Manvell was not familiar with the appropriate response. He imagined this was how children experienced torment when outnumbered and cornered in London's streets by bullies for a handful of marbles. There was no rationale to any of it.

'Captain?' he said.

Coxon half-turned.

'Well, Manvell?' he said. '*Are* you having any of it?'

Manvell set his mouth, ignored the grinning Kennedy and his complicit captain. He turned on his heel, the door directly in front of him, the bright day beyond cutting through its frame. He marched towards it.

The pirate exploded with laughter and the room followed, as even those who had not seen the altercation saw a smart back walking away from a brother's pitted cutlass and guessed what had transpired.

Coxon made a white fist beneath the table. He took some rum to cover his disgust as the table and Kennedy roared and even the musicians lost their detachment.

Coxon, above all the jeers, could hear the door open and close – a coffin lid slammed.

The pirate put back his cutlass, stabbed a breast of the hen with his dagger.

'Fine men you have there, Cap'n!' He slipped the greasy white flesh into his mouth as he sat. 'What Roberts will make of them will be a horror!'

The door opened again. The bows slid off the fiddles with a whine and the room stilled in mid-pour, and suddenly the only sound was the urgency of the rats inside the walls.

Manvell stood in the doorway, sans hat and coat, his hand on the door.

'Perhaps I am misunderstood?' His voice thrown across the room to hit one face.

'In my association a gentleman settles his reputation outside, sir.' He put out his hand and beckoned.

'I will of course accept an apology if you wish to reconsider.'

Coxon did not turn but raised his mug to his lips again. His smile remained hidden as the pirate cursed and pushed himself up from the table.

Dandon pulled on his boots, then leant back for several breaths to let the blood drain from his head. He sat on a fragile cot in the white rooms of the cathedral of Bourbon. He scratched his face where his short beard had once been. He had removed it months ago but still mused by working on a beard that was not there.

It had taken two days to sleep well, the ship still swimming in his head, but now it was if he had never left bed and land. He woke late every morning, and at night found the chirrup of the insects comforting despite the lack of drink from the priests, which made him question their vocation.

Dandon's days had been dry. He had little rattling coin to slake a thirst which was also his hunger. He had lived with Patrick Devlin for four years and summed up that living as corks thrown to the sea and hens picked clean. Maybe he had lived beneficially on his friend and it seemed just so now that his own purse came short.

He stood and looked in the mirror over his basin. It had been one year to the next since he had looked in a mirror and he combed his hair with his fingernails and questioned why his beard had not grown back.

''Tis the drink,' he declared aloud, and examined his gold teeth in the smoky glass and picked the unleavened bread out of their corners.

'And it is not the drink,' he said and put his wide hat on and brushed down his eyebrows. He looked at his purse by his pillow. No need to weigh it any more than he had done for the last week. Not enough for a bottle, but why not just a coin or two for some relief? Four or five Dutch tin won't buy a house or a week's food so why not let it serve some purpose every day?

He heard footsteps coming down the long stone corridor and sighed.

The priests. The damned priests.

Five days Devlin had left him here with O'Neill's Porto brethren and the *Santa Rosa*. Five days of cornmeal and honey-wine.

Devlin had abandoned him it seemed, and when he thought deeper on it there were many 'occasions' when Dandon had not been present at the culmination of Devlin's plans. No matter. If Devlin felt him too inclined to drink, too useless for conflict, disliked his notion to go unarmed, so be it. Maybe the one had outgrown the other. Dandon would only add that to the list of things to drink to and for.

The footsteps towards his door were running now and Dandon steadied himself for the blast that was about to burst into his room. The door flew. A priest skidded in, his breath rasping.

'What is it?' Dandon said. 'The captain has returned?'

181

'Señor . . .' he waved Dandon to follow. 'A fight . . . there is a fight at the inn about to begin!'

Dandon crossed the room unimpressed.

'Is there not a fight every hour?'

'There are English there. And soldiers too.'

'. . . Soldiers?'

'Redcoats. And smart men with smart clothes.' He sped ahead. 'Come. Hurry, señor.'

Dandon followed. Redcoats? And smart, orderly clothes on Bourbon? That meant naval men and none of it could be to the good.

Dandon straightened his coat and plucked his shirt-cuffs to his knuckles, confident now that this was why Devlin had left an unarmed, drunken loblolly boy behind. Dandon went always unarmed save for his head and his tongue. Dandon was trusted to do the wisest thing. Trusted. Aye, that was it. Trusted. Not left behind at all. And that would do until the end of days.

Dandon looked through the shoulders of the crowd at the scene. A young man stood in shirt and waistcoat. A rapier-point to the ground, right foot behind, left arm across the small of his back and his left side angled to the figure oppo-site. The other hunched, cutlass flinching, dagger loose in his second fist. They were given a wide circle. Empty mugs held wagers, full mugs pointed and laughed at the prim statue of the gentleman.

'That is not one of my companions,' Dandon informed the priest. 'Do we all look alike to you?'

The priest pulled Dandon's sleeve and stabbed a finger to the two marines and the pirate's opponent.

'See!' he whispered. 'Englishmen! They come for Devlin!'

Dandon studied the young man with the rapier and the marines leaning on their muskets holding the young man's coat and hat.

'Not necessarily, Father. Even priests can't be that unlucky.'

Just two marines. No fear in two marines. A ship come for victualling, nothing more.

The pirates jeered both duellists, their fight slow to start and mugs already empty and the sun too hot. Manvell cleared his throat.

'First blood?' he offered, loud enough for the crowd to hear. 'That will satisfy me.'

'Aye,' agreed the pirate. 'But you won't mind if I slice something.' The pirate squinted with the sun over Manvell's shoulders, and then snarled his way into Manvell's reach.

Coxon came out from the door shielding his brow from the sudden whiteness of the square and beheld the cockpit before him.

No longer did Manvell seem to be the gangly, clumsy lieutenant who dropped instruments and apologised for his slipping shoes. For a moment Coxon could see the fortitude that had suffered a dead child. The constancy in him was about to be exampled and the anger discharged through his debole.

Manvell, motionless, recalled his Capoferro:

*If you have an encounter with a bestial man, that is, one without measure and tempo, who throws many blows at you with great impetus, there are two things that you can do: first, adopting the play of mezzo tempo, you will strike him during his throwing of a thrust or a cut, alternately allow him to go into empty space, evading backwards with your body, then immediately give him a thrust in the face or chest.*

But there would have to be subtlety here. Only a scene not a final act, so perhaps Liancour for a touch.

Capoferro and Liancour: the treatises his father made him read after every failed *prima stretta*, and which Manvell then borrowed to memorise when his father was not looking. As a boy he had never questioned why a Deal publican had insisted on such a practice for his son. He thought it natural for all children. Manvell was pale and thin, not tall or impressive in any aspect. As a boy he had cut a feminine and sickly shape. But he feared nothing and had never lost a fight in his life. He bumped into every door and tripped on every stair. But with a blade placed in his hand he could only be merciful. The dead would pile up else. A Deal publican had wanted his beloved son to survive.

He turned his breast to the pirate, opened his sword arm. The pirate grunted and lunged at his offered prize.

Manvell appeared to do nothing, yet the pirate's cutlass became trapped under Manvell's left arm and his wrist wrapped around the pirate's as if it had always been.

Cutlass and man in a vice. The surprised face Manvell's reward.

He moved then.

His rapier dashed and sliced across the pirate's dagger and severed the webbed flesh between thumb and palm which opened to drop the blade. The pirate gaped at his treacherous hand.

Then the rapier up, across and behind the cutlass's guard before the dagger hit the ground, and he had dragged and disengaged the cutlass from the other hand.

Manvell swept back, the cutlass now his. He held both weapons high. Became the statue again.

The crowd's cheers for their brother still rolled, the action too fast for drunken eyes to catch.

Then the lull as their brother stood naked of any blade and bled, and the gentleman somehow had two pieces of steel. 'First blood,' Manvell said.

The pirate looked to his hand, to the statue, to his dropped dagger and lost cutlass. He clutched his hand and shuffled to the shelter of the crowd where laughing hands pushed him away.

Manvell stuck the cutlass into the dirt and bowed to his combatant and the crowd. Whores applauded, pirates belly-laughed and John Coxon reappraised his lieutenant.

This was good work, he thought. Manvell had shown his honour and ability in a manner that suited the pirates' temperaments and virtues. No real harm done. The pirate's wound? A paper-cut in his trade and he would be mocked if he complained otherwise. Manvell had done well. The tavern would listen to them now. He nodded to Manvell across the shoulders of the gathering and Manvell returned the nod and scraped back his sword.

The crowd began to filter back to the tavern, an equal number set around Manvell and the embarrassed pirate, congratulating one, building up the other. Coxon began to turn back with them. He sought the heads that had been around the table and wherever Kennedy had got to.

He stalled at a flash of yellow.

Across the square a dandy was fanning himself with his wide hat and flashing his gold capped teeth as he bent to a priest's ear. The years melted away from John Coxon's life.

*Dandon*, he thought. Dandon from The Island. The pox-doctor that gamed to be French.

Devlin's man.

His hand went to his pistol, slowly, as if the angels were watching him and might shriek a warning.

\*     \*     \*

'That was most impressive,' Dandon put back his hat. 'But has little to do with me I'm sure.'

'Not your man?' the priest asked.

'No,' Dandon said. 'But at least I am come to where I can partake.'

The priest still held onto a portion of Dandon's cloth and plucked his attention.

'But the redcoats? We are in trouble, no?'

Dandon stiffened as the unmistakeable jolt of a pistol in his back reminded him of his wound from last year; a good square of flesh carved out by one Albany Holmes, its inflicter dead now but still it woke him every morning.

The voice that came with the pistol he had thought forgotten.

'Dandon is it not?' it said, and the pistol jabbed. 'Don't move.'

'I am unarmed Captain . . . *Coxon?*' Dandon raised open palms in supplication.

'You were unarmed when you took my ship, pirate.'

He grabbed Dandon's collar and jerked it to his face.

'Your priest friend can come with. We have years to catch up on and I'm sure he would like to hear your confession!'

# Chapter Nineteen

*D*andon had first met John Coxon a few weeks after his introduction to Patrick Devlin. At the time he thought Devlin a creature of his own making, fresh and new. Then came The Island, the French gold, and John Coxon, bitter and vengeful.

Another year, and the hunt for the letters of the Jesuit priest – the porcelain adventure – and Coxon had been there also. And it became apparent that Devlin had not cleared all his past as Dandon had assumed. Then came the diamond and the South Sea débâcle less than a year gone. Coxon's pistol in his back hardly seemed a coincidence.

When you meet a smiling soul, a devil-may-care fellow, you hope this is how they are, that they are genuinely free from mortal pains. And then they become too drunk or too sober and you discover they carry the blight of chains and stones that all men drag behind them. Did the Lord really die at thirty-three? What use that to any man? A ministry of youth? Or is it that after that age only suffering is to be expected.

Never mind. Dandon was far too sober to appreciate any of it. A pistol in the back. Go only with what that entails.

He sat with his tied hands across the back of a chair, painful to his old injury. The priest had been given the respect to be allowed to stand. They were in the wine room of the tavern, their privacy bought with Coxon's purse. Dandon eyed the barrels, even the splashes, in a sweat. He could not help it; this was the measure of his days when Devlin was not around.

'Captain Coxon,' he said. 'It has so been a while. Perhaps a drink to reacquaint?'

Coxon said nothing. He surveyed the man that he only knew as Devlin's barber-surgeon. His presence meant something. And a priest? That meant something too.

Coxon went straight for the throat.

'Where is your captain, Dandon?'

'Devlin you mean, sir?' Dandon sat up straight. 'Say it as so. Or can you not find the heart to say the name?'

'Devlin, then,' Coxon said. 'Where is he?'

Dandon looked between the men. Kennedy he did not know but he knew pirates when he saw them. The young man with the able sword was obviously attached to Coxon, but the pirate? Dandon would question as much as Coxon.

'Your adjutants look a little rough these days, Captain. Have standards slipped since we last met?'

'Kennedy,' Coxon put his hand out to Dandon. 'Introduce yourself.'

The pirate checked once to Coxon and got the eye he was looking for. He strode to Dandon and sent the back of his hand sharp across his face.

'Walter Kennedy,' he said, and the hand came back harder this time. 'Pleased to meet you.'

Dandon shook away the blow, his eyes smarting. He had heard the name before and most certainly from Devlin, but the context evaded him. The pirate remained standing over him. Dandon would not satisfy him with a look up into his face.

The priest ran to Dandon, behind him, his hands on his shoulders.

'Please!' he cried. 'Do not do this!'

Manvell watched Coxon's hands clasp and unclasp as he spoke.

'I will get to you, Father. I want to hear this man first.'

Manvell saw the change on Kennedy's face. The sheen of ecstasy that he might be given a chance to vent something on a priest.

The scene was unpleasant for Manvell, the setting itself bad enough. The squalor of the storeroom, the heat and flies, and the sordid backdrop of the island, a nest of villainy and eastern savagery. Yet Coxon's current manner lay far beneath all of them.

'Captain,' he said. 'Who is this man to be beaten so?'

Dandon looked around Kennedy to the pale swordsman. His escape had just begun. He tasted rum already rinsing away his blood.

Coxon scowled.

'You remember our lieutenant's dream, Manvell? This *thing* is the measure of his nightmares. A friend to the pirate Devlin. Hold onto this one and Devlin will follow.'

Dandon piped up. 'Are you sure you should wish that on this fellow, Captain?'

Coxon nodded to Kennedy again who wiped his mouth and the smirk off Dandon's.

Back and across, back and across, and the priest had to catch the chair from falling.

Coxon took a step towards, let Dandon take a breath.

'Where is he? Or would you rather I allow Walter a go on the priest?'

Manvell had heard enough.

'*Captain*! I insist to protest!'

Coxon, hands still behind his back, watched Dandon leer through his bloodied lip then turned and put his shoulder against Manvell's and spoke quietly to the wall.

'Manvell, do not think that any of this is an art that I wish to employ. Or that I hold any familiarity with this fellow above my orders or position. But it is imperative—' he felt Manvell's shoulder shift and he pushed into it harder, '—*imperative*, sir, that no division is shown before these types!'

'We condone torture, Captain?'

'Mister Manvell. You should think more on what I have achieved for my orders. For *our* orders. Ogle and Herdman are still waiting on word for Roberts. Fattening themselves and buying dresses for their mistresses. Where are we? Where shall we be tomorrow? Everything I have done has brought only the pirate towards, furthering our cause and orders. We will be back in Portsmouth with Roberts and Devlin while Ogle is scratching for crumbs. How would your father-in-law measure you then?'

He paused to gauge the weight of his words and saw only uncertainty.

'You may disapprove, but none of this is against the grain. You should consider yourself fortunate that your career has thus far been so spared.' He turned back to the priest.

'Father. If you are so concerned about the fate of this man then give up what you know and I'll release him.'

Dandon spat blood.

'Don't. I'll be his prisoner anyways.'

Coxon came closer, gave the priest his finest captain's voice.

'So you know something? You are Portuguese, no? The diocese here is French. How many are you? Why are you with this man?'

The priest brushed down his dusty robes.

190

'There are five of us,' he raised his head proudly. 'We are on a path of God, Captain.'

'Of God?' Coxon said. 'And what has that to do with pirates?'

Dandon rolled his head. 'Perhaps we wish to redeem ourselves, John. Like Walter here.'

Coxon was beside him, stared down at his bloodied face and pushed Kennedy back.

'Your redemption will come at the end of a rope. You have all assigned to it.'

'And what have you assigned to, John?'

'Do not use my name, pirate.'

'In vain, John?'

Coxon stepped back. The priest, Manvell and Kennedy all points of a triangle at him.

'Manvell,' he ordered. 'The pirate will come with us to the ship. Leave the priest. We'll get no answers here. And the pirate will have friends about.'

Dandon showed no concern.

'Have you not considered, John, that Devlin may have abandoned me long ago? That I am here on Bourbon under the charity of the church and the scrapings of my past associations? That I have no idea where Devlin may be? How I may be grateful that you at least will feed to save me from begging?'

'You seem fat enough to me, Dandon. And I know Devlin's loyalty. And you need to know some accuracies.'

Dandon cocked his head and Coxon saw then how aged he seemed since The Island and at the same time wondered about his own face. He gave what he had, just enough to let Dandon consider that he knew more.

'The *Virgin of the Cape*. Taken by the pirate Levasseur. Sought by Roberts and Devlin. Millions in gold. I came here after seeing John Leadstone. I know all of it.' He watched Dandon's face, saw the right questions.

'So why do you need me if you know it?'

'I have considered that I do not know where Devlin is to be. If I leave the priest, then Devlin will discover you gone when he returns, and I will not need to hunt. He will come. Come to find you.' Coxon looked to the ceiling as if confirmation lay above. 'I am sure of it.'

'Perhaps you overestimate Patrick's concern for my well-being, John.'

Coxon unbolted the door, let Kennedy clear their way.

'No, pirate. I know as well as you how much he values his associations.' He gave a complicit look, as men share when caught out foolishly in a storm, strangers wet together on the road.

'We are all lonely, Dandon. I'm sure Devlin is of the same mind once he knows that we are together.' He put his hand out for Dandon to join him willingly.

'What would he do without you?'

# Chapter Twenty

A Bohemian left-locked pistol lay on the table in the great cabin of the *Shadow*. Smart pyrite flint was held in the lock with a fold of leather and screwed down tight. A ball of lead set in the octagonal barrel, partridge grain on top. A strip of cartridge paper rammed to hold the shot. Beside the pistol a box of ready-made loads to hang on the belt or across the back of the man who had spent his breakfast making up the box.

He ate his eggs and bread and between bites made up his loads. He took a couple of inches of paper, rolled it into a tube, and wrapped it around the ball; the paper's base end twisted tight.

Taking another ball and a powder flask, ball on his palm, he poured the powder until it covered; best estimate for a quick load. Then, with his measuring ball removed, he tapped his hand of powder into the paper tube as careful as a country-house cook who could spare no flour.

Once filled he twisted the other end and his cartridge was made. With one he could measure the others and before his plate was done he had twelve in the wood inserts of his hardened leather box.

He had tools that could pour and measure for him but then his hands would not be blackened and smell, and the sounds would not be as sweet, the concentration of making not as soothing.

The intricacies and pattern, the one-two-three of it, formed a catechism to recall when the fury came. The loading was good. It had method and ritual that base men do not understand. If you failed it would not be for want of preparation or ability. It would just be your time.

If he fancied he would have the carpenter make him a dowel to measure his loads but as a pirate his gun often changed month to month and its bore just as much. But not this one. Not this one. He had kept this gun as much as he had kept the brown bucket-topped boots taken from a dying Frenchman years gone.

In battle he could bite the paper – the ball with it and held in his mouth pour the powder and save a pinch of it for the frizzen pan. Then spit the ball down the barrel where the breech tapered to hold it, the paper rammed to sit and trap the shot. That was a fighting shot. But a luxurious charge for the first shot: partridge grain and mutton tallow with beeswax on top to keep the shot in all day and proofed against seawater and running feet.

If successful against a man the wax and paper when fired could just as likely set the cloth of the receiver on fire. He would fall to his back with a shot to his belly and try to pat out the flames as his blood sizzled.

He had fixed a belt hanger to the wood, as he had seen gentlemen carry their pistols, but he prized its left lock over all. In the Marine Royale he had seen officers with left-locked pistols. The advantage seemed slight but enough, and on deck fights he had seen its worth.

Any gentleman carried his sword for his right hand, the pistol for his left. With a right-locked pistol – the common designation – the gun would sit near the sword in the belt, the lock facing out, to prevent snagging in the clothes or digging into the side all day. The right hand to go for it; the sword delayed. A clumsy circumstance. Or if set on the right for the left hand the wrist of the gun would have to be reversed before it could be cocked and fired, for the lock again could be hampered if set against the body.

Devlin had a left-locked pistol for his left hand.

Twice he had wrong-footed an officer by pulling his sword first when he spied they wore their pistol on their left. As expected, his opponent gallantly pulled sword also, before Devlin took out his pistol and shot them down while they tried to contort themselves to grab their own or just watched and waited. Either way Devlin gave them the shot and moved on.

The hanger negated much of this. Officers, over time, came to hang the pistol on the belt, or holstered, but merchants and noblemen still preferred the bolstering of sword and pistol around the waist. And as for pirates, the pistols were their most prized possessions. Slings of ribbons or linen tied around brassed finger-guards or hoops screwed into the butt for leather lanyards. All to fire once and, instead of being dropped to the deck, kept about you, hung from belt or neck, the metal cap on the bottom of the gun more than decoration as you clubbed your way along a deck. Those beautiful fish and maiden's faces crafted there were purely to shatter skulls.

Patrick Devlin stood and hung the pistol to his low slung belt. He took an antler-hilted hanger from the wall and fed it through his simple looped frog, no scabbard. The plain knuckle bow was unobtrusive and could still break a jaw.

He listened to the running of feet from the deck above, the echoing cry of *'Deck there! Land, Land!'* coming from the other world amid the tops. He went back to the table, to the map where a cobweb of rhumb lines had caught a string of islands like so many flies. He had marked a cross south-west of one of the larger islands. Five days at seven knots, and calculated for his reckoning for when they had only dragged five.

He reached the door before the knock and stepped out onto the deck and chided John Lawson back to his sails. Devlin did not need to be told anything. Yesterday flying insects had begun to appear crawling along the gunwales and, at his windows, one moth as big as his hand fluttered him awake. Gulls rested on the *Shadow*'s arms like rooks on a scarecrow's. Dew had appeared on the wood and ropes at dawn.

For a moment, the map still in his eye, he looked over the gunwales left and right as if the shores of Zanzibar and Sumatra were inches away, the actual world no more than the lines on the parchment. No sailor ever considered the world to be flat as a table. At sea he can feel the world turning beneath him, and him part of it, rolling with it, not sitting on it like everyone else and waiting for its storms to come towards. At sea you rode to them. Your world could change in an hour, and there, there off Devlin's starboard bow, were the white breaking waters and the small black pyramid on the horizon that promised a substantial island, and that his world could – would – change in an hour. An hour not to his design. It was the Earth allowing.

He pictured The Buzzard, Levasseur, alone with his treasure, his scant crew having already up and left with their share and him waiting to be rescued wearing a suit of gold. Or him gone too, some of his fortune buried and that would be the end of it or Roberts getting there first. Either circumstance would not be to the good.

This island had been well-chosen. Levasseur had used Bourbon as his base, and the treasure ship had been taken at Bourbon. From Bourbon's St Denis a direct course north would find it. A rule along the map from one to the other and the longitude only four minutes different, and since the longitude of Bourbon was known and the latitude between the islands mapped, Devlin stood on his sliver of wood in the Indian Ocean and knew exactly where he was. He could hold a hand across the deck and point to England. John Leadstone, Old Cracker, could look out of a window east across thousands of miles and see him now. To get back to Dandon they would only have to head south and keep to it. Aye, The Buzzard had chosen well. He could plot between Bourbon and this island drunk and with only the Southern cross. Had none thought of this before except the French pirate?

Devlin took the three-draw telescope from the becket by the binnacle and checked once that the man aloft with the greater view was doing the same to look for wood and sail before approaching. The island lay under an hour away. Soon it would be close enough to see any ships against her green.

Slow now. An orderly ship. Their greater number below deck, sail shortened and the guns set in the tops covered with blankets and sailcloth as if put there for drying. He let down the scope. They were alone on the sea. Peter Sam walked up from the main to him.

'This be it?' he said.

Devlin said nothing, which was enough. Peter Sam followed his study of the sea. 'So what are we to do?'

'Get rich, Peter.'

'We were rich.'

197

'Then richer. And for the last time.' Devlin became solemn then. 'How are the lads? How do they settle for going against a pirate?'

Peter Sam breathed deep. 'A French pirate. Who gives a damn for that? But this one sailed with Hornigold and Cap'n England, Howell Davis and Taylor. Longer pirate than you, Cap'n.' Peter Sam did not have to hold his tongue with Devlin and Devlin expected the same.

'I was with Davis when he turned. When you were in Charles Town.'

Peter Sam's turn to say nothing, which was enough.

'Ready a boat,' Devlin said. 'Bags to fetch water. Sack for fruit and a cradle for meat. A hunting party to shore. Me, you, Hugh Harris and the priest.'

'A hunting party?'

'Reason to be armed. Should we come across rogues that's our reason for being there. Too many numbers would cause a start.'

'I'll load for a fight,' Peter Sam affirmed and went down. Devlin went back to surveying the black pyramid now splitting into green peaks and an emerald skirt as they arrowed towards. He saw the shadow of the priest grow over the wood.

'O'Neill,' he said before the man could speak. 'You best get changed. You'll be coming ashore.'

The priest rested on the gunwale beside him. None had told him to wait to be invited to climb to the quarterdeck. 'Why should I disguise myself when I am coming with an honest request?'

Devlin kept to the island. 'And what request is that?'

'I want only the cross. I wish the man no harm.'

'Do you think he will just give it up? And do you think I am only coming to ferry you to your cross? I'm here for his gold.'

'It is not his gold. It is not your gold.'

'And is it the King of Porto's gold is it? Did his hand cut it from the earth?'

'It is beyond my interest, Captain. I want only the cross of wood within the cross.'

'Then why set it in gold?'

O'Neill stretched to watch a pod of dolphin boiling the water chasing fish.

'It is for the peasants. They admire gold. I would settle for the wood.'

'I could get my carpenter to cut something if you wish?'

O'Neill ignored the flippancy. 'If you want you could let me alone to petition Levasseur for the cross. If you think it beyond *your* interest?'

Devlin could see a beach now, no ship.

'A seven foot cross of gold? What part of that would not hold my interest?'

'Its heart. I would judge you do not care for that.'

'Judge now is it, priest? Your station has improved since we met.' He went back to his study. 'Go to Peter Sam. He'll get you clothes to come ashore.' He anticipated the holy response. 'They'll be suitably humble.' He turned his back to the priest, his mind pretending interest in the helm, O'Neill's company ended and he waited to hear the sandals descend.

Devlin did not know the name of the man at the helm. So many men over the years. So many dead. His long-standers were Peter Sam, John Lawson, Robert Hartley, Hugh Harris, Dan Teague. Will Magnes had stayed in Madagascar; the Dutch were gone, all paid off with two thousand pounds in their account as agreed. This man was a black Spaniard from Tortuga. The *Shadow* had Porto blacks as well, smart slaves that had been taught to sail and work in the trades. In the merchants they were still slaves. As pirates they earned like the rest, although most pirates paid them less, but at least paid, and at least allowed them the option to progress.

It had shocked assizes all over the colonies and in England that they found themselves having to hang black pirate quartermasters and first mates. Now almost a third of pirate crews could be black, their rise coming exactly as the rise in the trade of flesh since the end of the war, when Europe was granted that which had once been exclusively Spanish. The reluctance of people to be slaves over pirates baffled only the minds of the richest. Devlin had found it to be a consequence of the New World. The blacks were destined to become pirates. In their homeland they would have been slaves for honour, for debt, for war. In the New World they were mere chattel.

And Devlin knew something of that.

He had lived in a world where everything rotten or cheap or badly done was preceded by the word 'Irish'. Even on his ship the salted meat was 'Irish horse', the ragged oakum or hanging sheets 'Irish pennants'. He had signed on his blacks exactly as any other man, and anyone who objected was always free to make their case to him on land, by pistol or sword, as they chose. And that was always the end of the matter.

He nodded to the man and then returned his concentration to the sea. The island now stretched out before them, and another, smaller island surfaced at their head, white ribbons of water all around.

Devlin went to the taffrail, leant back on the wood to take in the expanse of sail and sky above and see as much of the island as he could. Wide canvas and blue skies, a sight to warm cold nights when old bones came.

He saw John Lawson swinging the lead from the chains to sound, but judging from the breaking waters the *Shadow*'s three hundred and fifty tons was at her limit. Anchor here and row in, as surely Levasseur had done. And again the question:

Where was his ship? Where The Buzzard? Where the gold?

More green, more islands splitting from the main as if just born, narrow channels between, and the first thoughts of barren hope began to cloud the scene of fruitful paradise. This was no desert spit of land; this could be London for its size, its peaks as large as his Ireland home.

O'Neill had told where Levasseur was heading; that had been only overheard, was not a promise or declaration. Suppose Levasseur had changed his plans, suppose O'Neill had misheard or, worse, was simply a lunatic priest on a holy crusade – and God Himself knew there was enough of those. Peter Sam cracked Devlin's glazed look.

'If this is the island his ship's not here. If he's on the other side, that'll be the lee shore. He be grounded there if he's for staying.'

'Anchor windward at the stern,' Devlin ordered. Windward to keep their head out to the sea. He had expected to find Levasseur's *Victory* doing the same. If The Buzzard had anchored on the lee shore it could have been with the intent to beach and careen but it would have to be bedded anchors and capstan heaving to get off again and all his boats to warp him out to sea. Why all that when there was a perfect bay to windward?

Devlin scanned the land. Beaches, black monoliths and individual trees could be discerned now. A jungle climb lay in their future.

'We'll go ashore and take that peak,' he aimed his arm out and Peter Sam followed. 'Scout from there.'

'Aye,' Peter Sam could already feel the ache in his legs. 'Maybe some savages will cut us down before we make it.'

'Or we meet Levasseur and his men.' Devlin slapped him away. 'Think of the gold, Peter Sam! Ain't this why we came to sea? Or do you still fancy Newfoundland for the summer?'

Peter Sam lumbered away, the only way he ever walked.

'Aye, Patrick. Ever for the gold.'

# Chapter Twenty-One

Quieter now as they rowed through the soft, crystal water, as the ship faded behind them, and only in withdrawal did it become apparent how full of noise was the daily deck. In the jolly-boat, in these serene waters, with just the sounds of oars as gentle as the patting of butter, the cries of curious sea-birds and the crashing of surf, an unbeckoned tranquillity descended upon the visitors as they tensed themselves for any movement in the trees.

They weaved through a sandbar, sometimes rowing back on themselves to gain the angle, all eyes to the white beach. Then feet in the water, their splashes and grunts perhaps the first brutish sounds ever broken on the shore. They dragged the boat up reverently as if walking into a church, every slightest noise echoing back to them.

Muskets were shouldered along with the poles of the cradle – not a ruse: hunting for meat would be a real thing. Canvas bags there were for fresh water, a cask in the boat to fill. O'Neill would not carry arms so he carried more of the rest. Devlin complimented him on his new pirate look. Without the robes his black beard and cropped hair gave him a Spanish manner and the pirates laughed at his new-found aspect. His blushing curses traipsed away from them up the beach.

'You know where you're going, O'Neill?' Devlin called.

The priest stopped.

'No!' he yelled back. 'Away from you, I know!'

Devlin looked to Peter Sam then back to the priest.

'You *sure* you don't know it now?'

'Well I assume we are for getting off the beach, are we not?' He continued to the first break in the trees where the palms went straight out from the forest instead of straight up.

Peter Sam and Devlin squinted at each other and followed on, Hugh Harris giggling in the rear.

Two hours of sweat and climbing and slapping at insects and Hugh had gasped enough.

'This must be good for me liver!' he cried. 'It hurts too much to be anything I might enjoy!'

Devlin said nothing but kept up with O'Neill at the front, his cutlass sweeping their path. They had passed through ravines and crossed waterfalls, testing the water as they went. Black parrots and colourful sparrows landed fearless on them as they pulled along, the birds yet to learn to flee from trespassers. The air was wet, yet there was so little of it, every step proved hard – yet none complained.

The rock turned to shingle and slate and Devlin instinctively walked with care. Then the blue sky became clear above the jungle and a single strike of cutlass cut naked the last green and cast it aside like a curtain drawn – and the sea yawned beneath them.

Another beach. White horses of water crashing for a mile all around. The others saw the same as he.

An empty shore. No ship. Nothing.

'O'Neill,' Devlin squared to the priest. 'Where is he? Where's The Buzzard?'

No ship, no man.

A long astonishment from O'Neill as he looked at the barren shore.

'What month is this?'

'July,' Devlin said. 'What matter?'

'So it has been three months since he took the ship.'

'What difference?' Devlin said. 'You said he was run to here?'

O'Neill scratched his head. 'But he did! I heard it. He would have to be here. He said he knew this place!'

Devlin lifted his blade.

'But he's not here.'

No ship on the windward shore. No ship grounded on the lee.

'Where is he, priest?'

'But he must be here! The cross must! It brought me to you! Brought me here! He has buried it, that's all!'

'That's *all*?'

Devlin looked to Peter Sam and then O'Neill was fast against a tree, his breath slammed from him. Hugh Harris pulled one of his Dutch over-and-under pistols and gleefully clicked it into life against the priest's cheek.

'That's all?' Devlin said again. 'Are you a madman who has brought my starving crew on a chase for a piece of wood?'

'You said yourself—' O'Neill stammered under Peter's weighty forearm against his chest. 'Roberts is after the same. You had the same word. *The same*! You were coming here anyway, you just needed to know where. Have I not provided so? The Lord's word!'

Devlin's cutlass prised Peter Sam away.

'I trusted that you were privy first-hand. What if Roberts has been here?' He put the blade back to his belt. 'What am I left with, priest?'

'The Flaming Cross is here, Captain. On my oath! All the treasure here . . . somewhere.'

'And how do you know?'

O'Neill pushed himself from the tree, wiped his face with his new white cuff.

'I can *feel* it, Captain.' He gave Devlin a fearless look. 'As can you,' he said. 'Can you not?'

Devlin turned away, looked over the blue and saw yet more peaked islands where men could hide. Beyond their present the horizon displayed a line of grey from east to west.

Bad weather behind them or in their future, the sun's heels clipped as it sank westerly into ominous cloud.

'Night in two hours. We'll camp down by the last waterfall. No fire on the beach. There may be eyes about. We'll make a plan tomorrow.'

'What about the ship?' Peter Sam asked.

'John Lawson has the ship,' Devlin had already begun to walk. 'Fire a musket at sundown and sunrise. I gave him to come if he does not hear.'

Devlin's back vanished through the trees leaving O'Neill with pirates. Pirates that were not captains.

O'Neill understood his measure in their world, lowered his head and softened his body to be subjected to their pushes and shoves down the trail they had cut for him.

Night coming. The party seeing only jungle green not gold. But at least no objecting enemy. No life at all other than the small and giant reptiles and the winged and now the darker, shriller bats over their heads.

John Lawson on the *Shadow* lit his lanterns, waited for the musket shot that eventually came and signalled that all was well and that his captain had made camp, with rum his pillow as the planets wakened to glare down and laugh at the folly and greed that they had seen for thousands of years.

On the morrow then. On an unnamed island, a thousand miles from any named shore. Try to sleep with treasure promised; England's schoolboys dreamt of the same with wooden swords beside their beds.

Sleep on treasure to come, a waterfall and the paradise sonnets of birds lilting in your ears. But sleep with an eye open.

Here be pirates.

# Chapter Twenty-Two

*I*t was the bosun's chair to bring Dandon aboard, unable, tied as he was, to amble up the ladder to the entry port. At least they had made his passage easier by tying his hands to the front.

Thomas Howard watched the body swing over the deck and his face paled as he recognised the faded yellow justacorps and the gold-filled mouth. He turned his back as Dandon looked about, curious not apprehensive, and Coxon watched the young man gulp and steady himself against a rail.

Dandon was led to the hold, and there were strained necks and whispers as the crew wondered on their prisoner. Curses too, for this must surely mean that some deed had occurred on Bourbon that would put pay to any dalliance or victualling ashore.

Down and down again, dimmer with each stair, the stench from the sand and gravel ballast rising like a fish market, the palatable farmyard reek of the manger rolling from the fore. Coxon at the van of the party, Dandon following, then Manvell and lastly Kennedy, grinning all the way.

'Such a pretty boat,' Dandon said. 'A real huckleberry, John!'

Coxon took him by the cord at his wrists; he half-dragged him to the manger away from the weighted and damp curtain that led to the magazine – Coxon best sure that pirates should be kept far from it.

He pulled the cord through a fairlead in the overhead, Dandon's arms were painfully lifted above him.

'Fetch manacles, Manvell,' Coxon said as he whipped off Dandon's hat and slung it away into the dark.

'Captain?' Manvell ducked forward. 'Can we not take the man on his honour?'

Dandon preened at the lieutenant. 'Quite right,' he sang. 'What he said, John.'

'Are you suggesting parole for pirates, Lieutenant?'

'No, sir,' he said. 'I apologise. His manner and cloth had made me forget.' Manvell went back and Kennedy filled his place.

Dandon tested the cord and the forte of the metal ring sunk into the oak above. Solid. He was not going anywhere under his own strength but still he seemed indifferent. Besides, more than once he had coerced the strength of others, Dandon being able to bend wills easier than iron. If Coxon knew him better it would be his mouth he would bind.

'A twin-decker, eh, John? You have done well.'

'How do you think she'll shine against the *Shadow*?' Coxon swung away without waiting for a retort. Manvell had returned, the dreadful rattle of chain trying to leap from his arms, and Coxon took the black irons.

'The men will be concerned about none to go ashore.' Coxon kept his voice just for Manvell. 'Go above, to both watches and assure them that we sail to Île de France for one day's easing and victualling. That will calm well enough.'

'Île de France? There is nothing there, Captain.'

'It will suffice for water and hunting. We'll leave as soon as able. Before night. Carry on, Mister Manvell.'

Manvell looked over to Dandon and down to Kennedy's sneer.

'Would you not wish my assistance further here, Captain?'

'I "wish" you to carry on, Mister Manvell.'

Manvell tapped his forelock and backed away to the stair. Coxon came back to Dandon. He fed the chain of the manacles through his hands like a rosary; let the sound and sight of the iron sink in.

He shackled Dandon's wrists over the cord so his hands still hung. Dandon tensed at the weight of the irons and shifted the ache now growing in his back and arms. Coxon let the leg-irons drop. Leave them for now. Show some compassion. Have something to punish further.

'I do not relish this,' he said. 'But I do not need another pirate walking around on my ship.'

Kennedy saluted from the bulkhead.

'Could you relish it less by lowering my hands some, John?' Dandon shook the shackles.

'Of course,' Coxon stepped back. 'But comfort is a reward. Perhaps the simplest reward. But earned nonetheless. And, of course, comfort comes with wine. For gentlemen.'

Kennedy giggled, pulled a gully-blade and slapped it in his palm.

Dandon cocked his head. 'Why this imbecile with? What have you done to deserve him so, Captain John?'

Kennedy was unsure what the word meant but had come to learn that most things spoken about him were impugning.

'Enough of that, dog!' he wagged his knife. 'Manners now!'

Coxon sat on a barrel and ignored Kennedy's words. He watched Dandon sweating now; the humidity of the air outside boiling the customary stifled air of the lower decks and searing Dandon's coat to his back. The removal of his hat only reminded how cool he would be without the coat also. Too late for the coat now, his hands being tied. He would have to be cut from it or talk and have his hands freed. All these things would count, Coxon knew. Count for information garnered. Men can proudly, willingly, take beatings beyond measure and never talk but sometimes a hole in a stocking rubbing against a heel for a few miles could break Hercules. He did not need to sweat and shout while Dandon's back ached, while his coat grew heavier, while his sweat pooled around his clothes, while his throat parched.

Coxon ordered Kennedy to fetch him a cup of wine and waited until he had loped away to answer Dandon's query.

'I am surprised you ask about Kennedy, pirate. I would have thought Devlin would have mentioned him.'

Dandon shifted his back to ease his shoulders.

'Why so? Who is he?'

Coxon feigned surprise. 'Your captain never told of his reason for fleeing London?' He gave Dandon a few moments to sift his memory.

'There was a murder, I recall. Devlin ran from. To save himself from incrimination.'

'He lived with a chain-maker. A man named Kennedy. And his son. A man who had generously taken him in. Found dead across his table with a knife in his chest. A man murdered and Patrick Devlin running for his life.'

'And *this* Kennedy?'

'His son. His son out for revenge. His son who will swear on a tomb of Bibles that Patrick Devlin is his father's killer.'

Dandon heard Kennedy's feet slapping back down the stair.

'I would not believe that, John.'

'But would you not think it possible? How holy has Devlin been since last?'

Dandon watched Kennedy reappear, pass Coxon his tin cup of wine and retire back to lounging against the bulkhead.

He tried to judge how he himself had been, the young assistant in Mobile, and how Devlin must have been a decade ago, before the pirate Devlin. Before the Bloody Pirate Devlin.

Devlin had been a killer the entire time of his association with Dandon. That came with his chosen path, and although Dandon had seen no enjoyment in it, the act had come strikingly natural to his friend.

He had an aptitude for it.

But Dandon had never thought about the time before Devlin had cast his lot.

Coxon watched his thoughts.

'Walter would have been about sixteen at the time. Imagine the impression made on such an age? Your father killed afore you.' He downed his cup, head back, let it waste down his chin and slammed it to the barrel with a gasp. 'That's good relief so it is!' He wiped his lips. 'It'll be a warm evening to come I'll say.'

Dandon looked at the tin cup. He could feel its cool touch, could taste the wine. He opened his mouth to speak but Coxon jumped on his tongue.

'I only wish to know where Devlin has gone, pirate. Whether he has joined with Roberts or not. I would not see that as any great betrayal ... if I were he. And he would expect me to establish that. Even without you, I'm sure. Have I not come this far? Would Devlin measure me less?'

Dandon hid his face against his hanging arms and Kennedy chuckled, resumed playing with his blade. Dandon tensed once again at his bonds, then hung and murmured into his sleeve.

Coxon leant in.

'Your pardon? What did you say there?'

'A *map*!' Dandon spat. 'A *map*! I will need a bloody map, will I not? *Damn you*!'

'Mister Manvell?' Thomas Howard almost ran into Manvell at the quarterdeck rail, Manvell returning from telling the watch at mess of the ship sailing before nightfall.

'What is it, Thomas?' He kept moving. 'I have to speak to Mister Jenkins. We are leaving this place, apparently.'

Howard stayed to him. 'That in part answers some of my question, but—'

Manvell cut him short, loath to answer the other parts of Howard's enquiry; the subject not needing quadrant or rule to reckon.

'Can this not wait for supper, Thomas? I have a whole ship to muster, as have you now.'

'That man,' Howard checked his collar for other ears. 'That man who came aboard,' his voice dropped, 'he is the man of my dreams.'

Manvell was unable to fully choke back his amusement at Howard's choice of phrase, his laugh confounding, under the odd circumstances, even as he made it.

'I'm sorry, Thomas, Mister Howard. Forgive me. Yes. The man is, how you say . . . the man you used to know. The pirate. Of old, as it were.'

'But why is he here? On board?'

'We are after Devlin are we not? This man is one of his. The captain has some great plan envisioned no doubt.' Manvell made to move but the anxiety on Howard's face held him.

'Are you all right, Thomas?' He put a hand on Howard's shoulder.

'Yes, sir. I just never thought . . . thought to see him again. I signed to be with Coxon. I suppose I did not think what that might entail.'

'But this man saved you? That is a good memory, no?'

Howard looked back along the ship as if trying to see down through the deck to the man in yellow.

'I can't think what I would say to him. He's a pirate. The world's enemy. A fiend.'

'Then don't say anything. Forget him. Do your duty. You were just a boy. He probably does not remember.'

'But I remember,' Howard said.

Manvell did not understand. Howard tried to share the jumble of contradictions that had become his reason.

'If I remember and do not say anything what does that mean?'

Manvell's feet scraped again to leave and seek Sailing-Master Jenkins but he twisted back for one more consoling word.

'I'm sure there is a philosophy scratched by a Frenchy somewhere which will go along those same lines, Mister Howard, and I would suggest to you that you do not concern yourself with guilt or compassion. As to what it means if you say nothing, may I offer that it simply means you are a *man*, sir. *That* is what it means. Welcome to our pasture. It is pleasant enough when it do not rain.'

He spun away, pleased with his wisdom, leaving Thomas Howard again staring down onto the deck and his thoughts travelling through to the hold like a spirit.

Howard had work to do. Manvell had appeared with orders. From behind he heard Master Jenkins arguing all the points of the compass why he could not be underway before the night and dictating sails to the bosun with the same breath. Soon Manvell would come back and give him orders; soon

Coxon might reappear and soon Thomas Howard would have to concentrate on how to hold his face at dinner when word of the Dandelion pirate went around the table.

He stared at the black mouth of the companion stair vanishing away, down into darkness. Coxon was down there, Kennedy was down there. Kennedy who had returned from questioning Old Cracker with scarlet fists. Kennedy was now below with Coxon and Dandon – Dandon, the pirate of his nightmares, and how confident could Howard be that he was awake now?

The earth could not be this small. Not small enough for Coxon to point his arm and find all that he needed, no more complicated than the pocket of a schoolboy or as limiting as his schoolyard.

This was not faith, not the faith he had put in Coxon, unless it is the faith of a man who jumps from a ship to the sea with the assurance that another will inevitably come soon enough.

Howard was used to the orderly world. As a midshipman he had his books to follow, to learn from.

'*Read this and do as is done.*'

He would do well because the books would tell him what to do. There was no emotion behind their covers. Just learn them and *do as is done.*

But there had been one book of instruction that had broken its ranks. The thirty-one page book had been as precise and didactic as the others but he had turned a page to find a flower pressed into its pages. Faded and powdery as a moth's wings but had been bright yellow once.

Before Thomas Howard had gone to sea another boy had read the dull pages and copied with chalk and slate the signals to chase; and then one day, one bright day, perhaps even his first, he plucked a flower from a Portsmouth road or his mother gave it to him from her breast – but one day he had put a flower in a book and changed the ordered world.

And it had been a Dandelion.

Dandelion. Not a flower at all.

He stared down the dark companion stair, longing for someone or something to break him from his distraction.

He jumped as a scream of pain came from the black below.

# Chapter Twenty-Three

*D*andon had laughed at first.

'Go to hell,' he said and laughed harder. Kennedy cracked him across the jaw, silencing the derision but helpless to strike the pride off the pirate's face. Kennedy shook his hand with the pain of glancing his knuckles off Dandon's gold-capped teeth and Dandon laughed again. Kennedy raised a fist.

'*Enough!*' Coxon pulled him away.

That was then.

Coxon had brought him to the wardroom and placed a goblet of wine at the hands still wearing their iron bracelets. Dandon drank fast, before the charts landed in front of him. He rattled the cup on the table for more.

Coxon ignored the request and spread the Indian Ocean before him. He tapped the map.

'Where?' he said.

And Dandon, his wine empowering him, gave his first 'Go to hell!' and brushed the map from the table.

'It is the drink I waned for!' he said. 'Now I am willed to silence. Unless you have more wine, John?'

All that was then. All before.

Coxon had turned his back.

'So be it,' he thought.

'Elicitation' Coxon had called it. Let a pirate go to a pirate. The scream had come later.

The wardroom had lanterns. It had candles and tallow lighters, oil, match and tinderbox. Coxon listened to Kennedy giggle again as he went searching the room for toys.

Coxon went to the partitions of glass and hinged frame that went across the beam of the ship, the door from the room.

'I will be back shortly. I have a course to set. Do you wish to tell anything now? To aid me?'

Dandon leant in his seat.

'Go very merrily to hell, John Coxon. And shame on you, sir.'

Coxon opened the door and called for a marine to stand guard. He set the man to his post inside the room as Kennedy came back to the table; Coxon left with his eyes down and turned away from the scene. He retired to his cabin, listened for a moment to the sounds of feet scuffling on the overhead and went to his desk for paper and ink.

Coxon heard the scream. The writing hand went to his sweating brow, then the sounds of the ship returned, covered like a tarpaulin, and the hand went back to the paper. He had little time. Manvell would be the one to take the note to shore, Manvell the one who disapproved the most, so remove him for an hour and hope that the pirate gave up what he had.

He dusted the ink and folded and sealed the paper, the gentleness of this act belying the act below, belying its consequences.

He went to his door and ordered the marine outside to bring him the lieutenant and Coxon went to wait by his stern windows and watched Bourbon becoming night.

Perhaps he could tell Manvell of the other letter, the other orders. Manvell was a good man and growing better all the time while his own character was being shamed. Manvell would understand then, understand that Coxon was not raving, not obsessive and tyrannical, and that although these were the characteristics of admirals who survived the war, to these young officers such action was unwarranted now. But they should know that he was not making orders.

He was following them.

The coach door knocked upon and opened with Coxon's call. Manvell swept off his hat.

Coxon studied Manvell's reflection in the diamond panes, as he had done on the first day. Manvell had changed. His eyebrows appeared less surprised and his manner had lost its edge of clumsiness. Coxon pointed to the letter on the table.

'Take that to the cathedral, Manvell, if you please. Best to the same priest, if best you can.'

Manvell picked up the letter and blanched at the name across it. 'Captain?'

Coxon lifted his chin for the question.

'This is to "Devlin." The pirate?'

'Do you know another?'

'May I ask . . . for why, sir?'

'You may,' Coxon stepped away from his stern. 'I wish to tell him that I have his man. Confirm to him that it is I – by my hand – rather than rely on a babbling Porto priest.'

'To what purpose?'

Coxon thought on that. If only he could impress on Manvell the image in his own mind of Devlin's fury when he opened the packet to read his and Dandon's names and the history inside the simple message, Coxon indeed would; but he had no brush to paint it with.

'He will come for us,' said Coxon simply. 'And then we will seek each other. His treasure will mean far less. Trust me.'

Manvell put the letter inside his coat.

'Aye, sir. We will be ready to sail on my return.' He snapped his heels, replaced his hat. Coxon raised a finger.

'Mister Manvell, did you hear a disturbance from below? Could you discern from the quarterdeck?'

'I did not, sir.'

'And Mister Howard? Did ... Thomas ... voice any concern?'

Manvell delayed just enough to indicate that he did not wish to speak for Thomas Howard.

'He was stood at the rail above the companion. A better position than I.'

Coxon understood. He should have summoned musicians to cover Kennedy's work. That would be the way in the future if the pirate did not talk. Manvell stepped to his task and Coxon returned to his darkening panorama.

Full dark soon. Somewhere Devlin sailed, under the same stars. If Dandon remained closed then Devlin would know him gone when he returned to Bourbon to collect and know further that he had Walter Kennedy to assist, and know the nature of that wretch. He had written it all under calculation that the pirate in his democracy would share his knowledge with his crew. They would all know why Kennedy had come. An accusation in ink. That might have some use.

A rap at the door – for thinking of the Devil has an effect – and Kennedy shuffled into the room, his hands blackened.

'Captain,' he wiped his hands through his hair. 'He wishes to speak to you now, so he does.'

When he returned to the wardroom it seemed a smaller figure that was slumped in the chair before Coxon. It was clearly still Dandon, still the once-smart linen and tailored breeches.

But now the body was as exhausted and worn as its tattered raiments.

Coxon remarked on nothing. He dismissed the marine, paler now than the ruddy fellow he had been when placed there. He returned the map to the table and stabbed his finger amid the whales and Spanish galleons. He pointed inside the Indian Ocean as if there had been no gap since he first asked and nothing terrible had blighted his ship.

'Where?' he said.

In the same light, inches away from each other, Coxon could see the waxy hands, greased from an emollient to help soothe something but making the red and blistered skin of the knuckles shine like crackled pork fat. Kennedy stood behind his work, beaming with pride. Coxon could not bear to look at him. He pushed a full goblet to Dandon. That would pass as a degree of sympathy.

'Where?' he repeated.

The chains made their loathsome noise as Dandon's hands trembled for the wine. There was no blood about them and there was a biting need in Coxon to know what had occurred when Kennedy and Dandon were alone. Judged from the hands there had been burning. Prolonged burning. He had heard that pirates in their inquisitions of prisoners sometimes entwined the obstinate's fingers with match fuse, lit and let it smoulder through the knuckles. He determined then that he would not question Kennedy. The man would surely derive some joy from the telling.

Dandon drained the glass, turned it over, let it drop and smash to the floor. He lolled his head to Coxon.

'So I have agreed to speak. And so shall I speak. A man of my word.' He raised himself in his chair and cleared his throat. Coxon's patience at an end.

'What island? Where the treasure?' Coxon said.

Dandon lifted his chains. '*Je vais vous raconter tout ce que vous voulez savoir.*' He fell back in his chair with a snarl. '*Malheureusement le choc de mes blessures a forcé mon cerveau pour retourner au Français de mes premières années. Parlez-vous Français du tout, Capitaine?*'

Still Dandon. Still the pirate.

'As long as the wine comes, Captain, I'll gladly be here.' Dandon pushed the map away. 'Your fiend tortures, and you ladle me with drink, and in truth it tastes better for it: *la foie coloniale.*'

He lifted the chains to his forelock and saluted. 'What a set we have in the world, Captain.'

'You think you're not to talk?' Coxon said. 'You think I'm gaming you?' He nodded to Kennedy. 'Take him below. Tie him back to the overhead. See how arrogant he is after a night hanging in chains.'

Dandon laughed.

'Oh, John! Captain John,' he shook his head in pity. 'By my not talking can you not see how I am sparing your ship? I work for you not against, in pity for your fates.'

Coxon pushed away from the table, took the map.

'Tomorrow then. And no more wine. Nor water.' He rolled the chart to carry it with him for study.

'You forget, pirate. I have known Devlin longer than you. Longer than all of you. I have sent to that Porto priest the word that I have you.' He ushered Kennedy to pull Dandon to his feet. Side by side. 'You and I both know that he will come.'

Dandon pushed out his manacled hands, elbowed the body beside him.

'So why this? Devlin never spoke of your manner thus! He had little word against you.'

'If you tell what you know I may save some time in hunting him. It will inspire the men to fill their lockers with gold. And if you are any man at all you will know . . .' He undid the pearl button at his right sleeve, rolled the shirt back to show the star-shaped scar where the skin had been sewn back and showed it to them both. He did not finish his line but tacked on another.

'The winters make it ache. He took my ship, and did this. A small thing but it suffices. Hate enough.'

'He met you under truce before,' Dandon said. 'Do your men know that? You let him go with the porcelain then. Why this fury now?'

'That was before. He has since almost brought down the king and nearly ruined the world. I have been ordered to him.' He opened the door and stood aside for Kennedy to drag his prisoner. Dandon struggled, threw a sneer at Coxon.

'Then I hope you get the moment to fulfil your order, Captain John. I very much hope that day comes to pass. You will hear nothing from me!'

Coxon shoved him on.

'I'll see on that tomorrow. The night may make you perceive differently.' He shut the door. He studied the scar, rubbed its ache before folding down the sleeve to cover it. He had not meant to do that, to show it. Such emotion was not like him. But perhaps if Manvell should see, that might help. Not for pity or to stoke loyalty but just for understanding. Sometimes, for the ignorant, pictures could help tell a story more than words.

# Chapter Twenty-Four

*P*eter Sam grabbed Devlin's arm. It was dawn and he immediately felt the green and the damp of his clothes from sleeping among the fronds and rocks. Peter Sam had shaken him awake and said something and Devlin's coiled body had jerked and sprung for his gun. Now he rolled up, fully alert, the pistol ready.

'What say you?' Devlin breathed and then saw Hugh Harris standing behind Peter, checking his guns, a musket leaning in his armpit. Peter Sam had woken him with words but Devlin had missed them.

'He's gone,' Peter Sam said, and added as if Devlin would not know, 'O'Neill has gone.'

Devlin looked about and still needed the word said again.

'Gone?'

Peter Sam wiped his bald head front to back and followed Devlin's eye scouting the trees.

'A water bag gone. I've looked about. I make we go to the boat.'

Hugh Harris belted his guns. 'I make we go for the bastard's head!'

Devlin said nothing. He looked up at the green, listened to the water, stood as still as the trees. He put his pistol to his belt and picked up his hanger and sheathed it to the same.

'To the boat,' he said, and Peter Sam and Hugh knew when it was wisest to be quiet around him.

They followed him down, the tropical air already boiling around them, aiding the rising of their blood. They hoped to meet a man of God struggling to launch a boat from the shore or better still his pirate allies conversing on the beach with him. They would have livers and hearts instead of bread and fruit for breakfast.

The beach gave them nothing. There was the *Shadow* sitting high on the crystal waters with her angular masts and rigging, her prow and clinker-built strakes all too foreign against the natural world surrounding them; but the beach was empty. The jolly-boat was gone.

The pirates spread out along the shore, each with his hand on the wrist of a pistol, and glared at a different patch of water seeking a priest rowing somewhere.

Devlin called Peter Sam to fire a musket to let the *Shadow* know they were still there, that all was still well and that he was still in command and shaping the world.

The crack shivered the trees and snapped them all into rolling thoughts.

O'Neill had taken the boat. He had withheld cards from their game and played them all for fools. Played their captain for the Irishman that he surely was. He plainly had no fear of them, and that was the worst part.

Devlin turned back to Peter Sam. 'I'll burn him down,' he said.

Peter Sam nodded as he reloaded from his belly-box. 'Where is he?'

Devlin cocked his head to the green island over his shoulder off the beach. You could build a bridge to it. 'He'd be confident to row there. I know two things.'

'You'd better,' Peter Sam's eyes were to his weapons.

'There's the gold there. He led us to the wrong island deliberate so he could keep us from it.'

'And?'

'He has a friend to go to.'

'La Buse?'

Devlin looked to the *Shadow* already lowering a boat.

'It had better be God himself to save that priest. There's no Latin or Spanish to damn that dog enough.'

They waited for the boat, spoke little, and played their guns and swords like the itches of wounds.

Dandon had hardly slept so he could not say that he had woken. He had heard the watches and the bells above him all night as his head lolled and his arms hung. It was more stupor than slumber. His pained hands rubbed against his head and he swayed with the ship. But comfort is not a thing to be measured on a ship. Nothing about it is so. It is simply learning to lessen *discomfort*.

His pose was not too afflictive at first, but after hours of it had ached like crucifixion. His back felt whipped raw, his arms swollen and, when he could no longer grasp the chain he hung from, his wrists had chafed against the irons about them. He looked to the goats and pigs and envied them; and then they snorted and he heard footsteps from the stair and straightened himself with a grinding in his spine.

Through the wood and lanterns he could not see who came but he would not give them a cracked voice. He rolled his tongue about his mouth and lips and tried to swallow.

A head peered at him from around the wood. It was a young face with a wiry red mop of hair, his collar marking him out as too smart to be the fellow sent to clean out the manger.

Dandon then saw that he carried a flask and a cobble of bread and he was suddenly no longer interested in the man himself. The figure came forward stealthily, as if Dandon might suddenly explode, and held out the flask of water.

Dandon showed his wrists.

'I do not have the freedom to take it, sir.' He wondered what trick this was. Would he be a lip away from the flask and then Coxon and Kennedy would appear and snatch it away? He behaved with that in mind.

'Who are you?'

Thomas Howard crept closer and popped the cork, a civil sound discordant with the stench and gloom and the blood.

'Does that matter?' He put the flask to Dandon's lips and tipped it, careful not to flood his mouth, and Dandon no longer cared about the honour of the prisoner and sucked greedily. The bread next. Howard tore it and fed him through the chains, past the smell of blistered flesh.

'My thanks, sir,' Dandon said, wary still. 'But you should go. Your punishment will be great.'

'I have been ordered to attend,' Howard said.

'That is not true.'

Howard felt himself blush at the words.

'Then perhaps I do not like to see men starve.'

'Even pirates? That's very enlightened for an officer. You will not go far.'

A regret for his compassion flared up Howard's neck and he tossed the rest of the bread to the goats.

Dandon lowered his head. He had only meant his words to turn the young man away from a situation that would not go well for either if chanced upon.

'That is more like it,' he said. 'Don't let your captain down.'

'I have been a fool,' Howard said. He took a pebble from a

pocket. 'All the same, keep this under your tongue and roll it in your mouth.' Dandon did not protest and took it like a pill. 'You are not as thirsty as you think and that will stave off your thirst.' He turned and ducked away.

Dandon aimed his words to the back weaving away through the supports.

'Thank you, Thomas,' he said.

Howard's head appeared from the last wooden pillar.

'You do know me?'

'I do now. Such a flurry of red hair I could hardly forget. And I remember, Thomas Howard.' He leant towards him as best he could.

'You have become a good man. Now go, before you are in as much trouble as me.'

Howard saluted automatically and then blushed at his foolishness. He bounded up the stair.

Dandon, revived briefly, surmised his lot and calculated how his fortunes were improving incrementally despite his empty pockets and dirty clothes.

Manvell he had seen disapprove of Coxon openly and now came little Thomas Howard – or rather not so little – now an officer and yet feeding a prisoner ordered to starve. These were things he could use. Pebbles, one by one to build a dam, he thought, and he rolled the actual pebble around his mouth.

The peril of others had been to underestimate and dismiss Dandon in the past, and he schemed now. Not callously or wickedly, but for survival. Devlin himself had gone on so long and so well not because of who he was . . . but because of who he was *not*.

They had looked at Devlin's shabby coat but not seen all the others, taken from those considered worthier, which he carried in his locker.

Only Coxon was the sputtering fuse. Coxon knew. Coxon did not judge by size of snake but by speckled band. But Coxon had let a pirate onto his ship – two pirates – for Kennedy was the rotten tooth lurking behind Coxon's shining fronts.

Dandon sucked on his pebble. He whistled at the goats and pigs like he owned them. They chewed on his bread with pricked ears. He settled himself into the ship's movement.

This would be a better day.

# Chapter Twenty-Five

*D*an Teague and Adam Cowrie manned the boat from the *Shadow*. Told of the priest's betrayal, they now rowed the others to the islet hard, despite and also because of the heat, for the heat sharpened all their hate. Five of them now. Five pirates against an Irish missionary.

O'Neill must be insane, Devlin thought, or had become part of that small percentage of holy men who turn devotion into obsession. He remembered Coxon once telling him of a Benedictine who in hermitage spent thirty years creating a three-foot tall Bible. At some point in his lonely task that monk chose to ink a massive image of the Devil on one folio and an image of heaven on the opposing page. He was mad by that time, Coxon had suggested, the monk being probably fifteen years into his task.

O'Neill's passion for the fragment of the cross handed down from his ancestor had surely given him a taste for martyrdom. Why would any man willingly affront pirates unless he designed to enter heaven?

Devlin worked for gold and for those who had signed behind him and for those who had voted him theirs. Four years their captain. Kings had reigned for less.

Only a madman could see worth in a sliver of wood, unless he were Midas. And that would be O'Neill's only hope now. Yet there was something enviable in a man daring so much for so little.

'Be ready,' Devlin said as they came to the beach.

'Where's the boat?' Dan Teague said it for all of them. Teague was one of the old-standers from before Devlin's time. A broad Norfolk man with more farm than sail in him and a passion for blood as limitless as Hugh Harris's. At times Devlin loathed them for their lusts, at others it was all he relied on.

Devlin looked about. White sand, the surf barely discernible against it. Dead, bone-like wood sprung out from all about. Whole trees had been tossed to lie there. Behind this tide of white bone were the living palms. They nodded morosely in groups of three, angled to the sea. One of them had tipped upright back into the jungle. Its base of roots exposed like a nest of worms and snakes. You could hide men behind it.

The white wood, the ripped tree. There were storms in this paradise. Fast storms.

Beyond the palms an impenetrable wall of green faced them. They walked the beach. There were huge white boulders strewn as if thrown by a giant of the peak above them, cast down to destroy Argonauts for disrupting his thousand-year peace.

It was beautiful, Devlin could see that, but an inhospitable beauty, like a desert. Isolation. The empty room. The dead man found alone in his bed.

'No footsteps save ours,' Peter Sam sang out.

Devlin called back. 'He landed somewhere else. Did you want him to see us coming?'

Peter Sam scowled and trudged along the sand to survey further along the coast.

Hugh Harris turned to the island behind them, now a kingdom green and rolling as far as he could see.

'We were on *that*?' His voice went high. 'Is that India?'

Devlin drew his hanger and slapped it in his palm. They turned at the sound.

'Our work,' he said. 'There's gold here.' He hacked his first steps through the green without looking back.

They followed, just as they always had and would, until the day came that he let them down. No iniquity in that. Devlin had signed for that day.

He delayed that day only with moments. Moments that became hours. Hours that became stories. Stories that became songs.

Up, was Devlin's plan. Up and measure their world as they always did, as they plotted across the earth from a ship's table.

Go high enough to see the ocean all around, see where your oak girl could go, where she could run. See where your foot and your sword could reach and where men might be hiding. Hiding from them. Hiding was the word, for that would be it.

Nobody ever sat and waited for pirates.

The island had one great peak. Too much sweat for them. Every step was a reminder of how far they were from youth and how close to that tobacco chair by the fireside. If a giant rested on that peak then let him have his peace.

An hour later and Devlin wore his sopping shirt tight as snakeskin and the air tasted thin. But he could feel the sea again and the sky began to break through the green and the others would not call a halt until he was done, so they pressed on.

The green retreated and sand and rock pushed forth again, then puddles of light, and at last the sun. A break. The sea. A westward vista. More islands, and those white and blue shades of waters like the pearls of the Antilles; and in the scheme of God's moulding that made some sense, for the latitude was the same.

The others set to slaking their thirst and perched on the great white rocks. Devlin stood still, overlooking the sea, but Peter Sam knew Devlin's pose. The only thing still was his limbs. Devlin was working, sensing all about him like a blind man feeling the breeze and asking you to close the window or light the lamp for it was dark.

Peter Sam would be drawn into his reasoning, and he waited for the questions to come. He drank a water-bag high and missed Dandon for the first time. The dandelion popinjay was better suited for Devlin's musings. Peter Sam just needed steel and lead standing in front of him.

'Peter,' Devlin called and Peter Sam dragged himself from the cool rock. He sidled up like a reluctant horse. This gold hunt was getting thinner and thinner. Were there not ships to be had despite Devlin's torture of the South Sea Company that had sent merchants to the wall? Sweating and chasing ghosts was not pirates' work. Illusory gold crosses were for crusades, not for codmen pressed in Bristol, peeled from tavern tables.

He came to Devlin's shoulder. 'What?' he said.

Devlin pointed to the sea below, ignoring the sullen tone. 'What you make of that?'

Peter looked down. There was a smaller beach far below enclosed by rock, the tide beating against with a booming roar like a distant gun. Beyond that the waves, breaking as ever they had.

'I see nothing,' Peter said. 'What am I looking for?'

'To the left,' Devlin said, 'about twenty feet from the rocks. Every third wave or so. You see them break?'

Peter looked again and saw the anomaly. 'A horseshoe of rocks breaking. So what?'

Devlin watched the white shape again. 'Does that look natural to you?'

'I gave up on natural-looking things a long time ago.' He knew when Devlin wanted to parade himself.

'I say if we get down there we'll see more rocks scattered around where it's been broken up. I reckon that's a sea wall. I reckon that's a coffer-dam.'

'What's a coffer-dam?'

'It's what I would do if I wanted to hold back the tide while I moved a million pounds into a littoral cave.'

Peter Sam's patience with Devlin's and Dandon's riddles was short at best. They read their big books together long into the night yet they were not gentlemen or educated to do so. They enjoyed them, he figured, and though strange to him he would rather follow a smart man than a fool. But sometimes his own ignorance grated when Devlin spoke like this.

'What the hell's a littoral cave now?'

Devlin patted the big man's back. 'I'll show you tomorrow.' He walked back, expecting Peter Sam to follow.

'You'll *tell* me now!' Peter Sam stayed by the cliff.

Devlin turned. His hands rested on hilt and pistol wrist.

'You have a problem, Peter?'

The others watched but pretended not to.

'Aye,' Peter Sam bid Devlin closer, face to face.

'You and I both know we have no bones between us,' Peter Sam gave out as respectfully as he could. 'Devil knows we don't. But these men are mine just as much as yours. If I decide this is folly it'll all be over. You're walking around in a dream, bewitched by these seas. You trusted that priest and

234

now we've nothing. We've a hundred men, Patrick, who don't eat dreams, so you'll tell me what's this about or . . .'

'Or what?' Devlin's hands had not moved from their respite on their weapons.

Peter Sam thought. Gave one wipe of his bald head.

'I'll have to do my duty by my men.'

'You agreed to this, Peter. I was the one with the doubts. You persuaded.'

'That's long gone. I can feel the guts of the men. You turn up rotten out of this and neither of us will have the final say.' He sent a hard look to the others sitting and waiting.

'It'll be best for both of us, Patrick . . . if they know I'm in with you.'

Devlin turned to look at the pirates, their eyes boldly on both of them now.

'That might be just so, Peter. Besides I'm going to need all their backs.' He pushed Peter's shoulder to join him and together they went to the men.

'Lads,' Devlin said, he and Peter standing over them. 'I thank you for your hard walk. We'll rest awhile. Let you know what we're to do.'

Hugh Harris threw a stone to chip and smoke against a boulder.

'Hoping we're to kill a priest,' he said.

Devlin drew his hanger and they flinched, instinctively reaching toward their weapons. He laughed and began to draw in the sand with its point.

'There's a formation, a shape, out there just off the shore,' he scraped the elongated horseshoe in front of them. 'It might not, but I think it could be a coffer-dam. Broken up, mind, to protect its secrets, but we could build it back. It'll take a lot of us. All of us to beat the tide.'

'What does it do?' Cowrie's voice was almost a whimper, unsure if there was danger in words like 'coffer' and 'dam' – words which sounded too uncannily much like 'coffin' and 'damn'.

He was one of the youngest of the crew but had been with Devlin in the gaol on Providence, had fought hard on the *Talefan* on a terrible day and had been invaluable in rescuing Devlin from Newgate. But he still feared the Lord more than the Devil. A plot to kill a priest was wrong. He had enjoyed the Sunday masses on board the *Shadow*.

'It's a dam, Cowrie,' Devlin's sketch grew more elaborate. 'To hold back the tide while men work behind it. These islands are full of caves, some of them only sea-caves, littoral caves. They be full of water but when the tide goes back you can get to them.' He drew a cave which, judged by the whispered giggles, reminded Dan Teague of a woman of his acquaintance.

'But they're still full of the sea. A dam will give them time to drain elsewhere. Time enough to move a million pounds of gold and jewels inside. You couldn't bury that, but the sea could.' He cut a waterline over the cave. 'Levasseur. Smart man.'

Hugh Harris studied the sand. 'So it's beneath us? The priest has gone to it?'

'No,' Devlin put back his blade. 'The tide will only reveal the cave for a short time. Even then if I were La Buse I would choose a cave that no man could take a boat into. I would say there is another way in. If a cave is big enough there is always a crawling hole to get to it. That's nature. The hole draws in the sea.'

Peter Sam saw reason drawn in the sand and his spirit rose to the hunt again.

'The priest has come ashore,' he said, 'and gone to this hole? Hidden the boat. So we find this hole?'

'No,' Devlin's tone was sorry. 'That could take months.'

Peter Sam was at his shoulder. Again.

'So what then?'

'We rebuild the dam,' Devlin said. 'When the tide goes out.' The pirate's motive crawled on Devlin's face, the rakish Irish grin they had come to know as the promise of jingling coin.

'And we go in,' he said.

'Blood?' Hugh Harris threw another stone. Devlin caught it in the air; sent it to the sea in the same movement as they gaped at his speed of hand.

'There'd better be,' he said. He wiped his ancient boots across the drawing.

Hugh O'Neill had been a priest for thirty years. At fifteen he was sent from Ireland to serve his diaconate in Lisboa. It was there that the story of his ancestor's relic first divined to him that his profession was more than just his mother's ambition.

The first Hugh O'Neill, the Earl O'Neill, the man who might have been king of Ireland, failed to raise a holy army to take on the English. But after his death he bequeathed to the church a gold nine-inch cross with a small glass tomb set at its heart. Visible within was a dull, dry splinter of wood that had passed through his family for hundreds of years. The Earl O'Neill believed that towing the cross behind their fleeing ship had calmed the storm that came across them and had guided him into France. It had been a miracle but his only one. It was God's will that an army would not come to save Ireland.

The priest O'Neill, with such a personal connection, was entrusted to take the cross to Goa and there have it set into the Cross of Fire, a gift of Indian gold from the archbishop and viceroy to King João.

And then a pirate intervened. And miracles ended there.

O'Neill checked above to the diminishing light. He was scrambling down a hole, kicking wet slate and stone before him. His dread was that pirate faces might appear in the mouth of daylight even though he had tossed away the black quartz stone that marked the gap. They would look for such signs. That thought carried him down and into the dark.

It was a confining descent and he had to scrape down on his back and push himself along with his hands at his face. His breath was hard now, the stone hot all around, and then the cool blast of air and the eruption into the enormous cavern as if the tunnel had never pressed so close.

He dropped onto the narrow outcrop, sending a rain of shingle to glisten through shafts of light as they fell to the well of water below. They splashed and rippled like excited fish.

He crouched and looked about the place he had left over a month ago.

A cathedral of a cave. Fifty feet above him the stone broke in places with tiny holes that shone like the piercing of stars and shimmered on the water. He pictured the hunting feet of pirates walking high over his head. Below, the lake glowed like jade and lured you to dive as all still pools captivate if you stare deeply into them for too long.

His entrance would have been heard but before announcing himself he crept along, away from the hole lest his voice carry too far. The ledge ran around and down the walls, broken into a ruin like so many castles from his homeland since the English came.

He knew he would now be watched then remembered he was in different clothes and called out before a shot sounded.

'It is I! Father O'Neill!'

Nothing returned. He jumped the last few feet to land at the edge of the water. There was no trepidation in his footsteps but there was a coolness about his skin that had nothing to do with the languid pool.

He moved away and into the dark again, into the other chamber where he had left some of his brothers and the handful of pirates that had remained loyal to their captain.

'I have come back! As I swore!' His voice rang back at him. 'I am alone!'

Still he was not met.

He began to think of the woodcut plates of Bibles and the fate of the damned and then just as his thoughts had begun to pull away the veil of his faith he had turned the corner, and Levasseur was there.

O'Neill put a fist to his mouth at the sight and smell of the floor of the cave. He crossed himself and brushed the blowflies away then looked up at the motionless figure seated above it all.

Levasseur.

Still he looked the captain in his blue wool coat and scarlet brocade hat. He had seemingly spent the weeks of waiting to make a throne of rocks situated beneath a perfect beam of sun. He had piled the gold about his feet like steps, had carpeted a path with it. Rubies and diamonds on his lap like breadcrumbs. He cradled the magnificent Cross of Fire, from his feet to his chest and it blazed in O'Neill's eyes.

Levasseur moved amidst the dead.

Levasseur was not one of them.

'You return, Father,' his voice gave no emotion and it is hard to read the face of a man who has only one eye, a leather patch over his other. 'I told them you would.'

O'Neill gaped at the twisted bodies draped towards the throne, their hands grasping at gold.

Levasseur moved his shoulder under the cross.

'For their sins they did not believe me.' He shifted again, towards, and beckoned O'Neill closer as if the weeks had been only minutes and the cavern floor had always been this tomb. 'Now tell me,' his soft French accent was slow and calm like the Calais privateer he once was. 'You have a crew for me, no?'

# Chapter Twenty-Six

*N*oon on the *Standard,* the day well begun. Readings, logs, purser's lists, quarter-bills for action, Manvell to make their time and place, confer with the captain and at the ringing of the bell make sail, make way. One more day recorded. But not all of it to be written.

Coxon set his watch and desk chronometer to the bell. Two hours would have them at Île de France. Water, meat, turtles and birds, some sand underfoot for the men. A few hours of hunting would cheer them and, as he looked at the lists, they at least had a good six weeks of small beer and rum. He would keep a happy ship with that alone but the promise of gold had become the talk of the lower deck and the word had spread of the captured pirate who knew where the gold might be. Aye, the men were no concern. One speech more and they would already be counting their share. It was his young officers that knotted and creased his brow.

He set to shaving and thinking on them. He soaped and scraped his neck and contemplated Manvell and Howard.

Dinner last had been formal and trying. He had announced to them all who Dandon was and what he hoped to 'derive' from his acquisition. He had watched Howard attentively.

'You understand the validity of this action, Mister Howard?'

Thomas Howard had sipped his water after his wine before he replied.

'I do, Captain,' he said. 'Questioning the pirate as to his captain's whereabouts will only speed our cause and course.'

Manvell dropped his fork to his plate and made the whole assembly jump.

Coxon wiped his mouth.

'Something disagrees with you, Manvell?'

'No, Captain.' He picked up his cutlery and went again at his Poor John. 'Nothing disagrees. But I am curious as to how goes the "questioning" of the prisoner.'

'He will need a night to rest,' Coxon said. 'I believe the past association of the pirate Kennedy will do well to wile out his ways and means.'

Howard stopped eating. 'He will speak willingly?'

Coxon saw the concern draw on Thomas Howard's face.

'I hope, Mister Howard. I know that you – in perhaps some addled memory – think this pirate worthy of your compassion. But I hope you also understand the business that we are about here. He will go hungry and thirsty. Nothing more. He'll talk then.'

'He'll be *burning* to talk, will he not, Captain?' Manvell looked to his plate.

The others, the doctor and the master, drank slow as they watched Manvell and Coxon lean on the arms of their chairs studiously. The study of men who had deciphered a cheating table of cards between them.

'He will, Mister Manvell,' Coxon decreed. 'He is the pirate Devlin's closest friend – him and a bald, red-bearded bear he keeps to protect. More than that he is his intellectual confidant. I doubt there is anything that Devlin knows that he does not. And we will know it too. Find the gold for our king. As ordered.'

Manvell nodded agreement. 'Should we not consider why he left him on Bourbon then? If they are so close after all?'

Coxon plucked the wine carafe from Doctor Howe's keeping and poured to his brim.

'For the man's safety I suspect, Mister Manvell.' He drank without pleasure, only need.

'Devlin must assume great danger,' he continued. 'So should we. But now that I have seen your sword in action, Mister Manvell, I have no fear of anything that might lie ahead.'

He saluted with his glass and ended the conversation with port and the tale of Manvell's exhibition to everyone's pleasure, save for Manvell who accepted his applause graciously, humbly, and drank with the same need as Coxon. And the day began to fade.


Coxon finished shaving. He stood back from the mirror's oval frame as if it displayed an oil of his portrait, the sea in the window over his shoulder. A Boston shopkeeper no more. His future yet to be written when he had considered it done. And it had been his boot-wipe that had brought him back to the ledgers. And that for the last time.

He threw the Dutch towel to the bowl. What would those ladies who bought his cloth and pins make of him now? Pushing their plain daughters at him like samples of sugar. He had retired, done his duty. He had fought in two wars and had hundreds dead under him from the whims of queens and kings. He was the old bull of the field, watching and waiting for the farmer's shotgun when the time comes to turn his land over to lambing instead.

The expected knock on his coach came and he reached for the waistcoat over his chair and flapped it on.

'Enter,' he called.

Manvell stepped in, his hat already underneath his arm.

'Captain.'

Coxon waved him in as he dressed.

'How goes it, Manvell?'

'All's well, Captain. I have convened a shore party for hunting. They are preparing arms and baskets.'

'I would like all the men to go ashore, Christopher. All the watches.'

'How is that, sir?'

'There will be action soon. When the smoke comes men need to remember something to fight for. Let them drink, let them walk on grass in the sun. That might get them through the hours in the dark.'

'They will fight for the *Standard* surely? For their king?'

Coxon looked away. 'The *king*? I count the *Standard* fortunate that we can bait them with *gold*. Have you ever been in action, Christopher?' He chose to push the name.

'No, Captain.'

'After a few broadsides you'll be lucky if you can remember the king's name. Or your own.'

'You expect such?'

'The only thing I do not expect, Christopher, is to *live*. And that has kept me alive in my service. Remember that.'

He left his coat, being comfortable in shirt and waistcoat. 'But broadsides? No, I don't believe so. It will not go that way.' He thought of explaining further but then better for it. It was too fragile to expose yet what he hoped from the letter he had sent to Devlin. A letter hanging in time, delivered from the past, but when Devlin read it Coxon would be in the room as if actually, as if speaking the very words.

'Pirates will avoid such against a man-of-war. It is deception we must look out for.'

'False colours and such?'

Coxon let out a frustrated breath. 'Only if I thought Devlin an author of poor drama like Johnson and as foolish as the pirates in his play. No. You should think more on your watch being taken from your pocket and you paying the pawn ticket to redeem it.'

'Sir?'

Coxon played his arm against Manvell's.

'No mind now. All the men to go ashore. Let them know. It will cheer their spirits.'

'They are spirited enough I feel. The gold is already spent.'

'Good. Then cheer them more. It will add up for the days ahead.'

Manvell understood then. The pirate had not talked yesterday. He had been played a little by Kennedy, he was sure, but Manvell had not seen. Now Coxon wanted an empty ship. The crew would need officers to attend. A pirate might – just might – try escape with such an opportunity. He might have to be shot down. He might have to be shot in the back. Perhaps.

'I feel I had my legs stretched on Bourbon, Captain. I would petition to stay and attend to my instruction.'

Coxon did not meet his eye. He held his watch and wiped the moisture from its face. The humidity was rising. He thought of the grey clouds that dogged their evening watch, the perspiration at every meal now, every window sweating.

'But let young Howard ashore, Christopher. Send him to find me some eggs to take back to London. That will distract him. Something gentle to take his mind off his dreams. I fear the pirate has reminded him too much of his youth.'

'He is a man now, Captain.'

'All men are children in nightmares. You shall attend him ashore.'

245

He thought of his own dream that restless night in Portsmouth. The waters sucking him down, the gold drooling from his mouth, the pirate laughing at him. He slipped his watch away as the bell above rang again.

'His nightmare has become real.'

Manvell set his own timepiece to the bell. 'May I assist in the questioning of the pirate, Captain? I should like to hear how a pirate talks.'

Coxon looked at him now.

'Of course,' he said. 'Why not?' He bade Manvell to the coach door with himself behind. 'If I should suffer Kennedy's stench . . . And you may lose your novel notions of "false colours" when speaking of pirates. Count your shoes when you leave him.'

The ship saw them come out together, but only Coxon without hat, without coat, cracked shoes and unbowed hair, as simple as if he were about to pick up holystone and swab bucket. And the officer shone beside him in silk and linen. And Manvell watched the faces above, and from the fore, and from midships. Faces drinking them both in. He shook his head at what had been done so easily.

'Come,' Coxon said. He indicated the companion stair as if it was Manvell's first time. 'Let me show you a pirate.'

Manvell took off his hat and stepped down. He watched the eyes of the crew follow him.

Nothing stayed secret on a ship. Their captain promised them gold, his first officer discord, leniency for a pirate who held the keystone of their dreams.

'Have I not seen one already, Captain?'

Coxon frowned.

'On Bourbon that is,' Manvell said. He tipped his forefinger to his brow and carried on below.

* * *

Kennedy was already there. He wiped his face clean of sweat and saluted them both. A terrible heat and closeness lurked within and Manvell had never been under the two gun decks before. This was just below the waterline, the air already used, and he could feel the pressure of the water all around. He pitied the pirate who had been there without water or food or fresh air for too many hours. The sound of the animals lapping at their buckets was torturous even to Manvell after only moments.

'Come, Christopher,' Coxon patted Manvell's arm. 'We shall see if he is more communicative today.'

They weaved through the wooden supports and barrels and past the main mast to the fore and the manger. The deck yawed as the wind came against their larboard bow, the masts angling away from them and not coming back. Chains swung against each other, lanyards creaked. In any other place these sounds would concern. The tremors of strain, the crack of ending.

Passengers unfamiliar with life at sea would appeal to officers every hour of their first days that the ship was sinking. A wicked mate would take them down to the well and show them the sea for real and roar with laughter as the hose and breeches scrambled up the stair for their lives.

Dandon hung in his chains, his back crooked, head deep in his shoulder, his hands above him. He was not a tall man – women from their bosom had pointed that out to him often enough – and the overhead had become a church vault to his stretched flesh that had now solidified and hated him. But he forced himself up at their approach.

'Good afternoon, gentlemen,' he said. 'I am afraid I can offer you nothing in terms of refreshment.'

Manvell looked for bruises about the face but could see none. He saw just an aching, tired man. Not too much punishment. But lessened dignity.

'You may find a seat about. I myself have adapted to do without.' He pretended not to recognise the lieutenant from Bourbon and the boat and affected a pained squinting. 'Ah, sir, you seem familiar . . . Manvell was it?'

Manvell stepped forward. 'I am Lieutenant Manvell, sir. You are well?'

'As well as to be seen. As well as any pirate on a king's ship.' Coxon set himself against a barrel.

'We like to keep pirates so, until they can be tried and hung fairly. Is that not right, Dandon?'

Dandon sought voices in the dark.

'Is that you, John? Right, you say? As you decree. The animals have eaten if that is what you have come for?'

Coxon leant forward.

'No, pirate, I have come to ask the same as yesterday.' He looked at Kennedy as he spoke. 'I trust no-one has harmed you? You are well, other than for food and water in Kennedy's company?'

'Is Kennedy here?' Dandon coughed. 'I could only detect the manger.'

Kennedy rushed forward, his hand set to swipe, but found it effortlessly gripped by Manvell's fist. Kennedy tried to shake free, his eyes locked with Manvell's, but the arm did not move. Kennedy's shoulder rolled, tugged, but his hand stayed in the same place, for Manvell's honed arm was steel-trained. And then it was gone, the fist opened, and Kennedy almost fell with its release, his wrist burning. Manvell did not look at him, and Coxon ignored it all.

'Stay back, Walter,' Coxon said. 'I'm sure the pirate will talk for some water and meat. Gravy and meat.' He stood from the barrel. 'And wine. Is that not so, Dandon?' He gave no time for an answer.

'Where is Devlin?'

Coxon stood close enough to smell the night and the wounds. 'Suppose I show you a map now? And we shall drink. Drink long and talk about old times. About how you fooled me.'

Dandon rubbed his face against his sleeve.

'If I say yes, John, you will untie me again. I will go to that room . . . again. I will drink . . . again. And then I will become my arrogant self . . . again. Because I have the long drop of wine in my belly . . . again. And that is all I want. So I will be tortured again.' He flashed his gold-capped teeth at Manvell. 'And we will do this . . . again. And again. And again.'

'So you will hang? For nothing more than to tell me where he is going?'

'No,' Dandon's body tensed. 'I will hang because I did not *betray*. Do you not know how that might feel, John?'

Coxon twisted away.

'Kennedy?' Coxon snapped his fingers. 'Another day of no food or water for this man. But nothing else. He will not be harmed.' He looked at Manvell. 'It will do no good.'

Dandon's mocking voice spun him back.

'I will tell you that there is a cross, John. A gold cross. With rubies along its sides.'

'The Cross of Fire. We know this. It was part of the haul. What of it?'

Dandon stood tall in his bare feet. His chains loose.

'It has part of the True Cross within. *His* cross – if you believe such. And did we not all tremble as children?'

Coxon stood still.

'What matter?'

'How do you feel Spain, or Portugal, or France, or even New damned Spain would respond to a man who could bring them such? How many Catholic galleons do you think you could go against?'

'Is that a threat?'

Dandon grinned. 'Ain't it always?'

Coxon turned to Manvell.

'Have you seen enough, Christopher? Do you see now? They are intolerable rogues.'

Kennedy spat on the deck.

'They understand only one thing, sirs. I can make him talk.'

'Perhaps we could get you to write down his confession?' Manvell said, and even Dandon sneered. Manvell acknowledged Dandon's look as he turned his back to the wretch. 'Kennedy, if you hurt a man enough he will tell you he swallowed Jonah.'

He ducked to Dandon, shielded him from them both with his back. He spoke low.

'If you will but tell, your trial will be at an end, sir.'

Dandon's look lightened.

'I am not so mired, sir. You should ask Mister Howard how well I am able to endure thirst.' He hoped Manvell could read his face. 'Not everyone on this ship agrees with John's spirited treatment. You should consider that it is our past experience that silences my tongue. I might be willing to divulge more to "new" powers, Mister Manvell. If I felt less threatened, that is.'

Coxon joined them.

'Serpent's apples, Christopher?'

'No, sir,' Manvell said. 'I need some air. It is like being in a barrel down here.'

'I had not noticed,' Dandon said.

Coxon led them all away from the prisoner.

'Kennedy, watch him. Entertain him with stories of how Devlin killed your father.' He took Manvell to the stair and called back over his shoulder. 'Think on talking, pirate. We will fetch fresh water at Île de France. *Fresh* water. Then we will be on our way. You have one more day.'

Manvell followed him up the stair.

'One more day? And then, sir?'

'We must be on. And our only need for *him* will be as bait.' He paused to wait for Manvell to join him. 'I do not mean as shark-bait, Christopher. It has to do with the letter I sent you with to the priests. I know how to stir Devlin's pot.'

'Of course, sir.'

They went on up the next companionway.

'Call me John when we are not in company, Christopher. I shall prefer it.'

'Thank you, sir.'

Coxon stopped again.

'I mean, thank you, John.'

And they ascended.


Walter Kennedy was alone with Dandon, and he let Dandon know just how alone.

'We be in at one of the Frenchy islands soon, my boy.' He ran a waxed knotted lanyard through his hands, just short enough to be mistaken for a watch-chain, long enough to sting when swiped across flesh without too much marking. 'Everyone will be going ashore. Just be you and me and old Coxon. What you reckon to that, boy?'

'Less of the boy,' Dandon snapped out a kick to Kennedy's shin and Kennedy howled at the bite. 'I'm older than you, dog.'

Kennedy kicked back, harder, just under a knee, and Dandon closed his eyes but made no sound.

'One more day.' Kennedy brandished his rope at Dandon's face. 'If you don't talk Coxon'll be done with you. I don't care if you talk. I ain't in no hurry or hurrah to meet Devlin.' He moved his face close to Dandon's ear, his sweat dripping into it.

'And I did kill my father, scum,' he hissed. 'Stabbed through his ribs. I can hear it still. I was a *real* pirate. With Davis and Roberts. A captain with my own ship and men. Devlin is nothing compared to me.'

Dandon winced from the sweat and the breath.

'I assure you, Mister Kennedy. Patrick Devlin has never once compared himself to you.' He tossed his head to the manger. 'Or to any other goat shit.'

Kennedy cursed, leaned back and swung, flaying his rope into Dandon's eyes. Still the pirate made no sound.

'I killed my *father*!' he yelled and then remembered the ceiling above and the bodies that might hear. He lowered his voice for Dandon's ears only.

'Think what I'll do to you when we've done with you tomorrow!'

He pushed Dandon to let him swing in his chains and settled himself to his whittling and mumbling.

Dandon slumped forward. Forget Kennedy, he thought. There were not enough brains to work on. Howard and Manvell would be the way. They were closed but not locked doors. He had enough to spring their latches. Besides, there would be a day soon enough when he would sit down again at a table with Devlin. He had to have some story to tell, and it would not be one where he just sat and rotted by the manger until Devlin picked him up like an infant.

Devlin had left him for a reason even if neither of them had seen it at the time. He soothed his eyes against his sleeve. Aye, they'd both missed it at the time. And he would not let Devlin down.

He laughed, and Kennedy looked up and threatened to throw his knife. Dandon dared it and Kennedy went back to shaping wood and Dandon laughed harder. This time Kennedy came forward, his knife in one hand, knotted rope in the other.

'What you laughing at, dog?' He was sharp enough to put his blade in his belt.

'Can't you hear him coming?' Dandon sighed now. 'It is written. The whole ship sweats with storms brewing. And you will die, Walter. I'll make sure of that.'

Walter striped him again with the rope, and this time Dandon turned his head for the knots to strike his temple and its veins, and the blood came like a trail of syrup in one fat and glorious line.

'*Damn!*' Kennedy wiped the rope through his hand and then looked horrified at his palm. 'Damn you!' And he ran for the manger and a bucket.

Dandon's head went back and he laughed even harder. That would do, he thought. Soon Manvell would talk to Howard over what he had said in their whispers. Howard would come again to feed his conscience. Howard would see his wounds. And Dandon would have his story to drink to. And he and Patrick Devlin would chime their glasses. And then that image faded, Devlin's face gone. Instead Dandon would die on this ship with welts on his wrists, stinking of iron, and with piss on his breeches.

He scraped his chains against the cool wound to rip it further and felt the blood trickle down his neck. Head wounds were the best to be sure. They bled well.

He watched Kennedy stomp the deck, pull his hair and curse his Irish temper. Then Dandon settled back to weakness, the gifted pebble of Thomas Howard rolling in his mouth.

But slowly the weakness was becoming less play. Truly dying now.

He thought on that.

And it was like reminiscence.

# Chapter Twenty-Seven

*T*hirty men he had taken from the *Shadow*, and all her boats. They rowed round, left their girl where she was, should they be observed.

They waited for the tide to withdraw and for the strewn rocks to show themselves. A boat beyond the tide was set to signal when the cave revealed its mouth, and Devlin and Peter Sam set them all to building the stones atop the horseshoe-shaped foundations of the dam that remained. But it would not be a single day's labour. It was slow work. Levasseur must have used his whole ship's company.

'See it, Peter,' Devlin waved his arm across the bay they were creating. 'Levasseur has a ship. A hundred men or more. He builds a wall to hold back the tide. To reveal a cave that a hundred men can walk a treasure into . . . and then he floods it. Why?'

Peter Sam watched the thirty men build, all of them happy in the heat, or greedy in the heat, for it was the gold that raised their ardour and labour.

'I don't know, Cap'n.' He knew when Devlin was tuning his fiddle.

Devlin set a foot against a rock, leant on a knee.

'To flood the cave again. To leave the haul hidden. Come back another year.'

'Or?' Peter Sam mirrored Devlin's stance.

Devlin looked confused and then read down the same page as Peter Sam.

'Say his men trapped him there. Turned against. As you might do to me. In my madness, that is.'

'Go on.'

'O'Neill only cares for the cross,' Devlin spoke carefully, shaping his thoughts. 'He's brought us here just to get back to Levasseur. The Buzzard is still here. Not just the treasure. The man himself. Why else would O'Neill deceive us? He couldn't get the cross on his own. He has men here.'

Peter Sam loaded his pipe.

'Aye. That'll be it. The Buzzard and the gold are here. And we're going in. There could be a line of shot waiting for us.'

Devlin went back to his thinking pose.

'Maybe we should just go.' Peter Sam lit and drew his tobacco into life. 'Think how the men will feel if we find an empty cave?'

Devlin waited long enough to hear a round of land and sea birds back and forth, conflicting, fighting, celebrating. Enough time to see the white spume receding from the shore.

'It ain't empty, Peter.' He decided and rolled his breeches to help his men. 'I can smell it. I've known it before. I don't know the story, but the gold's here.'

He stood beside the big man and slapped his shoulder. 'Else I'll give the *Shadow* up to you. With willing.'

He walked down to help his men. Peter Sam cupped a hand to his mouth to shout at Devlin's back.

'You're supposed to ask me if I wants it first!'

Devlin pretended not to hear.

'Dulcinea, Peter Sam!' he yelled back. 'Dulcinea! We have become men of La Mancha!'

He came down to the beach. The tide was sucking out now. It would take two tides for the cave to be revealed. Once the dam did its work the water would drain elsewhere, for the erosion of the cave would have created another channel out. And then they would be the first ones since Levasseur to see the black-mouthed entrance.

'What has happened?' O'Neill asked. He had picked his way through the bodies, fearful of Levasseur but drawn towards the only living thing. He sought life.

The Buzzard stopped him with a pistol's click.

'Hold, priest.' The pistol arm stretched to O'Neill's head. 'You have a ship for Levasseur?'

O'Neill raised his palms and took in the man before him. Lean and sea-worn as he ever was. Fine clothes now worn by the habit of waiting, of patience, his limbs as wiry as smoke.

The priest and the pirate. And the priest had better talk well. The floor attested to that.

'I have a ship, Captain. I have brought a pirate. They do not know where I am. I took them to the other island. But, Captain? Are you well?'

'Do you have any tobacco?' Levasseur lowered the gun. Hugged his cross.

'No,' O'Neill came closer. 'But the pirates have all. Food and wine. Tobacco and meat.'

'Good. I am sick to my lungs of fruit.' He leant forward conspiratorially.

'Come, priest. Let me tell you how I died.'

257

# Chapter Twenty-Eight

*T*he blow-hole into the cave had been the lifeline for The Buzzard and those who had stayed with him. They could scramble out, they could roll down food from the bounty of the island to grabbing hands. Water was given by a spring trickling into the cave. Birds could be shot – strangled, for they had no fear of men – their nests and the lizards' nests pillaged. But the gold remained sealed.

It had happened quickly. Violence faster than the swiftest hand could inscribe.

Levasseur had taken his *Victory* and his snow, the *Santa Rosa,* to an island given up as worthless. No stone sat engraved on the shore to claim it for another country. That had been in April. He had split the treasure with John Taylor and the Englishman had gone his own way, to the South Americas the taverns said. But Levasseur felt that if he were to settle down with his share the French encroachment on the Indian Ocean would be the best passage. He was richer than God. But even God had to buy legitimacy in this new age. He would appeal to his Crown – with a sufferance of gold, naturally.

He had lost his eye in youth from his love of rock-climbing. He had been a man scarred by the cliff-face. He had ventured into sea-caves as a young man as others had stumbled in and out of taverns. The earth was his friend. He had no fear of caves or doubts about his mastery over the waters.

Levasseur had sniffed out the cave, and the crew of the *Victory* had built the dam. By the time it had served its purpose his pirate crew had been living with the gold for over a week. And not just gold but diamonds, rubies and emeralds. The gold proved to be the ruined part of the great treasure, for much of it was not in coin, which would have fit easily into pirate pockets.

There were idols, ceremonial plates, chains, and an untold number of crosses – the golden adulation a king expects, but which pirate teeth found hard to bend to their more practical uses.

Dragged into the sea-cave, piled up, and yet once amassed against the rocks and the sand, the wealth seemed too mountainous for one captain to preside over.

In chests, in sacks, there could be order, fair division. But a hundred pirates staring at a cascading harvest of gold . . .? And they wanted more, of course. And they had chanced on the wealth easily, after all.

If they had spilled their blood over it, shared a painful victory, that might have counted for something. Instead they looked at their captain as just a lucky devil. And luck costs nothing. Luck deserves only a tip of a hat. Nothing has been earned or deserved.

Levasseur's men wiped grins from their faces, unhooked pistols from their belts, and climbed towards him up a hill of gold.

Four were loyal, but against the whole that was just a stand of bravado and cursing. The mutineers carried off the bulk of the gold, leaving some out of respect, but even that remainder fabulous enough: ten lifetimes' fortunes.

And they left the cross.

To them it seemed likely the cross had sunk the first ship that tried to carry it and now the pirates could blame their revolt on its bad luck. The cross had willed them to it. No doubt its gold had been hewn from the earth by heathen slaves for Catholic masters and was cursed by those who gouged it, and cursed by Satan, for it was Catholics that bid it done. The Devil's cross.

And let him to it.

They destroyed the dam on leaving to cut off the Devil, and their captain's voice. But Levasseur did not howl out at their betrayal. They would not hear his woe. The pirates broke down the sea-wall, took the *Victory* and sailed away, vanishing into legend. It was the right time. Rich men were now aboard and rich men slip away easily. History is full of such empty pages, and no-one ever hears of successful pirates, after all. Only those that swung.

The Buzzard now became prey instead of predator. At every tide the waters rose over the treasure to fill the pool that had always been there, and left its captives to stare like Tantalus at their unattainable fortune.

The fruit was unreachable, the water undrinkable.

Twice a day the tide withdrew just enough, but for less than an hour. Armful by armful the pirates and the priests removed the hoard to the higher slope, to a new chamber, and O'Neill presented a plan to Levasseur.

They had discovered the blow-hole and that through it they could get out, and they soon discovered that the mutineers had abandoned the *Santa Rosa*. But the captain and the pirates would not leave the life that the treasure promised and that they had dreamt of all their lives – or at least since that day they had crossed the boards of one life into another.

O'Neill had pleaded that they could all be saved, that they might fill their pockets with what they could and be free.

'You do not understand freedom, priest,' Levasseur had replied. 'And what of your cross? Would you leave that to this hole?'

'Then we get out and rebuild the dam,' O'Neill insisted.

'We do not have the men to do it before the tide. Each day the sea will push us back, destroy our work. And then there are the storms due to come. I know these waters.'

O'Neill argued that the men could take the ingots, the rubies and the diamonds, count their blessings in that, still be rich men.

'And leave my soul. And your soul?'

O'Neill lowered his head. His brothers had already set the cross against a wall, braced by stones; already they had returned to ritual.

'Then let me go,' he said. 'I will take some coin and six of my brothers and buy us a ship of men to rebuild the wall.'

'Share my gold again?' Levasseur brought his face close. 'Not again.'

'No. I will find good men. Hire them to the task only. I only ask the cross for my church. No more.'

Levasseur walked the cave, watched the pool rising, watched his four loyal men sweat and study him faithfully. He came back to the tall priest and scratched the scar beneath his eye-patch as if an answer lay behind the leather.

'Then go, priest,' he said at last. 'But do not bring them until you have met me again. If I am not satisfied . . . you and I will both die here.'

'We were robbed,' O'Neill explained. 'We went to Bourbon, with difficulty. South you said, but it was not easy.'

'You lost the gold?' Levasseur dragged himself from his throne.

O'Neill stepped back, away from the dead, and the undead coming on.

'Pirates,' O'Neill said, without apology. 'I tried to get back to Lisboa. Hoped to appeal to my king for a ship, and then the Lord intervened for both our souls, Captain. That is why I have been gone so long.'

'Two months and more, priest.' He was upon him now, his pistol still cocked and waiting. 'We are dead.'

'But I have a ship! And great men.' O'Neill backed to the pool. 'Enough to build the dam again!'

'You lost your gold. How will you pay them?'

O'Neill looked over the pirate's shoulder to the golden carpet.

'A share, perhaps? I have told about the cross but he expects treasure. I have not told him of you, Captain. I thought a truce. To rescue our men and the gold . . . but I did not expect . . . what you have done.'

'*Done?*' Levasseur stopped. 'I have done nothing! They wished to leave. They forced my hand. They wished my gold for themselves. It is your fault to be gone so long. To riddle them with doubt.'

'My brothers would stay. They would hold their faith.' O'Neill crossed himself. 'You had no right, Captain.'

Levasseur pulled another pistol.

'*Right?* You all want *my* gold! *Mine!*' He levelled both pistol mouths to the priest.

'You shall have the same weight in lead! *Damn you!*'

O'Neill raised his palms again.

'But I have a ship! It is done now. I have done as agreed!'

Levasseur moved with his pistols outstretched, aimed at ghosts.

'You test me, priest. You bring a ship and men. But it is Levasseur who rules here. I am your life and death.'

'It is a pirate I bring. A brother for you . . . to replace those you have lost. He is a reasonable man.'

Levasseur hid his face, his back turned. 'A pirate? He would have to be a prince to talk to Levasseur. Who, say you?'

'Devlin.' O'Neill hoped the name carried some weight. 'Patrick Devlin. And nigh a hundred men. I needed him to shape back here.'

'You had my Mortier.'

'I needed a man of the sea.'

'I do not know this man,' Levasseur weighed his pistols. 'You have failed, priest. Failed to resurrect.'

They both stalled as the pool gulped and the level sank away somewhere else deep inside the island.

Levasseur stepped to the edge. He observed this every day. But not now, not at this hour. He watched the moss appear, outside the time of the tide.

O'Neill joined him. Hope lightened his face briefly and he hoped the pirate did not see it.

'He is coming,' O'Neill said and swallowed the pride in his voice as Levasseur glared at him, his leather eye twitching. 'He is quite bright. For a pirate. And he is an Irishman. He will work with me.'

The Buzzard became the buzzard. He put a pistol to a priest's temple.

'Traitor.' He did not exclaim. No need. The cave amplified his voice. 'Baptist's head. Is that your desire? Your want?'

The pool gulped again and O'Neill palmed the pistol away from his head.

'He has men, Captain. You have nothing now. The Lord has provided. Your days of seclusion are at an end. Let me go to him. His men are hungry. He will want little.'

263

'You bring a pirate to steal my gold?' But this was not a question to be answered. Its answer was in the tension of a fist, of steel springs and pistol locks, a dog-head cocking to end all questions.

'You would dare steal my gold? *My gold*!'

And a buzzard fired both its pistols into a priest's face.

The muzzles flamed. The head, a veil of red, snapped back and the body stumbled mindlessly over the edge into the sucking pool. Only the powder burns and blood spatter on Levasseur's hands testified that O'Neill had ever existed.

Levasseur stood where the body had been and stared at the footprints in the sand. He scrubbed them flat with a foot and pulled himself back to his throne to reload.

He had already forgotten the voice. He heard only the peaceful dribble of the spring and the chime of gold at his feet as he dragged himself up. These sounds he had heard for months now. They spoke sense to him. Traitors' tongues clicked like the crickets, like the bones and teeth of dying men as they sputtered their last bubbles of bile. He heard the crows high above squawking about his pistol's wrath, laughter on the wing drifting in from a world now strange to him.

From the shore Devlin looked up to the cawing crows flying about the trees and registered the silence of the songbirds who paused in their courtship and wars. The animals had responded to some sound unheard by the men on the island. Peter Sam studied him.

'What is it?'

Devlin watched the crows return to their perches, listened to the birds begin again their romancing and bickering.

'Nothing,' he said. 'The birds.' And Peter Sam looked above.

Devlin waded into the clear sea, picked up another one of the flat rocks.

The wall was working; Levasseur was truly a man to measure.

The shore fell off past the beach. The stone started there and a hundred feet of it arced round the rock-face. Even with fifteen men set to the task of rebuilding the dam the tide was still beating them and Devlin knew it would have to be more men and another day.

He set his rock. Three feet of wall so far and the tide had held back but now it reclaimed, and the mouth of the cave had barely come into view.

He saw the crows watching them work, daring him with their caws and their preening. Devlin waded towards the cave mouth, waist deep.

The wall had been destroyed carelessly, hurriedly. What must have taken Levasseur's men a week to build would cost Devlin only one more day.

Peter Sam watched him move through the water and then the others stopped their work and turned to look. They saw Devlin make some decision and then he was gone, under. Through the crystal water they could see him swimming to the cave.

He rose once, at the mouth, his head just a few feet from the sharp rock ceiling that would effortlessly scalp him, and then he was gone entirely.

The water was not as beautiful below. The salt of life that gave it such clarity also stung his eyes and skin. Ten strokes in and the water had developed an eerie palette of subterranean gloom, and Devlin kicked up for air. He raised his hand to the ceiling to stop his head being split and looked about him.

He was in the mouth of the cave. He spat out the salt, eyed the opening beyond. The tide rolled over his head – a warning – and he went under again. Just ten more strokes and he would turn back; the silence and adventure were seductive but he knew he was chancing his life against the tide.

It was even darker now, a twilight; the softness of the water was gone and his arms had to work harder. He came up again and the the ceiling was not so close. Something had opened up.

The cave yawned, but an edge of panic twitched in Devlin's chest. It was that taut instinct that keeps men alive, and although he turned and dived his legs did not move and suddenly something travelled with him.

A weight pulled him back and he kicked against a heavy mass. Even under the water he knew its sense. He ducked his chin to look back and could not help but gulp and lose the air in his lungs as O'Neill's shattered face rushed up to his.

Its eyes were peeled in surprise, the gaping mouth widened by shot and split to the ear; but it was still O'Neill, and the priest's dead hands flailed over Devlin's arms.

He struggled, wrestled with the corpse's weight, his breath frothing and bubbling in O'Neill's hideous face. They rolled together, the body playing with him, the head flung back as if in laughter.

He elbowed aside the grotesque leer and the corpse spun like a drunk shoved down a hill. Several of its loosened teeth span away leaving trails of blood and the body was buffeted back with the tide towards the cave.

Devlin gasped upwards and had to push against the roof which now descended fast, pressing down on his head like the sod on his grave. He regained his arms and legs, steeled himself and aimed for the sunlight.

They watched him from the beach. The tide and the cave had won and Devlin crawled round the rocks to splutter and gasp next to his men on the shore.

'She comes in quick don't she?' Peter Sam hauled him up. 'Reckon she won't tide 'til the night now. We're done for today.' He saw Devlin's pale face. 'What were you about?'

Devlin held the big man's arm then bent over and sucked the good air. The cave had been hot. His chest heaved. Then he remembered his men judging him always and he stood up straight. Stood tall.

'Needed to see . . .' he had no breath. '. . . We need more men. Send the boats . . . go in tomorrow.'

Peter Sam moved to hide him from the men. They could not see him weakened.

He saw Devlin's hands shaking. 'What happened, Patrick?'

'O'Neill,' Devlin said. 'Dead.' He bent again to gasp hard. 'Shot.'

Peter Sam slapped Devlin's back to shake free the water.

'Good,' he said. 'Some fighting, then.' He lowered his voice and spoke to Devlin's neck. 'Now stand well,' he pulled him level, 'Captain.'

Devlin nodded, shook his hair like a dog and faced his men.

'The cave opens up,' he said to their expectant faces. 'I saw O'Neill dead.' He pulled off his shirt, ignored the old wound of last year that clawed at his back from his exertions and the salt.

'We're going in killing. And getting our gold.'

And the roar and pistol fire set the crows back into the air.

Always crows, Devlin thought. He watched their slow wings drag themselves from the branches. Always crows. Since the first time. Since The Island. Since the archipelago when he had set his path. They had been there then, when a dying French marine gave up his boots and the map held within.

Always a murder of crows. The world was their cemetery. Impartial. They will eat both sides alike and laugh. The birds landed calmly again, preened at him and seemed to await his word.

'We'll go in,' he said. 'Kill. Get our gold. Then back to Bourbon and Dandon. Buy the earth with our riches.'

He picked up his belt, his weapons. And his men.

The Buzzard sat on his throne. He had heard the shouts and gunfire echo up from the pool like someone else's dream. He had reloaded and thought on the other four pistols from his dead. He had powder for them also. He rocked back and forth with the cross against his shoulder.

His gold. His fortune.

And he had grapeshot. He had held with the pirate tradition of taking at least one cannon to shore, should it become necessary on a strange island to build a redoubt.

He tapped the six-pounder beside his throne like a favoured dog.

'Tomorrow,' he said to the walls. 'Tomorrow they will come. And warmly they will come to their end. *Et vivement ils viendront a leur fin.*'

# Chapter Twenty-Nine

*T*he Dutch had abandoned the island of Maurice in 1712 after almost seventy years of occupation. They had built a stone fort with a garrison of fifty and settled forty families at the north-west harbour, which they called 'The Camp'.

They cultivated tobacco, and not unsuccessfully. It went so well that the governor decided they should now be permitted to trade not just with their homeland but with any nation and company they pleased. The Dutch India Company thought otherwise and the colonists were swiftly retired to the Cape of Good Hope.

The second epoch began when the French ship, *Chasseur*, arrived in 1715 and formally possessed the island in the traditional manner. A boulder brought with them, a possession stone, scratched with the date and the Bourbon flag. The Dutch had only burned their colours into a tree. Presumably the tree could no longer be seen.

Île de France was born.

The French had held Bourbon for as long as the Dutch had held Maurice and now they had the sister island and planned to colonise it just as fruitfully.

But not yet.

It would be September 1721 when they returned in force. For now, for Coxon's men in July the same year, the island was as desolate as ever. Some pirates, some Maroons and some bold families from Bourbon had all settled in the island's south-east harbour, and so the *Standard* moored in the north.

Volcanic and as verdure-covered as Bourbon, the enormous island seemed just as inhospitable to those English hearts that had run from the labour of the fields. But the hearts yearned to see those fields roll again, and again hear village bells toll before their knuckles finally knotted. Still, it was a shore; still, they could make some English mark upon it.

Coxon stood beside Howard as the anchors fell. Howard was a man now but a few inches below his captain and Coxon had known him as a boy and so to him Howard still held that aspect.

'You will escort a bill to shore, Thomas. I want you to see if you can find some example of that Dronte bird. Perhaps we shall rediscover it, eh?'

Howard smiled but said nothing. Coxon ignored the silence.

'Gather any sort of eggs you can. Birds and reptiles. We will present them as a gift when we return.'

'I shall get some baskets, Captain.' He tapped his forehead and wheeled away. Coxon flushed at the young man's brusqueness then dismissed it as anxiety and looked toward the island.

He had noticed Howard's change of humour since the pirate had come among them, but no matter; that was not a captain's worry. He had no doubt of Howard's discipline or his loyalty and that was all that mattered. The young man could sort his own soul if he had enough pieces to do so. And he would have to if his career were to progress and be a true career and not just the biding of time. Or one of shame and humiliation. Coxon moved away from the gunwale, hearing and approving the excitement of his men and their coarse banter.

Manvell watched him from the quarterdeck. He knew Coxon to be a common man like himself but Manvell had the mantle of assumed nobility. The man had no wife, no family to raise him and promote him. He had earned everything himself. But what 'all'? His cloth was old, his shoes worn. He had no wig and his black and grey smooth hair was tied with a bow that might have been found as a marker in a bible. The crew could see it. They laughed with him, a man of the sea like themselves. He had promised them gold.

Manvell looked over to the volcanic pyramids of the island. They could almost be man-made and just swallowed up by millennia and the dense green forests. One of them looked as if it had a carved obelisk of a woman stood atop it, watching him back. Others had flat tables that could hold hidden villages and the giant extinct creatures of this world and any other.

They were small men coming to see the ancient races of creation, the pages of Genesis unfolding before them.

Manvell tapped down the steps to catch Thomas Howard before he went below.

'Mister Howard,' he called, 'a word, if you please.'

Howard stopped. 'I am on orders, Mister Manvell.'

Manvell pretended not to hear.

'I spoke with the pirate this morning. Your pirate.'

'He is not *my* pirate, sir.' Howard carried on. Manvell fell into step with him.

'I meant no offence, Thomas. An article of speech.' He plucked Howard's sleeve. 'He spoke of you.'

Howard stopped again. 'What did he say?'

Manvell checked the bustling ship for ears about them. 'He may have "suggested" that you and he have had words. Against the *Standard*'s orders. That you . . . aided him, somewhat.'

271

'I gave him some bread and water. Is that not what one does for prisoners?'

Manvell carried them both on.

'It is the Christian thing, Thomas. Understand that I am not reproaching. More. I am approving.'

'You will not report me?'

Manvell took a breath. They were over the companion. The boats were away and the deck no longer such a narrow beam without them. Manvell whispered now.

'If I do not report you, Thomas, I would have no choice but to consider myself a conspirator. Alongside you. Would I not?'

'I do not understand, sir?'

Manvell patted his back.

'Go to your duty. We will talk more on the island.'

Howard took the stair. He looked up to Manvell framed against the bare poles and the blue expanse of sky.

'We are all ashore?'

Manvell leaned over the hole.

'Only those of us not privy to torture it seems, Mister Howard.'

'You talk riddles, sir. The pirate is not my friend. You understand? He is a fool to himself. If he would but talk and offer his parole—'

'And would you talk, Thomas? To the enemy? How would you judge yourself then?'

'We are not the enemy.'

'That depends on one's perspective, Thomas, does it not?' He tapped his forehead and grinned as Howard ducked his head below.

Manvell turned on his heel to Coxon glowering at him past the main hatch twenty-feet fore, his hands clasped behind him. Manvell over-extended his grin and salute and went back to the quarterdeck, the indignant stare boring into his back.

An hour. Every watch would take its turn ashore. Five hours given for the task of hunting, gathering water, fruit. Of building spirit. Manvell and Howard in white shirts and straw hats leading the perspiring midshipmen.

Doctor Howe and Sailing-Master Jenkins remained on the *Standard* with a short-handed crew. Jenkins was too earnest in his sails and setting the men to repair to waste time ashore; Howe was too earnest about the claret in the wardroom, and the tropics were not friendly to already-peeling skin. He had yet to find a soap that agreed with sea-air. Every day felt just a variance on sandpaper. He took off his hose and eased his swollen feet on Thomas Howard's chair.

John Coxon came down the decks, past one set of guns and then the next. Twenty six-pounders above, twenty twelve-pounders below. On land you measure a gun by its bore, at sea by the weight of its shot, for weight is everything, every ship given its burthen to the last thimble, worked out with the same science that Flamsteed plotted his almanacs. The larger guns were set below for equilibrium on the water, but the armament was not always so perfectly aligned. Pirates especially could carry a set of guns as motley as their cloth, as rag-tag as their morals, the ship swaying as drunkenly as her crew. But not Devlin's, Coxon knew.

He had taught him too well.

He reached the lower-deck, now above the water for some respite to the man chained and his cattle companions.

'Is it supper already, John?' Dandon called. 'I have hardly digested dinner. You are too generous. I should have given myself up years ago.'

Coxon weaved his way to him.

'Still the whimsy, pirate? I thought that done.' He came under the overhead and stood beside Dandon. He saw Kennedy on a barrel, his head in his hands and then the dried wound on the pirate's face.

Kennedy sprang up.

'It was his fault, Captain!' he pleaded. 'He forced me to it!'

Coxon dismissed him with a shove to send him bowling among the barrels. There was a flutter in his chest but he was not as angered as he would have thought. He lifted Dandon's chin and met the sly eyes, and examined.

'It is not so bad, pirate. You have fooled Kennedy but not me. I will tell my men that you goaded him. As you did. I will fetch the doctor.'

'You would have to keep Manvell and young Howard from me, John. I would talk else. Say how I have been beaten. Or perhaps you could gag me? That would work well. How fine they would think you then.'

Coxon pulled the chains, Dandon wincing as the welts on his wrists scraped. Their faces drew close together. Both bared teeth. In pain. In anger.

'You think you are working on them, don't you? That they care what you feel? Over my command?'

Dandon wilted, then shook himself back to the arrogance that he was feigning to uphold. His eyes sparked again.

'What you say is what you suspect, John. Try to see what they see. Save yourself. Tonight I will tell Manvell how you risk the ship for your own grievance. Has he met pirates? I will sow him seeds, and he will grow his own oaks. And Thomas Howard will confirm.' He showed his gold-capped teeth. 'It'll be best if you let me go.'

Coxon snarled, pushed the chains away. The goats bleated as Dandon laughed. Coxon went slowly to Kennedy and the wretch lowered his head like a shamed dog.

Coxon looked back to Dandon.

'We are alone, pirate. I have made it so. This is your last chance to talk. To talk well.'

Dandon posed himself as nobly as he could.

'I am supposed to say, "or else," am I not?'

'Say what you want. While you still can. I have less need for you than you think.'

Dandon's humour dropped.

'Less?' he said.

'If you would talk and tell where Patrick is, where the gold is, it will remove you from this place to your own quarters and save my good men some time.' He sat on a barrel like Kennedy, his arms crossed. 'But Devlin will come to me regardless.'

He relished the inquiry on the pirate's face.

'I told you I sent a letter. I sent word that I have you. What I also sent was the location on the sea where I shall wait for him. Where I will set the *Standard* to wait for the *Shadow*. You could avoid that bloody day.'

'Why not wait at Bourbon?' Dandon said. 'If you are so inclined to believe my captain is coming for me there?'

'Surround myself with dozens of pirate ships in pirate waters? In a short bay? How fine.'

'So, the sea is where you will have it, John? Am I privileged to know where?'

'I can bring a map,' Coxon leant back on the barrel. 'I'll show you mine if you'll show me yours.'

Dandon laughed. 'I am glad that we have not allowed circumstance to devour our humour, John! Good show!'

'You should rather think on that I only need Devlin to *believe* I have you. And that if you continue to threaten mutinous thoughts to my officers you will not need to manufacture wounds . . . or perfect your silence.'

Kennedy leered at Dandon.

'As I said,' Coxon went on, 'we are alone. I could release you out of pity, out of your promise to talk. You could attempt escape, attempt murder. Kennedy would defend me. We have hours left to us.'

Kennedy unclasped his gully with a gleeful click.

Dandon paled. It was not in him to flush with rage. He usually had men in front of him to do that.

Coxon stood. 'It is too warm for me down here. I will fetch the doctor for your wounds.'

'It is but a scratch,' Dandon said, but his voice was weaker now and Coxon heard it falter.

'You misheard, pirate,' he said. 'I will fetch the doctor for your *wounds*.' He cocked a thumb at Kennedy and jerked it towards Dandon.

'No cuts, Walter. I want some word from him for when I return.' He looked back at Dandon.

'I've had enough of your blather. I thought you an intelligent man, pirate. You should at least have realised why Devlin is so able. He was under his post-captain for years.' He turned for the stair as Kennedy slipped from the barrel, hunched, creeping towards the prisoner with a wet grin.

Dandon shook his chains and Coxon turned his head.

'I know,' Dandon called, 'that you, John, became post-captain when it was Patrick who translated for his French officers! On the day you took him into servitude! He told me that! You owe him that, "Post-Captain".'

Coxon's face showed nothing. He brushed a fly from his shirt.

'But did he not tell you that he stepped forward to *save* them, pirate? Was that not the vital part of his story?'

He did not wait for a reply and ascended to search for the swollen and red Doctor Howe.

But not too quickly.

It was a sky of a honey-onyx hue when Manvell and Howard took the final boat back to the ship. Every anker of water, every trussed pink pigeon, every giant tortoise with its delicious liver already setting tongues slavering, had all worked to bring a rare air about the crew. They laughed, sang, helped each other hand over hand willingly, more as a crew at the end of their work than one approaching the cannon. Manvell mirrored their humour by leaning down from the ladder to haul up Howard, his boxes over his shoulders and about his waist so that he waddled out of the boat awkwardly.

On deck, only Jenkins the sailing-master, greeted them, a stranger next to them in coat and tricorne; the lieutenants were still in calico and straw.

'How went the island, gentlemen?'

'Very well, Mister Jenkins,' Manvell said. 'How goes the ship?'

'All's well, Mister Manvell.' He saw Howard's pile of boxes. 'Specimens, Mister Howard?'

'Yes, sir,' Howard opened one to show. 'For the captain. For presenting back to the board.'

Jenkins sniffed over the box. 'Eggs. Good, good. What creature?'

Howard looked to Manvell. 'Bats, sir. A flightless sand-bat, I perceived.'

Manvell looked up at the mainmast, turned his face away and fascinated on the oak so Jenkins would not see his smirk.

'Good, good,' Jenkins approved. 'I shall look forward to seeing more. Perhaps after supper.' He saluted and spun away. Manvell came back from his study of wood.

'Thomas,' he took out a kerchief and wiped his brow, 'you are a terrible fellow. We should change and report to the *Standard.* 'He picked up his own share of baskets and boxes. 'Come now. The trees and the sand have improved me immensely.'

Howard was pleased. He had avoided Manvell on the island, should he have had whispered more of his seditious words. He was not willing to forge conspirators' alliances over the giving of a drink of water.

He had seen pirates, and judged them with the dead he had also seen turn up when the pirates walked. But that one, Dandon, had shown compassion once. All Howard had done was make a return on that compassion. If it was against orders he would live with that. The island had performed its magic. The world of wood that swaddled them daily was a small world. It magnified everything. The island had reminded how large the earth really was. Looking back at the ship from the jungle had been the best perspective. The ship just a hundred and eighteen feet of wood. A conveyance. A vehicle for his duty. And Manvell clearly had a similar viewpoint. They went below with shared laughter.

Sailing-Master Jenkins looked back at the sound, then the shrouds beside him began to shake and hum and the yards above creaked painfully. He clamped his hat down and watched the giant palms of the island shiver like wheat. The boats, still being pulled up, swayed dangerously. Straw hats flew from the heads of the men straining to hold them.

And then it was gone.

It had been a warm rush of air from the island's mountains and he watched it roll away from their starboard and across the sea, now seeming to pull away from them as the *Standard* bucked in her chains.

Calm again. The air heavy and too still. He stood and waited for another portent. The men at the boats went back to work and Sailing-Master Jenkins bit his lip. He took out his watch, his log and pencil and walked to the quarterdeck.

Manvell and Howard came across Doctor Howe hugging a post outside their quarters. The wind had unbalanced him, he declared, and the lieutenants helped steady him, amused at the wine stains on his paunch and the fermented breath.

'You would do better to get some air, Doctor,' Manvell said.

'I would so,' he clung to Manvell like a cat falling down a curtain. 'But the captain had an exigence to inspect his injured pirate.'

Manvell and Howard looked at each other. 'Kennedy?' Manvell asked.

'No. The other. I gave him a draught. It is all he will need. Closing of the bowels.'

Howard let him go and slung his boxes off his shoulders and peeled down the stair.

'*Thomas!*' Manvell excused himself from the reeling doctor and his own baskets and ran after.

Howard saw the chains swinging empty. He heard Manvell come down behind him and ducked his way through the hold until he saw Kennedy and Coxon and the prone body lying on a jury-rigged table. He stopped and Manvell brushed past him.

'What has happened here, Captain?' Manvell's voice was calm. He saw Kennedy slink away to the manger.

'Good to see you return, Lieutenant,' Coxon was in rolled shirtsleeves, his hair pulled tight by its bow as if recently secured. He stepped aside to show the full sight of the pirate.

'I released him. Out of pity. He attempted escape. Or some pain to me personally. I should not have sent so many of you ashore. I think he saw his chance.'

Howard took a step towards. 'Is he—?'

'Dead?' Coxon said. 'Why would he be dead?'

Manvell saw there was no blood around the table and came closer.

'Escape? Where would he go?'

'To the island one would suppose,' Coxon shrugged. 'There are pirates in the south. He would know that. Fortunately, I was unharmed. Kennedy was able to subdue.'

Manvell looked over at an unmarked Kennedy.

'You are more powerful than you seem, pirate.'

Kennedy saluted.

Manvell bent to Dandon's face. The eyes were closed and swollen. The whole head seemed bigger. His arms over the sides of the table trembled.

'He is asleep,' Coxon said. 'The doctor's draught.'

Manvell straightened.

'Or beaten senseless.'

Coxon pretended confusion.

'Do you suggest something inappropriate, Mister Manvell?'

'No, Captain. I do not *suggest*.'

'You are not entitled to opinion, Lieutenant. Unless it be granted you.' Coxon stood close. 'The pirate took advantage.

280

Kennedy came to my assistance. They fought. The confines of the hold afforded him his injuries.'

Manvell took off his straw hat, feeling himself foolish in his shore clothes.

'Then I would like it noted in the log that I think this man has been beaten unjustly.'

'This *man*?' Coxon looked between the table and Manvell. 'This is a *pirate*, Lieutenant. We have been around this conversation before. This pirate holds vital information concerning the purpose of our mission!'

'Our mission, Captain – respectfully – was to join Captain Ogle and hunt for Roberts and Devlin together. It was not some glory lust for gold!'

'The gold has no part of it. That is for our men. Would you have me tell them that you wish to deny them so? I have acted on more pertinent intelligence which has moved us from our orders.'

'Yet you need more? And this *man* has it all!'

'I believe you were with me on Bourbon, Lieutenant? Was I not questioning pirates? Found Devlin's closest ally? Whom – I should add – Ogle would not know from a horse's arse, sir! There is reason in sending me to this sea!'

Manvell took a step back from Coxon's reddened face. He had not said anything that he regretted and he would pause before he did. His mouth opened, then a croak from the table made them both still and stare.

'*Thomas*?' Dandon coughed. 'Mister Howard?' He tried to lift a hand.

Howard was shaking. He clenched his fists and tensed the sensation away. He was drawn forward by the voice and the pained eye. Kennedy started also but Manvell froze him with a glare.

Howard was beside the table. He held the weightless hand.
He saw that Dandon's cheek lay in a pool of sweat and saliva.
He had nothing to wipe it away save his own sleeve and he
carefully lifted Dandon's head to do so.

'You are hurt, Mister Dandon, sir. You should rest.'

'. . . *Hurt but am not slain.*' Dandon almost smiled. He
closed his eyes and Howard softly put the head back to the
table. He smiled then.

'Good boy. Brave boy,' he mumbled and dropped his hand
from Howard's.

Coxon and Manvell stood silent as Howard withdrew.

'He's out again, Captain,' he said, and fell in between them
both.

They watched Dandon's back rise and fall. Manvell broke
the silence.

'What now, Captain?'

Coxon put a hand on Howard's shoulder.

'He will need to be restrained again when he wakes. He has
forced it on himself with his attempted escape.'

Manvell felt his stomach twist. The time had passed for him
to regret his words.

'I wish to comment in the log, Captain. The treatment of
this prisoner is not fitting to my station as the *Standard*'s First.
As entreated to me.'

Coxon took his hand from Howard's shoulder.

'We should discuss over supper.'

He thought on his papers. The orders over all others. The
*Standard*'s logs just tinder, Manvell's words worthless. Back in
England Manvell might become privileged; once Devlin was
done, once the king's honour had been restored. He would
understand everything then.

'But he shall be restrained again,' he said.

The bell rang above them. The ship was at last back to order.

'To supper, gentlemen. You can explain to me, Christopher, your sympathy over pirates who attack your captain.' Coxon walked away. 'Change your dress. Thomas, you will tell me of your specimens.'

'With respect, Captain,' Howard said, 'I should like to attend to the pirate and secure him. As is fitting.'

Coxon stopped. He did not turn to Howard.

'Granted,' he said. 'I will deliver you some pork pie. Kennedy will assist.' He ducked away through the dark.

Manvell tugged Howard's shirt, pulled him to his face.

'Good show,' he said. 'I will mention at supper. With the others. Have no fear, Thomas.'

Howard pulled his sleeve free.

'I don't, sir.' He threw his straw hat to a corner. 'It is a Christian thing. As you said. Do not count me with your conspiracies. If you please.'

Coxon ordered from the stair. 'Manvell! Come!'

Manvell leant into Howard's face. He looked once at Kennedy near the manger who retreated from earshot.

'He is mad you know. He endangers us all with this pirate. We have broken our orders.'

Howard looked back to the table.

'No,' he said. 'The difference is that he does not wait for orders and papers. That is how the pirates win. Too many simply wait. He is going for the throat. I have seen their axes and guns. He is becoming them.'

'*Manvell*!' Coxon bellowed.

Howard pushed Manvell to the dark.

'I know what I'm doing, sir. Do *yours*.'

Manvell took his hand, not offered.

'Come find me later,' he said.

Howard dropped the hand.

'You are the First, sir. Do as your position. *Please.*'

He went to the table, and Manvell could find no more words.

He followed his captain.

# Chapter Thirty

*T*he night now. Coxon was dressed for a dinner he had
no appetite for. The pirate had not spoken. He had
Kennedy wrap his own fists with soaked cloth and beat at him
in his chains, so that his hanging arms punished him as much
as the bludgeoning hands.

Kennedy smashed against his liver, at his sides, at his groin.
And still nothing came from the pirate except sweat. Not
even the lies that Coxon had expected. Only when Kennedy
himself folded over exhausted did the pirate speak, as Coxon
asked his question once more.

'Where is he, Dandon?'

The pirate spat. It strung from his lip and he shook it free
like a dog.

'Where he has always been, John,' he flashed his gold caps.
'In your dreams.'

Coxon paled. He stared at the pirate as if he had discovered witchcraft in the world.

'Take him down,' he said to Kennedy. 'He's dying.'

'I know a priest, John,' Dandon said. 'I know where you
can find him for my end.' He passed out with the grin still on
his face.

Coxon looked in the mirror, an old speckled glass he had
carried with him for more than twenty years. It had aged with

him. Almost black in places, warped and opaque, it reflected well. He lowered his eyes from himself.

He had starved the pirate and he did not talk. He had beaten and tortured him and he did not talk. He looked again at the mirror and let it reflect on the marvel of friendship he did not know. The emptiness of the room figured behind him. It held the absence of portrait frames he had bought and filled in his life, mementoes of intimacy.

There were only tools and maps and the books where he lived the lives of other men.

He gleaned the bright brown leather of the Cervantes volume Devlin had given him the last time they met. He turned to it, half-expecting it to not belong in the real world and vanish with the mirror.

He walked to the shelf and his hand was almost upon it when a knock on the door came and broke him from his reverie. He knew that knock by now.

'Come, Christopher.'

Manvell ducked his way in. Bright in a blue riding coat. In all the time they had been at sea Manvell's wardrobe, Coxon noted, had still not rotated.

'What is it?' Coxon asked as he tidied his waistcoat. 'A private conversation not fit for mess?'

It was approaching nine o'clock but the sky was still golden in the stern windows. They had been underway for two hours. Without a word from the pirate they were heading north-west, coursing for the Comoros for now. Coursing to meet Ogle and Herdman. The ship had become sullen that the gold was slipping away like the hue of the sky.

'No, sir, I mean . . . *John*,' Manvell dipped his head. 'I just wondered when I might make my entry into the log regarding the *Standard*'s treatment of the prisoner?'

Coxon sighed and lost interest in his threadbare waistcoat's loose buttons.

'If he talks would you still call him the "prisoner" or would he be the pirate then?'

'Would that matter?'

'No. No, I suppose not.'

Coxon picked up his hat from the table, thought on the letters that would exonerate him from all of this. If he could but share them Manvell would not stand so indignant and Howard would not look at him so ashamed. He had become an agent for men in black cloth but he now understood why. They operated so to protect. To protect those beneath them, even if it was just from themselves.

No matter. He still had tricks to press young men.

'Christopher, I have decided that the pirate will not talk. Questioning him further will not serve. We need to consider other avenues to find Devlin.'

'Perhaps the *Standard* would consider the return to our original orders?' Manvell hoped. 'Ogle and Herdman. And hunt for Roberts – and Devlin. Is that not why we are shaping for the Comoros?'

'In part.' Coxon spied Manvell's deerskin slippers and looked down at his own cracked, wooden-soled shoes. He should have married a duke's daughter; he should have attended more balls. Then he remembered that Manvell was only a publican's son and forgot his envy. He had done well, that was all.

'In "part", sir?' Manvell's hopes fell.

Coxon was still gazing at his own pinchbeck-buckled shoes with the sloping heels.

'It would be unfair to the men to join up and share their gold with other crews. I still intend to capture Devlin on our own. We more than outgun him. And your sword must be worth ten.'

'How would we achieve such?'

Coxon looked surprised at his First's ignorance.

'The letter of course, Christopher. The one you left with the priest. Its purpose was to let Devlin know we had his man and Kennedy. To let his men know that their captain had murdered Kennedy's father and that the poor boy wants revenge. And as Kennedy became a pirate because of it Devlin would have to accord with that. Accord to the codes they live by that pass for their honour. I had hoped that it might set their minds to doubting their captain. He might leave his man, captured, but not refuse to meet Kennedy.'

Coxon looked over to the worn Cervantes. 'But I knew he could not leave his man. He travelled half the world before for one of them. All for a porcelain cup. I have played him, Christopher. We will head for Juan de Nova off of Madagascar and wait for Devlin there. I have told him so in the letter. That is where we will have our day with him. It is the longer plan. I had hoped the pirate would tell all but when Devlin returns to Bourbon for his man we have won.' He clasped Manvell's shoulders proudly. Proud of himself. Proud of the lessons he was imparting.

'*If* he returns for him,' Manvell said. 'This is all supposition is it not?'

Coxon marvelled at the lack of instinct that some men seemed to possess. To him it was akin to fashioning a rope, tying it around the object of your desire and then waiting to feel a tug. Somewhere between childhood and manhood some men plainly let go the rope and fell to paper and laws – lost faith in the feelings which kept them from briers and nettles as children.

'Christopher, we know that Devlin was at Sierra Leone before us. Had the same information. He drops his man at Bourbon. Somewhere is his treasure. A Porto priest in a French church. The *Virgin of the Cape* carrying Porto gold. It is not supposition. It is a clock winding down.

'He will be on my footsteps instead of us seeking him. You will return to your father-in-law a rich man. Rich in service also. A captaincy shall be my recommendation. You will see it just so.' He gave as much as he thought he could deliver.

'There is much here that I cannot share, but hold that I have only the *Standard*'s concerns before me. Devlin may have already returned to Bourbon. He has the letter and we are only days away from glory.'

Manvell reached into his coat. Coxon's hands dropped as Manvell pulled out the folded paper.

Coxon did not see just the black seal and ribbon on the swan white packet but also a grey tombstone heaved into place, Devlin's name in Coxon's script plain on its face.

'You mean this letter, John?' Manvell said.

# Chapter Thirty-One

*M*anvell was on the floor, his hand to his mouth where the blow had struck. The letter lay beside him.

'You *fool!*' Coxon stood over him. 'You bloody fool!' He kicked Manvell down as he tried to rise.

'*Ponce! Punk!* Do you know what you've *done*?'

Manvell pushed himself up to sit.

He saw Coxon then. Stocky and strong with fists and solid feet and hating as he panted over him.

The man who had fought the French and the Spanish and then had to swallow them both as allies. The man sent to hunt for pirates.

'I have protected my ship.' Manvell wiped his lip. No blood. His strong jaw or Coxon holding back, as if smiting a child.

'You want to bring a pirate frigate upon us. Alone. When we could have two men-of-war to go against them. As per our orders. Go for Roberts. He who has taken hundreds of ships. Not your bloody valet!'

'*Coward!*' Coxon spat. 'You have lost everything!' He stood back.

There was pressure in his chest and arms, a need to vent more violence but he held it back. The tempering of a good man of strength. His head went light and the room brightened and he let Manvell climb to his feet.

'Do you think the pirates would not know of three warships on the ocean?' Coxon stomped the room.

'They would scatter like rats from a light. But one ship? One ship is a dare. A slight. A challenge. And me upon it. And Kennedy. That would be the game they live for. Draw them. Your obtuseness I'm sure will get you a fine place on the Board and a good country seat. Is your ambition, sir, just to the fattening of your arse?'

Manvell brushed himself down.

'I bow to your superior knowledge of pirates, Captain. But this has gone beyond. You have not acted as the *Standard*. With Ogle and Herdman we were to hunt, to protect. You have confided in pirates and slave-traders. You condone torture of prisoners. Your men lust for gold not duty. Even Howard says you have become one of them.'

He watched Coxon go to his desk and push upon it with white knuckles, his head hung.

'You have disobeyed orders, Manvell,' he said, turned away. 'I will charge you with that.'

'I will contest,' Manvell said calmly. 'My objection will be based on my log entry and my concern for the *Standard* and her prisoner.' He rubbed his side where Coxon's shoe had delved.

'I shall not mention the assault upon my person. Spirited as it was.'

'So we say to the men that we are not for the gold? That because of my First's insistence we are coursing back. Will that go well? Shall I make my speech before breakfast?' He swung back from the desk. 'I will take you from them. For your own safety.'

He went for the door, pulled the powerful marine through it.

'Take Lieutenant Manvell. Confine him to his quarters. He is under my arrest pending inquiry. Restrain him in irons if he protests. He is to be denied parole.'

Manvell shook his head incredulously.

'On what charge?'

'On *my* charge!' Coxon shouted him down and then calmed himself.

'Do not make me say it now, Manvell. You should concentrate on your defence. For the time when we return to England. Do not wish to let the *Standard* know now.'

The marine shouldered his musket and grappled Manvell into his ham fists.

Manvell held fast.

'It is my prerogative, Captain, to ask to have a man to mediate.' He stiffened but did not struggle. 'I ask for Lieutenant Howard.'

'No,' Coxon said. 'Thomas . . . Mister Howard will now be my First.' He let the marine hear him, eyed him just so.

'You have cost the men their gold. It will be for your own protection.'

Manvell smirked.

'You want to say "mutiny" don't you, John? In front of this man? I have seen how you work the common man.'

The marine's fists clamped harder.

Coxon crossed his arms. He had no need to say the word. The touchpaper lit.

'I *am* the common. You have forgotten that. Take him away,' he tossed his head to the door. 'I will inform the *Standard* at supper.'

The marine had to dance Manvell from the room and his beef felt the steel of the body held fast in his arms.

'You cannot silence me, John!' Manvell yelled, hoped for

more of the ship to hear as he was dragged through the coach. 'What I have done is for the good of the ship!'

'I'll make sure to tell the men's wives how well you cost them their share. For the good of the ship. That will feed their children well!'

He slammed the door, fumbled with the weak brass latch with fingers that seemed engorged. He put his hands to his stomach to settle the rising sickness and looked down at the unsent letter. The pirate's name glared up at him.

*'Oh, John. What will you do now?'*

He left it on the floor and went for a drink to steady his shaking arms. He needed to think. An empty chair at supper. That would be a conversation not conducive to their meal. Possibly the worst words to share between officers and words that he had never had to say before. Not in thirty years. He sank a full glass of rum.

No matter. Manvell had disobeyed his orders, sound orders. A letter to Devlin, a simple hook now slipped. So what next?

He splashed rum in his glass again and drank before his mouth had dried from the last – but paused and turned with the drink still at his lips as he noticed his window latches rattle.

They banged and pulled and pushed to be open and then stilled as the ghost that yanked at them let go and moved on.

Coxon walked to the casements and looked down at the water below that lay as flat as glass; and then, as if caught out by his observation, the sea bashfully went back to making undulating waves and a creamy wake.

A knock at the door turned him back round. He bid the steward in to light the stern lanterns. He did not know his name.

'Did you spy that wind, man?' Coxon asked.

'No, Cap'n?' the man opened the windows and tended to his tallow and candles on poles. 'Although it is about, Cap'n. North I reckons. This be a large ocean for winds. That's why no civil man lives here.'

Coxon passed the man his rum to finish.

'How's the ship? The humour?'

The steward gulped the rum.

'The whole is much enamoured for the gold, Cap'n. All of 'em hard for pirates, thanks to you, Cap'n.' He gave back the glass with a wink. 'You just say the word and we'll walk that pirate round the deck. He'll talk then, Cap'n, so he will.'

Coxon put down the glass.

'Much obliged. It may come to that, sailor.' He picked up the bottle and drank straight. Gave it over for the steward to do the same.

'The men are not afraid of pirates I take it?'

The bottle went high.

'No, Cap'n. Ain't you got one of Roberts's dogs aiding us? And you Devlin's master before.' The bottle came back gratefully.

Coxon tipped it in salute.

'I have an empty chair at my table, my man. If not for the impropriety it would suggest I should have you fill it. My officers could learn some appreciation from you.'

The steward blushed and gathered his things. 'If that be all, Cap'n.'

Both men marked their stations, the bottle corked. Coxon dismissed him and waited for the door to close before uncorking the bottle again.

Howard, he thought, as he drank.

I have lost Manvell. Him I thought the best. I must keep Thomas Howard to my side. Too late to go back to Bourbon?

Deliver the note? Perhaps wait a degree north, along the latitude? Catch Devlin in a net. But he could long be gone from Bourbon. Manvell has cost all.

Coxon's only hope was that Devlin would learn from the priest that it was he who took Dandon. That Devlin would also then hunt for him. Two needles looking for each other in a bottle of hay.

He drank away the worst of his thoughts and, in truth, the rum did ease, as it was made to. The rum eased him, and the sailor who had lit his lamps.

Speak to Thomas Howard at supper over tortoise liver, gravy and bread. He corked the bottle again. There was no answer there. The answer was in the youth. The answer always in youth. He picked up the letter.

Thomas Howard would hold the faith.

It had taken a run to Doctor Howe to secure some laudanum. The doctor could only raise a hand in agreement as he muttered into his pillow that the draught was exactly what the wounded man required and Thomas Howard applied it to a leather mug of rum and plied it into Walter Kennedy's hand. And Kennedy was not in the habit of refusing mugs of rum from officers.

Ten minutes later Kennedy had slumped to the deck and was snoring like the doctor, and then Thomas Howard had his arms under Dandon's shoulders and was hauling him to the gundeck. The first watch was at supper above. He had half an hour when the deck would be empty. His supper would be after the second watch. That was the only fact that he would be assured of. Between now and then he was chancing that no soul would come across him heaving Dandon up from the hold.

Dandon stirred awake and eased Thomas Howard's burden. They climbed together, their shoulders locked. Dandon protested aloud.

'Thomas? What is this?'

'I am getting you out of here, sir. Be quiet now.'

They reached the gundeck. Thomas had opened a port, had set a ladder from it and a boat waiting bobbing below. He had stolen a boat. When he had swung it over the side he had imagined its ropes around his neck.

Providently, no-one had seen.

The night had covered and no-one had seen.

Men were at supper one deck below and no-one had seen. Or cared not: had not cared to see an officer at some private business. Men had swung for less.

The rumour of the First being held in irons had already become fact. Turn your pipe to windward and let the young officer to his noose.

Dandon became strong now. He gripped himself against the gun as Howard slung a bag to the boat below.

'This is madness, Thomas! Hold now. I wish no part!'

Howard pulled him by his shirt.

'They will kill you! Do you understand? It is night. By morning you will be gone. Gone from me.'

'Gone where?'

'There is a compass in the boat. East and you will be back at Île de France. There are pirates there.' He set to whispering. 'Or west and Bourbon. Please, sir. You saved me once. I put your coat in the boat. Your yellow coat. Please move now.'

Dandon felt himself being pulled towards an open square.

'I am to leap? My faith is not that strong.'

'I have set a Jacob's ladder to the boat. Climb down.'

They shared hands in the dark like walking a rural lane at night. Dandon stared at a cannon's mouth as he let himself through a hole and felt the wind whip at him.

'We are moving!' he declared.

'Barely. Fore-course only. I will release the boat when you are free.'

'I will be crushed!'

'Are you not a sailor, sir?'

'No I am not! You have perceived me wrong, Thomas.' He tried to scramble back through the hole. Thomas Howard held him by his wrists and pulled his face to him.

'Go!' he pleaded. 'You must go. I cannot stand to—' He let the wrists fall to hands and Dandon's feet hit the slats of the ladder.

'You did me good once. See it as no more than that. I am willing to fight pirates. I will hold with my captain . . . but I do not understand what this is.' He let his hands slip and Dandon caught the lip of the port hole.

'Thomas, you will be in trouble for this.'

Thomas Howard stood back from the hole.

'I was in trouble from the moment I saw you once more.' He smiled and became the boy again and wiped his eyes. 'We have a tradition, I feel.'

'Aye,' Dandon said. 'A corrupt tradition.' And he vanished from the port hole.

Howard leaned out through the hole and saw that already Dandon was in the bucking boat.

'I will release you!' he called. 'You are belayed above. Hold on to the gunwales.'

'Wait!' Dandon cupped his hands to his mouth. 'Do I have wine?'

'Brandy. Wrapped inside your coat lest it break.'

'Bless you!'

'Fare well, sir! And thank you! I never got a chance to say it.'

'I have brandy, what else is there to say? But hold Mister Howard.'

Howard stretched further out of the port.

Dandon, his hands still cupped and masking his voice just for Howard, whispered up to the freeboard.

'To save your punishment! I can afford some small word! Something to give our good John!'

'But you did not talk?' Howard rubbed away tears now but only from the wind against the port and the spray of the salient sea.

'I give willingly.'

'I must cut the boat now.'

Dandon stood. The boat objected and Howard put his arm out motioning him to sit but still he called up.

'Tell John that the Portos call the islands "The Three Brothers and the Seven Sisters". It is the largest one that Devlin has gone to. Where the treasure lies. You mind me, Thomas.' He lowered his voice and saluted. 'You mind me, Thomas.' He sat as the officer vanished from the hole.

Mere moments passed, a rope hit the water and Dandon watched the ship coast away and saw a white face against the gunwale and an arm that waved and waved until he could no longer perceive it against the blackening sky.

He rubbed his swollen eyes and went through the hemp sack and his coat for the brandy buried under the cheese and bread. He found also a compass with a mirror and fishing line and hook.

He popped the cork just as the *Standard* stopped buffeting the boat and the sea opened up around him like he was sitting on the moon.

He took a long draught, becoming Dandon again as something like strength returned to his arms and he flexed his fingers that had become dead. He saluted the *Standard*'s stern lights with the bottle.

'Good boy, brave boy,' he said, and drank long.

Often he had drunk without tasting. He had now gone days without wine and to him that was like days without sunlight.

He was lost to the bottle, he knew that. But now and then one bottle came along that meant something.

He let it roll in his mouth, allowed the brandy to wallow down his gullet like an oyster. Too much of what he drank and ate was stolen. Rarely was it gifted.

He let the waves roll him. The boat had a sail and he would make something of that soon.

For now he hugged his brandy, for the burns, for his closed eyes and aching organs that had taken the blows of his silence, and lastly for the apothecary boy he had once been.

He hugged his brandy and wept.

For no-one could see him do it.

# Chapter Thirty-Two

*I*t had been a silent dinner. Thomas Howard apologised that a brief sickness had come over him and meant he was unable to attend. Manvell was in irons in the same quarter. For a moment Coxon thought on the words they could whisper to each other through the thin hemp walls.

His table spelled misery now. Just the drunken doctor and the dull sailing-master. He was unable to discern which of them was worse company and felt strangely disembodied as he watched them tediously chase their peas around their plates; Coxon saw the tragedy of himself seated and eating with them.

When they first met he had seen them as men holding out for their pension, forgotten and aged, wasted and dilettante. He had scorned them and chortled about them with his strong young men, his favoured companions, as stalwart as he saw himself in the mirror that showed no age. Now he was sitting in the dark corner table at the wedding feast with the forgotten cousins and spinster aunts; the table where the servants forgot to pour. The sound of cutlery scraping irritating his teeth like chewing iron filings.

'Doctor,' he said at last, leaning back. 'Perhaps if you were to pierce your peas with your fork. Might that suffice? Rather than concentrating on your tongue between your lips for us all to view and sweeping them with a broom.'

'Sir?' Doctor Howe flushed more than usual.

Coxon demonstrated with his own remnants.

'*La!*' He popped the pea satisfactorily between his teeth.

Doctor Howe followed, confused and unsure, like an ape given a mirror. He smiled bashfully as he skewered his strays.

A knock on the door was welcome distraction.

It was the bosun, Abel Wales. Since Manvell had been indisposed Coxon had made a point to learn the man's name. Abel wrung his cap through his hands and tapped his forehead twice.

'Beg your pardon, Captain, sorry to disturb.'

'What is it, Wales?' Coxon wiped his mouth and pushed back his chair. He knew the face of a man scared to talk but bound to do so.

'The man Kennedy is dead for the drink.' Wales wrung his hands. 'And we're missing a boat, Captain.'

He quickly moved aside as Coxon's advance looked set to collide with him. He stumbled on his last words, used them as a shield as he called after the captain.

'The pirate is gone.'


Coxon exploded into the mess. Instinctively men stood or covered their plates and mugs as if they were stolen. The only place to look was towards him and the bosun and his team with their belaying pins.

'Who let the pirate go? Which of you has done this treachery?'

He ducked through the water bags and isinglass lanterns expertly yet still seemed at full furious height to them.

'I will take this as mutiny!' He looked at them all.

'If the man does not present himself I will cast you all as mutinous! Every man will be punished!'

They looked back at him now with puzzled eyes. But he had seen those looks before also.

'Do not think it cannot be done!' He wheeled back to the bosun with accusing finger.

'That includes you all! You are all in this! If you do not find this traitor you will be cast as the rest! The dereliction of your watch is enough to get you the lash!'

He saw his arm pointing, saw it tremble. He pulled it back and drew from his past resolve to damp his ill humour, the same resolve from decades ago when French frigates glinted on the horizon and midshipmen flapped about his decks. He straightened his cuffs and waistcoat.

'I trust you, lads, to root out the criminal. Someone has cost you your gold. That is what has drawn my anger. My concern for you. It is troubled times for all of us unless you be kings and Whigs.'

He moved back towards the stair, through the bosun's team playing with their wood and knotted rope and found Thomas Howard standing waiting at the foot.

'It was me, Captain,' Howard said and braced himself. 'I let him go.' His face drained white, a boy again as Coxon loomed over him. 'No other is to blame.'

Coxon only felt his shoulder move but he was sure that it must have been only him that punched Thomas Howard's face and sent him skidding on his back all the way to the scuttlebutt.

He watched the lieutenant sit up and rub his face then climbed the companion for air, for space where there would be no other face to look at, but the bosun, Abel Wales, was already at his back.

'Captain?' he said and waited for the head to turn.

'What do you want done with him? With Mister Howard, Captain.'

Coxon straightened for a deep breath, put his hand on the man's shoulder.

'I'm sorry for my words before. I was angry. I must consider what has occurred.'

'And Mister Howard?'

Coxon withdrew his hand.

'This is an Article of War, Mister Wales. You will be part of the ship's court. Mister Howard will be kept fasting and awake. You will see to it that he knot his own cat by dawn.'

# Chapter Thirty-Three

*T*hey began at dawn. Thirty of them came now, rowed from the ship under lantern in the night from the *Shadow*. And the wall grew. And the tide kept back. And the cave appeared with the sun.

Devlin threw his mug of tea to the sand and came down the beach.

'That should do it,' he said and planted his hands on his hips like a boy admiring his first garden fort. 'Enough to take a boat in.'

Peter Sam admired less.

'We don't know how many are in there waiting. They'd have seen the water fall. Cocking their arms to us to come.'

Devlin looked back.

'Why would that hinder us? Only men. Only guns.'

'It's *pirates* and guns,' Peter Sam snapped. 'That's three or four guns a piece and grenadoes and maybe a cannon or two. As we would.'

'As we will,' Devlin said. 'Pound of lead for pound of flesh.'

The men began to return from the wall, slapping each other's backs. Peter Sam came in closer to Devlin, so as not to be heard.

'And suppose that Levasseur has gone with the greater part of the gold? That this here is his cave. Men protecting. That this is where they hide out and it's just food and a hold for dyes and sail-cloth and we're chasing a tartar?'

'Look at that dawn, Peter,' Devlin stood aside as if that was the only way Peter Sam could see it. 'If what you say was true it would be raining now and that wall would fall. Instead we've got maybe six hours before the water comes back. Let's to it.'

The pot rattled over the fire-pit and the ash blew and picked up the sand and Devlin and Peter were too slow to close their eyes as it swathed them.

They turned away, felt the wind-blown grains scratch their necks. Their men ducked and shielded their eyes as the sand danced along the beach like powder and whipped around the white rocks. The trees crashed like the surf, appeared to walk towards the waterline.

Then it was gone and all was still again. The birds recovered before the men and their whoops and whistles told each other of what had happened like gossiping market-wives.

Peter Sam brushed his beard and eyes.

'You were saying there, Patrick?'

Inside, beneath the earth, within the earth, Levasseur had not slept. He had sat on his throne of stone after he had made his preparations, his reparations, and waited for a sign in his own cathedral.

He heard the pool complaining as the wind pulled it away. He came to the edge to watch sand shimmer like diamonds in the shafts of light as air rushed through the narrow hole opposite.

Sign enough.

He looked down at the pool and the bodies whirling like driftwood.

That would shock them. He wiped his sweating lip. Slow them down with the horror of Levasseur about to face them.

He giggled his way back to the cross and patted it as if its gold were shoulder to shoulder in his conspiracy. He loaded his belt with pistols and cutlass and regretted that he had not taken the time to carry them to the outcrop of rock beneath the hole. But then he had been exhausted, having spent the night dragging the six-pound cannon up there to stare down, and the bodies into the pool to surprise.

He watched the water steady itself and become glass, and the sand drifted down on the bodies as they slowed in their spinning. A few seemed to stand in the water as if alive but bobbed like fishing lures as they swelled with the water. Priests and pirates linking arms and kissing, O'Neill's body chief amongst them, staring up with his black hole as if in song. The priest's arrogance quelled.

Levasseur went to wait by his gun.

They did not need a light. The water glowed beneath the boat, lit by the day receding behind them as they paddled further in, the oars out of the thole pins for silent running. The eight pirates were dappled with the supernatural light, the surface of the water misting in the heat as they cut through it.

Devlin was first, seated at the bow, then Peter Sam, always behind him. Hugh Harris, Adam Cowrie and the four others crouched at the oars and tiller. They did not speak. Any word would echo forwards to the cavern, announcing them as surely as gunshot.

The tide played against the walls and Peter Sam noted where the mark was greenest and alive: nine feet above their gunwale. How quickly did that nine feet fill? he wondered. How quickly would their boat and bones be crushed?

He looked back at the mouth of the sea-cave, as distant now as if looking up from the bottom of a well; and then Devlin put his hand to him and was holding out his other over the bow.

Ahead they saw a brighter green, alive by shafts of light like the lattice of the rays through the deck hatches. And then they reached for their pistols as the first of the heads revolved into view.

Someone cursed as a floating body turned lazily into the light. Devlin glared behind him as the miscreant's voice echoed around them and the pirate ducked his head away from his captain's stare.

They pulled in the oars as bodies flapped against them. Grey faces scraped against the boards. Flaccid arms appeared to try to push them back. Devlin shared a look with Peter Sam and then down at the carrion circling the boat like sharks.

Levasseur had heard the English oath and slid himself along the rock to the vent of the gun, the smouldering match wrapped around his wrist. He would only have to put the heel of his hand to the touch-hole.

A string sack of fifty half-inch balls of grapeshot waited in front of the bag of powder, already pierced. It was sixty feet from the gun's black mouth to where the cave met the pool. The powder would hiss and flare and crawl to its home. Then, that pause, that prick of doubt wondering if the trail had gone out, and then the roar and bellow and the flying carriage and cry of pain from the iron. And skulls and bones would become skulls and bones. Apparent and apart. Ragged with meat.

Levasseur's gun did not have the room to recoil. He would
have to leap clear; not knowing where it would spend its fury
with only a mountain to fly back against. And then he would
pull his brace of pistols and finish the job. And they would
leave his gold. Leave his kingdom. Join the rest of the traitors
and their stinking traitors' flesh.

He wiped his face clean of sweat again, checked the match.
And then they came.

They had turned an oar into a bowsprit as the bow peeped
out of the cave and their traitor's black rag dipped forward
into the water.

Did they think he would fear that? That he would shiver at
a skull in a compass rose with crossed pistols?

He saw the first of their huddled bodies, crouching like
cowards and he put his wrist to the powder and scuttled away.
Half the boat now and more bodies. He hid in the shadows, a
chameleon against the rock, as he had been for weeks with the
dust and the damp, almost a lichen. He pulled his pistols and
aimed at the bodies hiding in the boat.

Cowards. Traitors.

The powder's hiss vanished down the vent, seeking its
purpose. It met powder and bit down, came alive. And the
cavern exploded with its life. Life to end life.

The flag ripped, its grinning skull's teeth rent. The balls
chewed through the boat and the men. The thunder of the
cannon seemed almost visible and echoed cracking round the
cavern long after the gun had shattered the rock behind and
jumped to the pool. The water boiled as it swallowed, the iron
to lay there forever.

Levasseur shook the ringing from his head and levelled two
pistols. Dust fell on his arms, then chips of stone. He ignored,
fired down into the stunned bodies, the ones not already

wrecked, his shots muffled by the pounding echo now ripping stone from the ceiling.

He stood, panting, the cannon-smoke hanging.

He surveyed his work, dropped the spent pistols and pulled more of his guns to punish the interlopers.

The boat limped in now, its flag spread on the water. He puffed his chest at the bodies splayed all about.

Their grey faces were familiar. Drawn and putrescent. Their bodies fat and drowned.

A crack from the water and a shot sang and split the rock beside his head, sending dust into his good eye.

Only Peter Sam had been strong enough to heave the dead bodies into the boat. He wedged them into place and slipped over the side to join the others treading water and pushing the boat into the cavern. He had to hang onto Hugh Harris; Peter Sam was not the strongest swimmer.

They had left their weapons and loads in the boat, for wet powder was the end of the game, all except Devlin who held his load above his head and clung at rock and then had crept along into the cave as the cannon splintered the boat.

The water bucked, dust fell, the sound blinded, the cannon ploughed into the pool and Devlin had fired at Levasseur, calm as turning a page in a book.

Levasseur bolted from the shot, and the pirates went to the sinking boat for their pistols and musketoons. They held beneath the gunwales, the steel at their hip dragging, their bodies anticipating more lead and they looked to the cavern's smoking walls for a bank of enemies.

Nothing. Empty. A tomb. A grave for the already dead and broken now slumping into the water; drowning with the pirates' guns. Hugh Harris, with Peter Sam weighing him down, yelled as the pool took his twin Dolep pistols. He beat his fist against the water. The others sculled to the far side and watched Devlin find purchase and climb the wall as two more pistol shots peppered the stone around him. He did not stop and made the ledge as Levasseur ran to his stockpile of arms.

Hugh Harris struggled with Peter Sam wrapped around him like a cape. 'I thinks you too fat, Peter,' he said. 'Do me a favour,' he pushed him to the last wood of the boat still float-ing, 'don't drown.'

Peter Sam clutched the wood as Hugh followed his captain.

'Damn you, Harris!' he scowled and dug his nails into the boat.

Devlin belted his pistol. He pulled his hanger, cleared the ebony knife from behind his back. That would be the way now. Steel. Close quarters. Teeth and fists. There was only one man here. Nothing new, not even worth a deeper breath.

He pressed on around the walls. Soaked and heavy. An empty pistol and his blade running wet. Against the pirate who had taken the largest prize on the earth.

Levasseur set himself now to meet the man who would take it from him.


Outside, the other boats had heard the blast, had seen it quake across the water. High up against the mountain, against the green, they saw smoke rising from some other place attached to the cave. They picked up their oars and powered to the cave without word or hesitating thought.


Devlin moved to the outcrop where the cannon had been, where it had recoiled to smash against the rock, only now the rock had cracked, stone had fallen, was still falling, and what must have been a small fissure was now an opening. He looked inside and up. Light. The descent where O'Neill had run to, surely.

While he climbed he had not seen Levasseur when the pistols missed. Was this his escape? Had he run from him?

A ringing report at his ear and he ducked, the shot spitting stone into his hair where his face had been.

He crouched and spun. Levasseur was on the ledge behind, with another pistol set, and for a blink Devlin avowed the colossal image of a pirate.

Pistols and apostles holstered across the chest. An eye-patch, a scar running beneath and to his lip. A snake-like form wrapped in cannon-smoke and clothes that could have been a hundred years old and cut for other men.

A pirate.

And for a moment, just a moment, Devlin felt his sword heavy. Too heavy.

Then the pistol cracked and he could see the ball and flame, his eye attached to it as it blurred over the pool and the heads of his men looking up at him, Peter Sam's last of all, and then he watched his left shoulder slam away from him.

He had never been shot at from the front before. On that day last year with Trouin it had been a ball to his back, a larger bore. From across the cave, from old powder, this was like a schoolboy's shove. Still, a spark went off in his brain, his heart in his ears and against his ribs as his body shocked.

He fell back, his legs failing him.

But the sword held.

One hand stretched to the sand but the fist with the steel in it was white and declared his signature across the chasm, to that pirate form ruling its stage.

Devlin was far from done.

He stumbled down the shale path, holding the steel before him as the terrible pirate, larger now, pulled again.

Words.

There were hollered words following the shot but Devlin could not hear them over the breaking and splash of rock. He saw Hugh Harris's head and boots rolling onto the ledge before him.

One ally.

Devlin's wounded arm pulsed as he moved to Hugh, his shirt arm just blood, and he watched another shot fly towards him like an arrow.

The stone falling drowned the ball and Devlin breathed again. He saw the rocks smash into the pool among his cursing men. He saw Hugh's back running wet, coming to stand, and Levasseur saw it also.

'Nice eye-patch,' Hugh said to Levasseur and unhooked his hatchet from his belt. 'I lost my pistols,' he rolled the hatchet in his palm. 'You be dead for that.'

Levasseur pulled his head back and looked down his substantial beak.

'English?' A French scowl.

Hugh shook his head.

'Pirate,' he said and skulked forwards.

'Dead,' said Levasseur and fired into Hugh's body with a snap of his wrist.

'*No!*' Devlin roared and was on Hugh before he fell, his sword out to Levasseur across them both, defending pointlessly against lead. His men remained lost in the water and shouted up at what they had seen.

Levasseur's palms rested on new pistols. He paused to pull. Gave a captain a moment with his lesser man.

312

Devlin held Hugh with his shattered shoulder, dropped his dagger beside him.

'Hugh?'

Hugh Harris pulled the back of Devlin's waistcoat, dragged himself up.

'Just me belt, Cap'n,' he grunted. 'Good. Italian. Like your boots.' Devlin looked down to the new stud decorating the six-inch-wide leather.

'But fuck, that hurt!' he hissed. 'And the fucking cave's falling in!' He passed his hatchet into good hands. 'I'll be up in a minute, Pat.' His gut denied and he went back down.

Devlin let him to the ground, stood over him. Faced Levasseur.

The hatchet dangled, loop already about his wrist, pitted sword in the other. The same Welsh steel he had faced René Trouin with. More a shield than a blade. Worn with worth. Earned. His clothes dripped like sand in a glass, wet as the dead below.

Levasseur pulled iron and lead against steel. And the steel came on to the pistol mouths. As all battles commence.

The lead. The steel. Both metals of the earth and shaped by fire and men for one purpose: the mettle of men. Strength of muscle and sinew, command of nerve and will.

'*Traitor!*' Levasseur cried. It was the first time Devlin had heard his voice, but the word seemed familiar.

'I am *Levasseur*! This is *my* place!' He stepped back to the shade of his chamber.

Devlin came on.

'Your cave is falling. Done for by your own cannon. Come. Leave with me.'

'You come for my gold, traitor!' The pistols sat cocked in both his hands, yet the man coming on was not afraid. This the gravy of his days.

'My men are here,' Devlin announced behind his blade. 'We'll take what you have. The priest's cross. I'll spare you. Lay down.'

'*Spare me?*' They were within a dozen feet of each other, a killing ground. And Levasseur fired, threw his pistols and pulled steel before waiting for the shots' end.

Devlin stood the pistol fire and heard the whistle as it passed. He still moved, and that was good enough, and through the gunsmoke steel finally met steel.

Levasseur's good eye widened, his mouth white with spittle, and they ran the swords' lengths to their hilts, fists almost to the floor.

Levasseur gritted his teeth as he felt the hone of the arm against his.

'Who are you, Monsieur? Before you die.'

Devlin pushed him back.

'Devlin. Did O'Neill not say? And this sword beat Trouin.'

Levasseur walked his quarter.

'They sent Trouin after me, *pirate*! He did not find.'

'I beat him and found you. You should measure that.' And Devlin took his quarter also.

They circled once, and that brought Devlin to see the glistening from the chamber, the stone throne, the gold cross gleaming upon it. And Levasseur saw the diverted glance and dove at his new enemy, a traitor like them all.

Below, the men were pelted by the hail of rock. They ducked under the water in time to miss the largest shards but with every stone they knew the cave was nearing its end, becoming mountain again, eroding aeons of nature's work. Hugh had climbed so why not they? They crawled and clawed their way up.

Peter Sam still clung to the upturned boat. Back, toward the cave mouth, he could see the new boats coming and shouted to the others. His brothers were safe now. Above he could hear the sounds of battle that came down like hammer on anvil even over the commotion of falling stone.

The combatants were out of sight but in his mind he could see every swipe and clash, and the muscles of his arms flinched at the familiar sounds. He could do nothing to help his captain. To help his friend. He waited for the final sound to come. But he had no doubt who would prevail.

Devlin beat Levasseur back for a pause of words.

'This is madness. We'll all be dead. Put down, *Capitaine*. Come out with me now.'

Levasseur howled and swung. The forte of Devlin's blade sparked against the Frenchman's. He had fought René Trouin and after that every sword felt slow. His blade had grown past the butcher's boy of his youth.

'You will fall,' he said – he promised – his sword up and beside his head. Grace given.

'*You* will fall,' Levasseur cried. 'Fall in *my kingdom!*'

He hacked as if Devlin were only a tree, and the pirate let the blows come on to sword and axe as if from the wooden sword of an enraged child. He parried easily, only turning his wrist. He had tussled whores harder. He pushed Levasseur away each time with the boarding-axe. Spared his head.

Devlin had the lead in his shoulder, and the true wound from the god Trouin still biting at his back, but Levasseur was no match. He knew that now. His pain was just payment for the skill he had gained.

A pirate stood before him, the man who had stolen the greatest haul on the sea. And Devlin was his master. He had practised harder with his men on Sundays. He was already counting his gold.

He let the blade come once more and turned it effortlessly to the stone and held it there with his own blade like a vice.

He put his Cordova boot to it, snapped it like a dead branch and kicked the poor steel to the pool in the same movement. His only concern was that his men would avoid its plunge.

He stepped back, turned the axe in his hand, let Levasseur marvel at the stump of blade in his fist and fall to his knees. The eye patch quivered as the brow moved in surprise.

'The words you are looking for,' Devlin said, 'are "*Dommage, Capitaine.*"'

He pricked Levasseur's bandoleer with his sword, made sure the pirate could feel the pressure behind the quillions.

Levasseur looked up along the blade to the cold face.

'We are of the same age, Monsieur. Young enough . . . old enough . . . to have seen the war. No doubt you became a pirate . . . for the same . . . as did I.'

'This life chose me,' Devlin said. He took away the sword and put out his hand, the hatchet hanging. 'Come. I'll get you out of here. For another day.'

Levasseur took the palm.

'You say "chose", Monsieur,' he grimaced. 'That is the difference.' His grip shifted fast to pull the wrist to the ground, his broken sword against Devlin's throat.

'Nothing *chose* me, dog!' The eye-patch quivered again. 'I am *this!*'

He pushed forward as Devlin's ebony dagger hissed between them and embedded itself in the leather eye patch.

Levasseur fell back in a scream, balled up in pain at Devlin's feet.

Devlin turned to Hugh Harris holding his belly, grinning for one wink.

'You couldn't have hit his good eye then, Hugh?' Devlin put his sword in his belt, checked his hand to his throat.

'I was aiming for his neck, Pat.'

Hugh stood and joined him. He put his boot to Levasseur's chest and pulled the dagger free without a grimace at the sucking sound that came with it and passed it back to Devlin. Levasseur stopped writhing and waited for his end.

Hugh whistled at the sight of the gold cross.

'Holy—'

'Holy is right,' Devlin said. 'The priest's Cross of Fire.'

Hugh sprang to it, to lay both hands on the cold metal.

Levasseur rolled up on his side to watch Hugh try to pull the cross from its throne.

The fight had gone from him, tears of blood coursed from under the eye-patch. The good eye was dry.

'It is mine,' he said. He clawed at the air near the gold.

Hugh grunted with the effort. 'It won't move, Pat! Help me.'

Devlin's feet began to quake. The dust and shale were now falling like a mist, sifting down his back into his shirt and boots.

'Leave it, Hugh! We have to go! The roof is falling!'

'We can't leave it, Pat!' Hugh bellowed back and pulled harder. 'It weighs a tonne!'

Levasseur sank, his claw now a fist.

'More . . . It weighs more . . .' and his eye swivelled to Devlin.

Devlin looked away, ran to Hugh, pulled him free.

'Hugh,' he dragged Hugh's neck to look at the ground, at the carpet of gold and jewels. 'If you fill your pockets you'll drown. We'll get out and come back.'

He twisted Hugh's head to the hole opposite.

'Look! There's where the priest came in,' he pulled the face to his. 'Where we'll come in. Come back again.'

Hugh looked at the gold cross, at his feet spilling with gold coins that trembled and chinked with the shaking of the cave.

'Aye, Pat,' he said. 'Aye. You were right. I've seen it. You were right.'

'You tell them that. If we get out. Bring Levasseur.'

They turned and stared at empty space.

Hugh scrambled to the place where the pirate had been, swept his hands over the earth as if the body hid in dust.

Devlin went to the edge of the pool, looked down at his boats now dragging in the others.

'This is his place,' he said. He looked back at the gold cross. 'Not ours.'

He spun the axe back to his fist, threw his arm behind and hurled it at the cross.

The gold pealed as the axe sank into its heart and quivered as it stuck. He imagined the wooden splinter buried within gasping at the air. And then his vision vanished beneath the rock.

'We'll be back, Hugh.'

They jumped the edge as the collapsing chamber clawed at their backs, dust fingers grabbing at their heels.

Silent seconds under the water, spiralling down, their boots on the faces of the dead pleading up at them. They kicked away with bullets of stone bubbling down past them and then broad arms heaved them back to the noise of the world falling.

'We're going,' Peter Sam declared, and the oars played fast and the rock chased them out, never harming but only warning them to be gone. Only Adam Cowrie, some religion still pressed in him, crossed himself when at last they met the day and swore that it was the cross within the cross that had blessed and saved them.

'You think so, Adam?' Devlin said with his old grin, slapping the dust from his hair while Peter Sam made a tourniquet for his arm.

'I didn't see it doing the last king of Ireland any favours.'

# Chapter Thirty-Four

*T*he bosun stood to his duty. Thomas Howard had been restrained in leg-irons in the larboard gangway. According to the Custom of the Sea he was to be given twenty-four hours to make his own cat-o-nine-tails. Under the circumstances he had only twelve as subject to the requirements of the service.

Coxon had pulled from his shelf the Fighting Instructions, part of which detailed the Articles of War of 1661.

It contained thirty-five acts of discipline all derived from the ancient Laws of Oleron, the customs of the sea that made the oceans a law unto themselves.

Thomas Howard had contravened at least four of them. Only one of them did not have 'death' as its last word, and that would do. He read it again. Plucked from it what he needed.

*Every Captain Commander and other Officer Seaman or*
*Soldier of any Ship Frigate or Vessel of War shall duly*
*observe the Commands of the Admiral or other his Superior*
*or Commander of any Squadron as well for the assailing or*
*setting upon any Fleet Squadron or Ships of the Enemy*
*Pirate or Rebels or joining Battle with them or making*
*defence against them as all other the Commands of the*
*Admiral or other his Superior Commander upon pain to*

*suffer death or other punishment as the quality of his neglect or offence shall deserve.*

He put the book open to the table. The bosun, the other warrant officers to read and agree. No need to mention the other disciplines, the more appropriate. They all read too final.

Outside, the bosun took the offered ropes from Howard. He tossed the worst of them to the sea and selected the nine best knotted for waxing and splicing to a cut piece of hawser. He said nothing, and Howard kept his eyes low, out of the sun.

The bosun went to select his team, one or two of them to be left-handed. No punishment had been set but no harm in being prepared. The choice of left-handers would make a difference when they lashed against the right-hand stroke already laid.

Coxon had chosen the indictment both out of compassion for Howard and the fact that mutilation or death would require warrant from higher authority. Manvell was set for Martial Court, which would be at sea but back in English waters. He did not want Howard to suffer so, to crush a promising young career. And he needed the ship to see the way of the path of sedition. He closed the book.

'Agreed, gentlemen? Twelve lashes.' The most available without a court.

The bosun, purser, master, carpenter and cook all concurred. The First Lieutenant was understandably absent.

The whole ship's company mustered, Manvell included, their heads uncovered. A hatch-grating lay wedged against the gunwale and the skidbeams. At the sound of the slam of wood

Coxon read the indictment and offered Howard his chance to speak.

Howard stared at the grating. He pulled his shirt over his head, let it fall and stepped forward.

'Bosun's mate,' Coxon ordered. There was no need to raise his voice; the ship stood already hushed. 'Do your duty.'

Howard's arm was taken and he was walked to the grating, his cheek laid upon it as his wrists were tied to its sides.

The bosun handed the cat to the first of the six. Custom. Tradition. One arm out to the prisoner's left shoulder, the arm with the cat at the same level. He would sweep the full length of the arm across the back, keeping it straight until one arm replaced the other now behind. A pivoting move was decreed so no undue or sadistic force could be used and no man could pull his sweep. The bosun's only power over the rule was to bring a left-handed man up next. His sweep would cut the knots across the lashes. Bring new flesh out. Each man before he threw would run the waxed tails through his fist to remove the clots of blood for his fresh swipe.

No man relished the duty but it was part of the service, and no captain truly wanted it done to his working crew. What point taking a man out of work by wounding him? Every hand weighed as much as every barrel and sail, as every nail and carpenter's band. The punishment was present for the threat only. Mostly.

But this was an officer who had cost them gold, had freed the pirate who had helped take their good captain's old ship with Devlin – the ship where their brothers had been slain, where this traitor himself had served and watched them die. And besides – and the whisper travelled the ship – how often the chance to strike the better-born that took a whip to them at any slight?

There had been no need for lots to be drawn.

The hawser rope and its tails were weighed by the first to step up. He slapped it to his hands and Howard closed his eyes at the sound and tensed his back. Not the best practice, and the sailor grinned. The pup would learn that instantly.

He snarled away the grin and set his arm, but Manvell had seen enough.

'*Hold there!*' he cried and the sailor dropped his arm.

'This man does not deserve punishment!' He stepped from the ranks along the larboard gangway and stared Coxon down.

'Mister Howard,' Manvell said, 'was following my order to release the pirate.'

Walter Kennedy, standing behind Coxon, hid his joy with his hand. This day was growing lively now. He had expected himself to be punished for his drunken dereliction. Now it was as if he was in the gallery of the Bailey. Common salt Walter Kennedy, he who had killed his father and pirated his way around the world, at court on a king's ship. He rocked on his heels with glee.

'What, you say?' Coxon said.

Manvell stepped forward more, became the player on his own stage.

'I ordered Mister Howard. I must take the blame, Captain. I insist.'

'*Insist?*' Coxon's jaw clenched. 'Your indictment will come, Mister Manvell. It cannot be replaced by lash. If you are guilty, Howard is guilty. Still the same. He did not report your . . . mutiny.'

'Then I request that Mister Howard is judged by advocate. He should face the same law as I.'

The bosun and his team stood back, looking to Coxon only.

'Manvell,' Coxon rubbed his eyes as if weary. 'If you wish to put Mister Howard to a martial court I can assure you it will be more than his back that he loses. Is that what you want?'

'No, sir,' Manvell snapped himself tall. 'But perhaps a martial court will listen to how the *Standard* has truly been betrayed.'

'I repeat,' Coxon matched Manvell's height, toe to toe. 'The result will not be favourable. I am lenient enough to protect Mister Howard from losing his neck and his career.'

He nodded at the looks of the *Standard* upon him.

'As I would any of you. I do not hold the same for mutineers. As you, Manvell, have just confessed yourself to be. I will commend to the court your honesty.'

Coxon saw the pride fall. Manvell felt sure now that he would never see his child, twins or not. He would never see his wife's face again.

A cry from Thomas Howard silenced them. The whole ship fixed on the pale body stretched over the grating.

'No!' he bellowed deep, from his pit. 'None of this!' A broken phrase, almost meaningless. 'I bargained!'

The wind and the rigging were the only sounds.

'I bargained with the pirate! Nothing of this is Manvell's!' His shoulders sank.

Coxon pushed Manvell aside and went to Howard.

'Bargained?' His voice in Howard's ear. 'What say?'

'I meant . . . no harm, sir,' Howard said.

Coxon clasped Howard's tied fist.

'I know, Thomas,' he said. 'But this must be seen to be done. Below you spoke in front of them all. In front of the *Standard*. In front of the king. You understand? What did you bargain?'

'The island,' he said. 'The names. He gave to me the Porto names. Said you would know.'

Coxon pulled his hand away.

'Why not say this before?' His manner back to the judge in black cap. Howard turned his face away and Coxon felt the eyes of the ship crawl over him.

He left the grating. Faced Abel Wales only.

'Return Mister Manvell to his quarters. In his irons, Mister Wales. Punishment is to be rescinded. To be pending.' He addressed the *Standard*.

'Lieutenant Howard was not questioned fully, gentlemen. I acted in your good faith. Swiftly. Only considering your loss. It seems Mister Howard has gained from the pirate where your treasure lies.'

The ship roared. The cat was slung disappointedly over a shoulder.

'We will plot our course anew within the hour!' The roar came lustful now, blood under it.

The bosun went to the ropes around Howard's wrists. Coxon grabbed the thick forearm.

'Mister Wales,' he said. 'I will do it.'

He picked up the shirt and draped it across Howard's shoulders as his fingers fumbled fatly at the knots.

'My chambers,' he whispered to the head still turned away and watching Manvell being pushed below. 'You will tell me what you know.'

# Chapter Thirty-Five

*T*hey left the boats on their painters; they hadn't the will to set them back amidships. The pirates never found the gig that O'Neill had stolen and with another boat lost to Levasseur's cannon it had taken two journeys to ferry them all back into the *Shadow*'s folds.

The afternoon now, and those in the cabin who had been on the island contrasted in their dirt and sweat with those who had not. Exhausted. Done. Beaten. They had come aboard heavy, and not with the weight of gold.

Peter Sam passed round a bottle.

'So what now?' he said.

Devlin took his cue.

'The gold is there.' He looked at Hugh. 'Tell them.'

'It is, Peter. Tall as you,' Hugh agreed.

Peter Sam took back the bottle before it reached Devlin.

'And now buried under a mountain! For all it's good!'

'It was already under a mountain,' Devlin said. 'Now we know where.' He addressed them all. 'We have two ways, as ever. I saw the hole that the priest must have taken. We find that and go back in.'

'That could take weeks! You said the same!' But Peter Sam's side of the room was getting thinner.

'Or we leave.' Devlin carried on. 'Back to Bourbon. Get Dandon and keep the *Santa Rosa*. Leave the priests.'

'Back on the account?' Peter Sam sent the bottle into the round again.

Devlin said nothing. He drank when the bottle came and passed it back to Peter. That would do.

'To the vote,' Peter Sam declared. 'Now. I'll call them.' He put the bottle down, bowed under the door and to the deck.

Devlin's head lowered as he leant on his table. Some tension was loosening in the knots of his back, his arm forgotten. The maps and logs across the table lay under his eye, the pencil promise of his course etched. All the past weeks formed only a single line. Just inches on a map.

He dragged the bottle over them as Hugh came round the table.

'We can't leave it, Pat.'

'We vote, Hugh. The only ones to see it were you me and The Buzzard. Probably the last. Hard to make men feel for what they never knew.'

'We could blow that cave back open. I know we could. From the top down. Levasseur still alive down there.'

Devlin drank, made for the deck, cocked his head to the same for Hugh to follow.

'No, mate,' he said, his arm pulsing again beneath the cloth tied tightly around it. He needed Dandon to pluck and burn the lead from him. 'Not alive. I think The Buzzard's been dead for months.'

Coxon moved around the cabin like a new-hatched fly. He pulled books and charts from his shelves; his waggoner already open on the table, and Howard looked down at an Amsterdam chart of the Indian sea. Master Jenkins stood beside the young officer and saw the sweat running off him and pooling at his feet. The relief of not being lashed. He could feel the cold coming off him despite the humidity of the day which grew thicker every hour they spent in this other world. England he thought no longer existed. The world could not be large enough to endure such pressure that made him wake in sweat and aching head. England was surely a desert under the same. The ship steamed with it as if threatening to burn, her decks swabbed twice daily, the spirketting beginning to warp.

Coxon exclaimed in triumph as the right chart came under the memory of his fingers. He threw its ribbon to the floor and swept his eye between the Dutch and Porto versions of the same ocean.

He waved Howard closer and tapped his fingers at the scallop-shaped ring of stones.

'"The Three Brothers and the Seven Sisters",' he said, a strange affection in his voice. 'The largest is a direct course north from Bourbon. I should have foreseen that. No-one has these islands. They rarely appear on any chart.' He stroked their ink.

'I should have foreseen,' he repeated to himself, his eye gleaming for the first time since he had found Dandon. 'Pirates would know them well.'

Jenkins looked down at the smattering of islands that Coxon now revered like runes.

'So we course here now? Not to the Comoros? No Ogle and Herdman?' He pulled out his notebook.

Coxon ignored him. 'It is possible,' he looked up at Howard, paused quickly at the red cheek and yellow bruise at the nose and eye, 'that the pirate has deliberately confused and misled. How do you feel on that, Thomas?'

'I should like to get dressed fully, Captain,' he said. 'And then consider.'

'Of course,' Coxon rose from the charts. 'And I am promoting you to my First, Thomas, as promised, in the absence of Manvell.' He did not wait for a reply, only put his hands behind. To hide his fists.

'Mister Jenkins, set your sails. All hands to spirit us round. North, north-east in half a glass. Four days. We will run as if straight up from Bourbon and find Devlin there or catch him on his run.'

'And if we do not?' Jenkins closed his book. 'If we do not meet him, Captain?'

'Then we have lost nothing but time, Mister Jenkins. But the men will feel that it has not been for naught. We will give them action. Gold is running in their veins. If we meet the pirate they will still be damn hot. If not, we have lost only four days to meet Ogle and chase for Roberts. And if fortunate we may catch them both. What soul of them would object after what betrayal they have known?'

He sent his last words to Howard, waited for comment that did not come.

'They still want gold,' Coxon said and folded his maps, closed the books that he carried with him for decades. He had sent them to the ship when Manvell had sent only a tailor's closet.

He pushed Howard affectionately to the coach, as if the thrown fist, the grating and the naked back were just an Eton prank. Jenkins followed, shaking his head.

'Your first duty will be to report gun-crews, your quarter-bill. Two kegs of powder. Drill them well, Mister Howard. Make the carpenter swear for his lost barrels you will set for practice.'

'Captain,' Howard stalled at the doors between the cabin and the deck. 'This is feeding me with Morten's fork is it not?'

Jenkins switched his eyes between them.

'Explain?' Coxon said.

Howard rubbed his smarting eye. 'If I do not accept the First's post I will no doubt find myself back along the gangway. And if accepted I show my allegiance to yourself and brand Manvell with you.'

Coxon pulled open the door.

'Welcome to the service, Thomas. The outcome of everything in it hangs on such decisions. Right or wrong.' He ushered him out.

'You'll make captain yet.'

# Chapter Thirty-Six

eter Sam had been quartermaster on a pirate for nigh on seven years. He had served on three ships, with only two men set alongside him. Not above him. The pirate quartermaster was the soul of the ship, the captain only the voice. If the quartermaster said 'no' the wood of the ship bent under his word. Devlin knew this, knew that if Peter Sam's mind differed from his they would set their stern to the island and return to the sea.

But Devlin had treasure on his side, fortune within their reach. He would paint it for them, set it in their pockets. He at least cut the form of the returning warrior.

A torn shirt, blood soaked, an earned wound worn like a badge. He stepped into the sun, every part of the deck hidden by a crew waiting for the word. He walked to the quarterdeck to join Peter Sam.

'Men,' he called before Peter had a chance, 'are we not gentlemen of fortune? Sworn on the account?' He could not see their eyes for their shielding and squinting. It was past noon on what seemed like the other side of the earth now. In their past, he had given this speech before. When the gold had promise, when expectation was undiscovered country.

'I've seen the gold. Hugh's seen the gold. And the priest did not lie. A gold cross. Seven foot tall and blistered with rubies.'

Peter Sam folded his arms, gave his voice.

'The cave is destroyed. The gold is gone.'

'We have powder enough to blow new holes. Dig it out.'

'That'll take too long. Time we don't have to be hungry.'

Devlin walked. 'The priest had a hole to get in. We find that, blow it open. Our way to it. These plots are rich with turtles and devilfish and the birds walk into your pot. A few days' good fishing in the sun is all. We've sailed enough to get here. We can rest awhile.'

Peter Sam placed his hands on the rail and spread his shoulders. 'No life here. No trade routes. Nothing passing. I say we go back to Bourbon. Back to life. Get Dandon and the ship. Recruit more souls and have us a fleet. If Roberts is fleecing Africa why not us? That's where the gold is. And when we're done we take our winter in the Caribbee to fleece those who thinks themselves got away.'

A resounding 'Aye' rattled the ship and the birds that had been preening on the crosstrees took off with the same cry.

Peter held up a fist.

'This gold ain't going anywhere. I say fill our boots elsewhere and come back when we're fat. We buried it more than it was. Who can take it from us? Roberts is looking for it but only the priest knew where and we've done for him. It's our gold now.'

Another cheer. Devlin looked down at Hugh and Hugh lowered his head.

It was done.

'Is that what you want?' Devlin put up his arms, winced at his shoulder. 'No one wishes Dandon back as much as I. We leave none behind.' He looked at Peter Sam. 'Never have. But fortune is here. A few days' work and we'll be rich as kings!'

A voice came up from the back, and where Devlin's poacher's ears were keen weeks before there was dust about him now and he heard it as if from them all.

'I didn't sign pirate to work! And I fished this morning!'

The laugh lowered Devlin's arms. He went to the rail beside Peter.

'So to Bourbon is it?' he asked. And the cry came back and Peter Sam lifted his arm with his.

'Not for offence, Patrick,' Peter Sam said over the cover of the men's roar below.

'Gold ain't going anywhere, Peter. As you said. But you're wrong.' He let go the hand to rest on his pistol's wrist.

Peter Sam wiped his beard and watched the hand.

'You know that I ain't. You can feed them their dreams. I'm for feeding more than that. Let's to that popinjay to fix that shoulder of yours. Get yourself another good scar for them Maroon whores.'

Devlin brushed the earned dust from them both.

'How many scars before we die, brother?'

Peter Sam pushed Devlin's hand from him.

'A hundred is the order. And you and I got none about the face yet.' He shook Devlin's forearm. 'That comes when we're slow.'

A grey curtain set itself across their bow's horizon, in the future yet to be traversed. And storms perceived were another ship's present, island fishermen cowering in their huts.

The *Shadow* had sail and rudder to rule over the Orient's storms. It would be simple enough to tack away from the billowing grey cloud riding over the sea, the vibrant blue fading, the devilfish and porpoises running from their stern instead of playing at their dipping bow. Low creatures who could not command the waves.

The *Shadow*.
South to Bourbon. Perhaps some easy trade on the way. And why not? It was a pirate sea and there were no kings here save for them. Those regents were lording over the sugar, the slaves and the molasses another world away. They had forgotten the old oceans. Nations might have different flags, so long had it been since the *Shadow* had seen their colours.

The *Standard*.
'From backstay and mainmast,' Coxon ordered. 'I want him to see us when we come.'

Jenkins pencilled in his book. 'Why announce ourselves? To what end?'

Coxon clasped his hands behind his back. They were on the quarterdeck, watching the coop being moved to sit behind the skylight over the wardroom. The deck had become too damp for the health of the hens.

'To what end?' Coxon's voice sang and he broke a smile for the first time in days. Coxon's smile rare enough to shiver men's sensibilities. It was the grin of the tavern before men unscrew their fixed teeth and put them to their pocket and put their watch to their boots and go outside together. 'To make them *shit* when they see us of course, Mister Jenkins.'

He put his back to him and Jenkins tipped his hand to his forehead, aware that he had been dismissed, and went down to bellow at the bosun to raise flag and pennant.

Thomas Howard was the only other on the quarterdeck, by the lectern with the log and map. He had the traverse board for his study and to avoid Coxon's eye.

The *Standard* was coursing east on a close-haul, the wind against them, tacking a course deep into the ocean. It was late afternoon, the morning of punishment not forgotten, and the sun was blanketed in a granite cast that fitted Howard's mood and met the ocean at every corner; the customary dazzling blue had gone. There were whitecaps now, and even at four knots the starboard was a mist of spray. Every glass surface dripped, pair-case watches stopped in pockets. Howard held onto his hat as the wind clipped at his ears.

'These are the sou'-sou'west monsoon winds,' Coxon had startled him at his side. 'They blow south of the equator down to the north-east of Madagascar. From April until October. For six months they come. It is the heat from the land masses that creates them, India and Africa batting them back and forth.'

'Are we in danger, Captain?' Howard steadied himself against the yaw of the ship. Coxon showed no such movement.

Coxon held up a hand, his fingers together in a pledge.

'You see this, Thomas? It is the width of our outer planks. As Diogenes says, of those of us on the seas, we are only ever four inches from death.' He put down his hand. 'The Greeks know us well. They defined us as belonging to neither the living or the dead. Even when we walk the streets we sway and our clothes are of another place.'

'But do we head for storms?'

'Do we not always?' Coxon said. 'More ships are taken by hurricane than all the shot ever fired. You should consider if you have truly helped the pirate in releasing him in such a sea.' He waved over the ocean.

'You hear and see the white horses? They are coming.'

He moved away, left Howard to his traverse board and to contemplation on the white waters encroaching, surrounding like a sandbag wall growing ever higher by the hour.

Coxon had checked the binnacle and Howard's board as he spoke, had glanced at the map clamped to the lectern. Six more hours at four knots would bring them to the tenth latitude. Cruise that for sixty miles and back again, a man with a glass at every bow and quarter, a lookout aloft to see into their past and future.

'Mister Howard!' he called back from the rail. 'You remember my asking in Portsmouth about the oil?'

'Aye, sir,' Howard replied. 'Six barrels. I did not forget.'

'Good,' Coxon did not turn from watching over the ship at work. 'Good.'

Howard shook his head and placed another peg and string as the compass made another tack with the ship's bow.

Mad, Manvell had said, and Howard had dismissed the idea. But the ship yawed, and the sky was a single cloud of slate. And his captain had asked him about whale oil.

# Chapter Thirty-Seven

## Monday, 21 July 1721

*F*irst figure recommended fitting. Actual figures bracketed.

*The Standard.* 40 (44)
Fifth Rate. English. 1716.
Burthen: 531 tonnes.
Length: 118 ft. Beam: 32 ft.
Gundeck: 20 x 12 pounders.
Upper gundeck: 20 x 6 pounders.
Quarterdeck: None.
Fo'c'sle: None.
Chasers: None.
Swivels: 2 x ½ pound quarterdeck. 2 x ½ pound fo'c'sle.
Complement: 160 (105)
Commissioned Officers: Capt. 1. Lt. 1 (2)
Warrant Sea Officers: Mr 1. Bts. 1. Gnr 1. Ctr. 1. Sgn. 1. Prs. 1.

*The Shadow* 26 (38)
Fifth rate. French. 1715.
Burthern: 400 tonnes.
Length: 100 ft. Beam: 26ft.
Weatherdeck: 18 x 9 pounders.

Quarterdeck: 4 x 9 pounders.

Fo'c'sle: 2 x 9 pounders.

Chasers: 2 x 9 pounders bow. 2 x 9 pounders stern.

Swivels: 2 x ½ pound quarterdeck. 2 x ½ pound fo'c'sle. 2 x ½ pound larboard qtr. 2 x ½ pound starboard qtr. 2 x ½ pound tops.

Complement:

*Pirates.*

There was a halo around the moon the night before and sun dogs had appeared with the rising dawn. Devlin did not see the signs but they were recounted to him in the hushed tones of omens, as sailors give them in their profundity.

'Bad weather,' Peter Sam joined him at the rail as noon came, the sun gone into the sheet of grey when it should have been sighting their mainmast.

'That's sea dog's wisdom for you,' Devlin said. 'The only old salt I know wouldn't shake on my eggs this morning. Sign enough for me.'

'I wouldn't know,' Peter Sam scratched his beard, 'I puts gunpowder on mine.'

'Heathen.' A hearty slap to the big man's back.

Devlin left him for the stair where John Lawson, the bosun, waited at the foot.

'Set deadlights to the cabin,' Devlin ordered, and Lawson fumbled for his pencil and book as Devlin carried on.

'Storm sheets and stop sails. We'll brail them loose. Fighting sail, bald-headed. Bring one boat in, leave the others trailing.' He moved on without waiting for a word back, swept to Hartley, the gunner, a drunk of great endurance and miraculously still alive, the oldest of them now that

Will Magnes had stayed on at Madagascar. That was three years gone. Hartley was ancient at more than fifty. He craved rum and lime, lambswool and sponges and wood nails for his baize curtain to protect the sanctum of his magazine. He had no care for English powder, only Porto and Frog. You did not have to sift it from swindler's practice and he could range his nine-pounders as good as twelves with it. He had been a warrant officer in two wars, assigned to a ship when she was built. Devlin had asked once how he had become a pirate.

'I was drunk,' he said as if that were all.

'Sight for masts,' Devlin said and then Hartley answered a question from someone else.

'Six barrels of white, thirty-nine sacks, eighteen coils and garlands of balls ready, Cap'n. Been making grape for weeks.' He reeled below, Devlin usually only ever got to see the top of the man's head.

'*Cap'n!*' A cry from the fo'c'sle, urgent for a pirate and Devlin dashed, and heads looked up to follow.

A hand over the bow at the bowsprit. Devlin ducked under the jibs and needed no other word.

It was an actual curtain, on the horizon and up to heaven. It had folds, it mushroomed where the sun should be and it meant hard work in the hours when Indian rugs should be laid and punch and hens set out.

Somewhere out there fishermen had pulled into their islands, took their drying catch into their huts with their families and dug up their buried food. This was the time. It meant no fishing but it would be good water to drink and it was how their fathers had taught them. Only their fathers had not seen the giant wooden ships that did not fish and dared the wind. Their washed up bodies had made their pigs fat for generations. The sea gods were always giving and there was no sin in taking those who did not respect.

Devlin held out his hand, his fingers apart and over the dark fore. He counted as Peter Sam came up.

'A storm then,' Peter Sam said. 'What's she doing?'

Devlin took down his hand.

'About sixty times faster than us and just as wide. She's cutting right across us. "Tufan", the Indians call them. "Typhon" if you want Greek. Fucking big storm in English.'

'We should have stayed on the island, Pat.'

Devlin looked up at the big man.

'Well, fuck you now, Peter Sam.'

Peter looked about.

'White horses. Half-sail?'

'Already done. Storm set.'

'Turn back?'

'Take half a day in these swells. We'll slow and watch her pass.'

Peter Sam studied the pulsating cloud. The water beneath sat smooth as glass as the rain flattened the waves. 'There's no lightning.'

'She's warning us. If we time well, keep slow, she'll go afore us.' He looked up. 'We'll get wet is all. Dandon can wait another day or two. We got nothing to hurry for.'

A shout from the larboard quarter. Devlin's second time to run.

'*Sail, sail!*' and already the quarter was full and Peter Sam had to elbow heads away, his captain in front of him.

Devlin put his hand behind and a spyglass slapped into his palm.

He had not set a man aloft. Men took that post willingly on a pirate for he would have first choice of pistols if they met a prize. The heat had whittled down the volunteers and so he had lost the scope of perhaps twelve miles all around. At the gunwale they had maybe five. Devlin had kept the bell as his only discipline. A mistake now, he knew.

This was how pirates fell, how Blackbeard fell and the fall of all the rebels from Providence. They traded up to larger ships, left their hidden inlets and shallow waters. And then the navy came creeping over the horizon, their crews not drunk. But not Roberts. Devlin had heard he kept to English order, to articles of conduct fit for Protestants, tea his only drink. As the war-ship rode the glass Devlin's only curse was for his own culpability, his own failure. The spyglass was his punishment, silently bringing closer to him his ineptitude.

A twin-decker, a chessboard of gunports, a British flag. Her captain would have set a man above; the bow turning even now to meet their stern. He took down the glass. Kept it. One error corrected. Lesson learned. He had neglected to keep his tools at hand. How pirates fall.

'She's on us,' he said to the heads over his shoulders. 'But she's a porker like her king. We'll outrun. Our girl was cut sleek.'

'Two gun-decks,' Peter Sam said. 'If she catches she'll grind us.'

Devlin climbed a gun to the shrouds and faced the expectant deck.

'Lawson! She thinks we'll scare at her rag! We'll show her our black and the red. No quarter! Fighting sail!' He jumped and walked. Took his quarterdeck.

'Officers to me. Bring my coat.'

Coxon heard the patter of rain on the scope at his eye before it tapped his hat. The glass eye misted and the ship in his

341

sights became a fog; an artist's smudge only alluding to a ship in the background of a greater subject, three thumbnail strokes through the pigment indicating the masts.

He lowered the sharkskin tube and looked up to the grey. No rain now, just the shaking of the sails. Wales, Howard and Jenkins stood behind him. Waited behind him.

'Cut their stern, Mister Jenkins. Keep at it.' He looked toward the storm at their starboard.

'They should make east momentarily to avoid. Be prepared. They are running at four knots to our five. We will be in range in an hour and a half—' he felt the wind '—if we do not lose too much abaft. The wind is across him and behind us. He will struggle. The favour is ours. He would lose us else.'

Jenkins scribbled into his book. 'And they will be in range?'

'She has nine-pounders. She'll be lucky at three thousand yards. Battle at six hundred. No match for our twelves.'

'But we only have six-pounders on the upper?'

'For closing. Keep in three thousand yards and our long-guns will decimate.'

'How do you know this, Captain? The size of their guns and all?'

Coxon still did not turn from the ploughing ship. 'Mister Howard?'

Howard looked at the question marks on Jenkins' page.

'That is the *Shadow*, Mister Jenkins. See her red and black freeboard? Her high prow and short bowsprit? Closer and you will perceive she is clinker-built for hull strength. She has iron in her bulkheads also. That is Devlin's ship. I drew her myself four years ago.'

Jenkins closed his book from Howard's eyes. 'And he would have the same ship?'

Coxon's front blocked the *Shadow* now.

'He took her to the Thames last year, Jenkins. Raped the king. He has pride in that which he did not earn. It is his error. The pirates fail when they give up their sloops. Watch now.'

He stood aside for Jenkins and the others to see what he knew was to come. No need to see for himself, he was already away to his cabin, to his charts and log. The third time he would write the name. The last time he would write the name.

The square of red jigged up on the mainmast over, the larger black at the backstay, the skull in the crude compass rose, the crossed bone pistols beneath.

'Devlin!' Howard declared. 'That is the poison I sketched when I was a boy.'

Jenkins and Wales ran to their work and Thomas Howard kept his eye on the black.

He lowered his voice so only the sea could hear, could carry it to the pirate on its holy ether.

'No boy now, pirate.'

For an hour the wind played its orchestrals through the *Shadow*'s rigging, the cordage sighing, the usual complaining cacophony of the ship now aggrandised and increasing like a racing heart. Men's fists paled with the strain of the ropes or their grip on wood as they watched the bow of the man-of-war jumping water to gain their stern.

The fo'c'sle was no longer a place to stand as each nose of the bow sent a waterfall over and down her step to slip rivulets to the scuppers. They had unsheathed the guns but kept the tampions and the vents' aprons in her holes. Waiting for the time when it came to open gunports.

Devlin's arms were across his table, hands resting at the edge and assessing the Mortier, a swinging lantern above as the deadlight shutters blocked the day save for a hole for an eye or a musket. Peter Sam stood in front of him, his role to give the Devil's view of the world.

'No John's Company flag,' he said. 'No East-Indiaman. English. He's still on us. Like hands on a watch. We be the minutes and he the hour creeping behind. But that will change. Our head's already whipped in the wind. We'll be in irons soon enough.'

Devlin scratched a cross on the paper for himself, for the *Shadow*. He did not look up.

'You mean the sails in irons, Peter. Not us?'

He scratched another cross for the bastard ship, angled his hinged-rule between and drew the line.

Peter Sam grunted.

'I say roll the guns. He might run at that, even without the range.'

Devlin walked the rule for the next hour, another line as his mug of rum crashed to the floor.

'Save our powder.' His concentration was still on the page, reading the fathoms, looking for reefs. He scratched another cross for the storm. 'We'll need it.'

Devlin raised up.

'I reckon she has twelve-pounders broadside judging by her burthern. Maybe sixes or eights above them by that reckoning. We need to keep her angled away and at three thousand yards to stay out of her long-guns.'

'And can we?'

Devlin threw down his pencil. Peter Sam saw the converging crosses and lines.

'No,' Devlin said. 'We need to get rid of those twelve-pounders. Whatever she has above should match us.'

'Shall we write her a note asking to play fair?' Peter Sam

paced the floor, his hands gripping his cutlass and pistol, his bare arms flexed, aching to draw.

'You ever play "hand-in-cap", Peter?'

Peter stopped. His neck was red.

'No riddles, Devlin. I don't canter like Dandon.'

Devlin gave Peter his rakish grin and plucked his pencil from its roll along the yawing deck.

'We need a neutral to give us the odds for an unfair play. Forfeit or fight.' He tapped the pencil at the storm on the paper. Peter Sam watched the innocent pat of the pencil.

'You want to go *into* the storm?'

'Her long-guns are maybe five feet above the waterline. In there she'll have to keep them ports closed, 'less she wants to drown. Even the odds. She'll be as blind as us and she has royals and top-gallants she won't be able to use. We could break her down to two-knots and our smaller girl will fare better.'

Peter Sam appeared to chew on his red beard as he looked at the paper that he never had understood. But Devlin had pulled cards out of boots and sleeves before. But intentionally aiming at an Indian storm was a different madness.

'Can we make it before they're on us?'

'We'll warm them all the way.'

'Might tear us apart. We'll be fighting a ship *and* the gods.'

'So will they. Rather that than a king's ship take us to Execution Dock. That's how I'll have it, Peter. And you the same. I know that much.' He threw the pencil, filled his hand with a bottle.

'Besides, who'd have sand enough to follow?'

Peter's greater fist took the bottle before it hit Devlin's mouth.

'Aye.' He drank high, gave it back. 'Can't be another mad as you.'

\*       \*       \*

Abel Wales sped into the great cabin, his words as urgent as his feet.

'She's making for the storm, Cap'n!'

Thomas Howard came after him, a Monmouth cap over his red hair. Coxon lifted his head from the study of the chart weighted on the table. He placed a pewter mug over the lines he had made.

'Head two-points sou' sou'-east. Aim at her. Forget the stern. He has the wind on his beam. We will quarter large, Mister Wales, and gain.'

Wales ran from the room and Coxon smiled at Thomas, went to fetch his cloak.

'Mister Howard,' his voice chimed. 'Your larboard gun-crews, if you please. Chain-shot and bar. Lower your trucks for their masts.'

'The twelves?'

Coxon turned from buttoning his cloak that covered his chest and shoulders. 'Of course.'

'I have inexperienced midshipmen. Another officer would help.'

Coxon studied the intent on the young man's face. 'You mean Manvell?'

'He would be of great use to me, Captain.'

Coxon took up his tricorne, pointed it at Howard's wool. 'It would serve you better to wear your own. The water runs through the cocks away your shoulders. And no, Manvell will not be of much use. He has never fought before. We have experienced gunners who will suffice much better. The midshipmen can handle the upper.'

'I'm sure Manvell would work under parole, Captain.'

'I *do* have work for him, Thomas. And you to give it him.'

The whole room jarred, every glass and ceramic object jerking in spasm as the wind objected to the turning of the wheel outside. Coxon ignored Howard's reach for furniture to steady himself against the new camber of the boards.

'Take five idlers and rags, clothes if you have to, and all the sacks we have. Tell Manvell's marine I will let Manvell assist.'

'Assist in what, Captain?'

'I want them to soak all the rags in the whale oil and stuff the sacks until they drip. I have proportioned an hour to the task. I will need thirty-worth.'

'What for?'

Coxon did not seem to hear. Howard corrected himself that he had not addressed the *Standard* appropriately.

'For why, Captain?'

Coxon moved as if to pass through him and Howard stepped aside.

'That is not how orders are accepted, Mister Howard. Questioning steals time and sinks ships. Find my steward and fix deadlights to the cabin and wardroom. I am to the quarter-deck. Meet me there when done. Manvell will be under your quarter-bill.' He strode from the room.

Howard watched the black cloak sweep away, made to follow, then a stylus rolling against the pewter mug with a chime turned him to the table.

A disobedient hand picked up the mug set in the Indian Ocean. He cocked his head to correct the aspect of the lines and crosses triangulated on the paper.

Howard had plotted similar lines and bearings in his classes as a boy. Not the dull rigidity of the rhumb lines and mathematics of the art that the master preached but the ones in the pages at the back of his book. The secret folds where he planned his bold future actions.

Points converged, Coxon had drawn simple bows and sterns ramming together, and Howard's eyes widened at the point where they met, at the very eye of the storm, marked and as wide as his own.

Manvell sat on his cot and rubbed his free wrists where the irons had marked them. Ridiculously he thought of Dandon over himself. Empathy for another.

'So, he *is* mad,' he said. Sorry for them all.

Howard was on his knees before him in the cramped cabin removing the chains. The narrow room seemed to hang in space, rolling on a gimbal like the binnacle. With the vented door closed it became no longer part of the ship. It was a hempen and canvas box for whispers and dreams, as Howard had dreamt, as they had both dreamt of pirates, the lantern dancing their shadows around its walls in a mad jig.

'No,' Howard stood, dropped the chains, kicked them to a corner. 'Not mad. He has let you go. He has readied the ship.'

'To fly into a hurricane! After his damned pirate! And he wants his officers to make scarecrows!'

Howard plucked his shirt cuffs.

'To be fair he wishes *you* to fill the sacks. I will charge the long-guns. And he has let me speak to you at least.'

Manvell joined him in standing, put a hand to his shoulder.

'Then we shall speak, Thomas, in the moments he has spared us. Our position is both privilege and duty, you know this? Our privilege is to look after the men around us. Souls not able to speak for themselves. How goes the ship?'

'All willing. He brings them a fight. And gold at the end of it.'

'And how do we get out of Typhon's fury? Buy our passage? We will only be giving coin to Charon.'

Howard took the hand from his shoulder.

'Have you been drinking, sir?'

'How does one board a ship in a storm, Thomas? It is only the pirate's destruction he seeks. There will be no gold.'

'So we will sink the pirate. That was always our mission.'

'No. He *declared* it our mission. We were to meet Ogle and Herdman. Hunt Roberts and Devlin. Three king's ships protecting the waves. There was nothing of gold, nothing of chasing into storms.'

'So how would you have it?'

Manvell bit his thumb, stroked his wrists.

'I would see it as my duty and privilege to those who cannot speak, to take a ship away from the hurricane. Let the pirate be dashed. What would we gain?'

'A rope. For mutiny.'

'Nonsense. A martial court hangs more paper than men. The storm will be our defence.' He gripped Howard like a brother.

'We could take the ship, Thomas! It is our right. For our duty and privilege. No mutiny for vanity or glory. For sense!'

'Are you afraid, Christopher?'

Manvell released him, held the lantern's sway and steadied their shadows.

'No, Thomas,' he said ruefully. 'I am only afraid that when the inquisition comes I would not be able to defend my captain's actions. Or my own.'

Thomas broke their coffin of a cabin by spreading open the door, the marine outside waiting, pretending not to have heard as if the thin door opened on another universe.

'We have less than an hour now for you to make these sacks, sir. I have afforded all apprentices and servants to you.'

Manvell let go the light, watched its wild swing.

'Can I carry my sword, Lieutenant?'

Howard put his tricorne to his head for the cocks would run the water away from his shoulders.

'I would advise it, Christopher. And I permit.' He smiled, hoped he saw the same in return, and vanished from the doorway.

Even within the rising wind and rolling waves over the fo'c'sles, the toll of two ship's bells could be heard by both crews. They stilled and looked across the swells as if they were only men at their ploughs in the field and the sound were just from the distant church of another village.

Pirate and king's man held at their stations to listen. The bell summoning. The bell warning. It marked the hour. Its morose peal came at the same hour on days in port, the same hour on days with white-water at the gunwales. And it might always mark their last hour, so listen well.

The bell tolled slow and unnatural in their thoughts, its reverberation surely the cause of the tremble in their working hands, and it signalled the edge of the storm spitting at them for daring to enter.

The rain swiped razors across their sight, slashed from every corner of wood. The courses above were wrestled by enraged spirits, the men at their ropes deceived that they had some control over the wrath of nature, having long forgotten that civilisations before their own revered its fury as a conclave of gods. Nature was too variant and powerful to be the whim of a single malevolent force.

'She's still coming!' Peter Sam, amidships, shouted to Devlin on the quarterdeck. 'Chasing! To our forefoot!'

Devlin exaggerated a nod to show he had heard.

His enemy chased to cross them at the nearest distance – across their starboard side. A good move if she had bow chasers, as Devlin would have done, but he could see no guns there.

She was conning into her three-thousand yard range, jumping like a horse raised for the flats, powering hard but leaning away. Her broadside high, as she wished, her long-guns not threatened by the water. He would have to change that.

He had a minute to him. Half of that to decide not just his own action but that which was centred in his foe's mind.

A bluff. The prow cutting to make him turn away from the storm, helm-a-lee, and run. And some advantage in that, for the *Shadow*'s stern guns could bite and she would have the wind at her back. The bluffer lines of his girl would gain three knots to his enemy's hulk.

But that would be running. And no-one who had ever seen the *Shadow* had seen her stern.

Or not a bluff. Coming into range. With the weather gage she would take the wind from the *Shadow*'s lee, put her helm down and those ports would open and those long-twelves would stare at French strakes again.

His minute was almost done. He looked fore to the storm, the sea black as the sky. They might catch some warmth from their enemy before they made that maelstrom.

He went to the ear of the black sailor at the helm.

'Match his two-points. Across his bows.'

He stepped down.

'Lawson! Any sail to make that storm! Peter Sam! Hartley! Starboard guns. Run 'em out!'

# Chapter Thirty-Eight

'S he's coming about!' Jenkins yelled for all, spitting out rain and slapping his face. 'I see gun crews!'

'She do not have the range,' Coxon said.

'Maybe "she" do not know that!'

'He's keeping to the storm. Thinks we won't follow.' Coxon went to the rail, gripped the wet wood and looked fore to his bow and the black wall.

Jenkins slipped his way to join him, the deck already awash before the storm.

'He knows we can't,' he said. 'That's what it is. If we head east now we can rake his stern as he goes. Bring down something.'

Coxon said nothing. The veil between the two ships was too opaque, yet he sought the familiar figure about her.

Spraybows shimmered in the spindrift running off her freeboard, off the tops of the whitecaps bucking them both, a Viking Bifröst bridge between them. He strained his ear over the side, closed his eyes.

'Listen!' He pulled Jenkins to him. 'You hear?'

Jenkins took off his hat and tried to block out the wind and rain from one side. At first he could hear nothing but his complaining ship being shaved by the wind. And then it came, but he did not believe.

'A fiddle! Pipes? Flutes?'

'Two fiddles,' Coxon said. 'And fifes. He wants us to think they are enjoying. That they can yawn and afford to play while they fight. If they start to sing then we will know we have them worried.'

Jenkins put back his hat and gaped up at the black wall stretching above their masts. The sea and the sky formed one monstrous wave bearing down on their eggshell world.

'Get the sergeant,' Coxon said to the back of Jenkins' head. 'Get him to play us a drum. A beat to quarters. Make them hear *that*. Tell Howard to run out his guns.'

'But not to the storm, Captain?' He saw that Coxon's grip was white against the rail, his feet never moving despite the ever-changing camber.

'Let him taste our chain. Then we will load with shot from both decks. See if he likes the storm then.' He went to the rail above the deck, found a midshipman yet tasked.

'Get below and bring me Kennedy, boy. I'll have the pirate beside me now!'

Jenkins watched him parade the rail, no care for the battering rain, hands clasped behind, estranged from the light being sucked from the ship, the fo'c'sle already in darkness, a black line being drawn athwart like the creep of sun on a dial. He dashed to stand by the mainmast, already in shadow, and waved the stout sergeant from his cowering under the quarterdeck.

Devlin strode behind his guns.

'Quoins out, Hartley!' he bellowed and Robert Hartley blew a kiss on his smouldering linstock. No more time remained to delay the removal of the aprons from the guns' vents that protected from the rain; the tampions were already out, the ports raised. Their opponent had the advantage of his guns below deck, no concern about drenching. Hartley had four men to a gun, behind a wall of hammock netting. The quoins away would make slight difference. Even fully raised and with the timing of the great swells' uproll his nine-pounders were on the last drop of their range. Their shot would become part of the coral and not part of their foe's supper. Still, like the first smoking pipe and rum of the day, one had to get it over with.

And just the sound and sight of it might break some nerve over the way.

Devlin stood at the starboard quarter with Hugh Harris and his quartet plucking merrily and beating their feet. He could hear the urgent drum from over the hills of water. A response to his music to evoke a column of soldiers walking towards them over the waves.

He watched his guns roll out, their trucks squealing like the scrape of the fiddles. A sound not heard for months, a fine sound. It had eagerness about it, like children at play.

Nine guns on the weatherdeck and Hartley timed them in three rounds on three uprolls. Seconds between the discharges when men could uncover their ears and set to reloading the first.

The iron punched, the guns flew back hissing and steaming against the rain and Hartley passed his linstock and picked up another from the bucket to the quarterdeck, passing his captain with a wink. Devlin watched the shot cut and curve high through the downpour.

Only those suffering the weather on the *Standard* saw the spikes of flame, those below, by their guns, heard the nine cracks no louder than the distant barks of dogs.

Coxon saw Jenkins duck by the mainmast and men follow. Coxon stood straight, the privilege of office being to stand on the open quarterdeck, protected only by the bulk of hammocks secured around the rails.

He watched the shot plunge like black terns into the white waves, hundreds of yards from their wood, and nodded down to the midshipman by the companion to order Howard to fire his twelves. The midshipman vanished and Walter Kennedy appeared in his place, blinking against the rain, and Coxon motioned the pirate to join him.

Devlin watched his enemy's strakes lean and run wet as the uproll heaved the behemoth over its back. Still too far, too high a sea to spy the guns. When they went down she was swallowed up to her fighting sail, the sea coming from them to engulf the pirate, and then the *Shadow* came up and the ship was closer again.

He had not seen the guns' flare, just the wall of water as they again plunged down into the swell, but the rippling crack that echoed off their wood was there as if from the air above their masts.

His men dived to the oak. He watched the balls skim the fat waves and could not help but think of it as beautiful, an extraordinary sight. He flattened against the bulwark to watch the sky and sails above him.

Two hits out of ten. Chain-shot, and it had not met their masts, only their hide. The sea was indeed Devlin's ally. It was impossible to sight firmly on a rolling target. Just fire and hope. Devlin's hopes were the better ones.

He stood as his girl shrugged off the iron and Hartley let go his quarterdeck guns just as his first three fired again. That was the way. Keep on. Return a load before a scope could check for damage, keep them down, silence their cheers. But the nine-pounders still fell short.

Devlin congratulated Hartley then felt the lurch rise from his feet and he looked fore. He hung onto the deck-rail as the bow ascended, came to meet him.

And a memory formed in front of him to carry for the rest of his days.

He saw his ship cross a threshold, divided from day into night. A sheet of rain was falling down from the bow like a wall, his men and masts swallowed away, and then over him, pushing his head low.

Into the lion's cage.

He laughed and could not hear it. His laughter for his foe. He had needed to take away their twelves. Level the play. And that was done.

He looked to starboard, could see nothing past the rail, and then ten candles silently lit and blew out one by one. He grabbed a manrope, hearing nothing but the gods in his ears until the wood exploded around him.

'You see, Walter?' Coxon was shouting now, Kennedy sheltering beside him. 'Devlin supposed we would break. He does not know that I am on him.'

Kennedy, from his crouch, mouthed something but Coxon could not hear. He saw Jenkins struggle to pull himself up the stair.

'Captain,' Jenkins huffed. 'We must close the ports on the long-guns. If we continue we will drown, sir!'

'Tell Howard close the ports. We are within a thousand yards. The sixes will have some range. As will the pirate. Give Howard my regards for his last barrage and send his crews to the upper. We need to close, Master Jenkins,' Coxon's voice was plain.

'We hit them?' Jenkins' face lightened and then dropped as the the word 'close' filtered through to him.

'*Close*? Into the storm?'

Coxon ignored the question.

'See the ports are closed. See to Manvell and his task. I want those sacks to the deck immediately.'

'But, Captain—'

Coxon rounded on him.

'Immediately, Master Jenkins!' He turned back to the rail, steadfast against the rise and fall of his deck. He took up his scope, pulled up Kennedy to his side.

'Stand fast now, Walter. I wish Devlin to see us both clear.'

Kennedy was a rag-doll in Coxon's grip, kept his head low. The quarterdeck was too open a space for his liking. They were alone upon it. The *Standard* had a wheelhouse below, afore the belfry, so there was not even a man at the helm to draw fire. When Devlin's guns found their range this is where he would train them. Straight for the walk of officers.

'Stand still, man!' Coxon berated. 'I want him to see!'

Kennedy found some voice but not the growl of arrogance he had shown so much.

'Let me to work, Captain! I can be of use below!'

'Nonsense. You have nothing to fear. You are dead already.'

Kennedy slipped, was hauled back up as the deck ran from him, and Coxon still standing as if nailed.

'*Dead*?' Kennedy held to the lectern, Coxon's fist on his collar. 'How dead?'

'This day—' Coxon paused for a sheet of spray piling over them. He waved his spyglass to the quarterdeck over, barely discerned, but there. He heard his ship crash through the wall of water, into the storm, and a new hail of rain beat his shoulders.

He dragged Kennedy to his mouth as he watched the bows of the ships pivot towards each other, the cyclone splicing them together.

'This day!' He yelled. 'A man named Walter Kennedy will be hanged at Execution Dock. I have arranged it.' He relished the sight of Kennedy's wide mouth suddenly filled with water.

'It is often done. Take a man who has wife and family. Pay his debts to take your place.' He pulled Kennedy from the lectern and forced him against the rail.

'Look pretty for me, Walter. This is not the way I wished it. But it might do.' He resumed his wave, held Kennedy to his side like a brother.

'Your soul is mine now, pirate.'

The damage was just to the furniture. Splinters and shavings. The *Shadow* and her captain bore many scars from those foolish enough to attempt to defy them. Her skeletal prow grinned and went on as she had always done, as her captain had always done. Their wood and flesh were marked together.

The storm sea had a pattern to it. Its rise and fall ticked like a watch and the men on the *Shadow*'s deck could pace their work to it. The wind and rain were unending, but the storm was taking them in its arms. It had its own agenda and what seemed chaos outside became order within. Keep from its eye and the outer rim and it could be ridden.

Devlin looked to the sailor at the helm above. The *Shadow* had no whipstaff under cover for the man and the helm was exposed on the quarterdeck. He might drown standing at his post. Devlin had heard of such things.

He took the stair, crawled it like an infant and pulled himself to the wheel where the Spanish black held his course, shirt about his waist where the torrent had torn it from him.

Devlin put his hands over the black ones and together they set the wheel to its centre. Then Devlin prised those rigid, powerful hands from the wheel and lashed it to its course.

'Go below,' he said. 'Get dry awhile.' He patted the broad back, felt the welts of aged whippings under his fingers and the man understood only the command of the English words. He grinned proudly and struggled away.

Devlin did not know the former slave's name. He was not Spanish. He had been taken from a Spanish slaver from where he would be sold to a field. A slave. A slave priced to cut cane or pull a plough. This day he had coursed a beleaguered French frigate through a storm under fire from an English warship, his shirt ripped from him, his eyes reddened almost shut.

Devlin was alone now. He felt into his coat's left pocket. He had cut it so he could keep a spyglass or pistol down inside to the hem. He had a leather strap of Guineas rolling around inside it, a dagger and bag of powder and shot also. A pirate coat. His very cloth was armed. There was a strip of coin sewn inside the spine of his waistcoat also and a dirk clasped to his inside boot-top. Ready for a gaol, ready to be washed up on a beach.

He pulled the three-draw sharkskin and held his breath as he brought it to his eye. He waited until the ship levelled, seconds before she plunged again and he swept it across his foe, sought the quarterdeck to see who had entered the storm with him. The glass brought them hundreds of yards closer together.

Two figures shimmered, the chromatic lens painting an aura around them. One was in hat and cloak and waving his glass above his head. Wanting to know him. The other was hanging off him like a corpse. Trying not to be seen.

The glass misted and Devlin cursed and wiped it clear. He waited again as the ship plummeted and the sea ran around his feet. He rocked with it, wedged the scope between the fold of his elbow and aimed it like a musket as the ship fell before his eye.

The deck good now, the wind served to blow the falling rain away for one second of good sight.

And gave ten years' perspective.

He lowered the glass in disbelief just as Hartley's guns fired and he was shrouded in smoke and fury.

The vision had gone.

He coughed down the steps. Hartley yelled something but Devlin brushed him aside. His feet found Peter Sam and he pushed the slab of him round to face him.

Peter had ropes on both his arms, guiding the fighting courses like a kite as if the *Shadow*'s only hope was his might alone.

Devlin yelled into his face but Peter Sam caught none of it.

'What?' he bellowed.

'Coxon!' Devlin shouted again. '*Coxon*, Peter!'

This time Peter Sam heard, dropped his ropes, wiped the rain from his face.

'I seen him.' Devlin leant in. 'And another.'

The ship pushed them together as Hartley fired his next three. The twelves of their enemy were done now, ports closed, just as Devlin had planned. The pirate's nine pounders were the only cards in play.

'Who else now? Who haven't we killed?'

Devlin could not say. Not here. Not on the Bedlam deck.

They went hand over wood to the cabin doors banging wildly. They could spare a minute. The English warship had followed them into the storm. Their nines were firing, the long-guns of their enemy silenced. They could spare a minute, a sailor's minute. Hartley and Lawson were holding. Holding against an English man-of-war. A twin-decker. Hundreds of tonnes of wood, iron and hearts of oak. A weatherdeck a man's height taller than their own, a giant upon them, captained by the last man who had ruled over him. Bearing on him again.

Devlin needed a drink.

# Chapter Thirty-Nine

'Walter Kennedy.' Devlin spat the cork from his jaw and passed the bottle to his quartermaster as they rolled in the cabin.

'Who?' Peter Sam gulped the rum, both hands around the neck against the yaw.

'You remember me telling you about London? Before. A decade more. An anchorsmith named Kennedy. An Irish family that took me in?'

'Aye,' Peter Sam gave back the bottle. 'You said murder. The son done for him. We don't have time for this, Pat.'

The doors slammed, the bottles and books shook against their rope beckets, the one lantern throwing their shapes around and around, but Devlin would have his word. He pointed through the wall to the ship beyond. He would have some word to settle what the rum could not.

'That's the son. The wretch that killed his father. I ran to France because. Why him here? With Coxon?'

'We'll be asking him soon enough when they catch us talking instead of fighting.'

Devlin pulled back the rum. Drank and wiped his mouth, sucked the spill of it from the web of his hand.

'And Coxon? How him? The world's not that small.'

Peter Sam had heard enough.

'Not to chance. So he is sent. So what do we care? And he be pleasured to hear you wondering so.'

He went to the doors, cracked them open and brought back the rain and the wind.

'So let him come. You've taken his long-guns. Good for you. I ain't got the brains for it and I ain't Dandon to praise it. You want to know why he's here?'

He strode out to the deck, called back over his shoulder.

'Come ask him like a pirate!'

The nines fired again and Peter Sam became lost in the smoke and the sheets of rain. He found his ropes, stood with Lawson under the main. Forced himself to not look back.

And then he heard.

Heard the pirate Devlin once more.

'Shave me two points to her bow, Lawson!' Devlin called for the whole deck.

'To that slut! Warm her well! We've taken her long-guns. Shove them back up their king's arse, boys!'

He climbed the steps to the quarterdeck, their cheers behind him.

His quarterdeck. His wood.

Peter Sam kept to his ropes, his head running with the rain but high to his courses and the black sky above making the grey sails gleam. John Lawson caught him for one look. Too much wind for any word from Peter Sam. The big man cocked his head back to where Devlin courted.

He gave a wink to Lawson.

Word enough.

'Ah, Manvell,' Coxon rolled his fingers over the rail as Manvell trudged up the companion. 'You join us in battle!'

Manvell looked up at them both. Kennedy beside his captain, on the quarterdeck no less. He slid to the gangway and a manrope, the weatherdeck sparse of men, the gundecks hoarding them all. Only Jenkins and his gang remained and Manvell looked up to four clinging desperately to the yards, ready to make sail if the order came.

It had seemed worse below, the ship's movement more pronounced as Manvell lashed the stinking sacks. But above, on the deck, it was the noise that was in command, the wind and downpour drunkenly playing the wood and sail. But still his captain's voice speared through it all.

'Manvell! Where the sacks? Where your duty?'

In answer a troupe of sailors came up the companion after, sacks off their shoulders.

'Your order, Captain,' Manvell said. 'How goes the fight?'

'That is not your concern.' Coxon saw the sword, the gentleman's scabbard, the duke's bursary. He pointed to it and remarked as the guns fired again, his words lost in the wind and cannons' roar.

The rain ran around their feet, misting in the broiling air like the brume of a dawn field, and Manvell dared the stair of the quarterdeck.

'I am still an officer of this ship! I can be of service. I believe we have lost the twelves.'

'Lost? No, not yet. And you are very much of service, Christopher. I need those sacks over both gunwales.'

'And what mad— what foolishness is this now?' Manvell stepped on the quarterdeck. 'We are already fighting six-pounders against nines!'

Coxon grabbed Manvell's coat but only for him to hear better. Orders in his ear. Kennedy slunk to below the taffrail, hugged his knees, hoped now to be forgotten.

'Manvell!' Coxon yelled above new waters powering over them. 'Let me teach you something about these waters! Teach as I ever wanted, Christopher!' He pushed him from his deck.

'Set those sacks over the gunwale! Even apiece! For once, for your ship, do as instructed!'

The guns of the *Shadow* came at them again, punctuating Coxon's fury. Manvell and Coxon were the only ones not to duck, not to stare over the waves. Their eyes were only trained on each other, with one look to the swords at their hips.

'It would expedite my action, Captain, if I knew what good will be served.' Manvell swayed at the foot of the stair, his arms across it, supporting himself against the rise.

Coxon wiped himself of the rain.

'See it done!'

He returned to the rail, to boast against the pirate and the whistle scything through the rain, a visible fall of the chain cutting the water in the air between like skipping stones on a pond. He could see their links, frozen in space. The experienced men put their hands to their heads and their chins to their knees.

They bit their jaws and waited. Waited while the chain chewed the wood around them.

'We have range!' Devlin ran along his deck. 'She comes for feeding, boys!'

He made his fo'c'sle, to see that prow still coming. His words bolstered his men admirably but he was alone among them. There was a space around him where Dandon should have been. A wide space amid the drama. He had set Dandon down to protect him. But now he feared, prophesier to himself, that it had been more. He missed the yellow coat. Coxon against him. Good enough. All fair. But Dandon had been with him always when the cards had fallen.

On The Island with the French gold: Dandon. On the deck of the *Talefan* with Seth Toombs: Dandon. In Charles Town: Dandon. In London and Paris: Dandon. He was the penknife used to prise the stone from the heel.

Devlin had set him down. Walked without him in his pocket. And now his deck felt emptier without him. A wide lonely space. Wide and yet as narrow and lonely as the grave without him.

But perhaps Dandon not set down. Perhaps Dandon spared. Perhaps Devlin knew and chased that which he deserved. Devlin closing his own book, turning the final pages swiftly ever since the death of Valentim Mendes, the Porto governor whose hand he had taken, whose ship he had taken, and ever since the deaths of all those dogs that followed his heels. Names crossed off in his log.

The guns cracked once more from his enemy, nails hammering into his *Shadow*'s coffin. The time come to pull down the lid on his face.

He thought of the cross. O'Neill's legend of the Flight of the Earls. Had Devlin but persevered, had he faith, he could have had a cross that could still the waves.

If he had believed in fairy tales.

No matter. He had taken Coxon's long-guns, taken his sails with the storm and levelled the odds. There was no Lord, no miracle that he required.

Thomas Howard's head was at the square of a gunport as he checked the pirate. He had first seen her in the Caribbean and the ship seemed larger then. But he was a boy then. The pirates must be old now. Devlin lined and grey, surely, and their luck run aground. Still, he would not misjudge the monsters aboard her, those faces that he had seen with axes raised still vital, still engorged with blood.

A thousand yards of turbulent water heaved between them. Good range. If the waves had not taken his long-guns he would be grinding her to waveson.

The quoins were away from his six-pounders and he looked down the long row of the ten guns. Bare-chested men sweated before him, working to the beat of the drum; worm and sponge, ramrod and ladle in all their hands. They had spent days firing at barrels floated on the calms, not to hit them, that would be fiction, just to range. Three minutes to reload the hogs at their knees. But the black and red ship fired back, was not a barrel. She answered every call as if she caught and heaved the shot back at them.

The gundeck was level with the pirate's weatherdeck, and if Howard had the long twelves available he could answer to her hull and that would be the short of it, the mark of it. As it was now, and for these last minutes he was cascading six-pounder roundshot at the pirate's returning nine. And they were closing, the storm in charge, hauling them together. It would be grappling hooks soon enough. Weapon lockers loosed, grenadoe and musket, pistols in belts. Then cutlasses and flesh. Skulls and bones.

Howard took a moment to look down a gun at the ship beyond, the barrel hot near his cheek, the water rising towards him, its pattern marbled like fat Irish beef, like horse flesh. It slammed against their wooden walls like it – like horses tumbling. He wondered if that was how the waves got their equine name. He saw that the pirate's tops had swivel guns mounted, men aloft already. That would not paint pretty on the *Standard*'s deck.

We are too slow, he thought. The Mediterranean draft of the clinker-built pirate was like a lamb to a hog in their wallowing. She could cut in front and have at their bows while they lumbered through the molasses of the waves. They would need a miracle now.

A rough hand pulled him away to let them roll out the gun and then a midshipman yelled from the stair. A boy was calling for them to hold and Howard bellowed through the gloom, repeating the same. He looked to the window of the port again as a sack dropped before them and hit the water below. His gun-crews stood back, their tools to the overhead, and waited for his word. He had none. He looked to the boy who had a hand outstretched to him. The drumming stopped as the sergeant wiped the rain from its hide.

'Hold, sir,' the boy said.

'Hold!'

Manvell's gang had belayed to pins the last of the sacks. The oil-soaked bags ran along the ship, bobbing at first, then they dragged like the nets used to steep their meat, the sea creaming over them.

Manvell looked up to Coxon paying the bags no mind. His concentration was solely on the pirate. Manvell's gang of apprentices and servants loped away, their swiftly learned course of knots ably applied. Shelter now became their objective after the pointlessness of their task.

'Your farmer's bags are laid, John!' Manvell called and hovered to the quarterdeck stair.

Coxon raised and lowered his hand to the midshipman waiting and the punch of the guns echoed out from below seconds later. He watched for the guns' report against the pirate. Only five met the fall. Not a shiver of wood could be observed. He called Manvell to him.

'You may see better from up here, Christopher.' And Manvell came to the rail.

'To see what?' He looked to the cowering Kennedy. 'And what of *him*? Would he not be better served below?'

Coxon faced him.

'It was you that done for my first plans for Kennedy. My intention was to let Devlin's men know that I had him, along with their pirate. His crew may have questioned their captain's past. Do not suppose that they worship dishonour. We could have created discord amongst. At the very least we might not be fighting if we still had his friend. Had you not let him go.'

'I did not—' and then Manvell remembered his lie for Howard, 'I did not wish for this!'

'Nor I. But this is command, Christopher. Know it. And no, it is not this pirate I wish you to see.' He pulled Manvell to the rail. 'I have magic, don't you know?'

Manvell felt the ship steady beneath his feet and Coxon drew his sight to the wake around them.

'I was aware we were entering the season for the Indian storms. This whale oil we use for lamps, for grease, for butter. But it serves for war also.'

Manvell looked down the freeboard to the seething sea. The white catspaws began to walk away from the hull, began to cease lapping at the gunports, and he could see the bags now. The water calmed around them, as if a spell encircled the ship, the rain now flattening the waves like a housemaid folding linen.

'Oil, Christopher,' Coxon said proudly. 'Since the time of Pliny it has aided the fisherman and the warrior. The old world!'

Jenkins joined them at the sight of the marvel, gasping over the gunwale as the white water retreated, as the gunports ran dry.

'It is a miracle!' he declared upwards to the quarterdeck.

Coxon took no pride, glared down to the midshipman at the companion.

'Tell Mister Howard do better. Range the twelves again.' He puffed his chest to Jenkins.

'What we have is movement, Mister Jenkins. We can run round them now. Do that. It won't last. Hard to larboard if you please, sir! Wait for one round of the twelves.' He turned to Manvell.

'You see now, Christopher?' He leant on the rail as his deck sailed smooth. 'I have taken back what you have wrecked.'

Manvell swept a low bow in time with the sixes firing. The twelves would follow.

He gave Coxon his due, convinced he had met and seen the moment of which he would tell his grandchildren, if they would but believe. And if his court martial would allow.

'May I stay, Captain?'

'Not on my quarterdeck,' Coxon looked hard at the soaked lieutenant. Looked through him to the duke and the pregnant wife standing behind.

'You must dry, Christopher. Go below. Howard is to the twelves. See if you can man the sixes. I have only boys. If you can, try to do better than them. I will need the starboard battery soon enough.'

Manvell tapped his forefingers to his head. 'Aye, sir.' He took the stair in a jump.

'Christopher!' Coxon called.

Manvell looked up.

'On your parole, Lieutenant.'

Manvell genially gave his accord and went down.

\* \* \*

Peter Sam pushed through the gun-crew, slammed his fist on the gunwale. 'And what is this now?'

Devlin appeared beside him, small against him.

'How is this?'

They watched the great ship running, coursing as if on a different sea, a toy wheeling across a paper ocean.

'She's moving fast,' Peter Sam moved back as the lower-deck gunports swept open with a run of water. He dragged Devlin away. 'And she has her twelves!'

They all watched the first smoke, heard the sharp crack a blink later and then the black ball visible as it turned the rain to steam. They ducked before the nine other charges echoed through the storm. A long, sweating wait of only seconds and Peter Sam and Devlin, tight at the larboard bulwark shared them all, open-eyed, as the low hum came on.

The *Shadow* rolled, cried out against the iron. That which they repaired a year ago after fighting Trouin in the Channel busted open like old wounds. There was no good wood in the world any more.

Only half the shot had hit, but still the deck shook, leant, the guns falling back on their tackles.

Devlin stood, saw Hartley already up and to his linstock and powder-trails. He would cover his foe's sight of their success with his own prowess.

Devlin and Peter Sam ran to starboard, held the rail and felt it tremble, the water shaking from its wood as their guns fired back, the furore no longer a shock to the senses. Devlin leant over the side, Peter Sam instinctively grabbing the tail of his coat.

'We're holed,' he called back. 'Not below our water.' He thanked the storm. The rise and fall of it his design, his genius against whatever card Coxon had pulled from his sleeve. 'They will re-sight for that.'

Peter Sam pulled him back. 'I think he has another mind.'

Devlin did not see how his returning fire fared. He only saw the other bowsprit winding round, the ship yawing hard and the petticoats of her keel showing as she rose. Coming about. In a storm. She crashed and ploughed on. Towards him. In a storm. Not sluggish and mute.

*How?* It was the only thought in his head.

He could make forward passage. Ride the storm. Crush them within while he skated through and would win. But the larger ship was shaming his, and she would have the wind.

'What now?' A loud Peter Sam.

Devlin felt the cold rain, his old coat pasted to him. The short minute again. The sand-glass of decision. Sixty seconds to what? He stared at the ship, aware of his crew's eyes upon him.

'Devlin! What now?' Peter Sam said again.

He could helm-a-lee, make a run of it with their cleaner heels but that would be the first choice and thus the one Coxon would already expect, would count on. The storm was across them, leaning them to windward, forward movement dragged to a crawl, but they could run into the eye of the typhoon; Coxon would have to be mad to follow. But they might not ever leave from there. His ballad would not end well when the taverns rolled with it.

No. Ride the edge of it, as they were. Coxon had come in after them. Plainly he was not set for leaving.

He yelled for Lawson.

'Raise the courses! Make the staysails! We'll ride the lee. Ride the storm. A running fight. Conn for the reefs. We can still outrun her. She can't make the shallows.'

Lawson sprinted away, Hartley back to his guns. Only Peter Sam not moving.

'A running fight. Against her iron?'

'We can't move to close, Peter. We ain't got the wind of it. We can ride it out. Wait for him to make a mistake.'

'He don't seem to favour many of those.'

Devlin minded the sea. Watched the other ship come about, white water over her bow thrown off like a cloak. The wind was now Coxon's mistress, easing him round with a gentle palm.

He saw the ropes trailing along from her sides like baiting lines but still did not comprehend the benefit. His own guns broke him from his study and he waited for the roar to drown.

Less than a thousand yards now, fighting range, but his guns would be over their bow at best. The cloud cleared. He took up his glass.

Some holes punched through the headsails, sparse falling wood, spliced sheets flailing. Even through the downpour some cries carried but not in pain; just for work. Some good had been done but that would be the last of the *Shadow*'s starboard broadsides.

And Coxon's starboard was coming about.

A game of bowls; the *Shadow* the Jack, the *Standard* playing at them calm and orderly like Drake on Plymouth Ho. The starboard barrage only ten minutes since the larboard and the *Shadow* wailed, pieces of her calved painfully to the sea.

Hartley on the uproll gave again, determined to return fire before the *Standard*'s could pat each other on the back.

He caught her final quarters with his chain, all his nines within every inch of her span, and even Coxon was forced to duck as wood plashed around his deck. He waved Kennedy over from where he cringed beneath the taffrail.

'Come, Kennedy! Not dead yet, boy! You should watch this.'

Kennedy crawled. A whine and snap of wood and a sheet and tackle swung before his face to barely miss his skull. He scurried to Coxon's side, surely the safest place.

'He ain't for giving up, Captain.' Kennedy saw the guns of the *Shadow* angled to bear on their quarters. Coxon pointed. 'Our long-guns will catch them between the wind and water,' his voice rose fondly to the pirate. 'One more round of chain from the sixes and it will be grape I shall send across his stern. Clear his deck of bravery. Razors to his neck.'

Kennedy directed Coxon's gaze to the men in the tops of the *Shadow*, the masts leaning away from them, the men's backs over the sea.

'They got guns aloft. They'll bite back.'

'It will be his chasers and quarterdeck guns that will concern if we get within.' Coxon's voice lowered. 'But not much.' Through the rain he could make out a figure with long-coat and spyglass. A brain behind it no doubt fevered by battle and fervidly clouded by Coxon's companionship with creatures from his past.

Kennedy blew out a breath. 'As long as we don't get too close, Captain.'

Coxon took strange pleasure that the pirate had always called him 'captain'. No contracted version or the umbrage-laced 'sir'. But Kennedy had fancied himself one of Roberts's captains. He must have had some respect for the title he had collared so briefly. Perhaps he should purpose to keep him alive. After this he may be some use for cornering Roberts. See how the next quarter-hour went.

'No, Walter,' he waited for the cataclysm of his guns before he finished. 'I intend to get very close indeed.'

374

The music over the way had ceased. His sergeant's drum came now the only sound.

No rapid response arrived from Hartley's guns this time. The fog of sawdust played about their faces with the cover of the rain like smoke from a hay-fire.

The puddings and chain about the sails had kept the pirate's masts and yards good but Coxon's sixes were firing at a man's height and the *Shadow* showed fresh wood where the iron had swiped her skin and bone like an axe.

Devlin and Peter Sam held at the fo'c'sle. They watched the larger ship pass across their starboard shrouds, her guns pulled in. Reloading. All twenty of them.

The *Shadow* was still reeling from the momentum lost as she absorbed the cannonade. Hartley was already going below for the stern chasers, the gun-crews diving into the cabin for more bags of charge where it was kept dry from the rain. Devlin looked up to the topmen on the main and mizzen. They had set their swivels, firing down onto the passing ship with their smoke and flame. The topmen were tied to their masts. He could see their mouths gasping for air against the punishing downpour as they reloaded with their match burning in their calloused fists to keep it dry.

Hugh Harris had taken his minstrels below to the carpenter, to pump the well where the scuppers could not cope with the holes they had taken from the twelve-pounders. This was a ship's end.

Peter Sam ran to aid Lawson and his mates to free the hanging sheets that their enemy's chain had made.

Devlin walked slow from the fo'c'sle. He had ordered nothing. His men had all gone to action as a single thought. A portion of them had been at sea longer than him – the advantage in the democracy of the pirate. Work as want required. No need for command. Every man for each other and for himself, for it was his gold in the hold, his account. And it would be in another's pocket if he did not work and fight for it when the trumpets played.

He could see Coxon plainly now, hundreds of yards still between them, maybe two ship's lengths, but the man-of-war towered above them. His only defence was the narrowness of his beam. Half Coxon's guns would rake across their stern, churn into his cabin, his home, maybe hit the powder that sat there. The twelves would be at Hartley's level, two nine-pounders against five twelves and Hartley would have to be the devil not to die and their rudder would surely be shot away.

Coxon's sixes would hold grape, would pepper his deck with five hundred musket balls and his men would lie on their bellies and hope not to burn.

The *Shadow* was not able to close – too much leeway. But to head-to, to close, that would be the way. Send pirate against sailor. That might do. Common man against common man but his the better suited. The sailors would have the pirate's legends. If any of them had been at sea before they would all have some myth. But he could not board if he could not move, and Coxon was on his stern.

No decision now. Only instinct. He walked alone through the chaos amidships. He had one weapon not used, one play still to draw. He walked to his quarterdeck.

He climbed the stair and saw the great wood rising above his taffrail, Coxon's two gundecks' ports running with rain, the strange smooth water around the hull that he had given up considering. This man had been his master. He needed no other consideration.

He took the hailing-trumpet from its rope-housing around the wheel. One weapon not used, one play still to draw.

Himself.

And John Coxon.

Two ships, two crews, but under the sky, over it all, not much more than two boys on hands and knees pushing their toy ships around and around the grass until one stands up, brushes the stains from his knees and has to go home to supper. Just them.

'Captain John!' Devlin called through the brassed cone, his eyes over it on the black figure standing beside Walter Kennedy.

'You want me! Face me! Spare your men!'

Devlin lowered the trumpet and held the wheel for support. Waited.

Coxon slammed close his scope.

'*Finally!*'

He walked to the deck rail and called the midshipman at the companion.

'Tell Manvell and Howard hold fire!' He sent his next command to Jenkins.

'Bring her to!'

Devlin heard, unlashed the wheel and faced his deck.

'Heave to! Helm-a-lee!' And he pushed the wheel down to his knee. To come about. Broadside to broadside.

And the rain eased as if to gratify.

And the storm was worn of enough of herself to spare to listen.

# Chapter Forty

*M*anvell and Howard climbed to the deck under the rain curtain over the companionway, their shirts steaming, but there was little respite in the open from the stifling decks below. The air heavy all around. They looked over to the pirate under a hundred yards from their own gunwale. The length of their decks was similar but the other a good jump down. They stood for a moment. Apart from the five marines with their muskets ready the deck was without animosity. The guns below waited. Manvell looked up to the tops of the pirate where black shapes stood behind falconets and waited. And then his eyes passed down to the bobbing quarterdeck and he chilled. He saw Patrick Devlin for the first time. And his captain was hailing.

'*Patrick*!' Coxon disliked the trumpet, a foolish-looking tool, but its power through the sleeting rain had use. 'I know of the gold! I know of the priests! And the island!' He paused for the words to fall in Devlin's ears, for him to weigh them. And then he took a breath.

'You are outgunned! You will not prevail! It is only you, only your head that is required for your king!' He lowered the trumpet and found Manvell beside him.

'Captain!' Manvell pulled Coxon's cloak to him. 'What goes on here?'

Coxon shrugged Manvell from him.

'I am at my duty, Manvell. Petitioning the pirate's surrender. Would that not be better suited for your temperament?' He turned his shoulder. 'And don't touch me again in front of him.'

Manvell stepped back and glared away Kennedy's grin. He looked down at Howard's confusion.

Bide, his eyes said. Bide.


Peter Sam joined Devlin. He had seen the officer grab Coxon and declined to do the same in front of the enemy.

'Devlin! What plan is this?'

Devlin's eyes remained fixed on Coxon as he spoke.

'He says he knows of the gold. Knows all. That might serve.'

'We don't have the gold.'

'But he don't know that.'

He moved away, to lean over the rail without the trumpet. He cupped his hands across his mouth.

'What gold, John?'

Coxon looked back, ignoring the roll of the deck.

'He thinks me a fool.' The words only to himself. He raised the trumpet.

'You remember Kennedy?' He shouted across so Devlin's men might hear. 'He has joined to bring you to justice for the murder of his father. I tell your men I have been to Sierra Leone. I have heard all! It is over!'

Peter Sam raised his head at the accusation of murder.

He had believed his captain when he had told the tale. He believed him still. But a king's ship had brought a young man a long way to tell a lie. He looked at Devlin's back.

There had been a young lad favoured by Peter Sam. Black, black hair, and skin with the luminosity of the moon. There had been Seth Toombs. There had been that night on St Nick, the Verdes, where Devlin had been the only one to return alive. He had believed that tale also.

A long way to bring a boy for a lie.

'So it is murder you want of me, John! Murder I did not do. Gold I do not have!'

The storm rolled them, furious that both ships had decided to sit her out for conversation. She had done listening.

'Do your men know how much you lie, Patrick? That is how I found you! How I always find you!'

Devlin climbed to the gunwale, climbed to the shrouds.

'Then come find me!'

Coxon did not pause. He dropped the trumpet, threw off his cloak and pulled himself to his own rail, ignored the press of his belly against his ribs.

'Lower your black rag,' he called. 'Give up yourself. I'll spare your men.'

Devlin pushed back his coat. To show the pirate, to show the pistol, the cutlass.

'Not this year!'

Manvell had heard enough. He gripped Howard.

'Go to the twelves. Fire. I'll form the men to board.'

Coxon had ears long used to hear the words of officers in any weather. He turned against the shrouds to Manvell.

'No!'

Manvell and Howard looked up to their captain in the rigging.

'Lines!' he ordered. 'Haul us to them!' He nodded to Jenkins to follow the order if Manvell did not.

'I will go aboard.'

# Chapter Forty-One

*T*he water, churning like milk, gave too much movement for boarding planks, the *Shadow*'s weatherdeck too low besides. There was no room to launch a boat between but maybe they could derrick one across with a party aboard.

But that was not swift enough for their captain nor the pirate.

They stared across as the grapples were away from them both, the ships hauled together.

Coxon ordered a hook to the *Shadow*'s rigging, in front of his crew rising from the decks below with cutlass and pistol. Manvell darted to grab him back then remembered the command not to touch.

'*Captain*! This is lunacy!' he bellowed through the rain against his face, cascading now from the two ships' yards like gabled roofs as the wood met.

'We have the advantage! He will hold you to ransom his escape!'

'Then you will be captain sooner than you might have hoped, Christopher.'

Manvell climbed up.

'Let me, Captain. My sword is the greater. Allow me the chance to restore my honour!'

Coxon kicked him back.

'You have a wife, Christopher. Children to come. A future.' The wind dropped for his last words. 'This is mine.'

Coxon took his rope, walked the ratlines, his coat whipping about his legs. He paused to look through the grid of the shrouds to Thomas Howard holding out a pistol butt to him. He reached through and brushed the weapon aside, his hand left out for the other to take. Howard reached, shook it.

Coxon nodded.

'There are sealed papers in my desk, Thomas. Should I not return, Lieutenant, they are yours. You may understand my recklessness then.'

He climbed one more step as his back hung over the water, he held for it to come back again and turned to Devlin grinning at him from his own rigging.

'No pistol, John?'

Coxon pushed off, swung to the *Shadow* and landed on his feet like he had done this all his life.

Like a pirate.

'There is not a world yet,' he let go the rope and drew his cutlass, 'where a master needs a pistol against his servant.'

Devlin dropped to the deck to join him. His blade scraped out. A final sound.

Never had he done this frivolously. Never once for show.

It stayed unsheathed until done.

Howard and Manvell watched their captain and the pirate and felt the men pressing at their backs, all eyes on the ragged long-haired brigands staring them down. They stumbled as the storm began to turn the two lashed ships and they took hold of each other's forearms as if dancing.

'Thomas!' Manvell yelled. 'I suggest that is you who is in command now! What order you?'

Howard steadied himself against the mizzen and pulled Manvell to its shelter.

'I think the oil will not work for much longer. The storm will wreck us both if we stay together,' he pointed upwards to the spars fencing against each other. 'She will take us down I fear. The pirate is taking too much water. I think he knows it.'

'So he will want the *Standard*, will he not? That is why he has brought us to close. To board and take us. The twelves will end it. We could fire. Cut free and run!'

Howard pushed Manvell's arm from his own.

'We will still have all of that for a time yet. And we still have the captain, sir.' He wiped his face, hoped Manvell could read it better now.

'You were not *there*, sir. I was. You do not want to give them reason to board. There is something between the captain and this man that even I do not understand.' He looked down to Coxon and Devlin circling around each other's cutlass lengths.

'I think the storm will grant them a minute or two.' He looked at the heads crowding about.

'Manvell!' He pushed the bodies away from him, his voice urgent. 'Where is Kennedy?'

Coxon was on a pirate ship and the woe of that circumstance surrounded him in all its motley-clothed discord. He ignored them save for the sight of the ones he knew.

The leather waistcoat, huge body and red beard of Peter Sam; the lean, scarred one who had owned his pistols for a time – that one had been on The Island and on Providence. He had been alive for a long while. Mark him. Some other younger faces that seemed familiar from the cells on Providence also. It was shameful that he knew them, shameful that he knew the man before him. He had been fighting that shame for too long.

'Patrick,' he paused in his carefully-paced walk. 'Would you not want to know how I know of the gold?'

Devlin checked to Peter Sam then to Hugh, put his blade to his side, tapped it against his boot where the tip dripped water to the deck. The hilt sat dry in his palm.

'Hugh,' he ordered. 'Back below. Wood and water.'

Hugh rubbed the wrists of his pistols and slipped away.

'There is no gold, John,' Devlin said. 'Trust me. You find me empty.'

Coxon lowered his own cutlass.

'That is not how Dandon had it.'

Devlin's sword turned in his hand and Coxon savoured the enmity from across the oak boards.

'He held out long. Kennedy worked it out of him. Eventually. The Porto islands where you have been. The Buzzard. The gold cross.'

Devlin's head went down, his hat covering his face, the water streaming through the cocks.

'Where is he?'

Coxon pulled his blade through the elbow of his shirt to rinse the rain. 'He is my prisoner. He gave up all that he had.'

Peter Sam cursed and Devlin raised his head to cut him down. Coxon saw the look, dived on it.

'But Dandon protected you all!' He ran his gaze over the pirates.

'He only gave what he knew when he learned your captain was a murderer before the pirate! That he ran from London with blood!' He turned enough to show his back to Devlin.

'Did he not tell you so? Murdered he who had taken him in? How many murders to make him captain?'

Peter Sam listened, watched Devlin's lowered hat.

They had made him captain when only he had returned that night in the Verdes. Seth Toombs had survived alone, had they known it, but Devlin had shot him through the mouth soon enough to silence him when the chance came. And there was Thomas Deakins – Peter Sam to hold him close no more.

'This true, Devlin?' Peter Sam stepped from the wall of men. 'Who else did you kill to get this ship?' His hand crept to his blade's pommel.

Devlin looked to his quartermaster, opened his mouth only to have it cut by an Irish voice hailing from the fo'c'sle.

'All true!' Kennedy shouted over the deck, and the heads swivelled to look at him. He had slipped from the *Standard*, had taken advantage of the grappling ropes and the wood so close together. From a king's ship to a pirate. And he knew pirates.

'That dog killed my father! My name is Captain Walter Kennedy.' He jumped the steps.

'Captain Kennedy of the great pirate Roberts!' He sucked in the looks and whispers that the name evoked.

'Brought from the noose to have my due,' he pointed to Devlin across the deck, 'with *that* man there.'

Devlin walked forward, Coxon forgotten.

'I didn't kill your father and you know it.'

Peter Sam stood between them.

'As you didn't kill Seth? As you didn't kill Deakins. *My* Deakins. And the rest?'

Kennedy could feel his time arrive, his chance. Coxon had hanged him back in London this very day. He had been newborn this day and now was back among his kind. He could not have planned it better.

'I call my right as brethren. By sword, by pistol, for my slight!'

Devlin looked up at Peter Sam.

'This is not the place, Peter. We don't do this. Not you and I.'

Peter showed nothing. There was chaos here. The beating rain, the king's ship. Confrontations will out under such, will end under such.

Coxon rang his sword against the bell.

'Enough!'

The ship upon him again.

'My orders are for Devlin! Give him up and I swear you no harm. Be free with your gold. All of you free with your ship! What do you owe him who has brought the king upon you?'

Adam Cowrie walked out of the line. Showed Coxon the fat scar in the palm of his hand where a poker had been rammed for stealing a pair of clogs.

'We don't owe him nothing. We don't live like that. I got this scar and six weeks for owing somebody. Reckon you owe, too, Cap'n. That's why you're here. We takes all what we could never have. Neither borrower nor lender be. That's Shakespeare, Cap'n.' He put a hand out to Devlin. 'And *he* taught me that when men like you would have me shovel their shit.'

Coxon pushed him back, lifted his sword.

'Good for you! *Patrick*!' He came on. 'Kennedy can wait! If your men won't deal than I shall!'

Devlin walked away from Peter Sam, a palm behind to order him to hold.

'Give me Dandon. Show him to me,' he mirrored Coxon's sword.

Coxon began to circle again.

'I have orders for your head. Subdue me. I'll give you your friend.'

'And my ship?'

'That's for their next captain to decide.'

'I beat you before, John. On The Island, remember? Nothing's changed.'

Coxon stopped walking, his feet set.

'Everything has changed!'

He thrust forward and Devlin hit away the blade, gave his pistol to the crowd with his free hand and pulled his dagger with the same. Coxon stiffened at the speed of him.

'John,' Devlin was calm as they walked the wet cockpit of their fight, the crowd shifting back. 'I ain't your boy no more. I done this many times. I'll show you your back through your chest.'

Coxon shook his head.

'Not this year!'

He thrust again, turned into a sweeping strike with a turn of his feet and still Devlin's blade was there.

Nothing grand. Not under the rage of the storm. Devlin had fought Trouin and that had been glorious, but that was on a clean summer deck on still waters. Here the deck yawed and the two of them pitched and brawled like drunkards across the sopping oak.

Nothing of skill showed in their hacking; their blades struck clumsily and Devlin tossed away the advantage of his dagger to grip wood for balance. Peter Sam stamped on the black blade as it slid to his foot. He picked it up. His now. To give back or to remember by.

Elbows to jaws, knees to guts, steel and brass filling their senses as their guarded knuckles closed to their heads.

Above, the men in the tops kept their swivels to the deck of *Standard*'s men craning to view, Howard and Manvell keeping order, holding onto the shrouds for a better look, and they gritted their teeth when Coxon slipped to his knees as the ships turned in the squall, the storm reminding everybody where they were, under its eye.

The pirate took a breath, held out a hand. The captain beat it away, steadied himself with his sword into the oak, saw a gap. A boot out and the sweep of a leg.

Devlin's back hit the deck and he looked up blindly at the rain firing into his face, his masts rolling in circles above. He came up slow.

He would not give quarter again.

They hunched over to keep their weight low, cutlasses to the deck. Together they wiped their mouths of the rain and sweat and again charged.

Years before they had spent Sundays sparring when Mass was done, the captain seeing the promise in an Irishman that could read. The captain teaching the young man the art of the astrolabe and Davis quadrant. He might have become a sailing master under Coxon's tutelage, aspire beyond his birth. Instead he had become the pirate when Coxon had been taken from him. Devlin's first act of piracy had been petty – to take Coxon's own sword and silver case of lighting pine-sticks bequeathed from his father. He had probably eyed them through all their years together and always dreamt of taking them, unknowing that Coxon would have willed them to him. He had after all no hearth and wife waiting, no son at his knee. Instead he had spawned a pirate that had pissed on every step of his career. And now he sold yards of cloth in Boston, brought back to the king only for his knowledge of the damned. All his years of service reduced to sniffing out his old steward's arse from the stench of others'.

His cutlass's scalloped guard punched into Devlin's face, scraped up to his eye. He did not wait for the blood and punched it again, the crunch rolling up to his shoulder.

Devlin's head went back, hand to his face, white shirt open. No room to thrust so Coxon swiped, rain arcing off his blade, and watched the watery red seep through the shirt, its boldness inciting enough for a back slice and another glorious stripe of red running with the rain drained down the pirate's ribs while Coxon's chest filled with the sight.

Devlin fell back. Arms caught him, hands across his chest as it drooled with his blood. They pushed him forward with private abetting slaps and then looked at their hands, looked down at their bloodied palms before the rain almost instantly rinsed them clean.

Devlin's vision was blurred: a white shirt and black coat was before him, sword up, defending with two inches of steel. He shook his head clear just enough to see the silver edge flying at his head.

His guard caught it, ran down to meet the other and slammed it back with all his weight to hit the snarling face that he could no longer remember.

Devlin staggered to wood, steadied himself and as the cold blood on his body reminded him, recalled where he was. He sensed his open back, the feeling of space on his spine, and twisted from the sword whistling through the rain.

He watched the blade cut and stick deep into the wood, the arm heaving to pull it free, and looked along it to the bared teeth and wide eyes.

He raised his cutlass high.

The cutlass was short to stay clear of ropes when boarding and swinging, was crude and heavy to cut canoes and carcasses of meat. It cleaved. Ordered for the purpose.

Devlin tasted his own blood, the salt of the tropical rain in his mouth. The spice of slaughter. It cleared the fog for him to recognise the face just enough.

He held back the hacking blow, slipped his edge to Coxon's throat, felt the flesh hang over it and used his free hand to prise the fingers from the stuck sword one by one. His strength proved greater than Coxon's resistance to it – one finger prised back and free for every year Devlin had served him. His hand was now a fist and he sent it flying to the sternum of his former master with a hammer blow that slammed him to the deck.

He stood on Coxon's arms, sword tip to throat. Coxon bucked for a moment, enough for pride, and Devlin let him do it.

'That's it finished, John,' he said. 'We're done for the years.'

His blood dripped on Coxon, the rain spattering it like freckles. He pressed the blade just enough to draw pink, a shave for his men to see.

'Give. And give me Dandon.'

He did not expect the laugh.

'He is gone!' Coxon mocked. 'Escaped! To the sea. Dead I hope! I have nothing for you. Nothing!'

'So why do we do this? I promise I have no gold.'

'Am I lying about Dandon? As you lie about the gold?'

The blood brought sweat to Devlin's lips. More spice to grind with his grist. His eyes swam unfocused with the wounds about him.

Just push down with the cutlass. Push down through the neck to the deck. End his past.

He faltered. The wind and rain battered his reason and the roar of the world dulled as if he were already under the sea, back to diving into the pool of Levasseur's cave. He needed to rest, to sleep. He tried to recall the names of the faces of his men about him; the mystery of a ship against his broadside.

Kennedy whipped a hanger from an idle belt and ran across the deck.

'A coward is it?' he cried. 'I'll show how a pirate deals these dogs!'

He slapped off Coxon's hat, pulled him up by his hair just as the fog slipped from Devlin and he heard the howling cry as Kennedy drove his blade through Coxon's chest and twisted it free.

'That's the way of it!' Kennedy held his sword high. The blade was clean, the blow too fast to even carry blood.

His mother swept into the bedroom, her dress as white as the curtains that billowed out from the summer window.

'John Coxon!' she frowned as she bent and gathered up his school-clothes. 'Am I to spend forever picking up after you, young man?'

'No, Mother,' he said. He was as tall as her and that was not true.

'Not forever.'

The clothes fell to the floor where she had stood and now vanished. The curtains blew harder, wider, rolling above his head. They were sails now, grey with the smut of cannon. They came back and forth through the window in heartbeats. Only the beats were the wet sound of a mop slapped to a deck. Grey sails. Rain on his face.

'It's a sucking wound,' Peter Sam said to Devlin as they looked down at Coxon's bubbling chest. 'His lung has gone. Drawing air through him. He's not even here any more.'

'What'll we do?' Devlin asked, watching as Coxon's eyes looked through him glassily.

Peter Sam pulled his pistol, pushed it past Coxon's lips with a terrible scrape of iron against tooth, and fired with a hand over the barrel to cut the spray of blood. 'We do that,' he said and turned Devlin to Kennedy who was dipping his blade out to them both.

'You see, lads!' Kennedy laughed. 'That's a captain's work! Let me spare Devlin and I'll lead us to glory, boys! I be your captain now! I've come from Roberts and escaped London to find my way again!'

Devlin could see the fear in the slitted eyes and the bravado of the bully – but without the meat and muscle to back it up. He looked back to Coxon's slumped and portly shape. He suddenly looked heavier than before. Heavier because his lungs had expanded, had shifted in his chest, and his neck had swollen as the air had ballooned there. His face was a bloody mask.

Peter Sam pushed him round to where the *Standard*'s men were all leaning along the gunwale and staring down. Manvell and Howard hung in the shrouds.

'Do something. Before they do. We're taking in water.'

Devlin saw only Kennedy.

'Axes.' Devlin was breathing hard. 'Cut us loose. They can't fire close or damage themselves. Make sail. Get ahead. She has no chasers. We do.' He stroked the blood from his face. 'And give me a minute.' He took his dagger from Peter Sam's belt and with his cutlass crossed the planks to Kennedy.

'One minute.'

Peter Sam bellowed his orders and every hand that held one slammed a boarding axe through the ropes that bound the broadsides and the *Shadow* got more scars for her end of days.

A handful of the *Standard*'s crew had climbed the gunwale to leap. The sudden heave of the deck as the tension snapped from the ropes drew in their courage. And the storm had not done with them yet.

The ships pivoted and spun apart. Together they had been almost eight hundred tonnes of wood and cordage but torn loose they were paper boats in a drain hole and the tempest let them know it.

Kennedy's heels tripped back from the bloodied form coming on.

'Now, Patrick. I just did what you could not. Don't be showing these lads that you're sorry I took the life of a man against us. I'm choosing to fight. You be the one choosing to swallow. Let thems declare on who they want as captain. That's the way.'

Devlin did not speak.

He had words. He had platitudes. He had Virgil and Shakespeare ready to sprout and vilify. But men that are only 'things' deserve only silence.

Manvell, from the shrouds, watched the pirate captain as he advanced. He had seen Devlin and Coxon fight, then had seen Kennedy run Coxon through. Now, now as the ship pulled away, only two men existed on the deck before him.

Howard was below him, shouted up.

'We could fire the sixes, sir!'

Manvell looked down.

'You are in command, Thomas.'

'Your advisement, sir?'

Manvell raised his eyes to the guns set in the tops.

'They have not fired. They could cut us down if they wished,' he said. 'And I want to see this.'

Kennedy swallowed, wished for a pistol and then Devlin was inside his sword's length and had cut his edge across Kennedy's wrist.

The hilt fell out of his hand as if he were already dead, the blood falling with the rain and he clasped the severed veins with his good hand.

He gasped at it. He had never even seen it happen and still Devlin came on, too close for the cutlass and then Kennedy's eyes looked down to the dagger sticking out of his chest and he had not seen that either; as his father had not seen.

He fell to his knees and still Devlin did not speak. Kennedy felt his chest pulse against the blade. He gripped his wrist tighter, fought the need to let go the staunching of the blood to pull the dagger free.

Then the blade had been pulled – too precious to lose – and he was in the air, tumbling over the side as Devlin cradled him, lifted Kennedy's knees and, pulling him up by his throat, sent him into the sea.

Devlin sank against the gunwale, his wounds draining him again now his lust was spent. He watched a shark leap on the body and hoped Kennedy was not yet dead enough.

There were birds on the fish's back, and the thrashing of more sharks, the rolling white bellies that always followed the ships. He looked up to the sky clearing, the rain only coming down now and not from every angle, great wings and cries about the crosstrees.

Sharks. Birds. Life coming back to the sea. The edge of the storm.

He looked to Manvell watching from the shrouds. Devlin's cutlass and dagger went back to his belt. Done now. Put away. He tipped his fingers to his hat and at the man in the shrouds.

*For another day. I have avenged. Avenged him.*

The figure nodded back.

*Aye. Another day. I have your face now. Your ship is holed. If you taunt I will destroy.*

And Manvell climbed down the shrouds.

Devlin swung back to his crew, to the *Shadow*.

'Any other want to call for captain? I'm yet only half-dead.'

He saw only the backs of heads and he clasped his ribs, leaned with his ship, with Peter Sam, the doubts no longer on his face.

'Out of here,' he said and the *Shadow* heeled to his word.

# Chapter Forty-Two

*T*he main course fell, the *Shadow*'s quarterdeck already at the fo'c'sle of the *Standard* and Devlin yelled for Lawson to brace them back.

'Hold!'

He knelt by Coxon's body and brought him forward to his shoulder, dead arm along his back. He tried to stand. Peter Sam caught his stumble and Devlin pushed him by and rose with his old master over his shoulder.

'To them. Not us.'

He staggered to the gunwale, his eye on Manvell and Howard, and waited for the ship to gain. His hand went to the rail to steady his legs then returned a breath later to holding the arm draped about him.

The derrick came and Coxon's body was lashed beneath his arms and swung across. Devlin painted red by both their bloods.

He watched the body being lowered to the *Standard*, watched Manvell and Howard carefully unbind him, and then let Lawson give the cry to slip away. He took his hat and threw it across to their deck.

Howard saw it travel, watched it fall along the scuppers. He would pick it up soon enough to prevent some liar proudly claiming it as a token. He tapped Manvell's shoulder.

'I went for the papers, Christopher. As the captain said. I thought them orders.' He put them out to Manvell, the seal broken: a purple seal.

'Maybe you were right. This is madness.'

Manvell stood away from the body, opened the vellum cautiously against the rain and then understood why Howard had no fear to bring them out upon the sodden deck.

He passed them one under the other, again and again. Three times, like shuffling cards, hoping something might appear upon their blank sheets.

'Did you break the seal, Thomas?'

'He told me to. Should he not return. I do not understand. He charged them with such importance.'

Manvell looked at the halves of the seal. Symbols he did not recognise. He tore them loose, pocketed them and crushed the paper to the deck.

'Never mind,' he said.

The bosun, Abel Wales, had already draped Coxon's cloak over the body, the blue and red face shrouded. Manvell nodded his thanks.

'We're going to take him home now,' he said.

Devlin picked up Coxon's hat. It fitted as poorly as all the others that he had never bought so that did not matter. Peter Sam stood beside him and Devlin held on to him.

'I need Dandon,' he said. 'I need binding.'

'I'll do that,' Peter pulled him up for the sight of the men. They would not see him weak. 'We're going back north. Back to the island. We need to repair. Right soon. Hartley has the stern guns should they want to warm. You sure they don't have him?'

'He's slipped them. Like a dog in heat. Like *we* don't have the gold.'

'Not yet,' Peter Sam hauled him towards the cabin, his strength keeping the limp body upright.

'The storm and your past has wished us back.'

'It's the cross.' Devlin spat his blood. 'It don't want to be left. I reckon that now.'

Peter Sam lessened his pressure as Devlin whimpered. He carried him softer.

'Don't be getting holy on me now, Patrick.' He held the chin up as it fell, for no-one to see, and closed the doors behind.

# Chapter Forty-Three

*The Riberia Palace, Lisboa port. September 1721.*

Two months later

*T*he system of government by the Cortes was dissolved with the succession of King João V. He was absolute monarch, Prince of Brasil, and in less than two decades of his reign his country had dug and pillaged fortunes that Spain could not aspire to in four hundred years of exploration and exploitation. But no iron fist directed his rule.

Science and culture, religion and art were his principles; galleries, academies and libraries provided for his people. His empire was in its Golden Age, above even Spain, and now that the French, English and Dutch had squandered all their wealth into paper and companies Portugal's affluence and influence became the mark of nations. Their trust still abided in the fruits of the earth: gold, diamonds, timber, and, with its wealth, architecture that would have made Rome envious.

Let the swine build exchanges and brothels. Lisboa climbed to the sky with cathedrals and opera houses.

But João's last ambition remained unfulfilled. The wish, the need, to establish Portugal's Catholic church with that of Rome and Spain; and for that he had bribed and courted cardinals and ambassadors with relics, diamonds and beautiful young nuns for years. But there had come no confirmation. Not yet.

The courtier outside the music chamber waited for the Cristofori pianoforte to pause and opened the door before the music sheets turned. He crossed to the plain instrument, His Majesty's new toy.

'What is it, Melo?'

The king, in a black and silver suit, contrasted with the solemnity of the instrument before him.

'You seem agitated, Melo?' He had not looked up from his page, the soft sound of the instrument enough to carry on conversation. A portly, pale figure, hair already receding at thirty-one, he wore his Ramilie wig even in bed.

'Do not dwell on your words.'

'Your Majesty,' Melo bowed expertly, with his black cane mirroring the action of his foot backwards like a third leg. 'I have great news from the ships.'

The palace was built adjacent to the port with the shipyard alongside, a maritime palace for the great explorers of the earth. Whenever an English or Spanish ship 'discovered' a new island they inevitably found generations of Portuguese goats and trees already planted. The Portos did not claim them. To their captains they were only larders and carpenters' stores for their greater passages into the unknown.

'What news?' João paused only to tut and take a stylus to those of Scarlatti's notes he disapproved of.

'It is the *Santa Rosa*, Your Majesty, the ship that sailed with the *Nossa Senhora do Cabo*. She has come back.'

João looked at him now.

'She was not lost with the other? The priest O'Neill is with?'

'No, Your Majesty,' Melo bowed again. 'Some of the priests have come. But Father O'Neill is no longer amongst us.' He sniffed and gave an almost Gallic shrug. 'At least not alive.'

'Speak, Melo.' João returned to his corrections.

'They have come with a tale of the loss of the *Nossa Senhora* to the pirates. They would also like to present to you the coffin of Father O'Neill. They are outside but . . . it is apparent that they have had some . . . "assistance" in their passage, Your Majesty.'

'How do you mean?'

'I believe – by my understanding – as I follow the discourse with the brothers, that the priests are here by the mercy of . . .' he hesitated to find a better word but none was forthcoming. 'By the mercy of *pirates*, Your Majesty.'

'Privateers? Our privateers?'

Melo winced.

'No,' he said. 'I would believe them English, Sire.' He gestured to the doors which opened on his command. 'And not privateers at all. If except of their own device.'

Coffins are unmistakable objects when walked into a room, and unforgettable when carried on the shoulders of eight pirates.

Devlin and Peter Sam walked at the front, the coffin bright and freshly made, wide enough for two men, as plain and long as the pianoforte. They set it down heavily in the centre of the chamber with a puff of its wood dust and Devlin removed his hat – Coxon's hat. The others stepped back and saluted as the priests they had fetched from Bourbon bowed into the room.

Devlin had stood in such rooms before. He knew enough to wait until spoken to.

João stood and Melo lowered his head as his king considered.

The one with the hat and long-coat was surely their leader and he raised his chin to him. The king spoke with an Italian accent to his English.

'Melo says you are pirates? Is this true? Explain.'

Devlin put his hat to his thigh and stepped away from the coffin.

'My name is Patrick Devlin, Your Majesty. I rescued your priest O'Neill. He died in service to you. I respectfully return his fellows.'

João saw the weapons at every corner of flesh.

'You bring his body to us? And you come to us armed? Out of the same respect?'

Devlin grinned.

'Just wanted to make sure we get out again, Your Majesty. And I never said I brought his body back.'

He kicked the coffin lid to the marbled floor. And the gold within lit the ceiling.

João and Melo came forward. They looked down at the gold cross emblazoned with the fist-sized rubies.

Melo was open-mouthed, crossed himself.

'It is the Flaming Cross! The Goa cross! It is here! How is this possible?'

No such humour for a king. Not even an eyebrow raised.

'The Cross of Fire,' João affirmed. 'Stolen by pirates. We ordered it made. We had thought it truly lost. How did you come by this, Captain?'

Devlin kept his eyes on the king.

'O'Neill told that you sent him after this. He knew where the pirate Levasseur had taken it. He led us to it. I brought it back.'

João pursed his lips. 'We did not send him. We have not seen him since he left with the ship and thought him lost, as the ship, as the gold.'

Devlin looked at Peter Sam. The priest had been an adept liar. Kings had no need of lies. João saw the look.

'No matter. This cross means much to our Church and our people. Do you know what it contains, Captain?'

Devlin ignored the piety of the query.

'I don't bring it out of charity.'

João scoffed.

'No, of course. There should be reward. And what of the pirates that took it? This "Buzzard" and . . . Taylor? You are English. How do we know you are not he?'

'I'm not English.' He cocked his head to the priests. 'And you can ask them.'

'And The Buzzard? What of him?'

'We saw him once. Not when we got this.'

They had coursed back to the island, made good their repairs to the *Shadow* and blasted through the rocks above to get down into the cave. Levasseur was not there. Only the ghost of him and his dead all around. A month of labour then back to Bourbon for the priests. And no Dandon, but his story recounted by the priests.

Coxon had taken him. That much true. Where he was now was their last mystery and the king had the same thought that Peter Sam had raised the night they left Bourbon for Lisboa.

'But why would pirates bring such a treasure back to its home? You would be rich all your days.' He took his eyes from the pirate and the golden coffin, walked the line of priests who bowed at his passing, Melo followed on his heels in exact step.

'I want a letter of marque,' Devlin did not turn, his admiration was on the pianoforte. He often forgot that men made beautiful things beyond the crudity of cutlass and pistol. He had seen nothing like it. Another world he had long passed from.

'I bring your cross for my allegiance.'

João halted his inspection of the priests and Melo almost walked into his back.

'You wish to be a privateer? For Portugal? We have no war.'

'A man of mine is missing,' Devlin faced him. 'He's in Indian waters. I could use papers for the ports.'

'You seek one man?' João came back to the coffin. 'Is he a lover?'

Devlin felt himself blush. 'No, Sire.' He looked into a king's eyes. 'He is my friend.'

João smiled. 'You would search the Indian sea for just one man, Captain? *We* have many friends. Many friends that do not deserve such an endeavour.'

Devlin hung a thumb near his pistol.

'I don't. And there is something else.'

João raised his chin higher, his brow shifting his wig.

'The less you talk, Captain,' he drawled, 'the more you seem to say. Go on.'

Devlin took a breath.

'I have had altercations with some of your governors.' He tried not to say the name. It was not the pirate's way to carry guilt against those dead by their whims, and Valentim Mendes had been no saint, but his death had come in that garden in Charles Town and Valentim had assisted him that day, if only in the hope to have the opportunity to kill Devlin himself.

'I would hope that the cross, and my offer, may settle that. For me.'

João took in the lean form, uncommonly still, the dried blood on his boots and buckles, the sharp eyes watching and waiting on every word.

'We know not of what you speak but take your word on it. Very well, Captain. Portugal can always use more men upon her waves. Melo will see to your papers. We are indebted to you for the return of our Church's cross. The Cross of Fire will further our position in the eyes of Rome, as was our original intent. And we had faith that such an object could not hide from good men.' He genuflected to the cross, no pride that his head was the lowest in the room; unseemly for a king and Melo lowered himself prone. João crossed himself as he rose, saw the cut in the heart where the axe had smited.

'However, the *Santa Rosa* cannot be appointed to you. She belongs to her port. To us. And we understand it customary for privateers to sail their own ships. It is simple to arrange purchase for you if you wish? That is if you are in ... "adequate" funds, Captain?'

'I have my own ship.'

It is quite a feat to shock a king.

'You have brought a pirate ship into our port? To our palace?' He looked down at the water outside his window, the dozens of masts.

Devlin stood by Peter Sam.

'As I said,' he put back his hat. 'Wanted to make sure we get out again.' He bowed, slapped his men to leave. Melo led them to the door, Devlin tipped his hat to the grateful priests.

João went back to his pianoforte, tutted at more of Scarlatti's notes, called back to the pirate.

'Captain? What happened to the rest of the gold? The *Virgin*'s treasure. You have knowledge on this?'

Devlin held by the door, touched his hat that fitted better every day.

'Most gone, Your Majesty. The ports say Taylor took his share to Panama. The Buzzard and his men had a disagreement. Mutiny. They left him and your boys here for dead. We only found The Buzzard. He had done for O'Neill.'

'So they took it all? These mutineers?' He touched a low key and let it hang. 'These "other" pirates?'

Devlin brought his hat through his hands, his rakish grin giving all of the Irish rogue and the gypsy selling you your own horse.

'Like I said,' he nodded to the coffin. 'I don't bring it out of charity, Sire.'

João went back to the wooden keys, the soft touch sensual, the sound angelically peaceful compared to the hall-filling harpsichord.

'We hope you find your friend, Captain,' he waved a hand in dismissal. 'We would almost fear for the world if you did not.'

Devlin squared his hat to his head. Kept the grin hanging like the pianoforte's note.

'Your Majesty.'

He closed the door. Left his new king.

Left to find his friend.

# Epilogue

*T*he uppers of Christopher Manvell's shoes were deer-skin, the soles shark leather. They kissed most floors, but the black and white tiles of the corridor echoed his confidence as he strode along.

The doors opened to his approach, a darkened room beyond. It was August but the room was cold as he crossed the threshold and the doors clicked softly shut behind him.

The candlelight from the table and the shuttered windows pricked at his eyes, their glow permitting his gaze to sweep the room. He saw the smutty outlines of paintings recently removed, liveried men with kerchiefs about their faces standing behind him at the doors. And the white masks coming slowly forward from the back of the long room.

'Do you not announce yourself to your superiors, Lieutenant Manvell, when you enter chambers?' A muffled voice. Manvell could not tell which mask spoke. He cleared his throat.

'I have been sent from Walsingham House, sir. I do not know what this building's official capacity represents, beyond victualling. Nor whom I address, sir. Not when they wear masks.'

'It is called security, Lieutenant.' The other white face now.

'Yours or mine, sir?' Manvell's voice snipered from the dark.

'Both, Lieutenant. Both. We understand that you return from your sojourn with Captain Coxon. Unsuccessfully we might add.'

Manvell was taller than them both and straightened himself even more.

'Most unsuccessful, as the voyage ended with Captain Coxon's death. Had you not heard? And why am I here? Who are you, sirs? I was told that I would receive my orders here.'

The masks turned into profile as they shared a look.

'We are informed that you are the Duke of Beaufort's son-in-law, Lieutenant?'

'And that implies . . .?'

'A great deal. Or nothing. You should understand.'

'Then you misunderstand, sir.' Manvell came forward. 'I am a publican's son. I married a good woman. Not for her nobility. You misjudge me. I have no society that grants me privilege. I work for my king. I will go to Walsingham House.'

The masks froze.

'You know, Lieutenant, that Walsingham – he whose face is etched above the door of your Board – was Elizabeth's spy-master general? Even if you were not born a gentleman you surely have gleaned something from the horse you have spurred your heels into?'

Manvell's hand gripped his sword.

'You dare speak of my wife, sir?'

Silence. The masks came together, whispered together, then lifted in unison so that Manvell could not tell which one spoke.

'She is due again, is she not? A birth lost before? Such a pity. And the duke has suffered considerably since the collapse of the South Sea Company. There is much you need to discover when you are home. The duke is one of many nobles who have suffered financial pain.'

Manvell did not loose his grip on his sword's hilt.

'I will go home when I am released from my ship. And I do not think that anything you have to say has any meaning to me.'

'Not Devlin?' one of them said. 'That must have some meaning surely?'

Manvell let go his sword.

'I have given my report.'

They moved to behind the table.

'And Coxon's orders not part?'

Manvell had nothing to hide.

'There was nothing on them.'

'Yet they were sealed. The seal broken. What does that mean, Lieutenant?'

Manvell went into his waistcoat, pulled out one half of the purple seal, sure he should keep the other. He tossed it like a penny to a beggar at the mask's feet.

'It means he was betrayed.'

A foot upon the seal. 'No,' a black gloved finger raised. 'It means he knew the value of trust. Of secrecy. And of reward.'

'Captain Coxon was a Norfolk parson's son,' Manvell extolled. 'I am a publican's. And just as provincial. You measure us both wrongly from your towers, sir. I am done.'

He put back his hat, turned to the door. The scarfed guards barred.

Manvell wrapped his fist to his hilt.

'You may ask the gentlemen if it be wise to delay me, sirs. I'm sure such detail has been granted them.' He scraped the blade an inch, sure the glint in his eye reflected.

They looked to the masks, something given, and stepped aside. Manvell pushed back his blade with a snap. A perfect sound. He made for the door, a sharp voice like a slap stayed his hand.

'It would take a captain to bring us Devlin, Lieutenant. Out of war this is how commissions can be sanctioned. Great destinies can be made for those who know the pirate's face. Great destinies.'

Manvell opened the door, flushed the room with light. He had words to reply but they choked in his throat as he saw Thomas Howard a step from the door, waiting to enter.

Howard's face glowed, his joy at seeing Manvell at the place where he had expected the end of his season. Manvell closed the door, marked across the floor the count of his steps to kill them both.

'So you will inspire the boy with your lusts when the man refuses? Loyalty to his captain his coin? Is this our navy now? The pocketbooks of companies?'

The masks did not move. Took turns to speak.

'No. Not companies. Prime ministers. Kingdoms backed by companies.' They pressed forward. 'And he is hardly a boy.'

They came on, but mindful of the sword's length that might still appear.

'You would let Roberts and Devlin to their work? Let them stop a third of your country's trade? The African work almost halved. Is this not as noble as war? Is half-pay your ambition? Your captaincy papers will be signed on the morrow. Your wife proud. The duke's credit restored.'

Manvell listened, his head lowered. The masks noted the hesitation their barter had coaxed forth.

'The pirates have plays now. Ballads. Where are yours? Where are Coxon's? Who will remember him now?'

Manvell lifted his head.

'I will remember him.'

'And you will honour him. Why would you not? Or would you rather let Howard to the task?'

Manvell stepped closer. 'Captains Ogle and Herdman? I would join with them? And what are they promised?'

'Knighthoods. Would that suit? They will be the first men ever honoured for the extinction of pirates. Think how that would ring around the world.'

'And am I only here because I have seen the man's face? Howard and I? Is that our worth?'

The masks dipped respectfully. 'That has worth. That gives you purpose.'

'Written orders,' Manvell demanded. 'No blank vellum.'

The masks bowed.

'There is only one small discretion . . . *Captain* Manvell.'

Manvell posed indifference.

'It has come to us that Devlin is now a privateer. Under the Portuguese. That must be handled . . . delicately. Do you understand?'

Manvell pulled the door open, flushing the room with light again as the masks retreated.

'My blade is ever "delicate", gentlemen. I will see my wife now. Howard will be my First. Your letters will find me with the duke. Good day, gentlemen.'

He slammed the door behind him and began along the corridor, taking Howard's arm. Thomas Howard slapped himself free.

'I have an appointment, sir!'

'You are with me, Thomas. We were sent here together apparently. And apparently we are set together also.'

He walked on, let Howard find his step with him as he took the piece of wax from his waistcoat, examined it minutely as

411

he strode. The figure of a bull, a sea-serpent's tail. He would enquire upon it.

'Accompany me to my wife, Thomas. We will receive our orders there.' He put the smooth token away.

'We go back amongst pirates.'

# Author's Note

$\mathcal{T}$he story of Olivier Levasseur is one of the greatest tales of pirate lore. It is also probably one of the most fictitious.

For those who don't know the legend (I mean the one *after* this story) the myth is that at his execution Levasseur rips from around his neck a small metal tube and yells to the crowd something along the lines of: 'My treasure! To those who can find it!' at which point he tosses the capsule into the baying horde.

Inside is a cryptogram, a code of Enigma style proportions which has baffled treasure hunters ever since.

And it's all nonsense.

Well, mostly nonsense.

In between writing the other books in this series I was constantly researching this one as I always wanted to tell it, and others actually asked me if was I planning to do so because it is a pirate fan favourite, so in many ways it has been the book I have spent the most time on and the more research I did the less satisfied I became on any of the 'truths' attached to Levasseur.

The Portuguese treasure ship was real but if we start from Charles Johnson's account(1) the pirates are Taylor, Condent, England and La Bouche. I reduced it just to Taylor and Levasseur for simplicity. In Johnson's work a letter from a

Captain Mackra names a pirate called Oliver(sic) de La Bouche and Johnson only refers to the pirate as La Bouche throughout. Also the story has different accounts from different sources but we will stick to Johnson's for ease of understanding.

Johnson makes no mention of a pirate called Olivier Levasseur and it seems supposition to presume that the pirate that Johnson calls Oliver La Bouche is Olivier Levasseur. More confusion is that if we take for fact that Olivier Levasseur is nicknamed 'The Buzzard' or 'The Hawk' and is referred to elsewhere (outside of Johnson) as such why does Johnson not mention this fabulous nickname? This could be because Johnson's work concentrates on British and colonial pirates but the supposition that Johnson's La Bouche is Levasseur is probably Johnson's atypical error in mistaking La Buse as La Bouche, or they are two entirely different pirates; especially as in his introduction Johnson says that La Bouche was eventually 'castaway' when at the time of Johnson's writing La Buse would have been happily retired.

The largest French account of the story lists the the same pirates except that they name Captain England 'La Buze(sic)' and make no word on a French pirate at all, and another French account only mentions a French 'Corsair' and no others. Yet when Olivier Levasseur is executed almost ten years later he is called Olivier Levasseur 'La Buze(sic)'. All very confusing.

Johnson mentions that the ship contained three to four million in diamonds as the most significant treasure and no mention of a huge gold cross encrusted with jewels.

And there's the rub.

The Flaming Cross of Goa may be purely apocryphal; certainly there doesn't seem to be any reference to it outside the legend or outside the 20th century and unfortunately most

Portuguese records of the period were destroyed in the devastating Lisbon earthquake of 1755. Flaming crosses do exist and certainly a great deal of treasure would have left India for Portugal but obviously as the treasure has never been found it is all just legend and perhaps better for it. I am happy to take the legend of the cross and place it in the story as I felt that the cross had a certain metaphorical use in Devlin's fourth tale.

The Levasseur that I use is as accurate as I found it to be but it is his connection with the treasure for which he is famous that I wish to elaborate on.

Firstly we have to imagine the circumstances for French pirates at the time of the story. Like their British counterparts the French *forbans* were offered amnesty if they turned themselves in and were allowed to 'buy' their way into comfortable positions and even settle down with land and homes, if they were – ahem – able to afford it. But added to this was the fact that the great René Duguay Trouin was sent out to the Indian Ocean to hunt them down. That was certainly a more persuasive argument and French piracy on the African and Indian seas all but disappeared. Levasseur certainly seems to have taken this opportunity to retire and is known to have been the captain of a pilot for merchants entering the ports of Madagascar. The mystery is that although Levasseur would have bought his amnesty to become French once again he doesn't appear to have done so with millions of pounds worth of gold and jewels, but then again why would he? Pirate remember.

And so we come to Levasseur's buried treasure and the tantalising cryptogram thrown to the crowd. If you don't know the story look it up, I'm just going to settle a few myths on it.

Throwing his secret into the crowd at his hanging.

*An* Olivier Levasseur was executed as a pirate on July 17th (not the 7th as is often reported) 1730 on Reunion (Bourbon) island. The letters of the governor at the time record this but there is no account of such dramatic an event as the prisoner declaring his treasure for those who are smart enough to find it and flinging a code to the crowd.* I think that would have deserved a couple of words. Any mention otherwise outside the records of Governor Pierre Benoit Dumas is just as apocryphal as the gold cross and again purely seems to exist in the early 20th century.

What is the most confusing thing about Levasseur is the vast amount of non-information about him. Even his grave which many people cite as evidence is a fiction. The cemetery in St Paul, Reunion, was not created until 1788. Only the swinging sign next to the grave attributes it to Olivier Levasseur, La Buse, and since when did authorities bury pirates? The tradition on the islands was to dispose of them at sea. This grave has the trappings of a tourist creation (especially as you are encouraged to put coins on it for luck). There *is* a pirate cemetery, on St Marie, but this is for those that died naturally and were buried by their own kind.

Putting on my detective hat for a moment I (and others) conclude two circumstantial possibilities. The cryptogram that appeared in the 20th century is either a hoax, as it is not mentioned by the governor who hanged Levasseur or any eyewitness account or it is a confusion with a genuine series of cryptograms by a French naval officer, and bit of a pirate himself, called Bernadin Nageon de L'Estang.

L'Estang died forty-five years after Levasseur, on Mauritius (Île de France) and left in his will to his two nephews and his brother several cryptograms indicating caves where he had buried (or had known to be buried) treasure from English and Spanish ships, scattered throughout the islands.\*\*

L'Estang's story is mostly forgotten as it doesn't have the glamour of the pirate attached to it and at least two of the treasures, mostly consisting of goblets and coins have been found.\*\*\* Nothing is as romantic as undiscovered treasure from a pirate treasure map so Levasseur's story rings louder. I find that having two stories involving codes and treasure within fifty years of each other too much of a coincidence and perhaps the two stories have converged with the distinct plausibility that the cryptogram supposedly attributed to Levasseur is actually one of L'Estang's.

Either way there would certainly be a case to suggest that somewhere in the Seychelles or the islands of Madagascar there is a considerable pirate treasure waiting to be found, and waiting for nearly three hundred years. Certainly there have been, and still are, several treasure hunters who are convinced that there is, as are the Seychelles' governments themselves. The islands have a Treasure Act due to the enormous pirate activity in their history. This act states that any treasure found is subject to a fifty-percent levy unless the period of three hundred years has passed since its 'burial'. I believe that the hunters out there now know where the treasure is (you might be able to piece the most likely location together yourself from some of the clues I have put in the book) and they are just waiting for the period to pass. That happens in 2021. Wait and see.

It is a modern cynicism that people scoff that pirates even buried treasure despite the fact that two of the most infamous pirates, Kidd and Blackbeard both claimed to have done so. They believe it belongs to *Treasure Island* and Hollywood, yet they seem willing to accept that after the Romans left Britain many people buried their gold and silver in fear of being robbed without Roman rule as we read from time to time when it's dug up by some boy with a trowel and a magnet. I have a standard argument for this pirate scoffing:

'Do you carry all your money around with you?'

'No.'

'Where do you keep it?'

'In a bank.'

'And if you couldn't keep it in a bank? Would you carry it in your car? What if you had an accident? Would you keep it in your house? What if you didn't have a house?' (You see where I'm going with this.) By the end of the questioning I have them in the garden with a spade and a torch.

The irony is that it is the very real treasure of the islands themselves that might mean that the haul of Levasseur and many pirates will never be found. Almost every desolate area where pirates might have buried their booty in the islands is now protected by worldwide treaty and I don't mean protected by signs I mean by full-on machine-gun-armed sea and air patrols. The only Shell in the Seychelles is the . . . er . . . shells, and for the sake of all our children we should make sure it stays so. The survival of the Earth will depend on her undamaged lungs. But please, if this is your first hearing of Olivier Levasseur, Oliver La Bouche, La Buse, La Buze, or the other half-dozen assortment of names attached to the man, check out the story for yourself and if it doesn't stir something of the child in you and make you consider, just for a moment, of jacking it all in and buying a shovel and a connecting flight then you should check your pulse.

The pirate Walter Kennedy finally makes an appearance in this book, although he is hinted at in all the other books. A

418

highly unpleasant character, even for a pirate, and I have changed history in order for him to have an equally unpleasant end, but I hope someone will appreciate that I did plot and time this adventure so that when Coxon reveals that he has arranged for someone else to be hung in his place it was on the actual date. Thank you. I do find a certain sadness in his final fate and something that often sums up the very heart of being a pirate. A young man who had seen half the world and had participated in the sacking of forts and towns from one side of the ocean to the other and sailed with some of the greatest pirates of the age ends up being hanged a few streets from where he was raised.

And so to Devlin. Over the course of the books I hope you have noticed that Patrick Devlin has been getting darker. He's still the same crow and even if crows don't moult, this one has, and his rougher plume is growing out. What becomes of that is down to him and, hopefully, his loyal partners. But we're moving into 1722 now and I've made mention of the Great Pirate Roberts (we don't say Black Bart in the 1700s) so that might indicate where we are going.

I've killed John Coxon and I hope that is one of the marks of a Devlin tale. When you open it you're never sure who'll still be alive when you close it. But I'll promise you this:

*'Them that die'll be the lucky ones.'*

(1) 'A General History of the Robberies & Murders of the Most Notorious Pirates' 1724.
*There are also issues that condemned men would usually have their hands tied (though not necessarily behind their backs) and in the islands it was customary to do so with a 2lb weight tied around the wrists. Not easy to pull off a necklace

and throw something into the crowd, but, granted, not impossible.

\*\*It is also possible of course that L'Estang got hold of Levasseur's cryptogram thus further clouding the issue.

\*\*\*Not all treasure found gets declared. Almost every noble or well-to-do family in the islands has a rumour about how they got their money and there are a few stories of ambassadors and governors suddenly quitting their posts and returning to their countries with suspiciously good fortunes.

Mark Keating, November 2012.

Do you wish this wasn't the end?

Join us at www.hodder.co.uk, or follow us on
Twitter @hodderbooks to be a part of our community
of people who love the very best in books and reading.

Whether you want to discover more about a book
or an author, watch trailers and interviews, have the
chance to win early limited editions, or simply browse
our expert readers' selection of the very best books,
we think you'll find what you're looking for.

And if you don't,
that's the place to tell us what's missing.

We love what we do, and we'd love you to be part of it.

www.hodder.co.uk

@hodderbooks

HodderBooks

HodderBooks